Noir Ain't the Half of It

NOIR AIN'T THE HALF OF IT

Stephen M. Honig

To Laura,
who experienced some of these stories
and then had to edit them.

"If you're not dead, you're not trying hard enough."

—*Big Lou*

INDEX

AUTHOR'S STATEMENT

These stories are partly fiction and partly true. The problem arises when the author can no longer tell the difference. Life so informs imagination that whatever is written is a fact in the mind of the writer. Thus, those readers who know me will recognize people, names, incidents, things I have mentioned before; those readers must remember that nothing in this volume was completely true in real time, and that liberties have been taken which cannot be described.

My editor, the estimable Howard Wells, has suggested that there is enough autobiography here that there lurks a memoir waiting to be made whole. My life is too fractured and ill-remembered to support such an undertaking. The risk is too great that people would accept what is written as an effort to be accurate as to events. In fact, the accuracy here is to emotions and temptations, sprinkled with memories of a Brooklyn that no longer exists—and perhaps never did.

I

PEOPLE

I do not know any of the people in the stories in this section. I confess to having had the feelings expressed by all of the principal actors. I do however swear to you that the chicken in the first story was known to me during the sultry summer of 2018.

THE BIRDS OF MAINE

It was one of those gray-ish days for which the coast of Maine was famous; ashen clouds with modest threat of rain playing hide-and-seek with hazy sun. The beach, growing larger with the receding tide, was washed with the kind of indifferent low rolling waves that told you the storm was lurking somewhere over the horizon, but was not imminent. Daunted by the prospect of a less than prime beach experience, the summer vacationers had used the day to visit the discount outlets in nearby Freeport; the sands were sparsely sprinkled with chairs and towels, allowing the seagulls to descend in large numbers, strutting from site to site, pecking at bags and coolers in search of food.

Sitting in my beach chair, trying to finish my summer book, I scanned each of the new arrivals with indifference. Until the blonde in the deeply slit, long, blue-patterned skirt arrived carrying the red chicken.

⊷ ⊷ ⧉◆⧉ ⊶ ⊶

Carlos was feeling pretty good about his boy. Through the haze of cigar smoke and the encouragements delivered in angry bursts, his animal had been doing well. Very well indeed. The razors strapped to his scarred legs had already split open the dark brown contender and had neatly decapitated the one

12

with the blueish feathers; some of the guys in the front row had to wipe the blood spray off their faces, and one was so drenched as to allow the fingerpainting of a modest beard and pencil mustache to the delighted howls of the crowd. The next chicken was a wire-y little creature and, although looks could be deceiving, Carlos was optimistic; the Slasher had himself suffered only a nick on one wing and wings weren't important in any event; it was all about the leg action, wasn't it?

<hr />

She was mildly tanned, but not roasted like some of the other blondes of August. From a few dozen yards away it was hard to gauge her age; surely not a teen, surely without the globular thighs a woman earned through the accumulation of years. But my interest, for once, was not for the woman but for what she was carrying. I could not tell you if she was plain, attractive or repulsive. All I can tell you is everything about her chicken. She placed the animal gently, with two hands, into a large straw basket and placed a white towel over the top. She spread out a small blanket and unfolded a portable beach chair, one of the old-fashioned kind with the aluminum frame and webbed plastic woven seat and backrest. She bent down to the basket again, produced the seemingly calm chicken, and stood it on the top of the back rail of the chair. She delicately held her hands on either side of the fowl until assured that it had found its balance, and then sat down on her blanket and dug out some magazines. With what I would swear was an entire stack of *People*, she transferred to the chair, the chicken standing over her left shoulder. I could almost believe that the chicken was leaning forward, reading along.

Hope the thing doesn't decide to lay an egg right now, I thought. It is a long way down from its perch to the sand. Question: if you drop a fresh egg from a height of three feet onto soft sand will it break? Second question: if the sand is really hot, will it poach?

━┅━ ☰◈☲ ━┅━

There was so much noise that no one at first heard the footsteps. By the time Carlos saw the policemen, it was too late. He was promptly cuffed, and Slasher was scooped, carefully to avoid the razors. Carlos' wad of tens and twenties was seized from his fist, presumably as evidence, although based on history the money would be applied to the purchase of Scotch and cigars for the after-hours club the cops frequented down by the Saco River . . .

━┅━ ☰◈☲ ━┅━

The blonde must have decided to try the water, which was deceptively warm, the curve of the Gulf Stream carrying a faint memory of the Caribbean gently northward to the pine forests. She glanced backwards; the chicken was observing the fishing boats far offshore, not particularly perturbed and, being flightless, not much of a mind to try to soar along with the wheeling gulls and the darting swifts and occasional plover. With the confidence of a pet owner with intimate knowledge of her animal, she turned her back to her chair and trekked down beach in search of the now-rapidly-receding ocean.

I do not know how intelligent seagulls are as a group, but I surely can tell you about one member of the cohort who will always live in my memory as a particularly stupid example. This chicken on the chair was not cooked as a roast. This chicken on the chair was not layered into a roll with mayo and a leaf of lettuce. This chicken was not buffaloed, sautéed, fried, steamed, diced, sauced, or otherwise transformed into a gull-worthy meal. This chicken was sitting there, soothed by the distant sound of surf, minding its own business, as peaceful as any bird could be. So why the gull decided to swoop down and, presumably, try his hand at grabbing a beak-full is a mystery I will never solve. The gull struck the chicken somewhere around neck or head, knocking it off its perch. A bundle of gray and red feathers rolled a yard or two down the beach, all in a tangle. Emanating from this tangle was a mix of caws and hither-to unheard gutturals that sounded much like a muffled roar of rage.

The startled gull emerged for a moment, wobbling with surprise, and began to deploy its wings, having concluded that this was not a chicken cutlet moment, when the red chicken swiped out with one claw and neatly popped out the gull's left eye. I can now attest that yes, the blood of a seagull is indeed red. A weak caw was the last thing that gull had to say to the world, as the chicken then mounted the gull's back and began a systematic slashing attack with beak and claws. In a matter of a few seconds, the gull's head took another roll down the beach sand, only this time it left its body behind. Red specks populated the slope, a larger red pool began to saturate the ground just in front of the blonde's beach blanket.

The chicken calmly hopped into the basket and pulled the white blanket up over the top with its beak. The basket rustled for a moment and then was still.

Someone must have called the police, although I am not sure why. A small circle surrounded the officer, whose bicycle was left propped against the fence at the entrance ramp; he had trudged down the beach in his ungainly boots with grim purpose to observe the carnage.

The blonde was holding the red chicken and gently stroking its sides with measured care.

"No, he's not at all vicious anymore. I was in the water, maybe someone else saw what happened. But I got him at animal rescue in Portland. He was pretty beaten up when I got him. Someone said he had been kept by some sleazeball for cockfighting. I had come in for a kitten, but my heart just went out to this little guy." She looked fondly down at her pet, then looked up at the policeman with a winning smile. Her eyes were blue. She received no criminal citation. The policeman buried the gull, in two parts, somewhere down the strand near where the rocky cliff began.

＊＋—≣◆≣—＋＊

Carlos told the judge that cockfighting was a recognized sport in his homeland. The judge told Carlos that a six-month jail term was a recognized cock-fighting punishment in the Great State of Maine. In his cell, Carlos sometimes thought of Slasher; when he got out he would need to find a bird as gifted, if he was to rebuild his bankroll.

Scion of the Sucrose Kid

Abe Wasserman graduated from CCNY on a rainy early June day in 1986 with an undergraduate degree in economics. He never made the Dean's List in a single semester, a fact mentioned by his mother during the graduation lunch at the Stage Deli, but Abe was by then inured to his mother's cruel honesty. After losing his job selling sporting goods at his uncle's store in Rockefeller Center by reason of his unwillingness to tout the virtues of the $75 sneakers which he knew were Mexican knockoffs, Abe applied for and failed to land any employment while suffering the escalating sarcasms of his mother.

Unable to afford to move out of the family apartment on the Grand Concourse, Abe finally took a position as assistant vice president of sales at the lower Manhattan stock brokerage firm of Carrington and Sons. His first day of work consisted of a brief interview with the senior Carrington, a/k/a Hyman Ginsberg of the Bensonhurst Ginsbergs, who explained that Abe would start in the marketing department under the tutelage of the estimable star salesman known in the firm as the Sucrose Kid.

The Sucrose Kid turned out to be an Italian guy from Staten Island. He weighed in something north of 300 pounds, smoked unfiltered Camels one after another, ate incessantly at his desk with the residue dropping off his fingers and untrimmed beard onto his plaid short-sleeved shirt, and his armpits smelled like fish heads rotting on a pier. Abe sat as close as he dared and did as he was told: listen to the phone calls on the extra phone, and do not, repeat absolutely do not, speak a single word.

The Kid was one of eight or ten senior vice presidents in what was called the sales floor. Each spent the day cold-calling potential customers. Their pitch was always the same, based on a typed laminated card issued by the firm and propped up on each desk. Each call was placed to a name off a list given by the firm to each person at the start of each day. The calls began around ten in the morning, New York being a late-starting city. The lists were prepared by "researchers" and consisted of membership lists of bar associations, large law or accounting firms, members of city clubs from directories taken off the desks of receptionists, members of Chambers of Commerce purchased at four cents a name and, when times were hard, pages of the phone book for postal zip codes which suggested affluence.

Whatever unsavory aspects possessed by the Kid, once his prospect picked up the phone the Kid was as smooth as could be. Could that guy ever talk the talk. He was so sweet, so ingratiating on the phone, that he earned his moniker as the Sucrose Kid.

Now most of the vice presidents of varying seniority, working the bucket shop phone banks, followed the pitch on the card pretty closely. It was the tried-and-true way to build your book, the best way to ultimately make a cold call into a customer willing to designate you as his stockbroker.

And all the people on the lists were always men; women were simply skipped over, although whether because they were presumed broke or because they were assumed to be someone's secretary was not quite clear. Not that there were that many women to begin with.

The card left little to the imagination; the mantra of the firm was "trust the card, it isn't hard." Just do what the card says.

Sure, 98% of the people you call will decline, most will just hang up, others will tell you that they were going to call the police, a surprising number yelled that they were going to report you to the FBI or the SEC or the U.S. attorney. A few would lead you on, suggest they had only $100,000 to invest, but what did you have in mind? Others would curse at you or, worse, ask you to call back later because you had called at an inopportune time seeing as how they were at that very moment engaged in sexual intercourse with your sister.

And there were slack times, many slack times. Lunches for many of the alleged upper crust prospects stretched for a couple of hours. Around 11 a.m. or 5:30 p.m. were bad times as people might not have meetings but were anxious to get primed for lunch or for the subway home. Doctors were impossible in the mornings, doing rounds. CPAs were inaccessible from March 1 through mid-April. Lawyers you could never tell, but that's life.

The card was so often used, in one or another variant, that it was amazing that people getting cold-called all the time by boiler room brokers did not just hang up after the first five or ten words. And many did, but some listened and some small percentage got hooked; the theory was that the more calls you make, the better your chances of getting a sale. The card read:

"Good [morning/afternoon/evening], Mr. _____. I won't take more than a minute of your time, I know you are busy. This is NOT a sales call, I'm not selling you anything. Just wanted to chat with you, [try first name] – can I call you [first name]? Thanks. So, [first name], we at Carrington follow a lot of stocks and every once in a while, we see what we think is a great opportunity to get in on the ground floor of a really good situation. We keep our eye on the market, and we have our special sources, if you know what I mean. Well, I just wanted your permission, if we happened to see some special opportunity, something that we think is in your sweet spot, just right for your portfolio, in say a month or two, I just wanted to ask if it would be all right to just call you and share that opportunity with you. No obligation of course. Is that okay with you?

[If yes, follow up] That's great, [first name]. Just to be sure I don't waste your time, let me confirm your stock interests. Tell us again the kinds of investments you have made and how they are doing. [Make note of answers.]

[If caller seems nervous about giving you the information] Oh look, as your broker whatever you tell me is confidential, we here at Carrington have been representing some of the wealthiest people in New York, of course I cannot reveal the names of our clients, here at Carrington discretion is the better part of valor if you know what I mean.

Well, it has been a pleasure talking with you. Now you may not hear from us for a few weeks, maybe longer, but just wanted to introduce our firm and establish a brokerage relationship with you. Thanks for your time and best regards to your wife, uh, sorry her name is ??? [pause, record name of wife on prospect card]."

In the background, Abe could hear all the other vice presidents pretty much adhering to the script, but the Sucrose Kid didn't stay strictly to what it said on the card. And he varied his pitch, right from the start, not based on anything about the customer's information, but just, as he said, to "keep it fresh." He might start with a "look, I wanted to talk to you but my phone is ringing off the hook so I gottta make this quick," or with a "your friend told me to call you and any friend of your friend is a friend of mine." Or he might simply say, "look, my stock brokerage firm tells me to chat you up and try to sell you something, but we are busy men and ought to get right down to business." Once he started with "didn't I meet you a couple of weeks ago, you know, was it the Yankees game, your name is so familiar." Usually he would switch to the "I'll call you later" script but sometimes, if he felt the love, he'd just go right for it: "Look, I have only 450 shares of XYZ Corporation in my allocation, and I thought of you and wasn't sure but you seem like a nice guy so just tell me how many shares and I'll put you on the line with someone from my staff to get your details, set you right up."

But it wasn't all about the pitch, it was something about the Kid's tone, the sincerity pouring off his lips, oozing into the mouthpiece of his black handset, dripping palpably through the wire and dropping ever so smoothly and sweetly into his listener's ears that caught Abe's imagination. "He's making love to someone he doesn't even know and he is going to be rewarded with riches and thankfulness," Abe thought. He couldn't wait to get onto his own telephone and try it himself. Sure, he'd follow the card, the tried-and-true card, but every so often he'd segue into the Sucrose Space, take his own love of humanity and way with words out for a walk and see what he could do with them. Carrington and Sons was going to be fun and, given his aptitude and his degree in economics, his path to a future of wealth and power was assured.

But Abe was made to sit for another four days, an entire week, just listening to the Kid, and occasionally overhearing the pitches of neighboring vice presidents, before he was cleared the next week to pick up the phone himself. He was shown to his own small cubicle and given a forty-page list of names and phone numbers with no other information. He was given his own laminated card with the pitch printed on it in 18-point type. He was given a small pile of prospect cards to record the details from his successful conversations. He was given a pad of white lined paper, two ballpoint pens emblazoned with the words CARRINGTON AND SONS – BROKERAGE AND ARBITRAGE, a small thermos full of black coffee, and an encouraging smile from the Senior Carrington, who left him with a light pat on his shoulder and the semi-cryptic admonition to "stock 'em up."

FIRST CALL: "Good morning, Mr. Sperling. My name is Abraham Carter. I won't take a lot of your time, I know you're a busy man, but I just wanted to introduce myself and my firm. That's Carrington and Sons, we are securities brokers and right off I want to tell you that I am not calling to sell you anything."

The light was still lit, Sperling hadn't hung up, a good sign. Emboldened: "You probably heard of us, we represent many people of means in Manhattan." Sounding good. "You probably know that we follow the market pretty closely, are well-known traders," off into a riff of fancy, "and I just wanted to let you know that we would like to be able to call you in a few months if we happen to come across a special situation that . . . "

"Hold up, there, let me save you some time. First, I live in the Bronx. Second, I don't have a pot to piss in ever since my bitch wife ran away with the Kosher butcher. Third, my uncle went to school with that crook Ginsberg, the goniff, and if he were selling real dollar bills for ten cents on the street corner, I'd still not do business with that shithead on a bet. And you can tell him something else for me: eat hot death for what you did to my aunt Sylvia—may she rest in peace." Click.

SECOND CALL: Well that didn't go so well but who knew that he'd start by accident with someone who actually knew the Ginsberg family. What the hell is the chance of that? So, "good morning, Mr. DiCarlo, you don't know me but I" followed by an interruption by a reedy voice with a thick Italian accent saying, "Yeah and we gonna keep it that way, muthafukka." Click.

THIRD CALL: Must have gotten up with a bad case of the crabs, that Italian asshole. But third time's the charm: "Good morning, Mr. Liebowitz, my name is Abe Goldfarb and I represent the firm of . . . " Click. Huh, imagine that, I seem to be trending downward. Let me take a hit from the coffee thermos and try again.

FOURTH THROUGH UMPTEENTH CALL FIRST, SECOND,

THIRD, FOURTH DAY OF CALLS: "Good morning Mr. so-and-so (49 clicks here), I represent the stock brokerage firm of Carrington and (25 clicks here) Sons (2 clicks) and first off I want to assure you that I am not here to sell you anything (3 clicks, 14 "bullshit"s followed by clicks, 6 "fuck you"s followed by clicks). You may know that our prestigious stock brokerage firm is a well-known market leader with (an ear for that hidden situation that presents the opportunity for profit—4 clicks) (an eye for an inefficiency in the markets that might fit perfectly in your portfolio—12 clicks) one "or up your ass" followed by, well, a click (ability to earn returns in rising or falling markets—33 clicks) and I just wanted permission to call you some time in the next (couple of weeks—12 clicks) (couple of months—3 clicks) few hours (75 clicks and one "make that at least five hours, I am working my way through statutory rape of all your nieces and nephews" followed by—you guessed it: click).

Abe came into the office early on his fifth day. He looked like hell but it didn't matter, he did all his business over the phone (or at least pretended he did). The rings under his eyes, red after the third day, now were a palpable field of black tinged with blood-shot. He uncapped his CARRINGTON pen for the first time, took his blank pad of paper and started writing. He wrote and crossed out, threw out page after page, until he found the right tone, part frustration and part motherly anger.

FIRST CALL, DAY FIVE: "Good morning, Mr. Fisher. This is a cold call from a boiler shop in a second-rate brokerage house that, if I started off by telling you its name, you might look it up and hang up right away. I am supposed to say I ain't trying to sell you anything but I hear you ain't a dumb schmuck so let me say right up front that that's a crock." Pause. Silence on the line, but no click.

"Uh, Mr. Fisher, you still there?"

"Yeah, kid, I love it, ya got my attention. So where ya from anyway?"

"Uh, the Grand Concourse. That's in the Bronx."

"I know where the fucking Grand Concourse is, you dick. You new at this?"

"Yessir. This is my fifth day and I haven't had a sale yet, not even writing down someone's name to call them later."

"You go to college, kid?"

"Yessir. CCNY."

"Huh! Me too, class of '50.

Long pause.

Then Fisher: "So, let's hear your pitch."

"Really?"

"Sure."

"Well, I'm supposed to wait a couple of weeks and call you up and sell you some stock from this list they gave me."

"So, do you like these stocks, kid?"

"Well, Mr. Fisher, I'm new at this but I did earn solid Bs in all my accounting classes and frankly, between you and me, I really don't understand why anyone would buy them. I mean most of the people here they just follow the list, but I spent all last night looking up these companies and my guess is that the firm is just going to sell out their own shares at a profit and then these companies, well, I bet they just go down in value."

"Kid, you free for lunch today?"

"What? Lunch? Are you kidding? Uh, sure. Why?"

"Come to my office at 1, make that 1:30. Bring that list of stocks with ya. 455 Madison, 16th floor. Fisher Universal Industries. Just ask for me. Give me your name so my receptionist will know you to let you in."

"Sure. My name is John – uh, actually Abe Wasserman."

"So, Abe Wasserman, do you know what a short sale is?"

"Well, I've heard of it, Mr. Fisher."

Fisher laughed. "Just be here at 1:30 today. And don't forget your list. That's the 16th floor, the executive suite. Don't get off at the lower floors, that's where my staff works. At least those I have here in the U.S. Just ask for Fisher Senior. My son wants my job as President, but that isn't happening any time soon ... "

<hr />

Lyndon Fong graduated first in his class at Northwestern's Kellogg School of Management on a rainy early June day in 2014. He had read all the listings for the major brokerage houses and had set his sights on one of them. He had applied and was fortunate enough to be hired. He was told he would start on the marketing floor, but you had to start somewhere. After four weeks of personal and on-line training, Lyndon was given a cubicle, two phone lines, two computers with one locked on Bloomberg, a Keurig machine with an assortment of caffeinated coffees, an iPad and a list of graduates from Ivy League colleges, resident in the greater Chicago area. Flush with excitement, Lyndon picked up his phone, ignoring the hum of the other assistant vice presidents around him.

FIRST CALL: "Good morning, sir. My name is Lyndon Fong. First off, let me assure you that I am not calling to try to sell you anything. I am a vice president at the Wall Street firm of A. Wasserman and ... Yes, that Mr. Wasserman, and I am calling to introduce myself and our firm ... "

Don't Wrap Tight

You can always tell the newbies, ya know? They're always tellin' you they're cold. Sure, they're cold, cuz they don't know what the hell they're doing.

There's an art to it, ya know? Well, maybe not an art, just sort of a life technique, if ya know what I'm sayin'. If you're goin' to stay outside, cuz ya don' wanna deal with that shit in the shelter where ya can't get a nip against the chill and some asshole's gonna hassle you in the john or mess with your good boots, then you're gonna need some protection or you'll sure as hell gonna freeze yer kiester off if ya don't do it right.

So during the day it's fine, yer in the shelter early or late, yer eatin', yer in the subway ridin', yer in a Dunkin' spending an hour or two over yer coffee cup, or at least yer movin' all the time which is pretty important. But night, outside, that's a different thing because if ya ain't clued in, ya can wake up dead.

Reminds me of an old poem about some guy what froze himself and they threw him in a furnace cuz the ground was too cold to bury the sonofabitch and when they come to clean out the bones there he's sittin' in the middle of the fire, and he's yellin' "close the fuckin' door cuz yer lettin' in the cold."

So anyway this kid, maybe he's twenty, smells sour and his shoes got flaps flappin' when he walks which is super stupid, ya gotta watch yer feet ya know, an' he's got one of them chin whisker things goin' but stubble all over anyway, thinks he's God's gift, big dumb white fucker he is, it's mornin' an' we're on line an' he's coughin' and not lookin' too good, half red flushed and half white as the snow on the ground, an' he is still shiverin' and complainin' and to shut him up I sez, I sez "Kid, shut it, if ya can't live on the street then go home to ya mama's tits" an' he's all over me with "well if you're so smart" and I'm tellin' him at least I'm not shiverin' and plannin' on pneumonia like some people.

But he's so pathetic I ask't 'im where ya sleepin' anyway and he sez someone showed him a grate behind the West Street Superette, which I happen to know is a pretty good spot cuz the furnace vents there from the building and ya get enough heat durin' yer normal night so's ya warm enough not to, ya know, fuckin' freeze ya balls off.

"So if ya found a sweet spot like that, how come ya so cold, ya got a blanket dontcha, cuz if not ya can go to the office and getcha one for nuthin."

So he's got his blanket, got it stashed in a cubby over at the Catholic church which is smart, but he says he still froze his petuties off and I sez, that don't make no sense an' he says, now all sorta apologetic and like, maybe you got a way to show me. And he looks sincere, ya know, an' I sez well I can come by and tuck ya in tonight real sarcastic like, and then right away I thinks to myself well he's goin' think I'm comin' on to him which is not how I am but how the hell does he know that, but he's real serious and says, yeah, can ya, and me shithead that I am, I hear my voice tellin' him I'll be down there maybe tonight which is really stupid because why do I give a shit, so I dust him off an' grab my plate and take the last empty seat at Tortilla Tony's table and the kid, he's disappeared which was my plan anyway.

That night, gotta tell ya, it was so friggin' cold, stone cold, wind cold, wet windy cold, I myself damned near gave up myself and went over to Saint Anthony's, but Louie the drug guy, the one he always insists ya call him "Louis," he may be there, knowin' him, and him and me we don't get along no more by reason of that unfinished thing from the Fall which I don't wanna talk about. So I'm goin' to behind my hotel where the kitchen gives us some extra stuff sometimes and if the wind is blowing hard even lets us into the loading dock, and I'm goin' right by the spic Superette and I remember this kid and what the hell, I hook me down the alley and sure enough there he is on that big grate and it's blowin' hot and he should be all fine and I'm about to walk away when I take a closer look at the dumb fat sonofabitch and wouldn't ya know it, he's got his gray woolen stiff blanket wrapped all around him, he's fuckin' sleepin' on top of it and got the ends wrapped all around himself.

Well, no wonder he's frozen in the mornin' cuz he's got no heat trapped in there for when the boiler shuts down and stops spittin' heat out.

So I kick him, but gentle, just sorta nudge his ass with my boot and all of a sudden he's sittin' up and about to stand up and his fists is clenched and I see what's comin' so I step back a few and yell "Hey, hey you, hey you from breakfast at St. Anthony's, remember me I told ya I'd be ya mama and tuck ya in?" And he blinks twice and says "hey yeah whattaya want" and I sez "I'm gonna do you a favor if you get up." An' he looks at me and says something like it's cold out there and I sez somethin' like "no! did 'ja figga that out all by yerself or did someone give ya some help" and he gets up slow, big sonofabitch if maybe I didn't mention that ta ya earlier, and I show him how to drop the ends of the blanket down the grate and make like a tent and put yer jacket rolled up under yer head, and let the heat sorta build up inside yer cocoon like thing and that's how you stay real warm and don't wake up like you been blastfrozen in some meat locker.

And he sorta looks around and smiles and says thank you, real nice, cuz he's real appreciative. And he says, ya know man I had ya all wrong, so come over here 'cuz I got a bottle and let's have a swig to seal the deal, and I'm about to say "man it's dumb when it's this cold" but what the hell, and he brings out a bottle from his back pack and takes a drink and passes me the bottle and I salute him with like a bottoms-up gesture kind of thing, and as I'm leanin' back a little to let the booze get down my gullet, and then I feel the knife and it's the last thing I feel until right now.

And so to answer yer question, no I don't know his name but I can ID him sure enough, just let me see the mug shots.

M. Pierre—Fragments of Life

I've heard lots of not so nice things about Empee, but you better not tell 'em around me and my family. For me and my people – well, Empee is the salt of our earth fer sure. I'll mention just one thing, so you can understand. In Brooklyn one year, we was all so young then ya know – my daddy was laid off from the trucking – and pretty soon money just wasn't around, ya know. So I and the guys we're on the stoop just talkin' and my father walks out to buy some cigs, and Empee he says hey, what's with your pop 'cause he usually working right up through the dinner. And I tell him, "Empee, he got laid off and we on the welfare, ya know?"

And Empee, he is all about saying that is terrible and he knows this guy always needs drivers. So I ask him, what you know about people hiring people, we just a bunch of guys with no jobs, playing cards and hanging and all. And Empee, he is huffy about now and says, basically, look maybe I don't want to work but I could, and I know people, good people. So everyone is hooting a little, but Empee he gets the beer somehow so no one is landing on him real hard.

So that is like a Friday or Saturday and that Monday, someone calls my pop and says hey I hear you a driver and I got needs for that in my shop, you come down to DeKalb Avenue, and we talk about it. And don't you know Empee he got my dad a job right like that, didn't ever say anything about it except when I

30

tried to talk about it he said, Eliah, just don't talk about it, ain't no one's business.

And that was just once, there was others as Empee got older and started going into the City regularly, all dressed up, all like a mystery but he helped out lots of people I tell ya. Me too. That Empee, he knew who his friends was, I tell ya that. Cool ass card man also, I tell ya.

Ya know, one time we was ...

⊶⊶ ⟨◆⟩ ⊶⊷

For a first novel, Mr. Pierre has written on a rather strange theme, a fairy tale for adults but with purely child-like tropes. It is hard to categorize *The Further Adventures of Maximillian J. Pussycat* and this reviewer has been looking at fiction for a couple of decades now. The premise, that a pet cat is particularly equipped to carry the world's moral burden by reason of multiple lives, and the self-affirmation that comes from that perception, is stretched to its philosophical extreme by reason of the cat speaking to the world only through the mouth of its eight-year-old owner. That conceit makes it difficult to separate the profound from the infantile, provided there is a difference of course. And it is not clear what Mr. Pierre had in mind by referring to "further" adventures when there are no "prior" adventures within our frame of reference. The photograph of the author, on the flap, shows a small gray kitten of no particular standing; this reviewer suggests that in fact Mr. Pierre is homo sapiens, although not of the most robust tribe.

⊶⊶ ⟨◆⟩ ⊶⊷

Count 1: Violation of Section 10(b) of the Securities Exchange Act of 1934.

22. The government repleads all facts set forth in paragraphs 1 through 21 above.

23. In or about the Spring of 1992, Mr. Pierre revised the format of his Sunday afternoon radio program, away from a listener -participation discussion of positive energy derived from nearness to feral animals to a general monologue concerning the United States economy and the economy of Latvia.

24. In or about June 10, 1993, Mr. Pierre placed a series of short sales orders through his on-line brokerage account wherein he effected disposition of shares of all the companies traded over the Exchanges of the United States and Latvia engaged in the business of selling armaments to the Middle East.

25. In early July of 1993, Mr. Pierre began mentioning on his radio program, which by then had a listenership of almost cult-like magnitude among the aged 35–54 cohort, that a certain fictional feline appearing in a book previously authored by him in the early 1980s, believed that negative energy derived from the arms trade with warm climate countries could depress the market value of all companies within that space by a factor of 30%–50% over the next few months.

26. All stocks reasonably within the identified industry grouping thereupon began to fall in market value, and by mid-August had declined from their June 30 market price by an average of 55%.

27. On August 30, 1993, Mr. Pierre covered his short positions by purchasing the subject securities at reduced prices, generating a profit, prior to sales commissions and charges, of $7,111,723.35.

28. By reason of a manipulation in the information available to the marketplace for a group of companies the securities of which are traded over the exchanges located within the United States, Mr. Pierre conducted a fraud on the

marketplace by which the general trading public was damaged to the extent of approximately $7 million, in violation of the laws of the United States.

— • — ⩵ ◆ ⩵ — • —

The first time I married M. Pierre—yeah, right, I married the old guy twice—was in '75, in Rockville, Maryland, which in those days was just really a farm town. I was daughter of the man who had the only hardware store in Rockville, a big barn of a place with a loading dock out back from which daddy sold everything from rolls of barbed wire to fence posts to milking machines to I don't know what. I was a little long in the tooth by then, resigned to Rockville like a pleasant sentence to a lifetime of relaxation and without much of an interest in men; frankly, nothing had worked out and I felt I was sort of lucky not to have ended up like half my friends, on the bus to Baltimore to visit Dr. Tom, the famous Dr. Tom.

So this tall thin guy buys an old house, not even a real farmhouse, just a square box of a place on the outskirts of town, meant to be on the edge of things but the town never really got that far; red faded paint, dark though, going to grayish purple, rail fence, but nicer than it sounds actually, neat lawn and a new roof, daddy sold Harry the shingles and some paint to fix the place up for this new guy; rumor had it he bought the house for cash, sure it was only 25 grand or so but not a lot of people had 25 grand free and loose in Rockville back in '75.

And this guy, M. Pierre a'course, he comes into the shop one day early on looking for bigger lightbulbs, he can't see at night he says, the place is really sort of dark and he needs lots of light. So I ask him as a matter of politeness, why do you need so much light. I'm a writer, he says. No kidding, I say, as there weren't many of those in good ole Rockville at the time, what are ya writing? "A short novel about a feline," he replies as if he were

33

saying something normal like "the life of George Washington" or "a cookbook for egg recipes."

"Can I see some part of it?"

"Well," he says with some surprise, "it is not usual for someone to ask to see a work in progress."

"Yeah," I says. "Maybe not where you come from but here in Rockville, everyone knows everything about everyone. Where you from, anyway?"

"Points north," he says and I reply, "Ya gotta mean New York, no one from New York wants to admit it around here."

So M. Pierre, he gives me that famous M. Pierre smile, and I melt just feeling it all of a sudden, and he says with that smile, he says "I guess Rockville is just a friendly place so next time I come in I will bring you a chapter or two and you can tell me what you think." And I said that is fine with me, I will look forward to it, and we both smile politely at each other and I can see his eyes moving around me a bit and I think, at that moment, "hmmm, that's pretty interesting even though I am surely younger than he is, maybe not much but ... " We married that winter and I loved him but never knew him and when the baby died he stopped giving me that M. Pierre smile and we were divorced as part of his leaving Rockville with his book finished and off he went to New York and got to be famous and a media star.

About 20 years later, in fact October 18, 1998, by then he was what, well past 60 and I was a only few years behind him on that score, on that very date I am closing the store at 6 p.m. and thinking about going back to the house we shared, now in fact part of the thriving town of Rockville, in walks this distinguished guy, same grin, really nice clothes, and I read about him in the papers, a successful investor and he even did get to publish that book about the cats which I thought was pretty lame, man knew

34

damn near nothing about cats I tell you, and he says he's been thinking about me and would I like to pick up again and move with him to Atlanta which was where he was now living, having just gotten out the Federal Jail there for something to do with stocks and he had no reason to move onward, having nowhere to go; which led him to thinking, blah blah, and so if you were coming onto 60 years old and spent your whole life behind a wooden counter in Rockville, Maryland you would agree to move to Hades with the devil himself if he picked up the cost of the train ticket, and so a week later I showed up at this small cabin near the bus station in Atlanta and just moved in with my stuff and we were re-married and had a pleasant few years before one day I came home from the food store and his clothes were gone. He left a lot of money in the bank account, so I figured it was a clue that our relationship had run its course and I transferred the money to the store account and went back to Rockville which is where I now live, having sold the store and ending up in the only place where I had any friends to speak of.

I guess I was still married to the guy when he died, but I didn't hear about that until after, and was not mentioned in the obituaries the librarian found for me on the internet. Mr. Tucker inquired on my behalf but there was no estate left for me to make a spousal claim . . .

━┅━ ≖◆≖ ━┅━

I first met M. Pierre when he arrived at the Thompson Retreat here in Slocum, and I recall the day perfectly. It was a Saturday in the Spring of 2004, and the forsythia had been out for a few days. He came walking up the gravel path, dragging a small suitcase on tiny rollers that the taxi driver had gotten from the trunk. Tall man with straight white hair, neatly trimmed, wearing a sports coat which is not how most people dress when they get here. Hair white as the sheet on your bed. I was on the porch in my chair, and up the gravel path he walks, straight as an arrow, little stones shooting out behind the wheels on his luggage, just strolling up the path with all those yellow flowers on either side of him, like some triumphal honor guard.

He said, "Hello old timer" and I said "I bet you're older than I am" and from then on, until his passing, we were best friends. We talked business, he had his theories, but after a few years the government had to pick up his tab so I guess his business success was not so great, ya know? He showed me a book he had written but it was about cats so I took it and told him I enjoyed it but frankly I couldn't get out of the first paragraph. Damned cat talked and everything; he said it was a book for adults!

He said he had no people, and no one ever visited him. He got no mail. When he died all he had was his clothing and a pearl tie tac which Mr. Lattimore gave to me as a remembrance. I don't wear ties at my age, but I sometimes put it in the lapel of my shirt for decoration.

I do miss M. Pierre. Miss him a lot . . .

———— ≍◆≍ ————

"It is my pleasure to talk to you, class, on this beautiful day. I am from New York, and I did not know how beautiful it is in San Francisco until I got here. You are very lucky to be children here, and I am very lucky to be able to speak with you. Your teacher said you were a very smart class and so I am going to ask for your help. I have just become a teacher myself. I started studying later in life. I did not really go to school to be a teacher until I was almost thirty years old. I know that sounds really old to you. It is not that old, but it is old to start paying attention in school. I know you kids will not make that mistake that I made, I know you will do your homework and pay attention to your teachers and parents all along.

So I teach writing. How to write stories. I have an idea which we can discuss, an idea for a story. It is about an animal, a pet in a family. It might be a dog, or a cat, or even an iguana or a turtle. Does everyone know what an iguana looks like? Good. This pet is pretty special. This pet is very smart, almost as smart as you children, and can talk. Not pretend talk like in a fairy tale but can really really talk. And this pet has the answers to all the problems of the world. But no one will listen to him or her.

So what I want to ask you is, how do you think the best way would be for this pet, let's call her Max, to be able to tell the world the answers to all its questions? Who wants to start?

Someone can start, there are only ideas, no wrong answers, we are making up a story here. You? Good. And what is your name ... "

<hr/>

Special to the *New York Times*, Page 47, April 18, 2014.

Pierre, M., author and public personality, passed away on April 4 in Slocum, Georgia at the age of 80. He left no family and the cause of death was not disclosed.

Mr. Pierre, born July 15, 1933 in Brooklyn, New York, as Maurice Pender, had a meteoric career in the public eye, parlaying his one published novel, *The Further Adventures of Maximillian J. Pussycat*, into a wildly popular radio talk show that ran from 1978 to 1993. Born into poverty during the Depression and after serving several brief prison terms for various petty crimes of violence, Mr. Pierre was adopted by the Brooklyn Catholic Archdiocese under a special program to benefit underprivileged Brooklyn citizens. He graduated from Brooklyn College in 1963 with a degree in elementary education, taught school around the country for a decade, then removed himself to Rockville, Maryland, where he spent several years crafting his haunting novel, a tale of a highly moral pet feline who had finally found a way to communicate its thoughts to the world.

Mr. Pierre built a radio career on the book, at one time being heard over 656 outlets in the United States and Canada. His utilization of his radio program to manipulate the price of securities caught the eye of the United States government, and after conviction he served three years in prison at the Atlanta Correctional Institution. Having lost his radio pulpit, Mr. Pierre lived out his life in seclusion in Georgia.

Married once in the early '70s to Lettie Harrison of Rockville, Maryland, Mr. Pierre divorced Ms. Harrison shortly after completion of his novel. The couple had no children.

Norman Cattan, former programming head of Central Broadcasting Network, remembered Mr. Pierre from his heydays as a radio personality. "He never was flashy; he always was calm, understated. Not the kind of shock-jock people you hear on the radio today. Always had an interesting, softer angle on life. He got sidetracked by some problem with the SEC in the '90s. Never understood all that, why he did it. He was such a gentle, helpful man."

"The son of a bitch, he took all my money and never looked back. Damned right I'll tell you about so-called M. Pierre. He was born up North, New Jersey I think, or Massachusetts. Wherever, he came from dirt. He had no manners, but that guy had a lot of what they call charm, charm like the guy selling you vitamins on the TV, that kind of oil. Rap like a hammer. That shit about his being born in the South? Of people who were from the French? Don't you believe it. I knew the guy, ya see. Real well, I knew him. That's how he robbed me, son of a bitch, in this town in Oklahoma. Summer of '70, he arrived because he had been hired by the public school to teach English. Said he wanted to settle into town before the school year started. Hot as hell, that summer ..."

Dear Mr. Madison: I am writing about a pair of your thin-soled "Manhattan" model shoe, which I purchased in brown in Macy's, just a couple of weeks ago. I found that, through normal wear, the front flap of the sole on the right shoe has separated from the upper part of the shoe. The people at Macy's say that I must have mistreated the shoe, but I assure you I did not. I am asking you to send me a replacement pair, size 10W, or at least a right shoe, in brown, to the address below. I am in the media and I need to look my best at all times and would be pleased to comment favorably if you were to make good on your shoe at your earliest convenience.

As you know, one comment by a radio personality, either favorably or not, can have a big impact on the commercial success of any company, particularly a company directly serving the consumer.

I eagerly await your advice.

Yours truly, M. Pierre

⋯ ⋯

WIKIPEDIA ENTRY MAY 22, 2015

Pierre M, born Maurice Pender in Brooklyn, New York July 15, 1933, and died of natural causes on April 4, 2014 in Slocum, Georgia, American author, radio personality, investor.

Personal Life:

Mr. Pierre was born to poverty in a particularly depressed area of Brooklyn, New York of working-class parents. An indifferent student in school, Mr. Pierre dropped out of high school at age sixteen. There followed a period of petty crime and temporary jobs. He was then taken into a program run by the Catholic Archdiocese of Brooklyn, which paid his living expenses while he graduated from Brooklyn College with a major in education in three years.

Pierre traveled through much of the United States holding

various jobs in education until he settled in Rockville, Maryland, married Lettie Harrison in [? Information needed], to whom he was married for several years while he wrote his single novel, *The Further Adventures of Maximillian J. Pussycat.*

The novel was wildly successful and launched Mr. Pierre on a career in public broadcast described below.

Little is known of his personal life after the publication of his novel. [further information needed]

Writings and Radio Career:

Mr. Pierre's book—cast as a fairy tale for adults in which a feline, speaking through its master, explores the simple truths of life and the need to return to basics—topped the charts for fiction from its first publication in June 1978, for seven months, and remained a top seller through six editions and eleven paperback printings, the last edition being published in English in May of 1992. It was translated into fourteen languages and was the basis for two cartoon series on Cartoon Network, one voiced by Meryl Streep.

The most transparent and most quoted passage from his novel, *The Further Adventures of Maximillian J. Pussycat*, is set forth below, a soliloquy by M. J. Pussycat himself:

"You must understand. I am a cat! Mystery is my life. Or lives. I do not have only nine, you see. I have many. Each new day is a new set of lives, to live as if my entire life. If I bring joy that is good. If I rub up against a visitor to our home and she begins to gasp and wheeze because she is allergic to me, if she must be taken out to the fresh air in extreme distress, if she even happens to die on our porch, her air passages swollen beyond relief, her face blue-tinged as her chest heaves uselessly—well, that day of her life was not very good of course but, as for me, I still had the arm chair to lie in and my little girl who stroked my fur and who told me that it was not my fault."

Mr. Pierre was contracted to conduct a daytime talk show about any and all topics, first on CBN, beginning in May of 1980. His four-hour talk show was moved from the 12–4 slot to the 3-7 slot after several weeks, when it was clear that his drawing power, and simple way of phrasing serious life questions so that the solutions become obvious, had attracted a large following. Unique among talk show hosts, his popularity was highest during prime "drive time," and did not wane although he never had guests and had no formal training in any particular area.

In or about 199?, his program suddenly diverted to reports on economic matters and selection of investments, which triggered a sharp decline in his popularity. His show was moved to Sunday mornings only in 199?. In 1994 he was indicted by the U.S. Department of Justice for violation of the Federal Securities laws, was convicted and spent 3 years of a 4-year sentence in the United States low security penitentiary in Atlanta, Georgia.

Later Career:

[if anyone has credible information about Mr. Pierre after his release from prison, please propose supplementary information to the editors]

Selection from Eagle Scout Project Outline submitted by Scout First Class Maurice Pender, Troop 81, Brooklyn, New York, September 24, 1948.

"At the new beach park known as Jones Beach, located in Suffolk County, Long Island, there are three very long walkways from the distant parking areas to the beach houses and beach itself. On hot days, many people become tired and thirsty during that walk, carrying chairs and umbrellas and coolers and permitted beach toys. My project is to install water stations at 25-yard intervals on all paths, using pumping equipment, piping and water fountains provided by the Park. I have a letter from Mr. Robert Moses, Director of the Triboro Bridge Authority, saying that he will cause the State of New York to provide all materials including bubblers if our troop will dig, and then cover over, the ditches to bring the water along the paths. Work will be done during the beach "off-season." My Troop will provide the labor. We will have parents provide suitable food and transportation. My project will improve the park and cure dehydration, which leads to many headaches and is a factor in drowning accidents.

My thanks to Mr. George Richter, Asst. Scout Master, who helped me write this project proposal."

<hr>

Report Card
Spring Semester 1943
PS 216, Brooklyn New York

Absent: 22
Tardy: 13

Grades:

English Composition	B
American History	B
Mathematics	C-
Science	C-
Geography	D
Art	C
Music	A
Comportment	D

Maurice is a polite, respectful boy, always correct with teachers. He is often the center of disturbances, however, usually involving large numbers of children. He seems to make groups of children angry with each other. Teachers and our psychologist, Mr. Levitan, suggest that Maurice be taken to a consultation with a private practitioner, as he is a bright boy with behaviors that we at 216 do not feel experienced in addressing.

⊷⊶ ▰◆▰ ⊷⊶

Selected Street Interviews, Conducted by Murray Schlictstein, "Man on the Street" for WKKL-TV, April 10 to 16, 2014. Each interviewee was asked if he or she had heard that M. Pierre had died.

+ Really. That is too bad. Poor woman, sorry she passed.

+ Oh, that guy. I don't even think that guy every really existed, it was whaddaya call it, a fake name, a nom de plume for someone else, some famous guy. Urban legend I think. Pretty sure about that. Yeah.

+Great man, listened to him all the time for must have been a couple of decades. His novel changed my life. He made me understand that each of us has both good and evil, and that sometimes you don't get to choose which one of you comes to the table at a particular time. We are all part of the unpredictable world, you know! Goddamned genius. Hey, carpe diem.

+ Oh, did not know. Shame. Best shortstop the Mets ever had.

⊷⊶ ▰◆▰ ⊷⊶

Yeah, M. Pierre was my father. How'd you find me anyway?

I haven't had any contact with him for maybe forty years before he passed away. My mother told me I was a love child, that's the way it was on the streets. Hard times. Sometimes he would come

43

by, but after I turned 10 or 11 he just stopped. I cried about it, yeah, asked mamma why he had stopped, he was nice to me and my only father. It was years later that I once tried to reach out to him, he was on the radio of course, I called in but they would not put the call through. I left my number and explained why I called and the woman said she would be sure to give him the message, but I never did hear back. I guess he was just a fleeting memory for me, but I was just no memory at all for him.

It wasn't until Mr. Jamison, the guy who wrote that biography about my father after he died, came to see me, that I learned about the, well, I guess the alleged incidents. He had seen some court records about a case brought by my mother about some sort of improper conduct, but I told him, I don't recall anything of the kind. I think I just loved him because he was my only father.

By then of course mama had passed, so I had no one to talk to about all that . . .

This morning I was texting...

The other evening, at a small dinner, one of the hosts said: "This morning I was texting with a woman from Brazil." I cannot remember any context for the remark, which was delivered as if from a vacuum, so much so that everyone stopped talking, held their forks in abeyance, and metaphorically raised their eyebrows.

Struck by the anomalous nature of this remark, and the subsequent unwillingness of the speaker to provide further detail (leaving unfinished what promised to be an interesting story), perhaps as the speaker was annoyed by the tone of the reception her opening sentence received, I asked each person to write and to circulate to all a short story starting with the line "This morning I was texting with a woman from Brazil."

Now that many days have passed without receiving a single reply, even though my challenge at the time evinced general laughter which I took to be assent, I felt compelled to ask the speaker if she was now willing, in a more amenable atmosphere, to tell me the story that she had started. Politely, she demurred, the moment had passed she said, it would be uninteresting and furthermore perhaps on reflection embarrassing; she hung up the phone as quickly as politeness allowed.

I had occasion shortly thereafter to stop by the speaker's

house to drop off some books and saw, on the narrow table in her front hall, atop the day's newspaper and under a small pile of keys and a few dollar bills, her cell phone. With no intention of permanent theft, I scooped the phone into my jacket pocket, and upon driving around the corner I pulled over and found out that I lacked the password to enter the device and scan the memory. No matter what I tried, no success: her address, her nickname, the names of her husband and daughter and dog, a variant on her phone number. Later that night I gently dropped the phone into the mailbox slot on the post at the end of her driveway.

A few days later I called the counsel general of Brazil and inquired as to whether he had a count or estimation of the number of Brazilian women living in greater Boston. At first the counsel, a well-known business lawyer in a white-shoe Federal Street law firm, thought my call was some type of prank, but I convinced him of the seriousness, if not the logic, of my inquiry. He then pointed out that it was absolutely impossible to know the answer and, in any event, even if there were an official record, undoubtedly there would be no accounting for what he smugly assured me were almost uncountable illegal immigrants who busied themselves by cleaning the offices and laboratories throughout the region.

I hung up feeling crestfallen, and the thought that the Brazilian woman in question might not even be in Boston at all, nor in New England, nor even the United States, was no comfort. I imagined her a bond trader in Singapore, a prostitute in Amsterdam, even one of 88 million women in Brazil itself.

Searching for some link between the woman who spoke and Brazil, I perused Facebook, LinkedIn, the surprisingly robust 13,000 items which Google produced against my entry of her name (including many for an artist in Taos with whom she shared her name exactly). No clues about any connection with

Brazil or a woman from Brazil, not even in the older items relating to the speaker's decade-old and now abandoned career as a real estate broker. Her history just lay there in perpetual plain view, but without any entries that might help me.

I could not write a short story, as I had challenged the group to do. It would only be an invented story, after all, untrue to the real-life story which the speaker still withheld, a falsehood which might crowd out the reality to ill effect, squashing forever the true story that was sitting just out of reach, crying to be revealed.

There was a young woman from Brazil
Who was seeking an ultimate thrill.
She went back to Rio
And partied con brio.
That woman is partying still.

I could muster doggerel, it seemed, but it did not satisfy my needs.

Under moonlight dripping with Portuguese lilt
My mind went astray as do all who seek.
Atlantic waters lapping my shores
Gurgled the words "Brazilia Brazil...."

Serious poetry could not fill my needs either; my effort reminded me that I was a failure as a writer, even when attempting mere imitation.

I finally capitulated. I invited myself to the speaker's house, claiming some topic I needed to discuss in person, nothing earth-shattering mind you but best dealt with in person, and could her husband, now returned from extensive business travel, perhaps be present.

They are friends, they accommodated my request with good humor and no sense of the sinister. We exchanged pleasantries and opened and sipped the excellent bottle of Amarone I had brought as a lubricant for discourse. I then confessed my purpose, admitting in false self-deprecation that this quest struck even me as somewhat absurd. But would not the speaker now complete the story that she had started at dinner that night, the one that began "this morning I was texting a woman in Brazil"?

The pause after my request at some point became a tangible silence which I at first attributed to their being stunned by the ridiculousness of my inquiry. I almost expected laughter to break out, or an invitation to leave and take the remaining half-bottle of wine with me as they were both tired from their days and thank you very much for dropping by.

But then I noticed that the husband was glowering at the speaker, whose eyes were downcast, refusing contact with either her husband or with myself. And after this uncomfortable interlude, the husband said softly, "I did not know that you were still in touch...."

The speaker then looked up, ignoring me, and said with a hint of iron in her tone and more than a glint of defiance in her eyes, "I must have mentioned it at the party; maybe when you were downstairs getting more wine in the basement?"

The silence resumed and could not have lasted as long as it feels in memory, with each looking silently at one or another piece of furniture.

"You had best leave, Steve— if you don't mind." The husband had arisen and had extended his hand to me.

"Yes, yes, of course," I replied, placing my glass on the side table and standing up, no doubt too abruptly. I awkwardly gave his hand one cursory pump, to which neither of us exerted any pressure, as if robust physical contact would somehow acknowledge a meeting which was unpleasant and not easily erased. I walked to the hall and put my hand on the doorknob, looked back into the room, and saw them sitting silently, looking away from each other.

I opened the door gently, stepped delicately out on the stair landing, and glanced back.

"I'm sorry," I said over my shoulder, and eased the door shut behind me.

FIVE WOMEN IN AN UNTIDY OVAL

There were five women in an untidy oval, all seated in beach chairs. Or rather, arranged on top of the flat part of beach chairs where your legs normally stretch out, surrounded by random towels and magazines, all leaning in towards an ill-defined center point for an indeterminate discussion that bounced around shopping, kids, shoes, Saturday night dinner. All were tanned, well turned out in glittery bikinis, all toes neatly painted, sandals with pom-poms (no flip flops here), lots of gold.

My guess was early thirties, not late, but they had kids. Hard to tell. Designer sunglasses. Gym toned. Conversation told me in their forties but, well, they just looked too damned good to be that old. And then, there were those squeals . . .

Well to do. Edge of rich. Truly rich would be at their own pools, or one of those exclusive Boca beach clubs, not here at a hotel beach club which was apparently open to locals who could pay what was likely a hefty tariff. Large tote bags, draw strings on top. Expensive. But no logos. They are tuned in, they know that logos are so yesterday. But expensive no doubt; yes sir.

Out of the sacs came, randomly, now a cell phone, then a tube of coconut smelling something, bottle of vitamin water pulled from the deep recesses, sometimes pulling along with it some unintended detritus of loose papers, a lipstick, tissues, an eyeglass case, a tumble of keys—ah yes, Mercedes logo on the key fob.

My chair was close, unintentionally close, a logistic mistake by the hotel beach boy, who might have thought I would enjoy the view, or perhaps just did not much care where he plunked down some transient hotel guest. And yes, the view was – nice. Covey of blonde shiny hair, punctuated by one dark-complexioned (and perhaps even a touch plump-y, is that possible?) woman with slick black close-cropped hair. Several hair bands coordinated with bikinis.

The perhaps plump-y woman was closest to my chair, I had to look directly at her when I put down my *New Yorker*. Not enough spin classes perhaps? I perused her up and down one time for good measure; no wedding band.

I was planning to move, the tide had receded, I could drag my chair down the slope a couple of yards, dim the cacophony, replace it with sloshing wave sounds. Just about mustered enough energy to sit up against the pressure of the sun on my chest when a snippet of conversation stopped me. A discussion about New York. No, New Jersey. Some of the women were from New Jersey at some point. Not all. Three now were local, members of the beach club it seemed. The others—visitors from the North Plainview. I know Plainview, I think, somewhere vaguely west of the Holland Tunnel, a commute to Manhattan, maybe near Newark?

No deep New York-Jersey accents. How come? Schooled out of them? Replaced for some by what now passed for an East Coast of Florida accent, scrubbed of origin yet not Southern either. The pervasive connective "like" notwithstanding, a well-spoken if squeal-ish group.

Other women stopped by for cheek-pecks, reminders about tennis, reservations at some restaurant; meet my friend Rachel down from New Jersey, meet my friend Sarah from Temple, meet my friend someone from somewhere, you know Miriam don't you

Antonia? Antonia, the darker woman is Antonia, perhaps Italian not Hispanic? Why am I trapped into listening to this?

"Hi there, how are you girls doin'?" A male voice, not a very original greeting but delivered full of gusto, the promise of being interested in the answer. I turned my head slightly to discover a stocky guy of medium height in a T-shirt and blue shorts standing in the narrow space between my boat shoes half-buried in the sand and the edge of the women's oval. My view of his backside was superior, sitting on top of tan hairy legs too thin for the rest of him. Trying to look upwards against the sun, was that a small bald spot? Or a bad angle, maybe sun glare?

"Ya remember me, yes? Lou. Louis Rothman. The party at the boatyard, the one with the band. Just a few weeks ago. Sorry, don't remember your name . . . "

"I'm Cindy," replied one of the natives. "I do remember you, you were with Maya Whatshername, right?"

A slight pause. "Yeah, she was my date. You a good friend of Maya, are ya?" Some obvious trepidation.

"Not really, we just have kids in some things together. Why?"

"Oh, yeah," said with some bare sense of relief, "cause she just blew me off after that party . . . "

"So you're single!" Could not tell whose voice, what with the triumphant minor rise in volume accompanying this seemingly vital deduction.

"Divorced actually." I think, can you be divorced not "actually," perhaps merely theoretically? Why do I dislike this guy I don't even know?

"But it's okay," he offers, "we're still friends! Hey, mind if I sit down for a minute, it's kinda hard to talk down on you girls, you know?" In the awkward silence, he sits on the edge of Antonia's chair, Antonia's feet curling quickly away and under her. Lou is still talking about something I miss but which the group seems to find absorbing.

"Yeah, I get the kids every other weekend. Bought a big condo over on 3rd. That new building?"

The local women grunt recognition, and Cindy asks if the building is nice; yes with a concierge, he admitted that he needed all the help he could get. General laughter. I could believe he needed more help than a concierge could possibly deliver.

"So, hey, all you girls married or what?" Asked with a simple open smile. Wow, do I dislike this guy. Let me count the ways. My father, born almost a century ago and a stickler for refined speech, told me that "hey" was for horses not people. My mother, born with her own Victorian sense of good taste, told me that you did not ask that kind of question. My wife, born into a more modern time, told me that there were women and girls, and the cross-over point was somewhere in the late teens and that in our upper middleclass suburb calling grown people "girls" was a major political correctness faux pas. Why is this guy holding court with these, okay you got me to admit it, really hot women when he's talking shit like that?

No one says, coldly, "how do you come off asking that?"

What I hear is an energetic bunch of yesses, a modest pause, then Antonia softly mentioning a recent divorce while slipping her ringless left hand unconsciously under the edge of a beach towel on her chair. This good news moved Lou onto a more solid placement of his rump on Antonia's chair, just a minor wiggle forward which this time is not met with a reciprocal contraction of any female body parts. Followed by more talk about restaurants, don't these people have kitchens, plans for tonight, how long are you down here, I begin to drift way, I am thinking of the sound of the waves again, looking for my resolve to sit up.

"Hey, how about a drink? You girls want a drink?"

A bunch of quick no's, gotta drive, kid to be picked up, too early, too hot, drinking on the beach gives me a headache.

No worries for Lou, he is off talking schools, and the New Jersey geography, he is asking inappropriate questions about spouses, he finds out he went to the same college as one of the absent husbands, and (Lucky Lou) the same school as Antonia's brother! What year, what's his first name, what frat house, do you know if he knew my buddy Jake, actually Joel but everyone called him Jake on account of whatever. Names and years offered, Lou it turns out is 42. Cindy mentions she is 45. Against my intentions my head rolls right for another look. Pretty damn good for 45.

"You girls sure you don't want a drink?"

In Boston if I called these people girls they would offer some sardonic remark, at a minimum. At least, a chilling of the atmosphere. It feeds into my superior self-image to think, that in Boston, if I were Lou addressing this group, there would be a chilling of the atmosphere and surely no cocktails. But Lou is cruising, he's set at 80 and he is on cruise control, his hands are off the wheel, his chariot is humming down the road. "Tequila shots!! Let me buy you girls tequila shots. Just one, whaddaya say?"

Lou has hold of the group in some vaguely male way. Across the few feet of sand separating us, I can feel, palpably feel, the charge in the air. He is young, single, turns out he is a sports agent ("oh do you know that guy, you know who, he's the Giant's big running back, they play y'know like just a few miles from my house in Jersey ... "), his testosterone is sweating out of his pores, it is wafting into the oval and being breathed, infused, he is infecting the herd.

"Sure, okay just one but then I gotta go"—giggle giggle, all floating in the air while a seemingly triumphant Lou is off his rump with remarkable alacrity, hard to believe how quickly he is up and harder to believe how fast he is back carrying a small try of shot glasses. He must have tipped the bartender at the beach bar shack a twenty to jump the line and get back here so fast.

Klink, klink, skol, a toast to the beach, another toast to Antonia we wish her good luck, bottoms up, the beach waitress stops by to pick up the empties and another round gets ordered, then some more, who cares if my kid gets picked up and I'm sauced, half in the tank at three in the afternoon, I'll get the nanny to pick him up, hey can your nanny pick mine up, general laughter. I am thinking, I cannot believe it but I am jealous, I am embarrassed to be jealous but yes I am, jealous that this chunky, balding, divorced shitty-employed clueless inappropriate jerk has got five beautiful girls, dammit women, totally enthralled. Enthralled with talk about nothing.

"Say, Antonia, I don't know if you have plans for tonight . . ." Carefully timed tactical pause, this guy is good, I will give him that. Next thing I hear is that Antonia of course is excused from dinner at the Crab Shack tonight, we have a group but it's all couples, we'll catch up tomorrow. Next thing I know everyone is on their feet gathering their miscellany, everyone is air kissing and waving good-bye, I see Lou and Antonia already at the stairs leading back to the hotel, hands linked, she is hooting "I'll call you later," Cindy says she will leave the key in the same spot, Lou promises in a booming baritone "I'll take good care of her, don't you worry," and I glimpse Cindy and Rachel, the last to leave, stuffing their beach bags.

"Nice guy, can't believe he's still available," says Cindy. "Yeah, but it hasn't been all that long," says Rachel. "Shit, I'm late," says Cindy. "And do you care," asks Rachel. Mutual mirth, fading up the beach and then they too are gone.

I hear the gurgle of the waves.

I am calming down from my embarrassment about my angry thoughts when I sense a shadow over me. Looking up, I see Celine, our waitress, the young, blonde and blue-eyed and open-faced and small-nosed and lovely Celine.

"Excuse, me, sir, but – I'm not sure, were you with the group that just left?"

"No. Not at all," I snap, too adamantly, straightening Celine up as she tries to figure out what she did to offend.

"Sorry, you startled me, why do you ask, is there anything wrong?"

"Well, I have this open bar tab for three rounds of tequila."

THE FOUR HORSE

I tore up my ticket in disgust. My pony lost it at the eighth pole. This other nag, at forty to one no less, exploded out of nowhere and trashed the field. His jockey never even used the whip, for Godssake. My horse was sure to win; at least in my own mind. I mean, I go to the track plenty, I'm something of a student of the art of handicapping. Ever since I moved to Miami and became fascinated by the statistics, the huge quantity of information available about each horse in each race, highlighted by the various tout sheets for sale around the track, I was hooked. A worthy undertaking for an active mind in retirement, and each exercise of the art costs a mere two dollars.

Hialeah is a beautiful track, a rich, almost brown oval framed by tall palm trees waving in the Florida breeze against a tapestry of blue sky punctuated by scudding white clouds marching towards the ocean. It is a peaceful place underneath the pounding beat of the horses, and splashed with racing colors and peppered with people of all sorts, well worth a critical look and a random speculation as to provenance, wealth and personality.

And yesterday, a diminutive, well-tanned man caught my eye by his serene demeanor. One thing about people at the track; they typically carry a harried aura around with them. There is not a lot of time between races to figure out how to lay down one's bets if you are more than a two-dollar-on-the-nose kind of guy, and you need to consider not only the statistics you studied the night before but also the late scratches, the moving odds on the tote board indicating, perhaps, the direction of the smart money, and how your favorite pony looks in the slow walk to the starting gate. But this fellow, well, he was walking towards a cashier with a thin grin, holding what looked like a single ticket. And his dress was stylish but not in a race-track-y sort of way; sharp crease in his trousers, crisp oxford button-down shirt, well-cut seersucker blazer, and a pocket hanky matching the band on his boater.

But what really caught my eye was what I was able to see about his transaction at the betting window. It took a long time to process his one ticket, the woman behind the cage seemed to take forever to count out a reasonably large stack of bills. Unless he was getting his pay-off in single dollar notes, he had quite a hit.

You generally do not start a chat with someone at the track. It is just not, well, protocol. Single men at the track are often lost in the process, alone with their horses and strategies, jealous of their judgments, and in spite of the reputation of bettors giving advice to anyone who will listen, at least at Hialeah I have just about never seen anyone talk to strangers. But a few minutes later I found myself standing next to this fellow in the men's room, each of us relieving ourselves in the way that men in their seventies typically do—slowly, carefully, accompanied by a gentle sigh signaling success.

"Excuse me, sir, I don't mean to intrude, but you seemed to have the last race doped out; I had the two horse and while not the favorite I was very high on him."

He turned his head slightly and narrowed his eyes, taking my measure it seemed. "Come here often, do you," he asked.

"Yes, I do, a couple of times a week during the season, matter of fact. I find it – peaceful and beautiful. I love the horses, they are sort of stately if you know what I mean."

"Really? I actually never look at them. They are sort of irrelevant."

We each stood there, shaking off the last drops from our wrinkled tools, a couple of old men in the most awkward of moments. But I could not resist.

"How can you say that the horses don't matter at a horse race? I mean, we come to watch them race against each other, the whole thing is about the horses. Yes?"

We walked to the sinks together, at first in silence. Then he turned to me. "Buy me a cup of coffee?"

"Sure if you tell me how you doped out that last race."

"Not sure I'm willing to do that but I only bet the sixth race and I could use a cup of coffee."

We spent a pleasant twenty minutes or so just chatting. A widower like me, Carl acquired his mildly British lilt as a researcher with a team of antiquarians working in the mid-East; his life had been spent in preserving and translating ancient Hebraic scrolls found in cliffs some distance from the location of the famous Dead Sea Scrolls. Turned out he was doing graduate work at Columbia at the same time I was in law school there and we traded recollections of restaurants, events, what the city was like fifty years ago. Suffice it to say we hit if off pretty well, a couple of older guys who found out, by talking with each other, just how lonely they were while living under the sun in God's Waiting Room.

"Let me suggest we have dinner tonight," Carl finally said. "It is hard to find someone to talk to down here. I really don't like Florida at all, too damned hot and most of the people I meet are just plain boring. If it were not for my work, I would live in London. Or New York."

"You are working," I asked with some surprise.

He grinned. "Yes, I am working. In fact, you just saw me working."

I must have looked confused; I was confused. Carl reached across the small Formica table and patted the back of my hand. "Jonah's Crab Shack. Eight o'clock. I'll explain."

That night I took a cab to Jonah's, a restaurant I did not frequent on my adequate but finite budget. It was the kind of Florida restaurant where most of the menu consisted of seafood flown in from Boston to cater to the tastes of snowbirds who really never did get the idea of what Miami had to offer. But Carl had invited me and in the back of my mind I harbored the hope that he would think it appropriate to pick up the check also. He was waiting for me; the maitre'd smiled at me and said he would take me to Mr. Lester's table; seemed Carl was a regular.

We both ordered the grouper with an excellent panko crust and Carl mentioned in passing that he was paying so I should not be concerned when he ordered a $700 bottle of Le Montrachet and, as the evening wore on, he ordered a second. By ten we had been at table for two hours and the restaurant was emptying; even at expensive Florida restaurants it is an early crowd unless you are a metrosexual hanging at South Beach. Carl leaned forward, a small splash of precious wine landing in his cup of espresso.

"I have a question for you," he almost drawled. "Can I trust you? I mean really trust you? Because frankly I think you are a kindred spirit. We could be friends, or well, maybe that overstates it, but at least regular acquaintances, you know. So, what do you think?"

I hesitated, not because I thought myself untrustworthy but, rather, because I was taken aback. Then realizing that my delay in answering might be taken in a negative way, I started to answer and found myself saying what I feared was far too much.

"Sorry for hesitating, Carl. I just was surprised, that's all. You know, I consider myself a very trustworthy person, and loyal to my friends. I was a lawyer, as I told you, and I think the very best kind, a trusted advisor is the way I was often described. I am not sure that I want to intrude on you and burden you with any doubts, I did not mean to pry deeply into any secrets of yours. I was just frankly curious, you know." I petered out.

"I sensed that about you, which is why I am asking you, in what seems a formal way, to promise to take my information and keep it in confidence. Because, well," he looked down now as he made what seemed to be a personal confession, "I could use a friend down here and you surely are the most intelligent person I have met and someone who could actually enjoy what I could tell you."

I sat for a moment. There was, after all, no downside for me to hear Carl's story. It might be boring and disappointing. Or, it might be fascinating. I surely would not generally violate a promise I made to any person so I felt confident I could and would protect whatever Carl might tell me. What did I have to lose? "Carl, I would be delighted to be your friend. I like you and I like talking with you. I also like your taste in wines," I said in an effort to lighten the moment, an aside he met with a broad and reassuring smile. "If you have a story to tell, I would be delighted, anxious to hear it."

And here is what Carl told me when we retired to the lounge and sat until after midnight over snifters of Louis XIII cognac:

"It was in the summer of 1997. We discovered a small single cave about 30 klicks south of the Dead Sea site, just where the topography was changing from cliffs to desert. Not a promising site for caves; most are high up and easily defended and hidden, but there were some texts, Aramaic references to a people who lived between the Sea and the desert and who were revered as most holy. The leader of our team was one of these intrepid Israelis; as if each stone were a gift from the God of Abraham, each discovery a further proof of the right and entitlement of the Jews to the whole of their land. In any event, he sure as hell could find caves, I'll give him at least that.

It was deceptively near the base of this small escarpment, almost where you would not even look. Perhaps that is why it seemed undisturbed for so many centuries. We opened it early one morning, before the heat made it unbearable to work and drove us to our tents at midday, to sweat on cots, preferable to sweating in the choking dust. There were some evidence of fires and human occupation which we later used for dating, but the main thing was we were looking for amphora, the pottery vessels into which scrolls typically were stored. Since the cave was seemingly undisturbed, and far from the salty inland sea, any scrolls we might find could indeed be well preserved. And from what was recorded as a site inhabited by a holy sect.

So to make short some details which were fascinating to us, but likely not so interesting to you, we finally found a cache of sealed pottery of very great age and we carried them back to our laboratory in Haifa and began the tedious task of unrolling the enclosed scrolls, preserving them and finally deciphering them. Immediately we knew that these were of the most ancient sort, the writing was so primitive that it took some effort to unlearn the techniques we had used on the Dead Sea Scrolls so that we could translate what was written.

Now you will recall that when Moses came down from the mountain the first time, he was appalled by the heathen behavior of the Israelites and he smashed the tablets containing God's commandments to express his anger. I was reading a small scroll recounting this story when something caught my attention that was new and different, however. It began with the words 'and here is what Moses said unto me, Aaron, upon descending a second time with the Law, which Moses made me swear never to reveal unto the peoples.' I confess that I did not tell the rest of the team of this discovery; I wanted the personal rush of pleasure of being the only person on earth who, for at least one brief moment, knew this secret of thousands of years. I never thought that the scroll was written by Aaron of course, that would be too spectacular for words and in any event would run counter to what we knew of history and the creation of the scrolls. But the revelation, I must tell you, began to make me wishfully speculate.

And Aaron recounted in this scroll, which had been very carefully prepared and preserved with exceptional attention, that the original tablet, the one that Moses cast down upon the heads of the people and smashed to smithereens, contained not ten but twelve sacred Laws. I spent many nights, secretly while everyone else on the team sat in the cafes overlooking the Mediterranean, feigning vague illness so that I could sneak back to the laboratory and work on my scroll. I was looking, of course, for the missing two Laws, the word of the Lord. It seemed that Moses had in fact told Aaron the missing Laws, their content, but could it be that Aaron had not passed them down, had adhered to the instructions of Moses as the vessel of God's word and left these sacred Laws unrecorded, lost to history, known now only to the Almighty? Feverishly I strained over the text, word by word, slow progress in the midst of the ancient writings and the arcane words, some of which had to be coaxed into having meaning, a few of which were unknown even to me after forty years in the field.

And then, one night, my last night with the scroll, I found what I was looking for. It read, and I will never forget it, 'I, Aaron, unworthy of Yahweh's forgiveness but unable to control my desire to know all of His holy word, record here the precious eleventh and twelfth Laws of the Lord Most High, Blessed be His name, and here seal them in the most secret of all holy places in the wish someday, when the Lord deems the people of Israel worthy once again, that these scrolls be found and the Twelve Laws of the Tablets again be complete in the word of the Almighty, King of Kings.'

I read these two Laws then, by the dim light we used to make sure that the writings did not bleach out, and committed them to memory."

Carl paused and heavily sighed. He picked up his snifter, sloshed the amber liquid, breathed its aroma, gently tilted the glass and wet the very edges of his lips, his eyes closed, his mind transported. And me? All I could say, after a few seconds, aghast at the magnitude of the moment, all I could say was "Then what?"

Carl smiled. "I will tell you what. And you must not judge me ill. I adhered to the admonition of Moses. The Lord had omitted the last two Laws on purpose of course; there is never anything accidental in the word of God. God did not want these Laws revealed. I did what I had to do." Carl closed his eyes, and his head fell backwards onto his shoulders, limp and rolling.

"I burned the scroll," he whispered.

"Oh my God."

"Yes. I secretly burned it. I told the team nothing of it. It was just one of many scrolls, when we did the final inventory I kept silent and it was just recorded as unfortunately misplaced, but there were so many other unique writings in the other scrolls that no one spent much time worrying about it. The missing scroll was lost to history and to mankind."

We sat in silence for a few minutes. I could not contain myself, I had to ask, even though Carl had not offered, even though I was risking the destruction of our incredible bond, our unique trust, I had to ask.

"Carl," I started, but he held up his hand.

"You need not worry. I will tell. You don't have to ask. I would never have told you this much unless I was intending to tell you. I have your oath. I trust your oath.

"The eleventh law was, 'In a hard world to come, thou canst not find the power to scratch every itch.'"

It took me a few seconds to focus. "You are of course joking with me, Carl."

"Would you like to hear the last Law, the last of the twelve Laws of the tablet?" he asked.

"Yes, I would," I replied.

Carl leaned forward and almost hissed these words: "The four horse in the sixth race at Hialeah."

KILLER GIRLFRIEND

I didn't know what the word meant when I first heard it. I was paying attention, too, because when the judge is giving your sentence you pay real close attention, I gotta tell you. And in County they don't exactly leave dictionaries lying around for the population to peruse if you catch my drift. I mean, from context I could tell it was not good, what the judge was saying, and when she got to the meat and mentioned a few decades I realized it was not good at all, ya know?

So "misogynist" really, when you think about it, isn't quite right because I got in trouble because I loved 'em, not because I hated them. That's a long story but, then again, seems I have the time so let me tell you but I warn you, it isn't pretty and it proves what everyone says about if you didn't have bad luck you wouldn't have any luck at all.

One thing before I start which is this: I am not the literary type, and I realize I left a teaser at the end there, about bad luck. I am not going to let it hang there and come back to it at the end of my story and expect you to say "aha, I now know what that was all about, that was really clever!" So let me take it off the table right now. I was driving down Route 93 the day it happened and this guy, he taps my car from behind while I'm braking, so we pull over and then he starts yelling and pointing and damned if the impact didn't pop my rear latch and when I pull over the door of my SUV slowly lifts up and sticking out from under the tarp wouldn't you know it but there is Cecilia's hand and arm sticking out, white as snow but with some of the splatters of blood on it, just enough to freak this guy out and so he runs back to his car, locks the door, I see him on his cell phone so I hop in my car and slip back into the flow of traffic and slide gently off the next exit but the cops are right on me and next thing you know I am in a cell and the rest is, as they say, history.

So now you know the end of Cecilia, so to speak, but there is a lot to say about the beginning which was really pretty good the truth to tell. Not that the good part made the whole thing worth it of course, but ya gotta give the poor girl her due, she was hot and a hell of a great gal until later when—well not so much.

It was one of those evenings in the winter when the clouds broke just before night so your sky had those streaks of gray and some purple and some really dark blue-black behind it all. It's January thaw but it still feels raw, what with the sleet earlier and that Boston wind backing around from the North. I hate those kinds of days. So anyway it's Thursday which is a real party night in downtown; everyone is in the bars after work, what we would call "checking out the action" but what it really was, you're 32 years old, you're a guy or a woman but you don't have any plans so you and a few friends you find a bar that looks lively and you get a bottle of Sam Adams and you speculate about the other people in the bar, you sort of give them a rating if you know what I mean, and if you happen to be standing close to a girl, let's say, you try to start a conversation and those things can go any which way, but sometimes you actually do manage to keep your size 12 out of your mouth long enough to say something not so dumb, and you and your friends you talk with her and her friends and, once in a blue moon you get an invite to a party in someone's apartment in the North End or in Somerville, and all that you need is for that to happen once in a while and it keeps you coming back on Thursday nights just to stay in the game.

Just so you know, in my experience if you pick someone out and weave your way over to them and they are not right next to you to start with, you might think they were flattered and would be receptive but it doesn't work that way; I think, because, if you talk to someone next to you it's natural, it doesn't focus on the fact that you are on the prowl and she is obviously alone and looking, which is maybe a pathetic admission of how her life sucks, so she rejects your approach because you are reminding her that she is showing out her real predicament and who likes to be reminded of that? While if you happen to be right next to someone it's only normal human interaction, you look, you may smile, you make small talk about how crowded it is, what's your name, it's a real conversation among civilized human beings. Anyway, that's my theory though I guess in the foreseeable future I am not going to be able to test it out, except maybe in the men's shower room which I tell you, if the things you see on TV are anyway near accurate, is not my idea of a well-spent Thursday night.

The girl next to Harry, her name was Felicia, a nice old-fashioned name; I had a cousin named Felicia and I lost track of her but she was nice. Anyway, Harry he went to college all the way through the third year and he's pretty smooth, he's chatting away and then I think he says something like "would you girls like to meet my friends here" and she says something like "there are no girls here but the women might like to meet your gentlemen friends," with a smile that defuses any offense Harry may feel about making what is now known as a micro-aggression ya know, and he comes back with "there aren't any gentlemen here but I can introduce you women to my stumblebum friends over here" and everyone is laughing and talking and exchanging names and in the back of your head you are wondering why you had to go through all that preliminary shit but so what, you are where you want to be right now so don't argue with the road when you've reached home.

There are four of us and four of them which is convenient although it does force you to sort out rather than play the larger field. That's okay with me, I am not very good at sorting out or being selected when someone else is doing the sorting. And by some process you end up with someone you are mostly talking with, because in a loud bar it is hard to hold a group discussion, and my someone is Cecilia who I will now describe as she was that night, which was one of her better nights I might add.

The late Jim Croce sang about a roller derby queen and that came pretty close. Cecilia was not tall, though she did not seem short. She was really solid, which is different from fat. Her chin was square, her nose straight and strong, her mouth was small and pouty and her hair was blonde but you could see the dark roots in her part, which threw her hair left and right from the middle of her face. Her eyes were green and wide apart which I love by the way, and her eyebrows could have used a good plucking and while she was at it she might have lightened them a bit to sort of blend with her hair. But all this was hung onto an open wide face with nice pink skin, and her ears behaved rather than sticking out. I liked that face, it had the feel of comfort food, I felt good looking at it. It was the kind of face that made me not want to say something stupid, and that took some doing.

Cecilia and her friend Didi were roommates in an apartment near Malden Square, a suburb of no known attractions beyond cheap real estate near the subway line, but if we brought some beer and maybe some chips perhaps we could come over Saturday night. Sure why not, instant party. Identify the kind of music you like, come by around 7:30 or 8, exchange cell phone numbers if something comes up (a real date? a tsunami?) and sure, see ya then.

So now it's 11 on a work night and the crowd has thinned, we all feel exposed just standing around the bar with two ounces of beer warming in the bottoms of our bottles. We start the good-byes and there are a couple of hugs, I see Harry gets a handshake that surprises him, but Cecilia gently bends me forward from the shoulders and plants a mildly liquid kiss on my cheek, she catches the corner of my mouth just enough to make me think it was placed on purpose, and then gives me the full two green eye-contact look before she hooks arms with a friend and walks out of the bar. I feel good enough to order a shot or two but everyone else wants to leave so that's that.

I am no more tired than usual Friday morning, which means I am processing orders at the rate needed to earn the middle of the bonus target for my office, which is fine with me because I split my rent three ways and I got rid of the car and my refrigerator is stocked with brewskis and frozen burritos none of which put a major dent in my budget. Last summer I camped out on the Cape for vacation. I go to see the Red Sox in the summer but bleacher seats are a fine deal, around the fifth inning I cruise into the box seat area and can usually grab a better view from the empties unless it's a Yankees game. So if you catch my drift, I am totally solvent with at least four weeks of running money in my checking account and over $400 cash in a trophy cup packed on the top shelf of my clothes closet in case of some un-named emergency. What I don't have is a regular social life, and around 4 on Friday afternoon when my blood sugar is low and I am contemplating the Reese's peanut butter cups in the vending machine I remember the kiss and I have an idea which is to call Cecilia. But that is hard because she works and if I call later I am going to be accused of assuming she has nothing to do on Friday night which I assume to be true but just because something is true does not mean it is a great idea to mention it. Then I realize that if I reach out to her now then I am admitting that I myself have nothing to do on a Friday night, and what sort of a message does that send?

Well, an accurate message.

Uhm, maybe that is even worse?

Too much thinking, I think. Too much thinking has screwed up many a relationship, I think. If I thought more, I might realize that for me personally all of my screwed-up relationships, which category includes everyone I ever had, suffered from various sins of omission and commission, and foundered on the rocks of too much thinking, at least on my part.

I decide to send a text, the modern mode of de-personalized communication ranking just above Twitter on the hit parade of interpersonal cowardice. I start by describing that my evening plans have fallen through, which in a way is true because if I end up seeing Cecilia on Friday night then by definition my evening plan to drink a beer and watch the Boston Celtics on TV will have been thwarted. I know she is likely busy, I further lie, but just in case she happens by odd coincidence to have no plans through some unforeseen and rare set of circumstances, perhaps we could hang out? Even go out to dinner (I internally gasp, no one invites anyone to dinner unless they are sleeping together, and regularly at that). I judge my text sufficiently protective of my imagined cool reputation to either work or make her feel guilty if she declines, and I send it off. The transmission line moves slowly across the cell phone screen, landing finally on "delivered." I have done my worst, she probably won't even reply, well maybe she will, is she cool enough not to even reply until Saturday night when she says she has been so busy she just saw the text an hour ago, or will she never acknowledge and me too scared to compound the error by actually asking her; or, is she so totally cool that she does not care how cool she looks and therefore will respond immediately, in which case any answer she gives will be a ten-point win?

It is now 5:15 and I am shutting down my office electronics, locking my desk drawers and file cabinets. My cell phone, propped up by the base of my desk lamp, has revealed only one incoming call, email, twitter, text or activity in the last two hours, and I have wisely (I think) declined the questionnaire about the electricity used by my electric appliances. The world is giving me what I deserve; it is ignoring my entire existence, I am so low on life's totem pole that the robo-calls are avoiding me.

A long time ago my mother, rest her gentle soul, used to tell me that when all else fails, tell the truth. Or maybe I read that inside a Hallmark card, frankly I am not sure. For me, in order to tell the truth about myself, at least to another person, I must picture myself in the bottom of a large deep pit, holding a shovel and digging downward vigorously. I look out the window in Mr. Rafferty's office (the very office I may inherit if I continue to do average work on the invoices desk for another decade or so, and for now my outlet to the world as my common work area has no window except my computer screen), and it looks like a nice warm evening and I close my eyes a moment and immediately smell the wet muddy scent of a very deep earthen hole, I feel the shovel blisters on my thumb and pointer finger, and I pick up my phone and text again to Cecilia: "I lied before, I had no plans tonight, I am desperate and can feel your kiss on my cheek. IS there any way you can save me tonight?" I hit "send" without rereading, which would only lead me to edit out typos and the truth.

I am in the elevator going down to the lobby when there is a distant ping, it is someone's cell phone, when we hit the lobby floor I stand aside next to the fake bamboo garden and retrieve my cell phone and there is on the screen the first few words of a text, so I open the site. It reads: "I also have no plans and was afraid to tell the truth and afraid to lie. I will save you if you save me. The bar at Kelly's Public House at 6. C"

Hell, I should be doing handstands but all of a sudden I am sweating and unsure. Did I shower this morning? Why did I drop taco sauce on my shirt pocket at lunch? Will she notice I am wearing the same Chinos I wore last night? My beard trim is two days overdue, I must look like a panhandler. What will we talk about? What did I tell her last night? Hell, did I lie to her, or exaggerate? I cannot remember.

That night in my apartment we had sex until the sun came up. She stayed in my room until my apartment-mates went out for Dunkin' Donuts and then I hustled her out to an Uber bound for Malden. I showered, set my alarm for 3p.m., and fell asleep on top of a very wet sheet.

I predict that the thing I will miss most while spending the better part of my entire life in prison will be sand. To my experience, sand is the bedrock of the beaches along the Atlantic, and for a Bostonian that means the beaches of Cape Cod, the poor man's Nantucket. As a kid my parents would rent modest cottages a few blocks off the beach in Bass River or Dennis or Eastham, the working-class areas far removed from Hyannis or Wellfleet. There I fell in love with the two classes of sand: dry sand that you could brush off your skin when you got up from your blanket, and wet sand that got into your bathing suit while you jumped the waves or rode them into shore and that stayed there to rub your skin raw or that clung to your sunburn and stung when you tried to apply sunscreen on top. Both varieties raised pleasant images of simpler days, staying in cheap cottages or camping at the Audubon, spending all day drinking beer on the beach, alternately baking and soaking.

I only had two weeks of vacation and I always tried to take

those weeks in early July. While it left you with a whole working summer ahead of you, July days were full of sunlight and the beaches were cleaner and if you could afford a cabin they were more likely to have a clean working stove and less likely to have had the kitchen pans taken away by prior tenants. In July, C and I pooled our money and got ourselves a cabin a half-block from the Bay in a pretty fancy part of Truro, the part nearest Provincetown; it had a deck, a standing charcoal grille, and an outdoor shower, and the toilet bowl didn't run all night or sweat in the heat of the day and it looked like a deal to both of us. For me, the two weeks looked like heaven, and I was beginning to think of me and C as a permanent arrangement. Now I never mentioned marriage and so didn't she, like that kind of talk can derail any relationship faster than anything.

Cecilia brought with her a couple of wildly flowered beach dresses that billowed in the breeze, and mostly disguised her squared off body. When she went into the water her one-piece bathing suits were carefully picked out, I suspect, solid dark colors with lots of control and just a hint of cleavage and a small dark skirt rimming the lower edge to ease the transition from her body to her firm and stocky legs. She had the kind of ankles that unexpectedly pinched inward just above the heel, an attractive feature for a thinner person but for someone built the way C was constructed, a cause for concern; it was not clear that there was enough support to keep her legs from buckling. C's skin tended to blotch red in the sun and the uneven coverage of sunscreen left her with some tan streaks and some red patches that were painful to the touch. And the sun, during this particularly dry and hot July, did no favor to her hair, parts of which seemed to bleach white while the under-hairs alternated between ebony and brass.

My friends had stopped hinting to me that C was not much of a looker. It just made me angry. She was my friend; I could confess to her that I hated my job, that my finances were pitiful for someone my age, that my clothes were ragged at the edges (as if she could not see), that my friends were jealous of my having any relationship, and that my days, historically empty in almost every way, were now filled up but with only one thing, that thing being our relationship. For her part, C seemed happy enough and not prone to share her emotions. I came to read her through her actions not her words; some people are like that, what you see is what you get and indeed all of what you get. If you dig deep, all of a sudden you have exited the person and you are in thin air on the other side.

One night I stood in the shallow waters of a neap tide with my bathing suit around my ankles, my torso pitched out, the wind at my back, pissing into the black ocean. I turned to find C a few feet behind me. I pulled up my suit and for some reason, who knows why, I walked over to her, put my hands on her shoulders, took a dive into her green eyes and said quietly and evenly that I loved her. She smiled and stood on her toes and put a small kiss on the end of my nose and said quietly "that's nice" and took my hand and started walking down the strand, avoiding the clam and oyster shells in the moonlight.

It was, all of a sudden, Friday of our second week. We had spent our time on the beach and gone to Hyannis only once when it was drizzling; she bought a shell necklace and I bought her a dark metal ring, silver I think, with a large green stone set alone on top. I read *The Boston Globe* a few times but even down on the Cape, without working and moving between apartments and hanging out with friends, even there with lots of time, we never really had a conversation about anything. And I mean what was happening in the world or even about the Red Sox, but also, thinking about it now, we never talked about us, about the future. Our future was one day long starting each day at sunrise. For the first time we went to a restaurant for dinner, one of those seafood places with clam chowder heated up from a plastic pouch sent from some factory in Boston, boiled lobster in a large paper plate with a bucket for shells, cold fries, warm catsup, kids whining in the next booth, big windows looking out onto Route 6 and a line of cars slowly moving down Cape. We talked about packing up the house which would be no big deal, about who would sweep it out, who would strip the bed.

As we were bent forward, counting out our bills, since we split everything down the middle as usual except when occasionally I would say "hey let me" and then she would look up with those eyes and breathe "oh gee thinks, hon" and I would feel like a million. We squared up the bill and C reached out her hand, laying it gently on my arm.

"What's up? You okay?" I asked.

"We gotta talk," she said.

I felt an immediate chill. We had never talked, not in the way that someone starts out by saying "we gotta talk."

"Yeah, okay. Ya wanna talk while we walk?"

"No," she said sharply, looking around at the people still crowding the restaurant. "No," quieter, "we should talk here."

"You sure we should do it here? Because…"

"I think we need to split," she said evenly, quietly. She tried the green headlights on me but then she looked down quickly when she saw my face.

It took me a minute to get some focus. "Split?"

"Yeah. Stop seeing each other."

It took me another minute. "Why," my voice flat of any content beyond the one word, as if I had said "pass me a napkin."

"I just don't want to do this anymore," she said.

76

"You mean being together all the time? Is it because we aren't married?"

She started then. "No, no, it isn't being married. It's the—the first part."

"The first part?"

"The part about being together. I – I don't want to be together with you anymore. I have – enjoyed spending time with you but I want more."

"I don't understand," I said.

"I know," she replied.

"Jesus, C, tell me why? What have I done? Wasn't this vacation great? Haven't the last seven months been great? They were great for me!"

"I think that talking about it, that would be – unkind. Can't we just agree we had a – a lovely, a truly lovely time, and leave it at that?"

"So do you want some time to think, a time-out, is that it?"

C looked up, forced herself to look up, look right at me, I saw her through what must have been my tears. She shook her head.

"I don't want to hurt you, and I don't want to talk. I had to tell you and I wanted to tell you when you were happy, when you had good memories and all. I – I didn't know how else . . . "

"Is there someone else, then?" I asked.

She looked at me again, a small smile spreading out from her pursed lips as she shook her head. I think she was trying to be kind when she said "no, it's all about us . . . "

So looking back at my story there really isn't much of one, is there? People split up, they don't get along all the time, no big news there. I always thought they fought but I guess I have no idea, do I, having only lived my own life and sort of ignoring other people except as they affected me. I also always thought they would at least talk about it, but again what the hell do I know? I was never much for deep discussion and, I guess, C wasn't either.

I can't even say I was heartbroken, whatever that means. I don't think I ever was so exposed in my heart that it could be broken. I just allowed it to be contented and maybe, whatever love may be, maybe it is just a few ratchets further around than being happy enough not to want to change things. I don't really know, do I?

And that's the real point. That night I thought the failure was with C and my anger took it out on her. Now I am not so sure.

Maybe I killed the wrong person.

Just as well I got into that car accident. I still have no idea what I would have done with the body . . .

MISS MOLLYCODDLE

The slightly sweet dusky smell of a small cigar crept out from under the folds of the red curtain and into the bar. The rule, or was it a law, prohibiting smoking was not much observed, and certainly not in the private booths. Occasionally, a modest blue-gray puff could be seen drifting upwards, to be swirled out of existence by the ceiling fans.

Earlier Molly had just chewed the slender brown tobacco end; the cheroot was a rum crook, soaked in liquor until it absorbed the flavor and odor and sugars. Molly did not find the mixture of leaked rum unpleasant when sloshed around with her spit and her Jack Daniels and thought there should be a clever name for the combination, like one of those Asian drinks with fruits and umbrellas.

Miss Molly was newly retired as PE teacher at the Girl's Academy on the hill, other side of town of course. She had been something more than a fixture, something less than an institution; it was an early retirement by mutual decision. The current run of girls did not appreciate the advice about aggressive use of the curved end of the field hockey stick to slow the opposition and suspected with some accuracy that their coach rather enjoyed giving the lessons in real time. There had not been even a single mention of Molly's attentions to the girls who, over the years, few in number to be sure, had enjoyed receipt of the pain and had understood the invitation it was designed to convey. Those disclosures would come later.

Molly grew up near here; this side of town. She went to the town school; big, gangly, nasty around the edges, played girls basketball to be in the paint with elbows out, played field hockey although she found herself always panting for breath; the cigarettes from age thirteen onward did not likely help her efforts. Molly was caringly nurtured by her mother, a woman of faded refinement abandoned by her husband with three small girls at home of whom Molly was the youngest. The household rallied to protect Molly from the things that the world had already done to her, too late to do much good except to protect Molly from the ramifications of her diffidence.

As a young woman, Molly went to State Junior College and majored in physical education. She liked the locker rooms most of all, instant assumed closeness that did not require really knowing anybody. She liked smiling all the time, at least when she really meant it. Big boned and soft-tissued, with cropped hair and bitten nails, Molly dated a few guys who hung around the teams. She did not pursue a relationship, and none pursued her. Upon graduation, a friend of her mother's recommended her as an assistant coach, and thirty years later she was still at the Academy, one of those graying invisible minions assigned to the minor sports for girls who knew they needed to exercise and knew they had no knack for it.

The curtain pulled back a few inches, releasing a block of smoke and odor; the opening was an invitation to come and sit and hang out. You didn't come knocking before the curtain parted; Miss Mollycoddle came in and lined up her three whiskeys and two rum-soaked, kicked off her sneakers and pushed her sweat socks off each foot with the toes of her other, and meditated alone about her day. Since her retirement she had taken to sleeping later, rolling out of bed around nine, taking care of her toilet and smoking a half-pack of American Spirits with her Sanka. Molly did not take a newspaper and she only used her computer to check the lottery and to allow her sisters to send her emails they insisted on sending; sometimes Molly would read them and, sometimes, not. This day Molly had spent some time putting articles in her scrap book. She had a book for each year with articles about her teams. She had no favorites as to groups or individuals, and never much worried that her teams always lost about the same number of games they won. On occasion her own name would appear; she used a light yellow highlighter to direct one's eyes to that part of the article. Sometimes there was a picture of the team huddled with the coach but Molly often cut out those pictures and did not put them in the book; she did not much like how she looked in her track suit with her calves showing their meat below the knee while all the girls seemed to have tapering legs ending in pinched heels visible (or sensed) even through the thick game socks.

Her departing retirement gift, aside from a plaque and a five-thousand-dollar check, had been a flat screen TV; she had thanked the dean and faculty in a brief, muffled speech and had lugged the screen home herself; it was not that large, it fit in the back seat of the Subaru quite comfortably. The box was still propped against the wall of the living room, Molly was thinking maybe she would ask around the tavern to see if anyone would make her a good offer; her old set was smallish and not that sharp, but good enough for the soaps and she liked sitting close anyway, why get a bigger screen just to sit further back, seemed a waste. Besides, she would have to get someone to hook up the new one if she kept it, and she didn't know anyone who could do that for her as a favor and was not in the habit of paying people to do work around the old house that her mother left her after her sisters had moved on to the City.

✦✦✦

"Who's the dame in the booth?" I asked. The bartender leaned forward discreetly.

"That's Miss Molly." A pause. "She's a regular."

"Regular what?" I asked, thinking myself pretty clever.

Another pause, a scowl. "A regular patron," he explained with a touch of bored sarcasm. Molly might have been a sullen minor player, but she was a local sullen minor player; someone new to town didn't get to share that perception even if accurate.

I must have knit my brow or something, or sent some signal of my own annoyance, because the bartender decided to lean forward again. "Just retired. A coach of girl's teams at our private academy, Miss Molly."

"Yeah?" I swished my Rolling Rock around my mouth; the neck of the bottle tasted soapy. "I coach kids at the Y. In the City, ya know?"

The bartender shrugged; he was almost as bored as I was.

"Think she'd like to talk?" I glanced over, could not see much of her face but I saw she was nursing a whiskey glass. "Talk shop, ya know?"

"Well, the curtain's open so Miss Molly is what you might call in a receiving mood. Go knock yerself out." This with a shrug and a tone that gave neither encouragement nor warning.

I lit a Camel, stuck it in my mouth, grabbed the beer in one hand and my order case in the other and started towards her table.

I know the type, it's almost like a bad TV show, the bartender said to himself. Louie pretended to wipe some water spots off the shot glasses as the salesman slipped off the age-veined leather stool and searched for his balance between the bottle and what appeared to be a heavy black sample case.

Louie didn't own the place. His brother's widow did. She was too dumb to suspect his skim, but then again business was so slow in the recession that it almost didn't pay to grab the few bucks a night. If it weren't for a few regulars—Miss Mollycoddle had surely been one of those for some time, although her intake had spiked upwards since her retirement—the place would have slipped beneath the waves. Shutting down the kitchen on week-days felt like the leading edge of a quiet demise.

Thinks he's a smooth talker. From Mason City, thinks his shit don't stink, at least when he's out among us country folks. Thinks every woman sitting in a bar is just waiting for some out-of-town guy to try out his hardware. Thinks every woman sitting in a bar is looking for it, from someone who won't stick around to brag about it and mess up her small-town reputation. Fuckin' asshole, ya ask me . . .

Louie watched the creases in the herringbone jacket fail to fall out as the salesman receded towards the booth; too much sat-upon in the car, almost permanently implanted in the fabric. Probably just the coat from some old suit anyway, not a very good contrast with the beltless gray slacks that had slipped down just enough to bunch unattractively on his shoe tops. At least this one didn't have so much of a paunch that his waistband rolled over, showing elastic and white trim where the belt-loops should have been. Must keep himself in shape, Louie said to himself with little interest. The tavern was halfway from the old business center of Mason City and the new ring of businesses attracted by the last governor's economic development zone. Lots of salespeople came through, mostly end of the day, say 4 p.m. or so (although some did arrive around 11 or 11:30 in the morning, already beaten down and ready to spend a few hours before they filled out their call sheet with imaginary visits that were likely to result in orders in the next six months, make that nine to twelve). They pretended to be disappointed that the kitchen was shut, but a bag or two of Planters salted peanuts seemed enough to satisfy them, on the

83

house don't ya know.

Louie had worked at the Deere showroom for most of his life, right from high school in fact. His wife died, left him childless at sixty with an aluminum-sided house that plinked like a ukulele when the rain hit it from the side and a ten-year-old Dodge that needed a wheel alignment. The bar paid less and the hours were longer, but he was tired of discussing horsepower with a shrinking bunch of farmers who usually couldn't qualify for the financing package once they decided on a model. Besides, there really was no boss here, and most of his friends dropped in to chat from time to time, which didn't quite happen at the showroom. Louie didn't know about the cancer yet, but he'd be spitting blood soon enough – about the time Mollycoddle left town, in fact.

✦━◼◆◼━✦

Jake's left knee popped when he slid off the stool and his leg hit the linoleum, and for a minute it felt like his balance left him as his sample case pulled him left and almost launched his beer out of his right hand. Jake had hurt the knee playing basketball years ago and every so often it gave him a momentary pang until the bone remembered its place and settled into the socket groove.

This is a bad idea – maybe, he thought, didn't like the expression on that skinny marinka behind the bar. Never know how weird people are, and I sure didn't get any good vibes from the smoking babe behind the curtain. What the hell, whatayougottalose? he asked himself, and since nothing sprang to mind he kept walking.

As he got near the booth the residue of cigar smoke reached him. Jake remembered smoking his father's White Owls as a teenager; the cardboard odor as they burned down, the small bits of tobacco that peeled off the butt and stung a little if you accidentally swallowed them. He switched to cigarettes as soon as he could afford to buy them; his father was a cigars only guy when home, which was not much. His mother never let inhalations of

84

gasses interfere with her wine coolers.

Lousy trip, he thought. The recession had hit machine tool shops hard, no one wanted to upgrade and, if a bit or chuck was a little too worn, well it'd probably last another few months or you can always borrow a part from Joe or Fred, or just do without. No one was buying anything these days, not around Mason City anyway. Friggin' Obama couldn't fix a dripping faucet, let alone the manufacturing . . .

Jake was close now and would have stopped for a better look if he dared, but he didn't.

"In for a penny in for a pound," I thought, and I took a deep breath and leaned slightly into the haze and the residual whiskey air, narrowed my eyes to their cynical slits, and started to talk before I had to take a hard look at Miss Molly.

"Excuse me, sorry, bartender said you were a coach, I do that sometimes also; wonder if you'd like some company?"

I was leaning slightly into the booth, as Miss Molly was back against the wall, kitty-corner; one leg was straight out on the seat, the other sort of tucked up under her rump in a way that a guy my age would never have any hope of achieving.

A full-cheeked, almost puffy middle-aged face looked up at me, rimmed with too-blonde hair close cropped in back with short bangs across a low forehead. Her eyes were pale blue and a little washed out, but with a suspicion of a spark lurking in the corners. The mouth was small, pursed, without color; there was no make-up anywhere. Suspected fine lines at the corners of the eyes were hidden by the tavern light; her upper lip showed the slightest start of vertical ridges as her skin shrank back against her jaw. A couple of ruddy patches might have been from the liquor or just the residue of some ancient acne.

Molly shifted her body into a more upright posture, her gray

85

blouse catching against the Naugahyde of the bench behind her and pulling across her chest; looked like she could afford to lose a few pounds, but it was the kind of broad body that let you get away with not bothering.

"Sure," she said, waving the back of her hand in the vague direction of the opposite side of the booth.

⊷ ⊶ ⊷ ⊶

I see this guy coming towards me and right away I know. I just know. Doesn't happen much but then again most of the guys here are local and know better, and most of the guys who aren't local aren't here very long, and likely not once they get a good look when I've shoved the curtain back for a little bit of fresh air. He's either a teacher or a coach or just a plain old drunk, and he's City so he's got some sort of rap, or some story. No one ever walks up to you and looks you in the eye and says, "I'm bored" or "I'm lonely" and "I'd like to talk with you for a while if that's okay." Someone puts that on me, they can talk all night and me drinking Jacks and sharing my smokes too and maybe even something else though it's been God knows how long.

He's mumbling now but I hear "coach" and why not so I pick my ass up a bit so I am not aiming my pants-front right at him and I wave him a seat. My budget is set at three a night but I am sure he's good for a couple to supplement my mood, just so long as I don't mention that they sort of suggested I not be a coach anymore. This one's the type who keeps his wedding ring on his finger, as if you could hide the slight swelling and indentation after you've slipped it into your pocket. I like that kind of honesty in a man. Particularly if he looks like he's showered lately.

Life is good.

So this guy is Jake and he gives me his card and he's selling fittings and drills and things that do not interest me. He coaches boys, soccer and basketball, a City gym in what he says is not the best part of Mason. What do I do, well not much just resting up between jobs thinking of office work or volunteering at the Town playground, yes lived here my whole life yaddayaddayadda say if you're still nursing that beer do you mind why yes thanks —Jack and a couple of cubes is all. His face is thin and pinched and the skin is slightly gray under his graying stubble, and he chain smokes cigarettes and two fingers of his right hand are yellowed so he must do it a lot. Maybe he's my age, dark eyes close together, eyebrow growing across, looks like a wiry ape but spindly arms and legs and a slightly bagged sport coat hangs pretty straight so he's still sort of in shape, at least weight-wise, which is something someone in phys ed looks at automatically even if you are not possessing any sort of interest. The flap of his coat seems to flutter regularly at the edge of the table; his left heel must be tapping up and down at a pretty good clip.

So I figure I'll give him a little tweak to see how he rolls, seeing as how I am dumb country and out of a job and he's this hot City guy who coaches soccer and basketball in his spare time, and I ask him if he is staying over on this trip, and his cigarette pauses just for a moment on its way up to his lips and I know I have caught him off guard.

"No, just on the road for the day. Finished a bit early, didn't have time for lunch so I thought I'd just stop in to wet my whistle before I headed – uh, back to town." He couldn't get out the word "home" but wasn't smart enough to head off the moment; I'm thinking, "this is fun but that's ten points off." Followed by some silence while I am smiling inside and starting the second Jack he's ordered for me while he's on what is his third or fourth Rock and pretending to neaten up his cigarette ash in the chock-full plastic ashtray so he can collect his thoughts, think up his next line, and test it for tone and bullshit content before he opens his mouth again.

Jake gives it up. Would have bet you my five grand graduation bonus he was going nowhere. He puts his legs in vertical position while he is sitting down, so he can stand up when his farewell speech is over. "It was great talking with ya, Molly. Maybe we'll get a chance to talk again sometime." He's up now, leaving his half-drunk beer on my table, his black case loosely held in his left hand, the lower edge on the seat, the whole thing tilted towards him. He sticks out his hand to shake, and I give it a shake and a slight squeeze because by now I am really feeling great, five is right up at my limit not that I haven't on occasion topped out at a higher count.

"You take care and drive carefully, Jake." I look him in the eye with open lids and slightly raised eyebrows. I have big eyes. I know that this look makes people a little uncomfortable.

Jake is dropping a few bills on the counter and talking low to Louie, and then there is a wave over his shoulder and he is gone; the sunset invades the room for a minute until the door swings shut. I take another sip, I am near the bottom, my eyes are closed. I hum the Academy fight song for no reason, then sense someone near me and open my eyes. Louie is standing next to the table with another Jack.

"Here, on the house," he says.

"Thank you kindly, Louie," I reply. As he is walking away he says over his shoulder, "What an asshole."

I pick up my drink and tell it to Louie's back. "You got that right," I tell him.

88

STATE V. GLEASON

So, of all the curious cases I've had through my many years of practice, no doubt the strangest was the Gleason matter. Now that I am retired, and after so many years, I see no reason not to tell the whole story, not just what appeared in the public court papers.

It was in the late '50s, in the City, a time of residual racial tension. I was working out of a small office, just starting out on my own, taking whatever cases came through the door. Someone at the Bar Association gave the family my name, and one Saturday morning my door opened and Buster's mother peered in from the hallway, perhaps expecting an anteroom or at least a secretary; I was a few years away from either.

I motioned her to a chair and we introduced ourselves. She carried with her a hint of the pine-scent from the newly washed hallway floor mixed with a strong overtone of perspiration that bridged the short distance to my desk. I realized after she was seated that I had not risen on her entry; I think I was surprised she was a Negro woman, and I suspect she did not expect a white lawyer to get up from his chair in any event.

"Call me Mrs. G, everyone does," she instructed me in an inflected blend of Southern drawl and City terseness; she wiggled her bulk in between the wooden spindles of the chair, her dark blouse straining against her chest and her black skirt hiking dangerously up over her enormous black thighs; she sloughed off several sweaters and wraps, which I believe served in lieu of an overcoat. Her small brown paper bag she placed carefully at the edge of my desk, the top crumpled where she had held it.

I was still living in my late parent's brownstone, but the surge of Negroes moving North after the War was peaking as they followed jobs and presumed opportunities. Their invasion changed neighborhoods almost overnight, houses gobbled up block by block. Already, my white neighbors and I had begun to receive the phone calls from the real estate brokers; if we did not sell now at the higher price, later sales would be inevitable and would reflect the fallen real estate values that "those folks" always brought with them. The Negroes were coming, the Negroes were coming, they drive down prices maybe 50%, maybe more.

My young wife, like so many other brownstone residents, was beginning to both worry and then feel guilty about being forced out rather than staying to embrace our new residents who had to be okay, yes, if they could afford the high purchase prices being discussed ...

As Mrs. G continued to jiggle her bulk into submission, an uneasy détente with my oak chair that I thought I heard groan in its joints at one point, I had a chance to observe. I guessed she was one of those "cleaning women," always black (it was well before we started calling the Negroes black, actually; "Negro" was in fact one of the nicer descriptives) who would come to your house to clean. You would call the City Employment Office and "order" a cleaning woman, who would show up the next day in work clothes, sometimes carrying her own pail or shopping bag containing her favored cleaning supplies. In exchange for 75 cents an hour and a lunch prepared by the lady of the house, and in exchange for absorbing the pervasive odor of sweat unimpeded by then not-yet-popular deodorant products, your "domestic" would clean out your toilets, wash your linoleum, scrub the mottled gray surface of your gas range, and (if you were lucky and didn't get one of those "I don't do windows" types) would glass-wax away the City grime from your bay windows.

Mrs. G's bag contained fives and tens totaling $140 which, Mrs. G explained, was all the family could now afford, and would I please help her Buster, a good man who could be in trouble for, well, exposing himself — which was not as bad as it seemed if I would only go to the City Jail and talk to Buster and learn what she gently called "the particulars of the situations."

"More than once?" I asked quietly.

"Yes," she replied with some annoyance that I had bothered to confirm her precise choice of word, "situation—zzzz."

Buster was wearing blue jeans without a belt, a plain white undershirt in the old style with straps, and those black tall Keds sneakers with no socks and laces; the tongues drooped sadly over the top of his feet like a pair of panting and none-too-clean street dogs. I did not then have enough contact with Negro men to venture even a guess as to his age, but he was not a kid and he had no gray; maybe early thirties, or thereabouts? Buster was pretty close to thirty I concluded, one side or the other. He spoke with the flat nasal tones of the City with no trace of the South, unusual for his time and place. I asked him what he did for a living; he had no job.

"So what do you do with yourself when you're not looking for work?" I was trying to get a feel for the guy and did not have the touch for it.

Buster smiled but did not look down, rather engaging my eyes directly. "Don't do much, boss," he said in a sardonic, subdued drawl which he had acquired just in time for his answer to my question.

"Buster, please don't do that thing with me. I've got your rap sheet here and it shows five – or is it six, yeah six separate complaints for indecent exposure. That's a crime that puts you in the jug, Buster, in case you were wondering." My tone was emphasized when I tucked my chin onto my chest and looked at him through the tops of my glasses.

Buster came back diffidently. His mother had wanted a lawyer. Wasting her money she made the hard way, cleaning up – white people's shit. She musta hit the bank pretty hard, paying for a white guy to boot. Buster himself, he's gonna plead out and avoid the "dance where the Negro goes to the judge who assumes he's paying the white lawyer because he's guilty as hell and so he needs the boost of paying up for some white guy to defend him, so he goes to jail real fast for exposing his dick to a bunch of white women and he's broke also."

I recall thinking that his analysis was not far off the mark in all likelihood, but my job was to defend, not commiserate about the quality of justice. "Buster, please just tell me what happened. Did you do it, let's start with the first one? And if you did, what were you thinking, what the hell were you trying to prove?"

Buster sighed, and you could see him deciding that he had to go through the drill. He told me his story.

"We're hanging at Jojo's, on the stoop. It's the summer, ya know, it's hot as shit. No one's got any money. Louie and Stepp, they're working at the machine shop on Center, ya know? But the rest of us, we ain't getting hired so fast. Here my mama she's working in white people's houses..." Buster dropped his head and shook it; then looked up and looked right at me and continued: "and she's paying for me and everything" –his brow knits with a hint of menace –" and supporting me and my sister, and I got my high school diploma, my mother she pays for some classes for me to learn how to talk like no Nigger talk so I can get a better job that way but, ya know, I think it is hurting me actually, the man he wants me to shuck and jive and he just thinks I'm acting what I'm not like. Almost uppity." Buster pauses so he can give me his best glare.

"So most of our mamas, they're cleaning houses, the usual. And we don't like that so we don't think about it that much, all our money comes from some tired old mama with knees hurting so she has to ask my sister to rub them each night, some Negro woman with a crap life on her knees five or six days a week to bend and scrub for some white woman who don't work nowhere anyhow, ya know? Makes you . . . [long . . . pause, eyes roll upwards in search of the word, then quietly] sorta sad and pissed. Ya know?

So whaddaya gonna do? Can't afford no beers, ain't even mentioning some hard stuff. I keep looking for work and it ain't easy. Then one of my friends from school, he tells me he gets an interview at Wilson's, the big store downtown huh? And he goes in and the guy tells him they are looking for laborers, that's the word he says, laborers, not some guy who thinks he's some executive or something, ya know? The dude he say, we want someone willing to do the manual labor, not someone thinks he's on his way to some college."

Buster leans forward, this is his teaching moment. "So here we got all these fuckin' white bitches, sippin' their tea and watchin' my mama's ass, and Jo-Jo's mama, and Tyrell's mama, they're leaning on their hands and knees over a bucket wiping up the shit this woman's kids dropped on her floor, which sucks enough. But why that white woman looking so hard at my mama there? Why, I'm asking you now lawyer? You know? You wanna guess?"

I thought I knew. I knew I didn't want to answer; maybe he'll just answer his own question. Seconds pass; maybe not.

Buster waits long enough to know I am trapped, and he smiles. "Well, I can tell by your not answering me that you know the answer, just don' wanna say, which I do truly understand. So I'll tell it for ya, man. She wants to be sure my mama ain't stealin' anything. Stealin' her shit, ya know? Stealin' all her precious stuff, like mama's gonna grab her new Crosley TV and drag it home on the bus so we can all sit around and watch Amos and Andy."

A long pause.

"So fuck that. So I'm thinkin' what am I gonna do to punish those snotty white bitches with their fuckin' 75 cents an hour for my mama's ass waving in the air, scrubbing her white kid shit up offa the floors; and then it just come to me. Just like THAT!" A crisp snap of fingers; I get a glimpse of nails bitten below the quick, more like some little claws of some underground digging creature moving mud around his tunnels.

"So next afternoon I go out to Sunnyside, I take a stroll around, and then I sit out back the A&P, there's a back door there I see, and every once in a while one of them white bitches she comes out with a big bag of food, and then one comes out who I don't like the way she looks, sort of snotty in a fancy dress with flowers, don't even notice she's pretty or ugly or what ya know, so real quick I pull down my trousers and my shorts and I wave it all around, like hey look at my hardware, y'all."

Buster looks down for the first time in a while; he seems upset by his speech if not his actions.

I wait but he's done with his story.

94

"So, what happened?" I ask. I look down at the police report. "Says here you ran away?"

"Yeah," Buster is weary now, the good part is over for him. "She looks funny and then just turns away, then damned if she don' look back real quick like she don' believe what she seein', puts down her food bag real slow and neat and starts back to the store. So I hike myself up back together and run like hell. Don' know what she do next, I am gone from that place, fa sure . . . "

There is a long pause. Buster is talked out it seems. I scan the police report.

"And these different times, different stores all around Sunnyside, you did those too?"

"Yeah well, that's where my mama works mostly, Sunnyside, there a lotta money out there in Sunnyside ya know." A small smile. "Betcha you live there yourself, huh." It is a statement of fact, not a question.

"I live on Fifth."

"They break your block yet?" He's smiling again.

"Let's stick with you, not where I live. You're telling me you did this what, seven or eight times? Never got caught? Never said anything to these women? No one ever chased you, at least until this last one?"

No answer. I am ahead of myself, asking too many questions at once, he is closing up.

"Let's start out again. So you tell me you did the first one?"

"Yeah, I done it alright."

"And the other seven, no wait the other five?"

"Prob'ly. Only remember four others actually but sounds like maybe the fifth one was me too."

I am scanning down the report, looking for my next question; I see something I do not understand.

"What does it mean here, the women said that when you exposed yourself you sort of, well swung it around and it was – white in color?"

Buster laughed for his own amusement, low and short. "Yeah, that's why I guess I done all the other five, they all said it was white, a real white waving machine man. Ain't no one else gonna do like that, y'know?"

"Hold on there, Buster. Are you telling me that your ..." Hard stop. Buster smiled really wide this time, for me as well as to himself.

"Well, that would beat all if it were white, I tell ya," Buster said. Then he told me the rest of his story.

⊶ ⊰◊⊱ ⊷

We came to trial in Muni about four weeks later. Until then, Buster stayed inside his jail. Mrs. G brought me three more bags, each with about $15 in small bills.

"Leave him in," Mrs. G instructed. "Don't you ask no bail. He's like to do something stupid if you let him out. 'Sides, we ain't likely able to raise no bail anyhow."

"I have an obligation to my client. I might be able to get him out on recognizance, remanded to you, no cash bail."

"You gonna do your job, you gonna leave that Buster right where he is. You listen to his momma now, I'm bringing you the money and I'm tellin' you how this is goin' happen! Boy never so much stole a candy bar, don't care what he tells you. Boy needs help. Let him out on our block, you think you doin' your lawyer duty to help him. You ain't so smart you think that."

So Buster I left in stir, they call his case, he is brought in, he is wearing a nice shirt with a collar as I told his mother to bring him, but she is not in court, I guess she is washing some white bitch's floor somewhere. I wish Buster had better trousers, not the thing he was arrested in, and I wish he had shaven, he has a lot of stubble for a young guy, but by and large he does not look like the dangerous type. His Keds still don't have laces, they flop open above his ankles, the tongue flapping onto the top of each foot as he bounces his legs nervously under the defendant's table. The Assistant DA, I know this guy, he's pretty good, one of the few who looks at the file before he starts talking to the judge, he responds he is ready to go to trial.

"Is the defense ready?" asks the judge.

"Your Honor, I request a bench conference before we begin."

"Counsel, no one has said a word yet. You have a problem so soon, even before we start? We haven't even sworn the jury yet. Why don't we try this case, doesn't look too complicated, I see this is the first time your client has been to court, the boy's got his troubles as I am sure you will tell me, I don't even know why you didn't plead him out . . ."

"Your Honor, the charges are indecent exposure. He cannot be guilty as a matter of law and I ask your indulgence to approach."

The ADA rolled his eyes, but the Judge (Joe Henry, an old warhorse who has heard it all, but a decent and mellow fellow at root) holds up his hand and waves me forward. "But this better be good, Mr. Winters. Tell me fast, I am all ears, why he cannot be guilty as a matter of law. All five, six times, where he's been ID'd by good citizens in all of these – incidents."

"Your Honor, the prosecution will allege, accurately I might add, that all the female victims, or alleged victims, saw a white–member, well a white sex organ."

The judge's eyebrows raised slightly, he grasped the edge of his desk and pulled his chair forward a couple of inches and looked around me at Buster, fidgeting at the large oak table. He settled back behind the judge's bench with a slight smile. "Yes counsel, do tell."

"Well, it is hardly likely he painted himself white down there," I started.

"I am not interested in speculation and you may find this humorous but I would like to hear what you are trying in your own stumbling way to tell me."

"Sorry, your Honor."

The judge turned to the ADA. "Mr. Grantham, will in fact all witnesses, if asked, testify that the— testify as defense counsel has suggested?"

"Yes, your Honor. We are not—exactly sure what that means but all of them did mention that, but they also positively identified it; or rather, I mean, identified him. The defendant. His face, that is . . . "

"Your Honor," I jumped in, "I am not saying that Mr. Gleason was not the person standing before all of these women. What I am saying is – well, perhaps I might impose on your Honor to ask learned counsel about the white sweat sock my client was, shall I say, wearing at the time of his arrest."

The judge turned to Grantham, and I swear the judge licked his lips gently in preparation for laughter. Grantham for his part glared at me, and then softened his expression as he turned towards Judge Henry.

"Yes?" asked the judge.

"Uh, yes . . . " said the ADA slowly.

Henry turned to me. "I am, yet again, all ears," he said.

"Your Honor, I am not saying my client is not guilty of a tasteless prank. But the gravamen, the essence of the offense of indecent exposure is, well, 'exposure.' And my client just didn't, shall we say, expose anything to anyone."

"Mr. Grantham?" asked the judge.

Grantham sputtered, the judge began to chuckle and I could not resist.

"Perhaps the learned prosecutor can point to a city ordinance," I invited, "prohibiting the opening of one garment to reveal, however shockingly, yet another article of clothing?"

⊷ ≖◈≕ ⊶

Buster disappeared from my life. I think I was told that he moved away from the City. I have no idea if he did good or evil. His mama paid me fifteen dollars a week until my whole fee was paid– $400. All in cash, all in small brown paper lunch bags, all hand-carried to my office. After a while I began feeling guilty about the whole thing and I asked her to stop paying me, we were even, but Mrs. G would not hear of it.

Then about ten years later I heard from someone, a client, that Buster had passed away. I would have been interested in the circumstances, but they were not offered and I decided not to ask.

For years after, I got a constant flow of small cases of all sorts from the Negro community in the Borough. They dried up about the time that the nomenclature graduated to "Black." We held onto the Brownstone until it was one of the last ones on the block not sold to Negro buyers; by then, the price had shot upwards radically, and my wife and I found a lovely ranch house in Sunnyside that we could now afford. In fact I am writing this while sitting on the small deck out back, we are still here though our kids are long gone.

I have always insisted that we do our own house-cleaning, even when the time came when we could easily afford to pay someone to do it for us. My wife, long-suffering as they say in so many ways by reason of her husband, never pressed the issue, and I felt obliged to pitch in with the housework well before that became the fashion or, at least, the alleged norm. Perhaps, I do not know, my wife understood.

My own reason was really quite simple. I owed it to Buster.

II

In My Head

The first two stories in this section I invented entirely, the first while feeling alienated from the world after reading an issue of The New Yorker and the second when I was quite obviously feeling anger tinged with undirected violence. The third story, based on Mayan myth and described in its own introduction, captures the pull of the tropics and the disquieting languor arising from exposure to too much vacationing in the sun.

WELCOME TO MISSOULA MONTANA

Here I am, imagining that I am in Missoula which I think is in Montana. I have never been in, nor seen a picture of, this town, and am not even sure it exists or is in Montana, but I like to imagine I am there all the same as I like the sound of the name.

I am reading the *New York Times Sunday Magazine*. It is not what you are thinking. I am not reading it in protest against the arid existence I lead in Missoula, because I can imagine whatever I want to imagine, and I am imagining that I do not find Missoula to be arid at all. I find it peaceful.

We in Missoula seem wholly out of touch. People in the *Times* are enormously wealthy or anticipate being so. Numerous trust companies want to manage their money. All these women are Nordic blonde with neat crows' feet; husbands are politely gray and neatly trimmed.

They all seem to live in tall buildings in busy exciting cities, paying millions for condominiums smaller than the barn I have just imagined I have here on my ranch in Missoula. They allow their living rooms to be photographed but someone has come in and thrown away everything personal, and all the books and newspapers. Perhaps they do not even read, not even the Sunday *Times*.

Perhaps they do not read because they lost their eyes to cancer.

Celebrity urban cancer stars, they are courted to recover in hospitals and treatment centers all around North America. Runaway cells have no chance, these people all will be saved, and it does not say so but I am sure, I will imagine, that if they have any chemical or radioactive treatments these people will not vomit.

No one drives a truck. All drive cars of quiet elegance. They have wanted cars like this all their lives I am sure I imagine. They have counted the hours until they could own one, counted them on a time piece that is not only not a watch but also is something they cannot own but only care for on behalf of the next generation that, I infer or imagine, similarly will find that ownership eludes them. Next generation will tell time only on their electronic personal devices and perhaps then the failure to be able to ever own a time piece will not seem so anomalous or harsh.

They are an unanchored crew, there is a column telling them what is ethical and what is not. They write letters to authors using perfect grammar and terse phrases. They have never imagined Missoula and, if they have, they have not imagined my Missoula, or the real one. They are locked beneath the surface glaze of the hard white paper that carries their inked DNA. Even now, they are headed for the rooftop pool in the heart of the city.

I will imagine the fireflies are circling my barn in my Missoula and excuse me if I must turn to the end of the *New York Times Sunday Magazine* and imagine that I can know both the characters in German operas and the county in which Missoula Montana resides so that I can complete the crossword puzzle in ink. I take a wild stab at the occupant of Grant's tomb, it has five letters and appears to begin with a "G".

THE DREAM

I am in a bed, on top of a pile of bloody sheets. There is a loose cover, blood-stained, draped over most of my body. My head is twisted to the right, eyes half-closed as I squint out beneath my lashes. My left hand is twisted upward, under a lumpy pillow, the fingers grazing a metallic object that I seem to know is a pistol.

There are other bodies all around me, one or more on top of the bed with me.

Where did all those other people come from? Next, I become aware of jumbled noises. Near me, flies – a constant droning. From the floor, an occasional soft effluence, a release of some ill-defined moisture or gasses. No moans ... Why aren't any of these people crying out? Perhaps they are dead; or, perhaps, they are lying in wait as I am, deciphering the situation, trying to get enough orientation to respond.

From the next room, or what I assume to be the next room, a dull rumble of men's voices, occasionally punctuated by a husky laugh. I strain to pick out words but cannot. Could it be a foreign language?

Beyond all this, an occasional rumble, as thunder. Not thunder. Explosions, far away. A rattle of window glass follows each of the louder ones. It is night because it is dark and there must be at least one window in the room, and there are crickets somewhere, but not nearby.

Am I hurt? Shot, cut, beaten? The cover seems wet, sticky. Clearly blood, which I cannot abide. Why then am I so calm in thinking about this? In my dream, do I know it is a dream, so it doesn't matter? I try to drag my right hand up from alongside my body and encounter the cold flank of another person. I think that he could be dead. I know it is not a woman; or, do I just assume it? How much is assumed, and how much is real?

I slowly pull up on my hand, and its back drags along his clammy flesh. I am afraid to make a sound, or destroy too much of the silent symmetry around me, for I do not know how it is balanced. Slowly I wiggle each hand, move my mouth, my feet, try a deeper breath. Everything works without pain. I ignore the itch between two of my toes, and the cramp across my shoulders.

I fish for a hold on the gun under the pillow, and my left hand slips into position; I seem to know what feels right. With the gun as my protection, I run my other hand along my own side, onto my chest and belly, as far down my thighs as I can reach without disturbing the cover. There are some patches of unidentifiable moisture, some sticky, some just damp, but my fingers discover no holes or rips in my body. I have escaped whatever carnage befell the others, and somehow I slept through it or passed out or repressed it.

A voice grows close and the door opens a few inches. There is a pause, and more words are exchanged. I let my eyes open another fraction, and see a vertical band of light echoed on the floor. Suddenly, the door pushes wide, and there is a silhouette of a man in a cap; he is carrying a stick, or perhaps a rifle. I force my eyes shut and suppress my breathing. In this silence, my thoughts pound in my ears. Deliberately, the man moves across the floor, kicking at unresponsive bodies. I let a peek escape from my clenched eyes; he is bending over some of the bodies, and pocketing odds and ends that he pulls from them.

A sharp knock in one corner freezes him. I shut my eyes quickly. I am forcing myself not to move, and then I sense the knot on my face. I relax my face. Another tap from some unseen source, and the room is filled with the rattling of automatic gunfire. The slugs thunk into wooden walls, bounce off the cement floor, bury themselves into unyielding bodies with a viscous suction. I concentrate on not moving, but I must have startled because the gunfire stops and I feel his gaze toward the bed. I want to swing the gun barrel to point outwards but am afraid to move my left hand. He is closer, his breath a staccato mixing with flies and crickets. A voice yells from the other room but my man makes no reply; I hear him picking his way to the bedside. He is there, he is over me. I cease to breathe. The body to my left moves into me, in response to what must be a poke of the rifle barrel. I leave my weight dead and roll back against the force.

Another voice is now at the doorway. There is an exchange of gutturals, and the man drops spit on my face as he responds. My mind twitches in reflex, but my skin remains placid. In another few seconds he is retreating backwards over bodies and limbs. I feel his distrust as he stands once more at the door, his eyes scanning for any motion. Then the door swings firmly shut, and there is laughter from the other side.

I am in a bed, on top of a pile of sweated sheets. There is a loose cover, semen-caked, draped over most of my body. My head is twisted to the right, eyes half-closed as I squint out beneath my lashes. My left hand is twisted upward, under a soft feather pillow, fingers still holding long strands of hair.

There is one body next to me, curled and curved to fit into the convex spaces my own body defines on the mattress. I don't know how I got here; is this my new wife in our bedroom, or some past or future affair, or some hooker drunkenly taken to some hotel room at the end of a long business day in some Midwestern city?

I am afraid to move, to admit that I am awake. What will I say if I am addressed? I don't know my name, or the name I have used. I do not know if I have been sweet, or brutal, or inept; or if l have failed, or have given pain, or been the butt of her laughter.

Without moving, I allow my body to feel her, sensing better her length, heft. She is not as long as I am, but I cannot tell if she is full or slight. Twisting her strands of hair in my hand under the pillow, I know (imagine?) that it is long and blonde, fine but without shape and style; I now know that it falls straight unchecked from her head to below her shoulders, and I remember her ears peeking out on each side.

My mind runs across my body for signs; I am sure we have made love, but not often.

I am wet, sticky and caked. We have loved and slept, and we have not washed or stirred. There is no hollow ache in me; I am not spent. Did we choose not to continue, or did we just decide to sleep in that single mellow moment? Was it too good to spoil by more, or too poor to tempt a repeat? Or, was I just drunk again, dribbling off into a flaccid snore? How does she smell? A slight residue of flowers. A friend perhaps, or an acquaintance?

But what if she is a friend of my family, or someone from my office, someone whose morning-after brings awkward complications, or at least the need to tell and repeat a story until its details become consistent from both of us? I had long ago hoped to avoid those mornings.

She exhales heavily, stretches; parts of her torso and limbs lose contact with mine.

Then a long pause, as she remembers where she is and whom she is with or realizes that she cannot do so either. Slowly, she pulls away from all contact, and I feel her hand grasp the cover to hold it in place as she slides out and onto the floor. She lets the cover fall back, and its warm drape settles into the curves where her body used to be. Bare feet move across the room, and the floor is not carpeted; the stick and pull of her toes and arches squish into the dark air. A door gently closes behind her, and in the next moment a line of light appears on the floor, its shine dissipating as it spreads towards the bed. I open my eyes, and water is running.

I take this chance to strain against the dark, forcing my eyes wide to absorb the scant light from under the door. There is a pile of clothing halfway across the floor, a dresser and a mirror and two large windows with curtains drawn. Each side of the bed has a small table with a lamp, and I still hear the water so I grope and turn on my lamp – one click. I look at her end-table; there is nothing on it but a crumpled tissue with blotted lipstick and a plastic wine glass, resting on its side. Stuffy air masks a smell I do not know, and the slow whirr of the fan masks all sounds outside the room save the now dying trickle of water.

I click off my lamp and lower myself to the position I remembered. I wait and my mind waits, and we are both very tired, so tired because it is late and it is confusing and we are oh so very tired that we lack the energy to decipher it all, although we want to, my mind and I, except the bed is soft and the room is humming and I recognize the smell at last, it is almonds, and I love almonds, which are sweet and gentle things with romance and bouquet. My mind wishes to sleep, and I cannot deny it.

Sometime later, I awaken with a start. I know I am alone. Light eludes the drapery and outlines the contents of the room. The bathroom door is open. On her end table she has set the empty glass upright, and in it sits her tissue. I unroll the tissue and breath through it, drawing the air through the lipstick, but all I smell is almonds.

I am in a bed, on top of a pile of bloody and semen-caked sheets. There is a loose cover, similarly coated, draped over most of my body. My head is twisted to the right, eyes half-closed as I squint out beneath my lashes. My left hand is twisted upward, under a feather pillow so ancient that it has gone to lumps. My fingers graze some object that repels me but I cannot move away from it when I try. There is no link between my will and my body.

There are other bodies all around me, and they are all still, except for the woman pressed against my side. Her curves reach into the spaces my body leaves but we are out of sequence, and touch only roughly, bone upon bone. I know how we got there, this woman and I. We wandered down a street, into a hotel, came together over the sounds of the war that came ever closer, and then there were shouts, and gunfire, and as we sat up in amazement the door sprang open, men poured through it and then other men followed them, spraying gunfire and then settling their sights on each crippled body and pressing the trigger for a long time until the bodies no longer responded to the punctures and the thuds. The men looked at us in bed, and laughed, and one pointed his weapon at us but another barked a guttural command in the language of the country, and reluctantly they backed from the room, leaving us among the corpses.

We looked out beyond the curtain then, this woman who was stranded, as I was, for a night and day and another night in the airport when the rebels began their unexpected drive to the sea. She was from Germany and was traveling to the interior to see a sister; I was returning home from unsuccessful business.

Or perhaps she was a prostitute caught between the lines of war, attaching to any man who wandered into her view, even if he was not really there but just bouncing through his personal stream of dreams. Then we hid together in a dark room upstairs in an unattended hotel, I just took the key to room eleven from the slot behind the desk and made love in the emptiness and waiting because that night might have been our last through no fault of our own.

From behind the curtain could be seen that much of the town was afire, and men were walking and running, and the sky to the east glowed red. There was noise and bombs and small arms fire and crickets were dying in their fields as the fire swept over them. We returned to our bed and lay there because we did not know what else to do, and we smelled the bodies and their emissions, and the heady fumes of fuels and floating dust of burnings, and we made love and fell asleep.

I hope I gave her pleasure, although I now recall that she gave me pain. Then I tried to place my body so that our curves would coincide, but she was the wrong height, or she resisted subtly, or I did not remember how, but it did not work. Then the noise below grew louder and came up the stairs, and again men were in the room. I reached beneath my pillow for my gun, but withdrew instead long strands of blond hair, and stood naked on the shiny floor pointing strands of hair at them.

They overcame their surprise and laughed. He shot her many times, and her blood sprayed over the bed and splashed onto my naked torso. I tried then to awaken, but they saw my game, saw what I was trying, and moved to foil my escape in ways that I could not understand. I heard other voices, real voices then, and I tried to cry out, but the power ran out of me, and I lost that detached control that had carried me over and through that dream, that variegated dream, the infinitely repeated concentric circles of my dream, and the bullets hit me, racked me, finally disemboweled me, after all those nights when I was impervious, unassailable through all permutations of my story, my dream that I had played with, toyed with, edited and rewrote with impunity.

The bullets killed me as surely as if they were real, and I floated back into sleep. On my tongue, there was the faint taste of almonds.

THE WOMAN WHO LIVED AT
THE THIRD HOLE

Those acquainted with Cancun's history know it is a newly minted city, designed and built to attract American visitors at a measured distance from major U.S. airports. Thus, there is an edge of cheesiness and stale beer about the whole enterprise, into which are interspersed verdant tropical golf courses the patronage of which masks the fact that there is nothing to see or do unless you boldly rent a car and drive inland to the ancient ruins. But none of this means there is no mystery to the place. Mayan myth speaks of the beautiful devil who seduces men who come near her pueblo. Breathless recounting in your hotel room flyer recalls the time when mystery engulfed the Yucatan: "Be careful when you walk alone under a moonlit sky blanketed with stars... The winds of the Orient may blow over you, making you feel as though you are blooming like a tree under the rain. She will be there: Xtabay, waiting for you, sure to attract you with her perfume and envelop you in the elixir of her aroma. She is like the flower that blooms at dawn, damp from the night's weeping. And she, Xtabay, is much more than that."

I had stayed behind at the pool, grateful for the break from routine. We had been in the Caribbean for almost two weeks, and although four couples created enough interpersonal variety to make the time pass, it turned out that two weeks of constant conviviality was too much to expect.

The men had left for the golf course again, their false camaraderie unabated by the wet heat. The women had headed to town, shopping for onyx and silver trinkets. The pool sustained me, its blue-green-ness surrounding my limbs, pushing my pelvis up to the sun. The weight of the rays drove into and through me, enough to burn, not enough to sink me. By midafternoon, I again began to believe that I could tolerate a few more days of togetherness.

I was so enervated that, later, I joined the women in a cab to the golf club for the by-now obligatory margarita and taco party on the patio overlooking the last hole. By the time we arrived, the three golfers were into their second or third beers; protocol required no margaritas until the group had fully assembled. While stories of the day's hunt were told in raucous interjection, Paco moved among us with the large pale drinks, glasses rimmed in salt and sloshing in icy milkiness. Jorge delivered tacos midst gracias and mucho gracias; vacationers permitting waiters to enter into the passing intimacy of our tribe.

While generally more interested in the stories the women brought back from town, it was assumed that I would rather rehash the day of golfing. The tribal assumptions were strong, not worth resisting.

"And when I teed off on three, a woman came from the trees, flowers in her hair."

All side-eddies of conversation gelled around Ernst's remark. I feared that this interesting tid-bit would be swallowed in the meaningless flow of chatter, so I jumped on it.

"What do you mean, a woman? What did she look like? Old, young, did she speak English? Where did she come from? Did the caddy know her?"

Ernst turned to my wife with loud confidentiality. "I don't

know where she came from, but she headed right for your father, I'll tell you that."

I had been talked into a vacation with my in-laws in a moment of winter chill when the promise of a subsidized beach sojourn overpowered my judgment. What was that saying about repenting in leisure?

Dieter, my father-in-law, was a tall man, the kind of person who had presence. Not handsome, not thin, not muscular, rather his entire aspect was large and pleasant and open. The mystery woman might well have drifted into his orbit, as did so many new acquaintances.

"Yep," my father-in-law confessed after a quick sip and a salt-induced wince. "She walked right up to me on the tee. She must have been thirty-five or forty, very tan, with this big red flower in her hair. Long black hair ... "

"Well, was she pretty, or attractive or what?"

My question must have seemed too eager, or lacked the right touch, I do not know.

My wife gave me a look, but the golfers missed it; they grew into the implicit bonding of the story, pleased I had expressed an interest.

"Well, she looked like some flower child or something." Larry was my brother-in-law and putting the fine detail on things was not one of his attributes.

"Was she pretty or just dressed in golf clothes or what," I pressed. The eyes at the table were beginning to wander, and two of the women, clearly less enthralled than I over this oddity, had broken off into a side conversation.

Dieter twisted his glass, testing to see if there was anything hiding among the ice cubes or whether it was time to order a refill. "She was actually sort of worn out, lots of lines. She was white sort of, not real Mexican or anything, but sort of dark also; she looked like the sun had done a job on her. The hair was jet black, though. Couldn't get rid of her. Wanted to ride in one of the carts, can you believe that?" He twisted around, on the hunt for a waiter.

"Did she want money? What did she say to you?" With that, my wife shot me a chilly glance, one that said "why are you so interested in this story, just what the hell are you doing?" one that said "that's your last question, you're coming across weird here," one that said, "my family doesn't understand how obsessed you can get so just drop it." Her eyes said all these things and more, and also suggested a price tag I wouldn't want to pay if I persisted.

"No," Ernst said, "she didn't even speak English, only Spanish. The caddy, he was only a kid, he looked kind of nervous but said he was sure he had never seen her before." Ernst knocked off his drink and said his last in a conversation-ending tone: "We just finally waved her off, sent her away. I went to get my driver and turned back and, well, she just was gone."

And then we talked about tequila and salsa, suntans and sunburns. We admired earrings, discussed chip shots and bogeys. We debated dinner as if it were the national debt, and whether the local taxi drivers were to be trusted. We discussed everything except what I wanted to know about, and then we climbed in our taxis and went back to the hotel and dressed for dinner.

The next day we had rented a minivan to drive our tribe out to a distant beach for a day of snorkeling. I had drunk enough the prior evening to make credible my claimed stomachache, and after small fussings everyone went off without me. At least Laura did not offer to stay behind and take care of her husband.

I waited a half-hour, then dressed and cabbed over to the golf club. I had always intended to learn some Spanish before the trip. I consider it rude to go to another's country and expect the people to speak your language, regardless of the circumstances. But it had been a few weeks from hell in the office, not even clear until the last minute that I would be able to break free and take the trip. By the time I was able to open the Berlitz I was seated on the airplane, and my exhaustion allowed me only to scan the first pronunciation page before I fell asleep. And at the hotel and the shops and restaurants English had been no problem, and thus no incentive to learn even the Spanish rudiments. This made my next task much harder.

When I reached the club, the starter and the few caddies sitting under the straw canopy near the first hole either did not understand me or took some special pleasure in pretending to be confused. I could not blame them; if they came to my office in Boston and started asking curious questions in a strange foreign voice, I surely would have them summarily tossed out.

Wandering into the restaurant, I found only one lone waiter at this early hour. He was not familiar to me, not part of our false circle of family fun we had woven over the past several nights. "Is Paco around," I asked. "Jorge?" I suggested. Shrugs, and an indecipherable spurt of Spanish. I pointed to my watch, intending to ask for the time of their expected arrival, and shrugged myself; the waiter shrugged back.

Outside near the starter's shack was a glass-covered map of the golf course—the first few holes lay in a near straight line running away from the clubhouse. The third tee looked like a good eight hundred yards away, half a mile perhaps. As I stood considering whether I could get away with just walking out onto the course and strolling up to the third tee, a familiar face reflected back at me from the glass.

"Hey, Jorge." My enthused false tone echoed the drunken style of the tribe. I even gave him a soft, friendly slap on the shoulder. Did I sense his body recoiling, if only an inch?

"Tito said you were looking for me, señor?" His voice was flat, not so much unfriendly as guarded.

"Yes, yes, actually I was." We were standing in the sun in front of the clubhouse, and I didn't want to have this conversation in so open a place. "Let's go inside," I invited, taking a few steps towards the door, and he fell in behind me.

I tried to order a margarita for each of us, but somehow it ended up that Jorge stood up, made me a drink and served it. This did not create the intimate environment I was trying to create. I asked him to sit with me at one of the low tables, making a sweeping sign with my arm, but still he held back, looking around perhaps for a supervisor or another patron, but it was still well before noon and we had the place to ourselves. Trapped, he sat, leaning forward in the soft chair lest anyone think that he was lounging like a guest.

"I want to talk to you about the woman on the golf course."

After a moment he looked down; his eyes flared, quickly, instinctively.

"I am very interested in the woman who was on the third hole of the golf course yesterday." Nothing; I shifted to face him more frontally.

"I am very interested in the woman who was on the golf course. I am prepared to pay for this information."

Still the same stare. Polite attention, no communication.

I leaned forward until Jorge was forced to blink; in for the proverbial penny, here comes the proverbial pound: "I am willing to pay much for this information." Silence.

"Molto." No, no wrong language. "Mucho. Mucho!"

Well, Jorge had the empty waiter stare down pat. I stared my most intensely ingratiating but mildly intense stare, and he gave me back a big-brown-eyed-empty-I-don't-know-honest-señor-sir-por-favor kind of stare that told me he was a heck of a stare-er, and that I was on the wrong track.

"Well, do you think anyone in the kitchen might know about the woman on the golf course?" His eyes flicked towards the kitchen. "So there is someone in the kitchen who knows about the woman on the golf course?" Silence. Finally a shrug.

Then, flatly but politely: "Are we finished talking together, señor?" Well I thought, no actually we are not finished, I'm not finished, actually I am going to tie you to that fucking chair and beat you with self-righteous Yankee brutality until you bleed from the corners of your mouth and you cannot wait, just cannot wait to tell me anything and everything that I want to know about my lady of the golf course. Actually I want to hurt you badly for pretending not to understand me, I want to punish you for all the thoughts that I know in my heart you are thinking about me as we stare each other down, with you winning.

"Yes, sure we are done," I said. "Thanks for your time," I added, and immediately hated myself for adding that, dammit what a stupid habit that made me say that! Jorge, already arisen and turning, looked back over his shoulder and gave me a gentle smile.

I leave without paying for the drink, hoping he will follow me outside. No such luck. Although I hate golf, and am suitably terrible to boot, I find myself renting clubs, shoes and a caddy. Yes, I am playing alone. No I do not wish to be paired with another golfer or group. Yes I understand there is an extra charge.

117

No, it's quite alright, I am one of those curious Americans, I guess, who prefers to play alone, thank you. After interminable trivia, I am permitted to tee off.

My caddy is twelve, or maybe fourteen. His name is Raymondo. His eyes are large, almond-shaped, deep brown, and leave no room on his face for any other noticeable features. I toy with the idea of walking directly to the third hole, explaining as I go that I have played the course before and that I prefer it that way, holes one and two are after all so damned boring. My guess is that this will create more trouble than it is worth. Better to play the first two holes.

This is something of a problem. My driving game, always weak and embarrassing, is at a new nadir. My tee shot off the first squirts ten yards to the left and nestles deep into the taller fringe grasses. When Raymondo appears seemingly to suggest that I replace it on my tee, I angrily wave away his offer. I also disdain his club selection and attack the ball with my driver. Grass and earth fly in several directions. My ball squiggles out onto the fairway, no more than twenty yards away. Already four new golfers are mounting the tee area, and one or two are looking curiously at my position, which is improbable given my tee time was ten minutes ago.

I bend over and pick up my ball and throw my club at Raymondo. He's a kid, why bother to explain it to him anyway. Vamoose. Next hole.

The second hole is shorter and straighter. If this expedition is not to be a travesty, I must concentrate. I position the ball, address it, stare at its back edge, remember to keep my arms straight and swing up and through. The ball arcs slightly and Raymondo and I exhale in relief as it rolls cooperatively up the fairway. I am now desperate to be done with it, successfully done with it. I hit a wedge shot that actually lands where it is supposed to land. It rolls back towards the hole. In my real prior life, I never have hit such a shot. But now I really need it, need the shot, I am not playing for a score or for someone to say "hey, nice golf shot." I am playing for real, for keeps, for I don't know what but I know it's very very important.

Raymondo is looking at me with respect. Actually it is relief. I imagine he is thinking: perhaps this gringo will actually play a game of golf and pay me my twenty dollars and not go crazy on me, why do I always get the crazies, the starter has always had it in for me. I pull out the putter and without lining up the shot I sink a ten-footer. Raymondo smiles and reaches for the score card, but then he remembers the first hole and stops in confusion. I grab the card from his hand and stuff it into one of my pockets. There is a sign in Spanish and English on which I have focused: "To the Third Tee." Raymondo leads the way, to show me. I am having none of it. I shoo him behind me.

Glancing back, I do not see the next foursome. My quick clean escape from the second hole has bought me some time.

Through a small copse of trees, I come upon the third tee. It is about ten meters square, elevated above the fairway which slopes away in front of me. It is ringed with trees, but the trees are not very thick. Quickly I scan around in an arc. I see no one, nothing unusual. To my distress, the trees are so thin that in most directions I see through them, to the sky beyond. No dense woods to wander or to hide.

Raymondo has taken a wooden driver from the bag and he has teed my ball. My back is to the hole, oblivious. I stare, and he waits. After a minute or so, he taps me respectfully on the sleeve, but I shrug off the gesture. The breeze is picking up, it is after-noon, there are now a few clouds on the horizon, the afternoon thunderstorms may arrive today. The winds stir the trees, but it is a tease, the shapes I see are different shapes. Minutes pass;

Raymondo calls out "Señor?" I turn on him, and my face must scare him, for he drops the club and backs behind the golf bag.

I look behind me. That foursome is coming down the second fairway towards the green, I do not have much time. To relax Raymondo, I pick up the club, but again turn my back to the fairway. Slowly I walk a crescent around the tee, peering into the trees. They are now swaying in the breeze, and the breeze is becoming more insistent. Even the darkest patches now are spread against the sky by the growing gusts, but nowhere is there the woman, nowhere is my woman of the golf course. I am staring, I am staring, I am staring...

"Excuse me, fella, are you going to tee off or can we play through?" The voice is Southern U.S., too polite to betray annoyance. A perfectly reasonable voice with a perfectly reasonable question. I am startled.

"I'm sorry, but you've been looking into the trees for a couple of minutes. Mind if we play through?"

"No, no, not at all. I just got distracted. Please. Sorry." I force a smile towards him, which earns me a nod.

I place my club politely on the grass at the rear of the tee, and as their voices behind me began the ritual banter I walk off the course toward the clubhouse. I stare straight ahead, and on the ground I fail to see a crushed red flower.

◆——◆ ≡◆≡ ◆——◆

I just made it back to the room ahead of the group. I brushed the grass off my shoes, hung everything up as I had remembered it, poured most of the juice from the decanter alongside my bed down the toilet, and mussed up the bedding and my hair as best I could. Even so, I earned a curious look from my wife, after she saw my flushed cheeks but could not detect any trace of a fever.

I rejoined the tribe for dinner but cannot recall any of the conversation. I spoke only as necessary, given dispensation from joviality by reason of being under the weather. My wife's disposition improved by reason of the attention I afforded her, and she did not guess my design as I kept her margarita glass full at cocktails and her wine glass well-stoked at dinner. As I sipped and sucked my way through the evening, the assembled hoard sopped up its usual bounty of alcohol, and my bride rode the crest of the wave. In our room, she fell promptly asleep, while waiting for me to emerge from the bathroom.

Still, I gave it lots of time. I lay down next to her so that her thrashes would encounter familiar resistance. At last, that deep and steady snore overtook her; I knew that she was out for a few hours, indeed more. I gently let myself out the door.

The taxi driver tried to tell me that the golf club, even the bar at the club, was long closed, but for once the ignorance of the language worked in my favor as I insisted to be driven there. On arrival, he reluctantly took my bills. He had tried, I was no longer his problem.

Rain showers had left the course drippy and redolent of greenness, but at least the sky had cleared enough for the half-moon to light my way. I walked straight down the first fairway, and over the green, straight down the second and over the hill to the third tee. I passed through the bower made by the laden branches, as wind dropped water on my shirt and hair in big cold splotches. My trouser bottoms stuck to my legs in clammy clumps.

I sat for a long time on the bench without expectation, the water soaking upwards into me. I understood implicitly that waiting was required. The winds cleared the air, and there was the smell of flowers. I closed my eyes and waited. My clothes pressed moistly all over me, and a constant sweat, a dew congealed on my arms and face. The winds then blew more constantly, but the perspiration remained, as if painted on by a broad brush.

When she walked out through the trees, I was not surprised. Nor was she surprised that I was there. I was not the first to wait, nor the first to be taken. Her simple lined face echoed a gentler time. But time had taught her peace, and she imparted it with each stroke of her hand through my soggy hair. She held the strands upwards, and her breath dried each piece into a wisp. Her hair was dark, her dress plain, the color of whitened straw. She rubbed my neck, at the base of the skull where all the tensions connect. She touched my shoulders. She kissed my lips, gently and like a brushing, and there were flowers everywhere.

I am on a hillock overlooking the moonlit lushness. And where are the buried warriors who sat before me, kissed by this wind, at love in this myth? The guidebooks tell me that this Goddess of the Waters gave Cancun's waves their name, gently azure and green lapping up onto powdered sandstone beaches.

Silver trinkets and woven blankets sold from steamy stalls, bars filled with short white skirts tight around the tans, Corona beer on the beach – these things cannot sate my lust. But I believe, I pray my Goddess can. Her face first is as Spanish as any textured line that Goya ever painted, and then spreads and darkens into stout Yucatan features guarding burning eyes of deepest brown. She sits. I hold her hand. She dances; I feel her skirt skim around my shoulders as she twirls. There are castanets; there are drums.

We make love in my mind, and her passion is an aroma on the wind. It fills all my chambers completely. Beware the winds that carry the hint, the trace, the suggestion of the Orient. Can those winds blow this far, and come to rest upon my face? Is the Goddess of the Waters not a goddess at all, just a woman of this place, of all times in this very place? Could it be that Mayan myth is not myth at all, and that Xtabay is as real as the stones, as true as the ruins, as provable as the astronomy?

◆—◆ ☲◆☲ ◆—◆

I sat on the hill until false dawn showed over the distant sea. Sometime before, she was gone. I walked halfway back to the hotel before a passing truck gave me a lift. I balled my clothes in a corner and lowered myself, cold and naked, into bed; Laura's body nestled into mine for one chilled moment, then moved away. And I slept.

When she awoke, she was disconcerted by the crushed red flower.

III

GROWING UP

All of these stories are true in part. All are based on remembered events. Anyone reading this section must refrain from asking me which parts are invented, as even memory is invented as it passes through the sieve of our minds on its way to the written page. Note: you cannot take Brooklyn out of the boy.

HERKOWITZ' BUNGALOW COLONY

BIG JOHNNY O AND WHY I ALMOST MISSED BREAKFAST

THE CARD

LINCOLN TERRACE PARK

THE (REDACTED) BOTTOM LINE

SUMMER OF '46

(PUTTING IT) BLUNTLY

THE ORCHID

HERKOWITZ' BUNGALOW COLONY

There were rumors of improprieties, but Hershkowitz opened his cottages that year, and the families came for the summer as usual.

I should have started by saying that my memory is not wholly clear, about the details that is. I was eight or nine, and it was long enough in the past that facts gather their patina of nostalgic accuracy without regard to what might actually have happened. But with the onset of this summer, of each summer, I find myself thinking back to my last year there . . .

Ten small white cottages formed a wide arc around a spotty green lawn, punctuated with white-painted wooden Adirondack chairs, a couple of folding bridge tables that stayed outside in the weather all summer awaiting sunny day games of mah jongg and gin rummy, and a clubhouse of sorts up a small rise towards the woods and the blueberry bushes. Walkways of thyme and gravel were fringed by diverse flowers in no particular order. Tiger lilies predominated, and they made me sneeze.

Our cabin, as always, was number ten, so we had no neighbor to the east. Like the others, ours had a small kitchenette, two bedrooms, and a sitting room with a Formica table letting out onto a screened porch. The porch screen door slammed on a tight spring to outwit the wasps and flies, but those who passed inside promptly got blasted from the orange DDT sprayer we kept on a chair just inside the jamb.

It was hard to sleep some nights. We brought a large fan with us from the City, to stir the stagnant heat. Set up in the front room and facing into the two bedrooms, most of the airflow was trapped and wasted in an eddy of looping torpor outside the rooms. We sweated on top of our sheets, scratched our mosquito bites and tried to fall asleep to the crickets.

We kids rolled out of our beds and onto the lawn early each morning, sometimes with bats and gloves, sometimes (informed by invisible signal) carrying small tins to fill with blueberries for pies or to be served over ice cream. We would walk to the hotel kitchen to buy a glass bottle of milk for a nickel, a collar of cream floating on top which shrank as the summer wore on and the cows stopped providing that rich fatty froth. Rainy days brought out Monopoly and Parcheesi boards, or decks of pinochle cards, spread over the floor of one of the cabins.

Each Friday night the fathers would drive up Route 17 from the City, cars steaming and over-heating as 17 snaked slowly through the clogs at South Fallsburg and Monticello, joining their families after a week of working in their offices or stores. We were kids; no one of us imagined our dads, midweek in the fuming City, playing evening poker without carping wives, smoking forbidden cigars in Brooklyn living rooms with couches protected by plastic covers, or even doing things with their secretaries that would have no resonance in our minds.

Hershkowitz was a real person and a caricature of himself, short and balding with steel gray strands combed straight across his forehead, pasted to his skull by ubiquitous beads of sweat. A compact fat man in his fifties, his bearing was not improved by baggy white short-sleeved shirts, long dark trousers, white sox and black tie shoes, even on the hottest of days. His belt-end whipped free, unengaged by his trouser loops when he waddled past.

At dinner or hanging around the mothers' mah jongg tables to grab a cookie, we kids were aware that Hershkowitz was viewed that summer under some sort of a titillating cloud. Questions were asked, too oblique for our full understanding, but with connotations of impending excitement. Whatever it was, it didn't seem to involve the slot machines.

We all knew that the one-armed bandits in the club house were illegal. We were forbidden to play our nickels in them and had to restrict our gambling to early mornings when only children were out into the day. We often saw the town police cruiser, a black Hudson with white fenders and one round blue light on the front of the roof, parked near the club house, the cop inside talking to Hershkowitz; but the slot machines were always in their place after the cruiser lurched away in a light spray of dust motes.

"Five bucks a week," my mother would opine, without being asked, through a cloud of cigarette smoke.

"Nah, gotta be ten at least," countered Pauline as she loudly racked her tiles, soaps to the left, winds to the right.

There was something more, some undercurrent we did not understand. Glances at night towards Hershkowitz' rooms on the second floor of the club house, where the yellow lights burned late most evenings, shadows occasionally painting the rolled-down shades.

Some nights, I would turn onto my side, perspiration running down my neck onto my pillow as I searched for the coolness of sleep, and stared through my window at Hershkowitz' windows, imagining the activity within, those imaginings limited by my nine-year-old imagination.

It was August, still in the heart of the summer, the days when you could see the tides of heat hover over the blacktop of the road, the nights where the fireflies could be coaxed into empty mayonnaise jars with air holes punched in the lid, a bed of browning grass in the bottom to create a proper home for our glowing prisoners. It must have been a weekend night because my dad was sitting on the screened porch, his cigar smoke further complicating the moisture saturated air, filling the bedrooms with stale after-smell of dime Phillies. At one point, all of Hershkowitz' rooms lit up, and a few cars pulled into the lot behind the club house, away from the cabins.

"Party time," said dad. My mother grunted.

"Put away the cigar, will 'ya, Harry?" My father ignored her, not mentioning that her cigarette smoke was a pretty much constant feature of our family's breathing experience.

That night there were many shadows on the Hershkowitz shades. I could not sleep; it was particularly hot, particularly smoky in my room; the snoring of my parents mixed with the sound of the fan did not help, and my dad had placed the fan directly into his own doorway that evening, so nothing kept the mosquitos from finding my arms and legs on top of the thin chenille blanket. The moon lit the area behind the club house. From the angle of our end bungalow I could see moonlight bouncing off chrome bumpers and tail fins. I did not know how late it was. Well after bedtime, well before dawn, almost at the point where the moon would disappear into the trees, I jumped at the voice just outside my window screen. "Scootch? Scootch, you in there?"

"Yeah. Shit, Stevie, that you?" I was now upright in bed, not fully aware of what was happening.

"Who else? Hey Scootch, come out here, we gotta go look."

"Ya kiddin?! Look at what?"

"Scoooootch..." Long, low, coaxing. "Scootchie, get out here, will ya?"

"Yeah, yeah, gimme a min."

I pulled on shorts from the floor, stepped into my Keds, forget socks, unhooked the corners of my screen and lowered it onto the ground outside, straddled the sill and stepped down onto wet grass and weeds. Stevie, vaguely silhouetted by the fading moonlight, was at the corner of the bungalow, looking up at Hershkowitz' windows and I moved to him, tall weeds wetting my legs to match my sweat-sogged T-shirt.

"Watcha lookin' at?"

Stevie just kept looking up.

"My mom's over there," he whispered.

"What? Over where?"

"My mom's over there!"

"How do ya know that?"

"She went over after she tucked me in. Said my dad had to work the weekend in town. Told me I'd be fine, she'd be back in a little while, wanted to take a walk ... " Stevie paused. "Too hot to sleep." Another pause. "Watched when she went into the club house and then the lights came on upstairs." Something like a sigh. "She didn't come back." Long pause. "Gotta go over there." Very long pause, then "I'm scared. Ya gotta come with me."

"Now?"

"Yeah now, whattaya think, dickhead?" No sarcasm, just a statement of the obvious. Stevie began walking, along the edge of the grass rather than right down the open walkway. I followed silently. Too late for the crickets, too early for the birds, the wet swish of grass was the only sound over our breathing.

My father stayed through Monday to help us pack for the move back to Brooklyn. The police had wanted to talk to Stevie and me, what we saw, what we remembered of the other parked cars. Stevie wouldn't talk or couldn't. His father had come up the next morning, unshaven and gray and not looking at anyone. He spoke to my folks, gave me a tight little hug I did not expect, and then went back to his bungalow to stay with Stevie and pack their stuff.

It was exciting to talk to the police. The nightmares came only after we were back in the City for a while. I told the cops I was sad I had to go back to Brooklyn while it was still the middle of the summer, but I was mainly sad for Stevie because I was sure not having a mom was a bad thing to have happen. I told them all what I had seen, of course, not that I really understood it. In my head, it was just like a series of big photographs in the *Daily News*.

There were the chairs, I told them, the red colors, Stevie's mom sort of sitting up but with her head drooping down, and Mr. Hershkowitz who was on the floor and I thought he was sort of naked but also he didn't seem right 'cause he was bent in sort of a strange way I could not describe and that some of his body might have been missing but I wasn't really so sure about that last part, it was all so fast.

We pulled away in our Dodge coupe. I was on my knees in the rear seat, looking backwards through the oval window at the arc of white cabins, hazy through the road dust. It was the last time I ever saw the place. Stevie's father was dragging a garbage can out of their cabin and Stevie was sitting on the front step. I waved through the window, but I guess he did not see me.

BIG JOHNNY O AND WHY I ALMOST MISSED BREAKFAST

Muggy nights, I always had a hard time going to sleep. My old room felt alien now. Home from college for a brief visit, the walls seemed too close, the smells too familiar in an uncomfortable sort of way. The light came through the edges of the door to the kitchen; apartments in New York were always poorly designed, as the cost of comfortable design was too great for your average city-dweller to bear.

I think I was half-awake when I heard rustlings in the house. At 2 a.m., what was going on?

I slowly opened my door to find my father standing across the kitchen, buttoning his shirt. His trousers were pitched neatly over the back of one of the kitchen chairs as he stood there in his shoes and socks and boxers.

"What's up, dad? You okay?"

"Stanley, what are you doing up? I was trying to make no noise, not wake you and mother."

"Well, I'm a light sleeper, dad, you know that."

I think he remembered then; he and my mother would be up late playing cards at the kitchen table, the edges of the cards making a distinct click when they hit the Formica, and with me yelling from the bedroom for them to go to sleep already.

"Yeah, sure," he said. "I gotta go out."

"What's the matter?"

"Nothing, I told you nothing is the matter." He looked at me and saw he was not going to get away with the answer. "Okay. Johnny O was arrested. They have him down at the Tombs, lower Manhattan. I have to bail him out."

"Uncle John? When did this happen? What did he do?"

"He just called me. Good thing it didn't wake up your mother. She stirred but I grabbed it before it could ring a second time."

"He called you at two in the morning?"

Dad looked up with a smile. "Yes, he called me at two in the morning. Why are you so shocked? When you get arrested in the middle of the night, you're supposed to call your lawyer with your one dime. Who would you call, pray tell? Your girlfriend?"

"Wow. This is sort of exciting. How much is the bail, dad?"

He was pulling his pants on with one hand, steadying himself with the other. I was sure I misheard him.

"How much?"

He cinched his belt, some of the trouser fabric gently rolling over the top, prodded along by a small roll of fat. "I said, a hundred thousand dollars."

"Holy shit, that's a lot of money." Looking back today, to 1961, it was really a lot of money. Who wanted to sleep, get up the next morning and read Spinoza for Monday's exam, when people were in jail and their bail was a fortune.

"What the fuck was he arrested for," a question which elicited an annoyed glance followed by a single word, "murder."

"Murder? Really?"

My father had a sardonic side and lack of patience for stupidity, which made it all the more amazing that he loved me so much. "Yeah, murder. Here's how it works: you steal it's ten years, you shoot and miss its twenty years, you shoot and hit the guy and he croaks, that's a hundred thousand in bail and they fry you. No one can make that kind of bail." A pause. "Well, some people can, and those guys call their lawyer."

I turned back into my room. "Wait a minute, I'm comin' with you."

"It's no place for a kid. And keep your voice down, you'll wake your mother. She's not feeling well, you tell her when she gets up."

I am already pulling up my jeans over my sweaty shorts. "No, I'm coming, dad. Write her a note."

In a minute I am fully dressed: trousers, T-shirt, sneakers no socks, Dodger baseball cap. "I'm ready."

"Don't you have homework, Stan? Don't you think you should get a good night's sleep and do your homework? You need to get the grades to go to law school."

"Dad, I told you I'm not going to law school and this is exciting, I'm not going to miss this."

And so we are in my father's big gray Buick Roadmaster, with those ugly fins and bench seats wide enough for four people, and all of a sudden I realize we are driving on the Belt Parkway and we are going east, away from Manhattan.

"Dad, you made a wrong turn, you're headed out to the Island."

"No, it's okay, that's where we're going first."

"Dad, why are we going to the Island when Uncle Johnny is in jail in Manhattan?"

Now he was really grinning, the grin visible weirdly in the greenish glow from the impressive instrument panel with all those extra dials for RPMs and FM radio and air conditioning, all those things that had boosted the cost of our shiny Buick all the way up to four grand.

"Thought you'd never ask," he said. "Guess what? When the call came in and I looked in my wallet I said to myself, Joseph, I said, will ya look at that? You shoulda gone to the bank today like you intended. Because you don't have a hundred grand in your wallet so what are you gonna do about that?"

"Hey, dad, so what are we going to do?"

"I called ahead to Johnny's house. We'll pick up the money there and go into the City."

Oh, okay, I thought to myself and a minute later it occurred to me that not a lot of people had thousands of dollars sitting around their houses and I was about to ask when I remembered about Uncle Johnny and his house about half the size of our apartment building, with the security gate out front with always a man in the booth, and the interminable green lawn sloping all the way down to the Long Island Sound which seemed a zillion miles away, and I thought to myself that, yeah, would not surprise me if Johnny O had a million or so lying around the house, just in case he decided to buy another boat or fly to Italy or, well, just decide to shoot somebody and get arrested.

A half hour later we pulled up to the gate, which was still closed, but there were five or six men standing behind it, which was odd but then again visits to Uncle Johnny always were. One of the men slipped out between the fences, which opened

135

for a moment, and stepped towards the back door of our car.

"Just don't sit there, Stan. Open the door lock."

"What? Wait, sorry." I twisted around and pulled the locking pin up. The man stepped silently into the back seat. He was carrying a small dark leather satchel which he placed on the seat beside him. The seat depressed a good deal; the bag must have been pretty heavy, I thought.

All of a sudden the car was moving. There was no discussion, no one had said a word. It was all awkward, so I turned around and stuck out my hand. "Hi," I said, "I'm Stan and this is my…"

"Shut up, will you, Stan?" It was my father's voice, a bit loud I thought and clearly full of annoyance.

I turned my head, my body still twisted towards the back seat, arm extended and not yet shaken.

"Stanley, just turn around and face front and forget about the man in the back, will you?"

I looked over at my dad, who gave his head a jerk, back to front, just to make sure I had understood which way he wanted me to move. In the glare of an oncoming headlight, to this day I can swear that he was rolling his eyes upwards because of my gaffe.

So for forty-five minutes we drove in total silence. There were few cars on the road. We came over the Queensborough Bridge, never so empty as at four in the morning, and zoomed downtown, pulling up in front of a dirty gray building that could only be either a prison or a New York City public school. My dad stopped under the "No Standing" sign. I guess he then realized it was going to be strange to just leave me in the car, although at this point I had no idea what to expect.

"So how about you go inside and make bail," he asked as casually as if he were asking me if I wanted another pickle with my pastrami on rye.

"What do you mean?" I heard myself ask.

"What I mean is I want you to step out of the car. The gentleman will hand you the satchel. You will walk through those two doors there, and turn right, and go up a few steps, and you will come to another set of swinging doors. You will walk through those doors and you will see a desk with a policeman behind it. You will tell him why you are there, and he will ask you for the money and you will give it to him, and you will wait. When Johnny comes into the room, you will not say anything. You will then turn and walk out with him." He paused, and then that same grin. "And you need not tell Johnny what to do, he will know it will be time to go."

I managed an "uh-huh," or at least I think I did, and stepped out into the waning night. Somewhere the sky was beginning to lighten, but in the City you never could tell directions, the buildings always blocked the geography, you just got the light or the dark or the rain or the shine down on the street, coming between the towers from some location you did not know.

Our passenger stepped out of our car and held out the bag, which I took. I was afraid to say "thank you," and my silence seemed to be the wise choice as he turned away and walked slowly down the street towards Broadway without looking back.

I turned towards the building, and sensed my father waving his hand at me, pointing in the direction of the doors. Sure enough, in the first set, right turn, four steps, more doors, and then an incredibly bright room, neons hanging from the ceiling, and straight in front of me a tall desk, dark wood, and a fat policeman sitting on what must have been a high stool behind it.

He ignored me, which was strange as the place was totally empty and still. I waited. I cleared my throat. I was obviously doing this incorrectly. "Excuse me, officer," I croaked. My voice was cracky and high, not the tone I had hoped to convey.

"Yeah, kid, whaddaya want?" I did not deserve his looking up. He seemed to be reading something, although perhaps he was just studiously disrespecting me. It occurred to me I should have thrown on a suit jacket before leaving my bedroom, but it was a bit late for that now.

"I'm here to bail out Johnny O," I said with confidence.

"One hundred thou," he replied, as if asking for a ten-spot. He still had not favored me with his gaze. All I saw was the top of his cap, and the pink jowls of his lower face.

I reached up, holding the black leather case. It took all of my strength to lift it a couple of feet upwards.

"Fa Chrissake," he said, finally looking in my general direction, "take the fuckin' money outta the bag, will ya?" Apparently, I was so inept that I could not even manage to give someone a hundred thousand dollars in cash at four a.m. without screwing it up.

Speechless, I fussed with the clasps, there were two, and put the case on the floor as I could not really hold it up and deal with the neat clumps of bills. I reached into the case, bent at the waist, grabbed two handfuls of money, reached up to my eye-level to place them neatly on the top of the desk, bend and repeat, bend and repeat, my back and arms began to hurt, God there were a lot of bills to add up to that much money, and then thought well that's no surprise is it, bend and repeat, bend and repeat, until finally the case was empty.

"That's it," I sighed, not even aware I was intending to speak.

The policeman stood. He looked old, really old, with a short white mustache, several chins, and what looked like female breasts underneath his sweaty shirt; the room was still and hot and he was not handling the heat very well. He swept the money off the desk with his forearm, and I could hear it dropping with successive thumps into a drawer. Then I heard another drawer open and the same thump-thump. I guess desk drawers in police stations hold about fifty thousand each, they were not built for the bail for Johnny O.

I fought down an urge to ask him why he hadn't counted it. I guess people like Johnny O are stand-up. They don't chisel you on the bail money, I guess. What did I know? I was still in college ...

I heard a rotary phone being dialed; three numbers, then an audible tinny ring. "Yeah, Hogan here. Bring the wop up, he's been bailed."

He looked up. "Sit down, kid. You makin' me nervous." He waved towards a wooden bench a few yards away where I sat for what seemed like forever.

Then a door opened at the other end of room and out walked my Uncle Johnny. One thing about Uncle Johnny, he always was well dressed. In fact, long time ago I asked him about his suits and jackets, I was just a kid but even then I thought his clothes were "unusual," and he showed me some different fabrics up in his massive bedroom, you could walk into his closet, it was bigger than my bedroom at home, and showed me what hand-stitching looked like, I had never even known there were different ways to sew a suit but I saw that my clothing was not sewn like Uncle Johnny's.

Johnny was wearing a blue pinstripe suit, alligator belt, pointy loafers, silk shirt, no tie. The usual, now that I think about it, but at the time all I could think of was that most people never in their lives looked that nice, forget about just stepping out of jail.

"Hiya, kiddo," he said, and gently raised me from the bench and gave me a friendly push towards the door.

"See ya soon," said the policeman as we reached the door.

"Fuck ya mother," allowed Johnny O, all in his usual even voice, throwing the remark over his shoulder as the inner doors swung shut.

We walked to the car without talking. I was afraid to say anything and Johnny was not in the mood for chit-chat. Instinctively I opened the front door and Johnny sat right down in my old seat. I slid into the back. My dad rolled away from the curb.

"Rat bastard douchebag," said my Uncle.

"Later," said my father.

And we drove down to the ocean, over near Floyd Bennett Field, before it was renamed Kennedy International, before the President was shot and eligible to have big things named after him, and no one said a word, and my Uncle's head lolled back on the headrest and I could swear he started to snore, the gentle snore of the righteous.

Johnny awoke when we bumped into the near-empty parking lot of a silver-bodied diner, its shadow casting a long rectangle of deeper blackness on the macadam.

"Good, I'm hungry." Johnny stretched his short arms in front of him, then reached for his door.

"Me, too," said my father, who was always hungry.

Wordlessly I opened my back door and was halfway out when my father walked around the car and looked down at me.

"Stay put," he said.

"I'm hungry."

"Just stay in the car, please. I have to talk to my client, and that has to be confidential. You can't be there."

I collapsed back into the seat and my father was gently closing the door when Johnny O's head appeared. "Relax, Stan m' man," said Johnny O. "We gonna take care of you. You, you're a real nice kid, ya know."

"Thank you, Uncle Johnny," came out of my mouth. He reached in and patted me on the cheek.

"Real nice kid," he said with a smile, and then the door closed and I was sitting in a parking lot, in a dark car, all alone, with the sun now glinting over the reeds at the edge of the ocean, and a couple of gulls strutting over the pavement, pecking at what was left on the ground.

I must have dozed off but was awakened by a knock on my window. I looked out and two waitresses with little caps were standing outside, each holding a tray. I jumped out and handed the food onto the back seat.

"You got eggs scrambled, bacon, sausage. You got a bagel, rye toast, toasted English. Ya got a short stack of blueberry pancakes. You also got cheese blintzes, coffee, juice, chocolate milk."

I just stared. Then I broke out in a big smile.

The other waitress smiled back. "The guy in the nice suit? He said you wanted to be alone but were hungry and didn't know what you wanted so he ordered you all of this stuff. Said it was fine, you were a nice kid."

I'm sure I sort of beamed, standing there with the two of

them staring at my back seat full of all that food, coffee cup on the floor so it wouldn't spill, napkins and utensils all over the place.

I turned to the two of them and said a simple "thanks." They looked at each other, giggled, and the pretty one said "And he gave me five dollars to do this," and she leaned towards me and gave me a huge wet kiss on the mouth.

I watched their backsides hustle back to the diner, turned and began to figure out how to eat all that food. In the window of the diner, I saw my father and Uncle Johnny talking at their table. What I did not know at the time was that Johnny O was going away for the rest of his life. But he was always okay by me.

THE CARD

"Why are you so worried about your cards," she asked in her precise English, muddied only slightly by vague mid-European overtones.

"Well, gotta look at my cards and see what I got," I answered.

"Certainly take a look but how hard is it to understand five cards right under your nose? After that quick glance, look where it is important to look."

We were on a foldable card table on a small stone patio behind my Uncle Charlie's house; small neat brick ranch, three bedrooms, two bathrooms, no garage; "fourteen nine but only a hundred down," advised my uncle, bathing in the good luck of the GI bill. It looked like a castle to me, coming from my brownstone with no grass in sight. A worn deck of Bicycle cards, the blue ones, were spread over the canvas tabletop.

"Well, Grandma, I can't see the other person's cards, can I?"

She shifted in her nylon-webbed beach chair, her tightly bunned gray hair bouncing in one motion on top of her head. Her thick legs, wrapped in inscrutable beige leggings, stuck straight out from under the table; I imagined all sorts of veins, bumps and maladies embossed on those legs underneath; I had not, in all my ten years, seen her actual legs, at least that

143

I could recall.

"You can, Stephen, if you know where to look."

I glanced behind her but of course there were no mirrors, no window reflecting her hand. I sat quietly, waiting. My Grandmother was always patient, never raised her voice, lived with my Aunt and Uncle and younger cousin in the suburbs of New York City in what seemed to me bucolic wonder.

"You look at your opponent. That is how you know that person's cards."

"You mean, if they smile you know they have a great hand," I said as I pounced on an idea I could grasp.

"Yes, yes. But what if he is lying? Smiling to only make you think he has a good hand? That's not cheating you know."

"Maybe because he bets a lot of money?"

"Yes, yes, that too. But maybe he's bluffing?"

"What's bluffing?"

"That's lying to you by betting a lot of money. He hopes to scare you away even if you have a good hand."

"Oh," Now totally confused: "so what am I looking for, exactly?"

"His body. Does he look tense, like his bet makes him nervous? Is he sitting back, like he knows he has you beaten? Is he in a hurry to bet or has he thought a long time about his bet? Is he in a hurry for you to bet, one way or another?"

"Those would be good things to know, Grandma, but how will I know them by looking at someone?"

She smiled, the sad sage smile of the old. "If you look hard enough, you will learn to know," she said. "Now, look again at your cards and place your bet."

I had a pile of pistachio nuts in front of me. I bit my lip for a moment, then counted out ten and placed them neatly in the center of the table. My Grandma immediately threw her cards in the middle, face down, and signaled for me to pass my cards for a shuffle.

"Wait," I said, now really unhappy, "why aren't you playing the game? You get to bet and then you get to throw down three of your cards and get three new cards, and then we both get to bet again."

"I know you have a really good hand. My hand is okay, but it is not likely going to beat you this time."

I stared at my three Aces and I think my lower lip even quivered a little. "How do you know," I asked.

That same smile. "You bet too much. You bet too fast. You are too young to really understand bluffing. You were too interested in your own cards, and you told me all about them by how you played them."

I tossed my cards despondently into the middle. They fell face-up on the table. My grandmother's hand froze over them, she looked up at me and prepared to speak. I had no idea what I had done wrong, but I knew, just knew, that I was about to find out.

＋—◆—◆—＋

The sweat poured off my face and made the neck of my T-shirt a darker blue. My glasses slid down my nose every time I looked down at the concrete on top of my front stoop leading into my brownstone. Lou and Stevie S (there were so many of us Stephens that our parents all identified us with a letter for our last names) sat on a lower step, their bodies turned towards the surface. Julie from upstairs and me, we sat on our haunches up top. In the middle, a large pile of nickels and dimes. In front of those three, a small pile of silver coins. In front of me, a large pile.

"Fifty cents," said Stevie S, fingering a short stack of dimes.

"Whoa, it ain't the last card, ya can only go a quarter," I said.

"Yeah, says who?" Stevie S's hand started to drop the dimes into the center pile.

"Cut it out, Stevie. Ya know the rules!" Julie reached out and pushed Stevie S's hand to the side; a couple of dimes dropped out onto the second step, bounced once and flew onto the sidewalk and began to roll down the street.

"Now look watcha done, ya fuckin' douche," allowed Stevie S in a sullen plaint as he stood up and pursued his dimes. "And I don't like the deck," he spit out. "'Next time, I bring my own deck!"

"Fine," I yell at his back as he bends to pick up his money. "I can beat your ass even you bring a deck you marked."

Stevie plunked himself back down and quickly made change so his bet was a quarter. "There! Ya happy now?"

I looked at my hand, I was the only other person left in the game. Two pair, jacks and tens. Not a bad hand for draw, no wild cards. And I could draw another card once I bet.

"Hurry up, dummy," said Stevie S.

I waited a minute, then carefully placed my hand face down on the remainder of the deck. "Take your money," I said.

"Crap." Stevie S threw his hand into the middle, face up;

three kings. "You are luckiest son of a bitch in the world," said Stevie S, as he picked up the coins.

I looked down at my pile of silver and smiled the sad sage smile of the old. I might only be fourteen, but I still had the biggest pile of nickels and dimes.

—•— ░░ —•—

"Hey, Stevie! The Delta Chi convention is coming to New York in a couple of weeks. At the Astor! Hundreds of pumped-up frat guys drinking cheap booze and throwing up in the halls. Do you know what that means?"

Marty never did say "hello" or "hi it's Marty" or anything else to start a conversation. He was right into the message from word one, and in truth the voice was so distinctive that you never confused him with anyone else.

"Hiya, Mart," I slowly drawled. "How are you doing? How are things in Philadelphia? Are you studying hard? What's your favorite subject?" I always tried to divert him, it was a fun hobby and I knew it drove him crazy.

"Asshole, listen to me. In fact, listen into the phone. What sound do you hear?"

"Let me guess. A college sophomore breathing heavily and that can mean only one thing!"

"Ka-ching! Ka-ching! I hear the sound of cash, lots of cash. I hear the sound of Lincolns and Hamiltons and Andrew Jacksons!"

"Marty, bills don't go ka-ching, coins go ka-ching. And since we are having this cryptic one-way conversation, what is Delta Chi and why do I give a shit?"

"Ah, mon ami, permettez moi! Delta Chi is the big fraternity for those rich College kids who are Greek Geeks. Surely at Columbia you have heard of fraternities, oui?"

"Sure, of course, they run the whole length of 114th Street. So what?"

"Well, I am talking earlier today with a guy I know, he's in Delta Chi at Penn. I play cards with him sometimes. He stinks. He alone could almost cover my tuition bill. So he tells me that he is going to this annual convention and I ask him, like what's that all about, and he tells me they have meetings and then they drink and walk around Times Square looking at the people and going into Ripley's and maybe take a train down to the Village, but this guy, he loves playing poker and there are these big money poker games late at night, sometimes until dawn, and everyone is drinking , and the pots are big and he's going to play all night because he loves playing poker with the guys."

I have forty pages of Plato to read. The book is face down on my desk, I am standing at the wall phone that serves our suite of two bedrooms and a common room. I want to get back to Plato, not because I love it but because I would love to just finish it. "So what's this got to do with the price of tea in China?"

"Ah, mon ami," more of his bad mock French accent, "this is how we make what we call 'la moolah.' From these drunk jerks. I moi-meme will come up on the RR early that evening. You will take the subway to 49th street. We will meet for a light healthy dinner with no alcohol, a couple of cups of black coffee, and around about eleven we stroll into the lobby of the Astor, find a card game, and we play til dawn."

"I don't want to spend a night playing poker. Exams are coming up ... "

148

"Stevie, listen to me. This is not social. This is business. Most of these guys can't play for crap even when they are rested and sober. We are going to clean up. And by clean up I mean hundreds each easy, probably thousands. See, we play sober, we each grab a beer and nurse it all night so no one notices, we just play our game. You and me in the same game, for safety ya know? That may cut down winnings but still it's safer. Probably we hit two games, maybe three. We dress regular but no school emblems or anything, we tell them we're from somewhere, I'll figure out a chapter from which no one likely is attending, Texas or somewhere."

"Marty, I don't want to do this. And what if we don't win? Cards are cards, ya know. Hey, you aren't going to bring one of your special decks, are you?"

"No, course not. And I don't want the shit beaten out of me either. No need, these clowns will be real marks. Tell ya what, I'll stake you, give you say $500 for starters. End of the night, I'll give ya the $500 to keep. You just give me anything ya got over $500. If you're busted, I'll give ya five from my own money. No risk. I'll even give ya more depending on how much you and I win. Or either of us. Ya can't lose, mon ami."

"Marty, they're gonna figure out we're ringers and beat the shit out of us."

"Not us, pard. Just you!"

"What!"

"It's a joke, jerkoff. It's a joke. C'mon. you know my old man doesn't have enough money to send me here, I gotta play cards and this is easy pickings."

I let out a sigh. " When the hell is this?"

"The eighth and ninth. Ninth is best, they'll be even more

wasted the second night."

"All right, all right but listen. If I get nervous or anything, we're gonna have a code word. Like 'hey, aren't we supposed to meet Harry about now?' and if I say that, I don't care how well we're doing, you gotta say like 'o yeah' and we cash out and leave. Ya gotta agree to that because you, you get buried in the game, you want the bread too much, you gonna run through the warning signs and get us killed by some drunk football jocks who are figuring out what we're doing."

"Whatever you say, boss. You wanna slow play the night, you wanna cash out, it's all your call."

I close my eyes and exhale. He is always doing this to me, I have no resistance. He is my best friend. He has bailed me out plenty. He is the excitement in my life, truth be told. Truth be told, he had me at 'ka'ching.'

"Yeah, okay okay, you're on." I am sorry I said it but I had no choice. "You pay for dinner also," I blurted.

"Anything you say, Stevie; anything you say. Just remember: ka-ching." The line went dead. I picked up Plato, but all I could think of was poker on the front steps of my brownstone. Marty was the only one who was a winner. Except of course for me...

The Astor had seen better days. Actually, I am not sure that is true. The Astor lobby looked like the kind of fake-gilded public space that never had a better day. Two stories high with elaborate crystal-festooned hanging chandeliers dangling from plaster-molded ceiling ovals painted white with tinged edges of gilt, heavily carpeted with mock-oriental wall to wall of a dark cherry red hue, populated with numerous worn leather chairs and an occasional mock-Chippendale wooden settee, the lobby absorbed large numbers of noisy people without really welcoming them. Ashtrays on pedestals, some over-flowing

150

with cigarette butts, stood at attention next to many of the armchairs.

And across this crowded and confusing space trod large numbers of perspiring college men, many in school T-shirts and shorts, boat shoes without socks, a mild odor of sweat blending peacefully into the residual tobacco overtones of the ambient air. Older patrons looked up in either amusement or annoyance, but neither reaction pierced the attention of the students; freed from committee meetings and the "grand conclave" at which the national officers announced the growth of membership and the new rules against violent hazing, their conversation revolved around cheap dinner options and asking "where's the action."

We looked like we belonged, Marty and me, because we were of the proper vintage, proper attire, proper vocabulary. However, unlike the others, fun was not on our minds. Filled with half a cardboard crusted pizza and a giant cup of bitter coffee, I wanted to find a men's room and then a subway uptown to the dorm, particularly as the chemistry exam had been rescheduled from today to tomorrow, and I was not sure I had the stamina to play cards all night and remember organic structures at dawn. Marty was so keyed up that I was afraid to let him ask about card games at all; he was walking through the lobby in predatory fashion, his head stuck forward, his lips pursed almost to a pucker. I was probably projecting, but to me he looked like a hustler in a dirty polo shirt.

"Leave this to me, will ya? And fer Gozzake, will ya take a chill pill?"

"Look, Stevie, I'm fine, you're moving too slow. You're too cautious. Let me handle this."

I gave him a look that drew him up short.

"What?"

"Marty, you wait here. Drink a piping hot cup of shut the fuck up."

I turned away without waiting for an answer, walking slowly among the clusters of chairs, my head inclined towards the carpet and my brow knit in false consternation. Picking a small group of seemingly gregarious guys, I veered in their direction and looked up. As I approached they turned out to be bigger than I had originally imagined, but I had eye contact with one of them so the die was cast.

"Hey, man," I began, ever a cool introduction.

"Hey, bro," said the big blond with the acne pits and unwashed hair. "What's shakin'?"

His shirt said "Duke."

"You from Duke?" I asked cleverly.

"Yeah. You?"

"My friend and me, we're up from Utah." I jerked my head slightly behind me, not even towards Marty who, hopefully, was leaning against the pillar where I had left him. "I'm Stan. You guys been to one of these before?"

A series of half grunts, some affirmative. I stuck out my hand and met Lars, and his buddies Pete, Choco and Lance; an unattractive cadre but you know what they say about beggars.

"Hey, yeah, it's our first time and I was wonderin' maybe there's a card game going on we could join."

"Ya know, lots all over but we, we just aren't here to play cards." He smiled and looked around his quartet, eliciting nods and a random "you said it" from Choco; or maybe it was Pete.

"Right," added Lars. We're gettin' a cab and going to the Village and grab some beers and look at the creeps." He paused for effect. "You ever hear of a bar down there, McSorley's I think, my dad said he used to go there when Chi partied, ya know, in the day." His head bobbed up and down for punctuation.

"Nah, never heard of it," I lied. "So tell me, what floor you on where they're playing cards?"

"Try eighteen," said Pete. Or maybe it was Choco. "There were a couple last night, kept it up all fuckin' night, good thing I passed out or I never would'a gotten any shut-eye." He laughed the shallow laugh of someone who said something that wasn't funny and looked around the circle until everyone gave him a quick smile.

"Hey, yeah, maybe we will. Thanks for the tip. Have fun at McCarthy's," I added.

"Yeah thanks," Pete/Chaco replied. "Later," promised Lars, and as I turned away I thought to myself, sure as hell hope not, you must be six-four if you're an inch, asshole.

Marty was not where I left him, no surprise, but at least he didn't get into any trouble, he was seated on the edge of a settee, his legs bouncing on the balls of his feet.

"Eighteen," I said.

"Great. Let's get goin'."

"Sure. And Marty—stay cool, hear? And if I say we gotta meet Harry ..."

"Yeah, I know, I know. Don't worry about me. And here ya go."

He stuck out his hand and gave me a roll of old bills, ones on the outside, held together with a thick rubber band. I slipped the band off on the way to the elevators and flattened the wad so it didn't bulge out of my pocket. Never did a lot of money feel so unwelcome against my thigh. The folding gate on the elevator clanked shut and the elevator operator, wearing a cap with some fake badge on it, collared shirt and jeans below, drove us up to eighteen. By the time we were at about fifteen, you could already hear the din.

"Hey, Marty, look at the time." Gray light was invading the room through the dirty windows, illuminating the pizza boxes, beer bottles, Seagram's Seven bottles, tequila bottles, cups filled with cigarette butts, a mirror coated with white powder residue, two guys asleep in arm chairs, and six guys on the floor around a rearranged coffee table covered with playing cards and piles of bills.

"Whose deal is it?" asked one of the guys. I had promptly forgotten the names. I was tired, this was our third game, I had no idea how much money we had won but it was a lot, the bills were bulging in my pants pockets, pulling the fabric of my jeans across my crotch in a most unpleasant way.

"Me, gimme the cards will ya," said another one; all this group were from NYU, which was making me uncomfortable from the start, it was in New York, I knew a lot of kids at NYU, and I would have preferred another game with guys from Pittsburgh or Cincinnati. And these guys they were really stinko, dropping farts and belches and passing a bottle around really fast, this one was either gin or vodka, something clear like water but certainly not water. We were killing them at poker, and I didn't want them to get the idea that they should be, physically, killing us.

"Mart, it's what, shit it's after four, Harry is waiting for us, we said ya know?"

154

Marty looked up, a happy glaze over his face although in the last five hours I doubt that either of us had finished as much as a single beer. It was the flush of lust, an animal rictus of victory.

"Yeah, I know but ya know what, Stevie, fuck 'em, I'm having too much fun." I realized I had forgotten to call him by our agreed fake names, he was supposed to be Mel and I was Ray or Stan or who the hell could remember, that's what I had remembered until just now, when the fatigue got to me. Now I knew we had to split.

"Marty!" Loud and sharp enough to quell the chatter for a minute. "We gotta go, like now."

Eyes narrowed as the rest of the table paid attention to the two of us, something that was not exactly a desired result.

"Whattaya got going at four in the fuckin' morning?" the kid with the dark glasses asked with a touch of suspicion; his umpteenth cigarette was hanging from the corner of his mouth. "Ya got somewhere ta go, Stan or Stevie or whatever the fuck ya name is?"

Marty had his opening. "Hey, go to the room, make sure Harry is okay, alright, if ya so worried about him." He turned to the group. "Asshole picked up some chick in the lobby, who knows what sorta shape she's in, ya know?" He snorted for effect; everyone relaxed, laughed.

"Ya, go ahead to the room," Marty said, easy and slow like he was talking to some younger brother who was a pain in his ass. "I'm gonna stay and play with the guys for a while. I'll catch you for breakfast. Okay?"

I was end-gamed; couldn't stay now, couldn't extract Marty at this point. Damn fool, dangerous shit, I thought. "Yeah, well fine, see ya later," I said as I stood up with a slight wobble. "Wow, too much beer and booze."

The big one stood up which gave me a scare but he stuck out his hand. "Thanks for playing. You were pretty lucky tonight, ya know?"

"Guess so. And everyone at school told me to be careful of those guys in New York."

He chucked me on the shoulder, I gave the room a group smile and went out the door. I was going to stay down the hall to spot Marty if there was any trouble, but he seemed okay and the guys were pretty mellow even if they were loaded. I figured it would be weirder to hang around, so I called the elevator and the old coot running it paid me no attention and drove me down to the lobby and mumbled a good night.

There weren't many places to get comfortable and invisible in the hotel lobby at four in the morning, but there was a men's room off by the bar. The bar was shut but the bathroom was open. I stuck my head in; no one in there, and all the stall doors were open so no one was hanging out on one of the toilets. I locked myself in, took a long satisfying piss and carefully pulled out the bills crammed into my trousers. There were a lot of small bills so I was not too optimistic, but then I started to count and didn't stop until I emptied my left rear pocket which turned out to be stuffed with twenties which I must have segregated at some point, along with a few U.S. Grants. I made the pile at just over $2300. Gotta say, I had a big grin on my face.

About then, I heard the front door swing, and then the long loud splash of someone emptying his horse bladder, and then the burping whoosh of someone throwing up a whole lot of miscellany, after which a soft "oh, fuck" and a few gargles with water from the tap after which the front door again swung and I was again alone. By then, the acrid smell had infiltrated my stall, and I got the hell out of there, through the lobby and into what turned out to be a warm and misty dawn.

Marty never showed up at the Chock full o'Nuts on Forty Eighth, which was our rendezvous point if separated. We were 15 years away from cell phones, there was no way to reach him. I went to Penn Station and stood on the platform for the first two trains to Philly in hopes of catching sight of him, but then I had to hop a cab back to campus and take my chem exam.

I got a B, which was a gift from the gods. Marty got two broken ribs, three missing teeth, a mild concussion and a crushed coccyx bone at the base of his spine and had to sit on an inflated rubber tube for six months until it healed. He was found without watch or money in a hotel stairwell.

I sent him all the money but he sent back five hundred. I guess a deal's a deal.

—◦—≧◦≦—◦—

"We're here in the lobby of Caesar's Palace in Las Vegas, Nevada interviewing Stevie Newhouser, winner of the 2019 Masters of Poker championship. Stevie, first, congratulations."

"Thanks, Candice."

"Stevie, this is your third tournament win in the last two years but this has got to be the biggest. Five Million Dollars and a platinum and diamond bracelet appraised at almost two million more. What do you have to say about all that?"

"Well, first off, that's a shit-load of mon—uh can I say that on TV?"

"Stevie, you know you can't and you know you're live but I am sure all your many fans will forgive you because, after all, you are King of the Hill and you are entitled. So tell us, how did you do it? Did the cards fall for you just right?"

"Candice, the cards just fall the same for everyone. Anybody tells you poker is luck doesn't know much about poker. It's just like life, ya know."

"Really. How do you mean that, Stevie?"

"You keep your eyes open and make your judgments based on the facts that life tells you. Same with cards. You just slow play your opportunities and then the world comes to you."

"The cards speak to you?"

"No, the players speak to you. They tell you what they think. They may not know it, but they speak to you."

"Well, Stevie, whatever your secret, you are again the champion. They don't call you The Card for nothing. One last question, if I may?"

"Sure, Candice, fire away."

"How in the world did you learn to play poker the way you do?"

The Card smiled and his eyes rolled back into his memory.

"Mein bubbie," he said.

Candice knit her brow, and the station went to commercial.

LINCOLN TERRACE PARK

Herewith, the history of Lincoln Terrace Park in Brooklyn, New York, from c1948 to c1957. Why would one care about this history? It is my history. Why would one care about my history? Perhaps you will not, though it also is the history of a slice of time and place.

It is 1948 and I am six years old. It is December and it is cold. I am holding my mother's hand and walking down the center pathway of Lincoln Terrace Park. It is morning. We are walking East towards PS 189. The sun is in my eyes. My muffler is bunched around my neck. My hat has fold-down earflaps which extend down to the edge of my pea-coat. I am being walked to the first grade, as I am every morning, to the dark-haired Mrs. Zimmerman, the beautiful (I think) Mrs. Zimmerman. The teacher who pulled me aside, first day, and told me that she knew all about my being thrown out of kindergarten for calling the fat ugly Mrs. Saltz too stupid to be my teacher. I told her that Mrs. Saltz was indeed stupid; she did not recognize that the airplane Kenny made out of an empty cookie box was missing its vertical stabilizer. Mrs. Zimmerman nodded sagely and told me that we would get along just fine.

My mother walked me to school every morning that year, and

every year through fifth grade. When I reached sixth grade and was Captain of the Safety Guards, wearing a white belt with silver and dark blue badge attached, helping cross the younger children over dangerous East New York Avenue, I felt demeaned to be walked by my mother, but that liberation was five years in the future that chilly day in December.

"The Park" was the core of my world view. It started less than a block away from my brownstone and seemed enormous at the time. It had baseball fields and cement chess tables and basketball courts and two tennis courts and green lawns and big trees. It sloped sharply downward from Eastern Parkway, ending at East New York Avenue at the foot of the hill. It was where we played when not on the street, it was the path to school, it was where my father had started taking my friends and me to pretend to play baseball, most Saturday mornings weather permitting, as we stumbled around the dirt kiddie diamond in our Dodger-blue caps and wooden bats too heavy for us, sipping our chocolate Yoo-Hoo drinks to protect us from dehydration and dust.

The geography was known to me through practice; no one had or needed a map. Lincoln Terrace Park occupied a steep hill, with flat terraced areas, starting at the peak along the southern border of Eastern Parkway and running an overlong block and a half mostly between Rochester Avenue on the west and Buffalo Avenue on the east. The Park descended its hill, sometimes precipitously, seven short blocks. My house was on the east end of Union Street, the highest street of the seven; you could see the trees from the steps of my brownstone. We were, all of us, loyal to the kids on our block, of which there were many; I never thought to count them but today, decades later, I can remember perhaps twenty boys, although that is not so remarkable. Eight of us were named Stephen or Steven for reasons of simple popularity; we were none of us aware of any famous Stephen in the early 1940s.

A word about Eastern Parkway on the north. It was a major

thoroughfare across the Borough before there were major highways or restricted-access roads not subject to cross-streets and stop-lights. Conceived in grand style with a central roadway and side-lanes in each direction, separated by a narrow strip of grass and trees and occasional benches, it was a palpable boundary to our neighborhood. After the end of the Second World War, it became a regular parade route. Every Veteran's Day, and I think on VE and VJ days, a major military parade would run for several hours past the northern rim of the Park. There were vets from the Second World War, still young and smartly turned out, fitting for the most part in their uniforms. There were marching units from the First World War also, in stranger uniforms and different hats and helmets, soldiers we observed with quiet respect although they did not march with all the great armament of the WW II guys: large guns, open trucks with seated ranks of soldiers and, above all, great grinding noisy tanks, one after another, enough tanks to retake Germany we were sure, and if we yelled and waved sometimes the men would swing the gun turrets for us and we would cheer.

Add in floats and trucks advertising on their flanks local stores now long gone—Abraham and Strauss was my mother's favorite because they carried pants that were stiff and durable and not made of denim—and politicians in open Cadillac convertibles and, incomprehensible to us, an occasional car with a few men in squared dark blue hats, upright and saluting—soldiers of the North's Grand Army of the Republic, carried in style up Eastern Parkway along the parade route that began far to the west at the Grand Army Plaza, that broad open space dedicated seventy or so years before to the men of Sherman and Grant, a link to an inconceivable past that over time has come to seem even more surreal.

We would stand with our backs to the metal spiked fence that bounded the Park, facing the parade and paying close attention to the men, the arms, and the occasional troops of Boy Scouts

161

and Girl Scouts and high school bands to see if we could identify kids from the neighborhood who were lucky enough to march. Small American flags appeared everywhere, distributed free and waved energetically, their golden pointy peaks at the pinnacle of each flag glittering in the mid-morning sun.

At the western border, there were no car roads heading into the Park; the streets that ran up to the Park on the hill, starting with Union, all terminated at the Park; Union and President and Carroll and Crown and Montgomery (where my best friend lived in an ample deco apartment house of yellow brick on the corner) and ending at East New York Avenue. On the east, Buffalo Avenue was tree lined on both sides, as a triangular rump of the Park jumped the street and continued, tree-filled and without walking paths, on the other side.

All the magic of the Park was either inside, of which more later, or in the geography to the south and west. South just across East New York Avenue was our Public School, kindergarten through grade six, a sea of first- and second-generation Jewish kids punctuated with what seemed to be a dozen or so Italians in each grade. One of the paths through the Park terminated across the street from the School and it was to that corner that my mother walked me each morning until I became a crossing guard myself, and officiously held out my arms or waved them like windmills to direct the little kids each morning and afternoon.

To the west, the Avenues were named for many blocks for the cities of Upstate New York, for reasons never quite clear. My father had remembered moving from the Lower East Side to a nearby street, just north of Eastern Parkway, before 1910 when almost all these streets were laid out and paved but with no buildings on them; his father, my grandfather, told me that when he had first seen the neighborhood it was mostly farmland. As you trekked west, leaving Buffalo and Rochester Avenues behind, you reached the commercial center of the neighborhood, Utica Avenue, itself running up the hill parallel to the Park, with its food and clothing stores and delicatessens and the only air conditioned building I had ever seen until I was about twelve years old and taken into Manhattan to see Mary Martin in Peter Pan on Broadway, the Carroll Movie Theater (where upstairs I went to learn piano until the kids on the block followed me one day and saw where I had gone and shamed me into refusing to play).

If you trekked west then, past Schenectady and Troy and Albany and Kingston Avenues, you finally reached the most important building in our lives, more alive than our homes and certainly more imposing than our school: Ebbets Field. The Brooklyn Dodgers played here, seventy-seven glorious home games, almost all during the day, often one admission buying a seat for two entire games, the now-long-abandoned all day festival called a double-header. During the school year my father would refrain from work and take me out of school and we would walk to the ballpark and buy a couple of box seats, five dollars covering the most expensive location for two, in those days easy to get on the day of the game. There I could see my idols, whose statistics I knew by heart, updated indeed from the very most recent game by reference to one of the newspapers; the *Herald Tribune*, the *Post*, the *Brooklyn Eagle*, the *World Telegram* and *Sun*, the *News*, the *Mirror*, the *Daily Forward* ... I never saw anyone read a *New York Times* until I went to college.

Baseball games those days were a challenge for a young boy; all the men wore business hats and many smoked cigars. If you sat on your haunches, the men behind you told you to sit down, and if you breathed you choked. But the ballfield was tiny, you were on top of the players.

In the summers, we ate from the ice cream trucks. The favorite ice cream pop or cup was the Elsie Bar or the Elsie Cup, named for Elsie the branded cow. Ten wrappers or cup tops and a quarter bought a general admission seat behind a pole. From there you could sneak anywhere. Our streets were scoured clean. And if by chance you did not have either the wrappers or the quarter, you would stand on Bedford Avenue in front of the plate glass window of the car dealer – was it Buicks, I don't recall and I refuse to look it up because it does not matter, and we would pound our gloves and wait for Duke Snider to hit the ball over the right field wall so we could catch it as it banged on car hoods and nearly but never quite crowned a pedestrian. And the beauty part—you never missed a play, all windows opened wide against the summer heat, radios and an occasional new-fangled television blaring the play by play out into the daylight, commentary by the ole Redhead and sometimes that new kid, Vin Scully, who you had to admit was pretty good at it though nothing like the ole Redhead describing to us Brooklyn kids how so-and-so was now in the catbird seat.

On the west border, the street I crossed to reach the Park itself was Rochester Avenue, the steepest of all. Here there was the mythology of place for at the top of the hill on the Park side of the street, at the apex where the Park fencing met Eastern Parkway, here was the start of that stretch of history we all called Dead Man's Hill.

We all knew, as we were informed by the older kids who had been informed by the older older kids, that in the old days the mob would rub you out but that was not humiliating enough to express the contempt that your particular mob boss felt for the lately deceased. No, the body would be dumped in the trunk of some car, no mean feat at the time where large car boots were unheard of since no one really took long trips by motor car—bad roads before Ike built the Interstates, gas rationing in the war, and who had the money or the vacation time anyway? The car was driven to Dead Man's Hill and the body unloaded onto the sidewalk alongside the Park. The bets were laid and the bound body would be placed athwart the sidewalk and then given an even kick to start it rolling. Down it would slowly twirl, we believed. At some point the body would stop, or veer and run into the side fence or a parked car; the game ended and the person guessing most closely how far the corpse rolled picked up the bets.

The time came when we all knew these stories could not be accurate, but we told them to the younger kids anyway because that is what you did growing up in the neighborhood – you told the stories and traded the dime comic books and played stickball in the street and played Chinese and Hitting Away and Box Baseball.

And what was the Park, then, aside from the walkway from home to PS 189? It was where we went when we were tired of being hassled by the police for playing ball in the street. From Spring to Fall, during weekends when school was in session, and almost every day when school was on vacation, it was baseball games and sodas and which pick-up team could call themselves the Dodgers. There were handball courts where you hit hard black balls against the concrete walls until you got stone bruises underneath your leather gloves, and where sometimes you cheated by taping a silver dollar to your palm underneath the leather so that the pain would not be so intense. There were picnics with family, cousins who lived nearby because then, families lived nearby, even in big cities.

On occasion, the Park came alive with an event larger than itself. Sometimes there were championship softball games or handball tournaments. Sometimes there were semi-pro basketball games. One time, famous people came to play on the tennis courts, not that we kids were attuned to the niceties of tennis, which we viewed in our ignorance as a sport better suited to Westchester where, everyone knew, all the kids were rich and were driven to school in Cadillacs.

━•━ ≍◆≍ ━•━

One day, when I was in ninth grade and hanging out in my advisor's office, Mr. Green asked me if I played any chess. I told him that everyone I knew played chess; we would go down to the Park and watch the old men sit at concrete tables, shifting on their towels draped over the cold rough concrete seats, hunched over their boards, playing with agonizing slowness, or sometimes with amazing speed when driven by their ticking timers in games of "lightning," and we knew these were quality games because we could barely follow them and even our block's best player had sat down a couple of times and lost his dollar with great alacrity to these old men with stony expressions who gave no encouragement but stuffed the bills into their coat pockets and signaled the next "mark."

"Why you asking?"

"Because there is a player who lives in New York who is about your age and he's going to be the greatest chess player in history. And he is coming to give an exhibition in Lincoln Terrace."

"Yeah? I bet old Schmuhl can beat him. He beats everyone."

"Maybe," Mr. Green said, "but I wouldn't bet on it."

Green, he was a crafty one. He never did say I should go watch, because then it was unlikely I would. He never even told me where or when. But that night I looked at the Chess column in the *Brooklyn Eagle* and, sure enough, Master Bobby Fischer would be at the main promenade at Lincoln Terrace Park to play all comers next Saturday. The Parks Department was taking reservations for seats to play against Fischer. It would be for a dollar a game, Fischer would be there for two hours, and they were taking 120 reservations. I told my friends. Sounded like fun.

That Saturday dawned chilly, dank and still but at least there was no rain. It was a typical Brooklyn late November day. The wind gusted spasmodically, and you could feel next month's snow on your ears as a promise. It would be cold on the cement seats, and cold standing with the observers, but the thought that a twelve-year-old was going to challenge all our great old men was too good to miss. We were also interested in how this would all work. There were exactly ten tables at the promenade; we made it a point to go and count them. There were 120 reservations. My friend Mendez had gotten one of them; seems twenty slots were reserved for people Fischer's age. That meant they would hold, what, sixty games an hour. Six games per table. Ten minutes a game. Are you kidding me? This kid is going to play everyone for an average of ten minutes a game, walking up and down the promenade to do it? He was going to get slaughtered. We couldn't wait to see the kid humiliated. Imagine coming to our Park and disrespecting us that much!

There were a lot of people standing around when we showed up. Some were running the event, wearing topcoats and business hats. There were many adults, and we did not recognize most of them. A few tables had metal police barriers around them to hold back the observers. Those had the largest crowds; we guessed the better players were going to be seated there. A few minutes after eleven a clump of people approached from the Buffalo Avenue end and then they parted to disclose a young kid, dark hair, no hat, tall and thin. He walked with a slight stoop and didn't look up. People were talking to him continually. Then a bell rang and someone with a megaphone called out "first ten players" and, almost instantaneously, another bell followed by the call "commence play."

A few of us worked our way to the front of the third table, the last one with the barriers, and there was Schmuhl. What luck! He would kill this kid and we would have a front row seat. We called out encouragement to Schmuhl as he took his opening, pawn to King Four, but then someone in a coat told us we had to be quiet so the players could concentrate. Almost immediately the tall kid approached the table through a small break in the crowd that one of the organizers kept open. The kid barely glanced down. His thin hand reached out from inside his car coat, the end of a red sweater sleeve showing a fleck of some old food, a piece was

167

moved, Queen's pawn, and he was gone. We heard talk moving down the line of tables and then, all of a sudden, just as Schmuhl had moved his second piece, there was the string-bean again. He did not break stride as he slid a bishop out of its rank and he was gone. Schmuhl seemed not to be surprised as he promptly moved another piece, and then there was Fischer again and then again and again and all of a sudden there was a shrug from Schmuhl as he flicked his King over on its side with his wizened index finger and conceded the game, then stood up stiffly to make room for the next player. I had a new watch, a gift from my parents for my Bar Mitzvah, a real adult watch, a Benrus! I looked down. Seven minutes. Seven minutes!? What the hell . . .

We stayed until 1:35. The event was promised to continue until 2p.m. but by 1:30 all 120 players had conceded or had been mated by sneak attack. The man with the megaphone congratulated the kid, who was asked to say a few words.

Looking down, he thanked the players for an interesting after-noon but did mention that not one of them had really given him a hard time. A sullen mumbling from the crowd accompanied the kid's departure, again surrounded by the adults in dark topcoats as they rapidly retired in the direction of Buffalo Avenue.

As the crowd dissipated, I moved to a cluster around Schmuhl, who was known as the best in the Park. I only heard fragments, but I did hear "never saw it coming" and "fucking arrogant goniff," the Yiddish word for thief which seemed to me particularly ungracious since the kid had beaten Schmuhl in seven minutes in a fair game in front of half the neighborhood.

We walked across Rochester to our block, and I realized none of us had seen Mendez play his game.

"Hey, Mendez, how'd ya do?"

Mendez pretended not to hear as he turned towards the entrance to his apartment house.

"Mendez, you pussy," screamed Joel, "How'd ya do in the chess game?"

Mendez quickened his pace but as he grabbed the metal handle to the apartment house door he half turned his head and called over his shoulder in a matter-of-fact tone, "Fool's Mate!"

We couldn't stop laughing.

Joel yelled after him, "What was yer plan, Mendez? Trick him into thinking you wuz stupid or something?"

But Mendez by then was well into his lobby, safe from our scorn.

Mainly, though, the Park was a comfort. It was cool and green and it was not like the street. The alleys smelled like cat urine in the summer but the Park smelled like grass. You could play pinochle on your stoop with your body twisted around as you sat on the steps, or you could walk into the Park and sit down on a blanket or even sit at a table and play like your parents played. You could listen to old men caressing violins and speaking with deep European accents as the sun set. You could see the older kids do things with a baseball that you could not do. You could play basketball, and hope to be a shirt and not a skin because you were a bit fat around the middle, but sometimes you got picked to be a skin so you just took off your shirt and played extra hard.

You could go to one of the larger fields and lie down on your back on clear nights and see the Milky Way, which you thought was a hoax when it was first explained to you until your parents first took you to that field so you could be shielded from the lights on the ground and see for yourself. The Park was the place where the stars came to visit Brooklyn.

And of course, there were the used car tires. After the War, used tires, bald and with their inner tubes, again began to appear on the streets. During wartime one never left rubber to rot; it went to the war effort. But after 1945, tires were a problem, too big to jam into garbage cans and the trash trucks would not pick them up. No one had even heard of a municipal dump. You left them around and they got used somehow or, more likely, ended up in sparse backyards filled with dirt and a few sprouting flowers.

So on occasion we would find an old tire and we would stand it on its end and send it on it edge reeling down Dead Man's Hill, on the sidewalk that abutted the Park. Now Brooklyn sidewalks were seldom repaired and being poorly installed the individual cement squares tended to rise and sink in their own ways, breaking the initial level surface into a series of discrete and slightly skewed planes. If a tire made it a quarter of a block without falling on its side it was a noted miracle. Random events being – well, random – every so often one of those bad boys would get rolling, pick up steam and next thing you knew you had a new world rolling record, three quarters of a block or, more often, a record expressed in car lengths.

One such day we were rolling a tire, a big one, it must have been from a medium sized truck, and it just slowly gained speed and seemed to right itself whenever it hit a concrete seam or displaced paving plate. After a few seconds we began to follow it, walking quickly and finally running at full tilt down the hill, our Keds pounding flat-footed on the pavement as we began losing ground and as the frightening tire took on a life of its own. We hoped no poor person would exit the Park at President Street or Crown Street and step in front of the wheel, and we began yelling out warnings, drowning each other out and becoming less and less helpful as the tire now was ahead of us by two entire blocks, rocking and bounding down the dead center of the sidewalk.

At the base of the hill, the street curved left as it melded into

East New York Avenue. It was a blind corner; cars took a soft turn to head up the hill. No one told our rolling tire that it was supposed to turn peacefully to the left. It bounded headlong into oncoming traffic. There was a loud horn that did not stop blowing. There was the clatter of the police Ford being T-boned by our tire, then veering hard left and running head-on into a bullet-nosed Studebaker that had the misfortune of descending the hill and encountering the police car as it was pushed across the center line.

Our view was superior. I don't think anyone had a better view than we had.

Well, actually, likely the cops had a better view. And whoever was driving the Studebaker. We looked at each other in silence as the crackling sound of crunching metal faded away.

"Shit," said Mendez.

"Poor fucking Studebaker," Joel exhaled.

Then someone yelled "run!" and suddenly we were running up the hill, which was pretty hard going so we all wove as a flock of birds across Rochester and down Carroll and we didn't stop until we hit Utica and the four of us pushed into Harry's Kosher Deli with cold sweat pasting our T-shirts to our bodies. It was mid-day Saturday and people were holding numbered tickets, waiting to be served white fish and derma and knishes and chopped liver sandwiches. Our entry caused everyone to stop and stare; but only for a moment.

"Hey, you schmucks," said the man behind the counter. "I don't care you in a hurry, take a ticket and you wait like everyone else."

"Fuckin' kids," said a gray-haired lady I had almost run over.

We all began laughing without being able to stop, and that infuriated a fat lady in a purple flowered dress; she was clutching a numbered ticket and I guess it was a really low number and I

171

think she feared we would disrupt her place in the line. That's when Harry came around the counter and none-too-gently shoved all of us out the front door.

That sidewalk on Dead Man's Hill also was the reason we finally left the neighborhood. One day, a few years later, I was in my third year in high school and I had been playing handball in the Park and it was getting dark. I got on my bike and started pedaling down one of the paths. When I got to Rochester Avenue, I turned up the hill. I was never much of an athlete and always a little overweight, except for those times when I was a lot overweight. My motion slowed and I was just getting off my bike to walk the rest of the way uphill when a younger boy approached me from behind a bush and put a gentle hand on my handlebars, stopping my progress entirely.

"Nice bike," he said.

Well, he was right. It was new, a gift from my parents, a Schwinn Black Panther. This was before three speed bicycles became status symbols. The Black Panther had a thick central panel between the seat and the handlebar post which contained four batteries powering a rather neat horn you could blare by the push of a button.

"Yeah," I said.

"Get off," he said. Underneath his white T-shirt you could not see any muscles. His jeans hung on him; he had no discernable butt.

My lightning-fast Brooklyn analysis was that I was being robbed. Or at least that some ridiculously small kid, whom I could have kicked halfway across the street, was actually trying to scare me into giving him my bicycle. I responded in standard Brooklynese to this insult.

"Fuck ya mamma," I replied.

The kid seemed to turn towards the now-dark phalanx of bushes rimming the Park and said in a small controlled voice something like "looks like we gonna have to take it."

I woke up in Kings County Hospital two days later with a broken nose and two cracked ribs. My mother had already picked out our new apartment in an area of Brooklyn where the blocks had not been "broken." We moved later that month. My father bought me another bike.

And it was a shame, too, because I had great affection for the Park and we moved to a fancy area with no character and no parkland.

But then again, the Park was no longer the Park of my youth. By the time I was sixteen the neighborhood had changed and, I guess, so had I. My friends and I never went to play baseball anymore; we had other things to do. The Park had become dangerous at dusk, lethal at night. The neighborhood fathers had tried to stem the tide that transformed the Park and its environs, but to no avail. One evening foray into the Park with baseball bats thrown over their shoulders, just a peaceful walk in the moonlight to stake out ownership, made no difference in the long run. The fathers had to escort us to Hebrew School at the Temple north of Eastern Parkway to prevent us from getting shaken down by small clusters of kids who would demand quarters and open and close their push-button knives for emphasis.

The tall gawky kid who used to come to the Park some weekends to play lightning chess on the concrete chess tables that lined the central walkway, strolling quickly past each of the ten tables, moving his pieces immediately on reaching each chess board, never losing, collecting a dollar from each child, teen, adult or old man who lined up for his chance to play, stopped coming to Lincoln Terrace. Rumor had it he now was playing at tables in Central Park in Manhattan, but no one would take the train to the

City to play against that Fischer kid; you could never win, anyway.

After we moved away, I would sometimes get on my replacement bike and come to the Park after school to play handball with my friends, but then you are a senior, you have other friends and interests, you are writing essays for college and then, poof you are gone. You go back once, a few years after college when you are in New York for a visit from another City, and you slow your car as you cruise past your old house and you drive around the Park but it just looks and feels too dangerous, too alien, to even stop. The Park now is a history, warm in the telling but you are no longer of the place.

Today I Googled the Park. I found a map, nothing else. A few businesses using the name Lincoln Terrace pop up; most are not even in New York. I promise myself I will now go visit, take a look while I still can. After all, Brooklyn I am told is now "hot," no one can afford to live there anymore. I suspect I will not keep my promise. Places are not a geographic location. Places are a memory of you at a given time. You can find the street corner, but you cannot find the hours of your memory. They have rolled and bounced down the hill of your life, gaining speed, causing glee and excitement and damage, and have disappeared around the corner.

All you get is the memory of a distant thud and the tinkle of broken glass.

THE [REDACTED] BOTTOM LINE

My father was not your conventional New York City lawyer. Back in the 1950s, lawyers donned suits and took the IRT or the BMT into Manhattan. They arranged their *Herald Tribunes* and *New York Times* into subway folds, thin vertical strips to be held in one hand while their other hand grabbed the overhead strap, which allowed them to read in their narrow standing space while swaying with the lurches and screeches as the subway car navigated the numerous twists of the tracks snaking beneath the City above. You did not place your paper in front of your fellow straphanger, invading his own reading space.

If the bottom of your paper happened to obstruct the seated passenger's view, or if you readjusted to balance against a particularly egregious lurch and thus planted your wing-tipped foot on top of some seated passenger's high-top sneaker – well, that was the price they paid for sitting down in the first place.

Our Brooklyn Brownstone had a marginally heated back room, a porch with flimsy insulation and single-paned windows installed decades ago as an afterthought. This was my father's home law office. His in-town office at 150 Broadway held most of his files, his secretary, and an occasional law clerk, but he was seldom there. Unless compelled to visit Manhattan for a hearing or court appearance, my father donned his baggy dark pleated trousers, strapped T-shirt in summer, plaid shirt in winter, and worked overlooking our miniscule dirt-covered back yard with an incongruous apricot tree in the only corner that got regular sunlight from between the nearby apartment houses. Two or three times a week, a Yellow Cab would shuttle files between Brooklyn and Broadway.

This office contained several old-fashioned bookcases with glass front doors that rolled upwards out of sight above the books, a pair of gray metal file cabinets, a dark red leather guest chair cracked from the harsh weather it endured on the porch, and a massive desk of some unknown dark wood typically covered with papers and a thin powder of cigar ash from ten-cent White Owls. Nearby on a rickety metal stand, a black Remington upright typewriter sat next to a pile of typing paper, letterhead and loose carbon papers resting on the floor.

The room smelled mildly of smoke all summer as the windows stood open to create circulation; with all windows shut down in winter, the smell was unbearable, leaks of nausea creeping through the closed glass-paned door into the kitchen and ruining mother's energetic cooking.

My room was safely down the hall, far enough to escape the odors and the occasional noise as my father and a visiting client would talk and yell; I imagined his clients, mostly middle-class business owners or truckers, were a particularly stupid lot, as my father always seemed to have to yell at them until they finally understood what he was trying to tell them. I would sit at my small desk next to the radiator, enjoying the warmth, doing my homework or putting stamps into my album, pausing each day to stand on my bed and rearrange as needed the small pennants I had thumbtacked to the dark blue walls, one for each of the sixteen major league baseball teams, reflecting their standings in the two Leagues after each day's contests. Over time, the holes in my walls got wider and the pennants less secure through constant rearranging, although usually the first pennant in each league did not change, as the Dodgers and Yankees dominated the baseball world while I was growing up a few blocks from Ebbets Field.

Normally clients rang the bell, my dad passed my room down the long hall that connected almost all the rooms on the first floor, they would walk together past me on their way to the office in the rear, the door would close with a click of the latch and a rattle of the glass, and other than occasional raised voices I would not be disturbed until they retraced their steps out to the front stoop after their meeting. Sometimes my dad would have a casual hand on a client's shoulder as he soothingly escorted the man—never once a woman—out the door. Sometimes they walked, my father in the lead, in sullen silence.

One warm day in the late Spring, the City humidity had made an early arrival, the office windows that let out onto the alley were open, the same alley that abutted my bedroom. My mother was not home. There was a hell of a lot of office yelling, it rolled down the hallway and was audible as an echo bouncing down the alley and entering my window a split-second after the sound from the hallway reached me. I could not follow the conversation but it sounded much like an argument growing more intense until, unexpectedly, the glass door was pushed open, its glass doorknob rapping into the wall at the end of its swing, and there was father, as I looked out of my room, hunched over like a crab, shuffling down the long hallway in a crouch, his head twisted back towards his client who had followed him out of the office. As he hobbled down the long hallway, my father's finger was pointed at the baseboard.

"You know what that is? Do you know what that is? Tell me what that is," said my father. Silence. He was now halfway to the front door, almost even with my doorway.

"Tell me what that is, you dumb shmuck. What am I pointing at? Tell me what it is." The client was standing in the middle of the hall, face beet red, fists tight. My father stood up, out of breath, all five feet five inches of him, his stomach stretching the fabric of his T-shirt which was soaked with sweat, a cigar stub still glued to his lower lip, his right arm pointed straight down at the floor.

"I'll tell you what that is. Ya know what it is? It's the fucking bottom line, you dumb asshole. You understand what I'm trying to tell you? What I'm telling you is the fucking bottom line. You gonna listen to me, or you gonna continue to be the dumb shit I think you are?"

There was a moment of silence. At first I thought the man was going to punch my father as he walked slowly up to him, but when he got near I saw he was slight of frame and even shorter and older than my dad.

"You know what, Mickey," the man said evenly, his face now pale and his tone flat and frightening. "You remind me of my old man. He used to talk to me like that." The man half turned and passed my father on his way to the front door. When he reached it he turned the handle, half opened the door, looked over his shoulder and spoke in the same cold tone.

"Ya know, counsellor, I hated my father. Coulda killed him a thousand times."

In the silence, the door shut softly and he was gone.

That night, after my parents talked for a while in the living room, my mother told me to pack up my schoolbooks and she loaded a lot of my clothing into a tan valise that my dad used to take when he traveled on business. I was driven to my grandmother's house in Queens, where I stayed for a week. I missed the last days of that school year, and I really missed my friends. There were no stickball games in my grandmother's green suburban neighborhood, no kids on the sidewalk playing boxball or up-and-over, no walls for Chinese handball, and nothing much to do except play rummy with my grandma and my aunt. When I asked, I was just told that

I had to stay in Queens until some business was settled.

Then one day, just as school had ended, my father picked me up and redeposited me on my block. My friends were there, curious where I had been, but the summer began, the wonderful Brooklyn summer of playing ball, and going to Ebbets Field where you could see Jackie Robinson jiggle along the basepath and do things we pretended when we played in Lincoln Terrace Park. Only Jackie, he did them better.

It was several years later, when my father deemed me able to "understand," that we sat in his office and he told me why I had been banished to Queens. Seems it took that long for the police to locate and lock up my father's client.

"He was a button man for Murder Incorporated," said my father through a particularly acrid burst of White Owl smoke.

"He was what?"

"Murder Incorporated. They did the wet work for the mob. Bunch of guys I grew up with. They were the Jewish mafia. That guy, he was a professional killer. Do you remember what he said, he threatened me." Another puff, released in slow contemplation.

"Mother and I, we just didn't want you around until the cops could take him off the street."

I sat there a bit and then said something like "well thanks dad." He said "sure" and I escaped awkwardly back into the house where you could breathe the air without choking.

I never thought of my father in the same way after that.

SUMMER OF '46

Murray was mustered out, finally, in the Fall of '45 and needed a job. One of the guys on the street worked the docks and was a vet himself. He couldn't get Murray a union card—those were like gold and weren't available unless you were related or connected and in no case went to Jews—but he introduced Murray to a trucking company, and Murray ended up driving a straight van for Lockheart, delivering furniture for Bernstein's down on Myrtle.

After the war, lots of families turned their attention to themselves. During the War, not a lot of people were buying dressers and sofas.

So Murray, his wife played mah jongg with her friends from the block every Wednesday night. The game moved from apartment to apartment, five women in their early thirties moving tiles with a clink and munching cashews and crackers and washing it down with a glass of cheap blush, laughing more as the night wore on. One night, at Harriet's, she was Murray's wife, my own wife goes into the kitchen and comes back to the table and tells Harriet, "hey that is one fancy new refrigerator you have in there."

"Thanks," says Harriet, and then lowers her voice as if saying something she shouldn't be saying, "it was a gift from my Murray. It's real quiet, not like that last one with the big bunch of coils on the top. It's almost like the old ice-box, ya know. No noise at all to speak of. And ya don't hafta dump out the melted water!"

So that weekend, maybe even Thursday I don't really remember exactly, the wife she says to me, "you should see the new refrigerator over to Harriet's, it's really big and quiet. If ya really want to surprise me on Mother's Day, why don't cha buy me one of those?"

She is looking right at me, knowing we probably don't have the money for something like that. I'm starting again at the bottom at the car dealership, there aren't exactly a lot of cars for sale, and nothing new is available; we are all waiting for the '46s to begin coming in, first production runs since the War, and they are not exactly flooding the market down in Brooklyn. Personally, I think they sent them all out to the suburbs, I bet you could find whatever ya want in Long Island or up to Westchester.

So she always could read my mind and she says, "hey Murray, he drives a truck, they can't be millionaires, if he can afford it I bet you can also ..." A smart one, my wife, knows just how to get under your skin, ya know, withouts ya being able to really get mad at her.

So next time the guys are down at the handball courts, I see Murray and I say my hello Sailor and he says his hello Soldier and I ask him, what's the story with you buying your old lady a fancy refrigerator?

"How you know about that," he asks, all of a sudden a little testy.

"Well, I guess it's no secret, it's sitting in your kitchen and all. My Shirley, she's over the other night playing mah jongg ya know?"

"Oh, yeah," he says.

"So if ya don't mind my asking, what kind is it?" So he tells me.

And I say, "sounds nice and my wife, she's sort of envious and I would love to be able to do something to surprise her for Mother's Day so, if ya don't mind, where'd ya get it?"

He lights a cigarette, hand cupped around his match, which is something I don't do when I'm in the park playing ball, because we're playing a buck a game and I like to be on the top of my ability, not sucking wind and spitting little pieces of tobacco all over the court.

Finally, he says, "Bernstein's. Ya know, over on Myrtle. Almost to Queens."

"I think I know it. Yeah. Expensive?"

He sends a straight jet of smoke in my general direction. "Well, ain't cheap." He pauses and then says, "we truck for them, so we get an inside price. Ya know, like an employee discount. But we ain't employees, ya understand, right? But, well it's sorta the same kind of thing."

"Wow that's great," I say, because ya know that stuff is expensive and I was really happy for Murray and Harriet, he's a vet like me and things are expensive these days anyway, and why shouldn't a guy get a break?

Wednesday night they are playing at Lottie Greenberg's place, in the big apartment house down by the end of the row of those nice brownstones heading towards the park, and I take my clunking pre-War DeSoto down to the shopping strip on Myrtle, which is open Wednesday nights ya know, and I walk into Bernstein's and I tell them I'm just browsing and where are their refrigerators because mine is beginning to give me trouble and they tell me they don't carry appliances, only real furniture, nothing for the kitchen unless I want a dinette set, nice stuff in wrought iron with that new Formica top if I'm interested.

I'll be goddamned, I think, but of course I don't say nothing because I don't know the score and if ya don't know shit, ya better not say shit, ya know what I mean?

That next Saturday morning it's raining and no one is going

down to the handball courts but late in the day the sun comes out and I take a walk down there just to see if there is water on the courts and a couple are pretty dry and there's Murray, a good player mind you, good with both hands and he doesn't even use the leather gloves, just his bare hands, he's finishing a doubles game and he's serving out, low and hard into the corners and these other guys, I don't know 'em, they don't have a chance. So they get done, Murray picks up his dollar, goes to the wire fence and grabs his Coke bottle and I come over to him.

"Got your serve going today, huh?"

"Pretty good," he says. "But those two guys, do you know them because I don't remember seeing them here except maybe once or twice and they ain't very good, ya know?"

"Yeah. I mean nah, don't know them except Julie told me they from Bensonhurst, just like to travel around and play different people."

"That's weird," says Murray, digging for his Camels in his small duffle.

"Say," I say, "I musta misunderstood ya the other day," I begin.

"Whaddaya mean?" He offers me the pack, taps the bottom and a smoke sticks its head out over the paper rim so I take it and light it with his matches, not saying anything, just enjoying my smoke.

After a half minute: "So, what ya saying?"

I look up real casual and tell him I went looking at refrigerators at Bernstein's.

"Yeah? So?"

I exhale and look out in the distance. "They don't sell no fucking refrigerators in Bernstein's." Then I turn to look at him. "Ya know that yerself, right?"

A pause, we are both leaning back on this tall chain link fence, we are both in the same section between the poles, the fence is sagging backwards so far that we are almost sitting down.

"Yeah sure, I know that." He spits out a tobacco fragment. "A'course I fuckin' know that, whattaya think?"

"Well, I don't know why you told me that thing ya told me. I felt like a schmuck and a half in the store ... "

"Hey, I'm outta my Coke. Want to take a walk with me to the corner store? I could use another. Come on, I'll spring for the nickel and buy you one also. And we can talk while we're walking, okay?"

We go about a half block in silence, heading to Hy's which is a soda fountain with maybe five stools, ice cream cones for sale, an ice box opposite the counter full of colas, ginger ale, seltzer, and Yoo-Hoos with that chalky chocolate aftertaste that I just love when I'm real thirsty.

"Ya know," Murray starts out, "driving a truck ain't easy and unloading furniture up and down them brownstones, ya know they ain't got no elevators like the apartments, ya can kill yaself."

"Uh huh."

"Yah. So things get banged up from time to time. They slip out of yer hand, they get a ding. Now if ya had it in yer house a while and your kid gave it a ding ya might yell at him but, well, shit like that's gonna occur, right?"

"I suppose."

"But ya can't deliver a dinged chair or table right off the truck, so ya ring the bell, ya explain and ya take it back to the store. And at the store, what they gonna do with it? Sometimes they can buff it up, fill it in, but sometimes it just ain't – pristine no matter what ya do. So whatta they do with it?"

"Ask your trucking company to pay?"

"Well ya might think but, well, that's just not the kind of thing a store is gonna say to the truckers, ya know?"

"Yeah? Why's that?"

So Murray stops, holds my arm to stop me and he's looking at me like that fire hydrant over there's got more common sense than I got. "You shitting me? You shitting me, right? So old man Bernstein he calls up Luigi Carrigio and he says, 'hey, ya know Luigi, your guys they banged up a $100 lounge chair real bad so you oughta make good on that?'"

"What ya saying?"

Murray looks at me. He says, "Picture this. Luigi is at his desk in Long Island City and this 78-year-old store owner calls and wants a make-good. So what happens? I tell ya what happens, Luigi, he says real slow to Meyer Bernstein, he says something like 'Well, Meyer, if ya can't get yer customer to pay for the chair then maybe ya just oughta give it to one of my boys over there.' And for a minute Bernstein is going to think about that, about how outrageous and wrong it is, and then he's gonna say something like 'uh, hey, Luigi, hell of an idea, why didn't I think of that myself?'"

I am beginning to get the idea.

"So," I ask, "you guys get stuff for free?"

"Well, not quite because ya can't get Bernstein to swallow the whole pill. So Bernstein, he says, look who could use a $100 chair for twenty bucks? Or maybe it's 25 or 18, whatever. And someone could use it, or their mother could, or next day they come in and say, Meyer I called my sister and she's interested.

So there's the deal."

"So, you can get stuff real cheap sometimes, yeah?"

"Well, yeah. Look, we don't pretend it got took offa the truck while we were carrying something else upstairs, that's being a goniff, a real thief. But this, I mean things happen and ya gotta accommodate the situation, if ya know what I'm saying."

We are walking again and about a half block from Hy's and I'm really parched but something is bothering me and I stop Murray.

"So how does that work when you end up with a refrigerator?"

"Ah, right. Well I didn't finish." Murray is warming to his task, he is having a great time explaining how business works with the trucks.

"My company, we deliver for most of the stores, right? So some of them carry appliances, right?" He pauses. He smiles. He gently whacks the back of his hand on my shoulder. "Kapeesh?"

"Huh. So when someone tells ya there is a refrigerator that's slightly messed up, maybe you get a shot at a deal? Smart."

So we go into the store that's hot as hell and smells from Hy's armpits I think, and we fish around in the big red ice box, pushing aside the floating ice until we each find a bottle of Coke, and Murray as good as his word plunks down the dime and then we're walking back up the hill towards our block when Murray, he lets out a little snort, then a little laugh, and then he stops me again by my shoulder near a bench on the side of the park and he invites me to sit down so he can finish what he was telling me.

"Let's say you wanted a new ice box, right. Like your wife, she's a nice person a'course, I know her and all, and I also know you, you from the block and you a friend and you a GI like me, and your wife says, 'how about one of them new Amana fridges that clean themselves and all' and you're thinking, who the hell can afford that kind of thing just back from the service. So let's say you come to me and you was to say, 'hey, Murray, what's a guy gotta do to get one of them things what cost like, $125 bucks cause like I seen you got one of them yerself and you ain't rolling in dough either.' So maybe I say to you I'll look into it, I'll see what I can do for a friend."

My Coke is freezing my hand but I am holding it real tight. I grew up in Brooklyn myself, ya know. I can almost feel what's coming, the way he's leaning towards me and talking really low but I can't quite get my mind around it yet.

"So then, let's say, I come to you a week later, and I tell ya, damnedest thing! I know this guy, he's got one of them things and its got a ding in it, can hardly see it, but it's for sale by the store, cause of the damage, for twenty-five bucks! And you say, hey that's pretty sweet but, they real big, how do I get it to my apartment, and I smile and I say, ya know we got trucks, don't worry about that."

"Ya kiddin."

"No I'm not," says Murray, taking offense I should doubt him.

"Well, I'd say thanks a lot, ya got a deal and I owe ya one."

Murray straightens up now, takes a slurp of Coke, and he's smiling.

"I got a question for ya, tho," Murray says.

"Oh well, what's that?" I ask.

He's got a grin now from this bench all the way to Coney Island and back.

"So, ya wife, what color fridge does she want? White, beige, or somethin' called avocado that looks puke green to me?"

187

Me and Murray, we got to be real close friends. I met a lot of people at the car dealer, and there was a tenner for every customer, and there weren't many things, other than automobiles, that I couldn't get wholesale. That whole summer of '46, it was a hot one and no one in those days had air conditioning, just fans that were just about useless, that whole summer we did a brisk business. Business was to be had in those days, the War being over and all, and the GI's wanting to catch up on the good life, getting married or having kids and everything.

Me and the wife, we even had enough extra to rent a cabin in South Fallsburg, up in the Catskills, for a couple of weeks. It was real nice, being out of the City, looking at fireflies and cooking dogs and burgers on one of them little charcoal grilles.

We picked up in the Fall where we had left off, of course, Murray and me, right up to when the cops came for him. It was terrible, the talk of the block. They sent him away, and then Harriet moved away, and ya know we lost touch and that was that. But Murray, he was good people. I mean, the fridge it lasted until 1968 and as for Murray, well he was stand up because, while for about a year I shivered every time my doorbell rang, Murray he never gave me up.

(PUTTING IT) BLUNTLY

I mean no discredit to the White Owl cigar, presently on offer in various shapes and fruit flavors for less than a dollar each. But no one has ever confused the White Owl with a Davidoff, or an Upmann, or an AVO. White Owl is, to my understanding at least, a cigar of the people.

In the 1940s and 1950s, while I do not have an exact recollection, I would bet a plug nickel that a nickel could buy a White Owl cigar. Modest research discovers that Phillies were a nickel and a pack of cigarettes a quarter in 1950.

My father passed away just shy of 101 years, and he was an avid cigar smoker for most of his life until he lost his taste for them in his 90s. Why he retained his yen for maple walnut ice cream and bourbon sours while cigars fell by the wayside is another story and not one that I know; during the years I grew up my dad smoked several a day but, alas, not one inside our house. My mother would not have it. So he smoked outdoors. Almost all the time. An occasional Philly but, for the most part, White Owl blunts.

The White Owl is a domestic American cigar manufactured since 1887. A blunt is, as its name compels, short in stature. I do not have a vintage 1950 handy, but today the cigar is five and one-quarter inches long. Once you bite off the tip, and stick the drawing end into your mouth sufficiently so that it does not fall out when you walk, the cigar protrudes from the plane of your face perhaps four and half inches, probably a touch less, and after a few puffs your smoke is a wasting asset, ending up a mere inch and a half long, pulled from your mouth to avoid a burn and held daintily to the lips by two careful fingers to draw the last few puffs before your cigar hits the street or the ashtray.

Why would a man not buy a longer cigar? They might well have been a better value? We are back to my mother.

My dad would not give up either my mother or his smokes, and his work schedule was such that he had lots of time to indulge both. As for cigars, there were those few halcyon days when, ensconced in our back enclosed room with six windows and a screen door, he could sneak a smoke if the wind was right; there were times when he could sit on our small wooden back porch, surrounded by apartment houses towering over our brownstone, and send fumes skyward while at his ease. But most of the time, he was on the pavement.

At the time, men wore hats. In the summer it might be straw. In the evening, a fedora. In the winter, something woolen was most likely. In the rain, something with a floppy wide perimeter. For my father, in all seasons it was a hat with the widest possible front brim. And I mean all seasons; if it was pouring there was my father exiting the wrought iron front door, down the steps and onto the sidewalk; if it was snowing, there was my father exiting the wrought iron front door, down the steps and out onto the thin veneer of white fluff that passed for a snowstorm in the City; if it was broiling hot, there he was in a polo, his ample stomach stretching the fabric out, a boater or the like on his head, out the door with his cigar being lit just as the door was closing behind him. In bad weather he would not carry an umbrella. He needed his hands free to adjust and nurse his cigar, or on many walks to light the second one. Off he would go in the night, generally in the

190

direction of the local stores although even then no one except the news store would let him enter with his fuming stogie, no matter how harsh the weather.

The hats might have kept his dark thick straight hair dry, but that was incidental. It was all about the front brim. He needed about four or five inches of overhang to keep his cigar safe. Particularly when it was raining or snowing or sleeting, the awning of his hat was the key to a happy walk. Observed on the street, from a distance he sometimes looked like a thug sent by central casting to appear in some urban noir movie.

There were times I would ask my mother why she would not let dad smoke in the house. Perhaps just one room we could seal off. Was she not worried about his catching pneumonia, thought at the time to be triggered by being abroad in foul weather?

"It's his choice," she would hiss. "Him and his damned cigars," she might mutter.

"But why?" I would wheedle. I liked having my dad around to play pinochle or hearts or to discuss what I was reading or what I did in school or to help me organize my baseball cards into teams or put my stamps into my album.

My mother generally would ignore the question, presuming the answer to be self-evident. But I came over time to understand that it had to do with the carpets, the thick draperies with swooping fabrics overlaying the drops and spilling off the brass rods, the green plush couch, the red arm chair, the upholstered ladies chair, all the trappings of elegance that in her mind made our house an Edwardian showcase. The White Owl was not a retiring bird; his effluent it seems saturated the fabrics, wormed its ashy way into the interstices of the fabric, and lingered to befoul the air of our elegance and, worse yet, cause the ladies who attended the weekly mah jongg session, prior to lighting their cigarettes, to sniff fussily and ask, "Betty, has there been someone – (half beat semi-dramatic pause) – smoking a cigar in your house?"

So many the night I sat curled in a chair in the front bay window, half-reading a book selected by my mother as appropriate "literature" or sneaking a Hardy Boys mystery instead, looking down the street in the direction of the stores for that tell-tale red dot in the night, the burning tip of my father's banishment leading him home, his Rudolf pulling his corpulent Santa's body back to hearth and child, closer and closer until he paused at the first step of our entry, took one final massively deep drag before flicking the stub into the gutter midst a spray of red sparks, and then threw open the door accompanied by the heat or cold of the night and also by the clinging sweet-sour smell of smoke that, for all my mother's rules about smoking, could not be banished unless she threw out the man's clothes each evening and, perhaps, also threw out the man.

"Fa Gadsake, Mickey, will you hang that coat and scarf in the front hall? You're going to kill your son."

Little did my mother know that having my dad back at home, cloying smells and all, was the best part of the evening. My mother would retreat to the kitchen, my father to the hallway, and I would stand in place and breathe in, as deeply as I could.

THE ORCHID

My mother left a pile of nondescript books when she died, and after a quick scan of titles I found no enthusiasm for sorting through in detail. Neither did I feel comfortable in throwing them out, or putting them in cardboard boxes along the curb with a small "help yourself" sign, a certain way of disposing of unwanted goods in our neighborhood without feeling guilty of committing waste. So they sat in the attic along with other boxes and piles of forgotten assets, clothing and magazines and broken sports equipment and dried corn ears that once hung on our front door and were long ago eaten clean by the mice.

There came a fall day when for no reason (vague fear of fire? vague sense of disorder?) I decided to climb the ladder and begin the process of triage: keep, sell, discard. The prospect was not promising; old children's clothing of indeterminate size and provenance, dried catcher's mitt, *National Geographics* stripped of their maps and inserts and displaying yellowed edges from years of heat. The books seemed the most promising, and with the slight hint of possible discovery to inspire the effort.

No sense in trying to build high drama about my discovery, it just happened, the thing simply slipped out of a thin book of poetry by an unknown author. Two pieces of tissue paper, both slightly soiled with dried oily residue, between which was sandwiched a small dried orchid. Its purple had faded to a pale lavender, its bouquet long dissolved into dust, its stem twisted and gone from green to gray.

The book was *Love Poems* by Catherine Caruso. Never heard of her. Put the flower and the book aside and spent another half hour sorting old books, a few classics, a few books presumably popular in the thirties, a first edition of *Gone with the Wind* that I promised to take to an antique book dealer in Boston, mostly titles and authors I had never encountered. I began to sneeze, the motes of dust floating in the beams now cutting into the air from the window at the end of the attic; time to descend.

After dinner, sitting down at the computer, I did a search for Catherine Caruso; over 2,000,000 hits. Catherine Caruso poems; a few Facebook hits; not likely for the writer of a book dated 1922. Catherine Caruso with the name of the publisher; nothing. A few pages into the search, I had millions of hits to go and still not a clue; a middle school student in Connecticut took second place in a poetry contest; decedents without biographies; a self-professed agnostic concerning Brussel sprouts (almost tempted to read that one, but resisted); a daughter whose father was linked to Al Capone. Not much to go on, unless dedicated to reading two million or more entries.

The poems were sparse, blank verse, rather pleasant, bland, precious and pretty. Flipping through, riffing the pages, a glimpse of blue led me to carefully turn all of the pages one by one; a blank folio after the title page bore a note: "To Bessie, With Greatest Fondness, Jake 3/1/33." The kind of handwriting that you don't see any more; some States do not even teach script handwriting in elementary school, the assumption being that every word will end up as computer bits, either typed by hand or automatically through word recognition software.

Who remembers the names of the friends of your parents, when your parents were young? When parents are dead, and uncles and aunts and friends and all that remains is a pile of old books in some attic of a son who himself is a grandfather? All that remains of your parent is the faded memory of more recent times, a stone on the ground somewhere and a bunch of faded pictures which, if you are lucky, are stuck in an album captioned with black crumbling pages and unglued mounting corners.

There's an idea. Into the den, into the lower cabinet, out comes the old photo albums you found in your parents' closet when they were both finally gone. Mostly used to find early pictures of aunts, uncles, grandparents, faces to show your children and grandchildren so that they can feign attention and then go back to whatever it was from which you distracted them, not to care at all until decades later when a couple of them want to build a family tree from the shards of evidence still available.

There she is, younger than I knew her, before I was born, before she was married to my dad, before she left for the City to become a dancer in theory, a bookkeeper in practice (and glad indeed for the job, it is 1932 and there aren't many positions for a high school graduate from a small town somewhere). High school graduation; all alone in white gown and flat hat. Dancing shots, sepia and cracked, publicity pictures perhaps, one or two with another dancer, but female, likely not our Jake.

Two pictures of a bunch of young people in period beachwear, sloppy pyramid of faces, fuzzy 3 by 5-inch glossy picture with perforated edges, taken by some Brownie Hawkeye or even some more primitive camera, who knows, an old Agfa with small bellows you extended by hand to move the lens into position. Gently I remove the pictures and look on the back; no names, one says "Old Orchard Beach '30-The Gang!"

There are no diaries from my mother. There are no letters tied together carefully with a red strip of ribbon. There is no one to question. That is a shock; I cannot think of a single living person who knew my mother on her twentieth birthday (3-1-33), or who knew her in a time and manner where some hint of Jake could be identified. By the time I tried to get an oral history from my mother, her mind had a tendency to wander and in the wrong direction; and then, she was gone. My own life's line sharply readjusts at that thought; I will write down everything, I will make my children film my every memory. When my memorabilia slips out of some book fifty years from now, it will be documentable, traceable, fixed in time and space and memory, footnoted for all who care to know.

In my dreams last night I asked my mother, my mother of when I was ten years old, to explain to me about Jake and the orchid. She smiled and told me to do my homework. She glanced at my father and lowered her voice and said that someday she would tell me, when we were alone and had a lot of time.

I woke up and put the orchid back in the book and put the book on a shelf in my bedroom. Someday my children will go through my pile of old books, triaging them—indeed, if at that time there is any use at all for actual books. I will tuck a copy of this story into the front of the book, and date it and sign it. I record now for posterity: this book and this flower were my mother's, Bessie Ida Tashlitsky, born March 1, 1913, given her by Jake for her twentieth birthday.

And somewhere the children or grandchildren of Jake have found a picture of some girl named Bessie and have been at a loss to know who she was.

Memo to Jake's heirs: Bessie was my mom.

IV

OBSESSIONS

If you are wondering if these are personal obsessions, or at least matters I have entertained, you would be mistaken. If you are wondering if I have observed these obsessions in others and am simply a reporter, you again would be mistaken. If you then ask, "so where do these come from," then please join me in having no answer. If you thus think that there is something disturbingly dark afoot here—well, everyone is entitled to one's own thoughts.

THE GOLFER

EVERYONE NEEDS A HOBBY

THE SHIRT OFF YOUR BACK

FINDERS-KEEPERS

THREE WEEKS ON THINGVALLA ROAD

RELATIONSHIPS REQUIRE A SOUND FOOTING

THE PRODUCER

THE GOLFER

Although it is difficult to remember exactly when it began, there are clues in certain memories: wet peso bills spread to dry on the table, a hacking cough from the chill, the sting of rainwater running through my eyes. Maximillian was to blame for all of it – at least at the beginning. After a while, I guess candor requires me to personally accept some responsibility.

It was one of those moisture-infused days in the tropics that gives definition to the concept of humidity. It was not just that the rain came; it rains almost everywhere in the world, and in one way or another all rain is the same. The totality of water was the defining emotion; the heated air itself carried a heavy burden of wetness, and the horizon blurred in thinning mists. Walls of the hotel, whitewashed against the sun, toned gray to echo the sky, and the palm fronds dulled toward blackness as they waved in the gusts.

The weather had been threatening for two days, and the tourists lolled in the heat, buying Mexican handicrafts and waiting for a beach day. The front desk assured me that the rains never stayed very long in Cancun, but the lush jungle visible from the balcony gave lie to his words. Although just being away from the City at first was vacation enough, by the time the drizzle settled into a constant pattern that third straight morning I had accumulated enough unspent energy to be tempted by misadventure.

Maximillian was well over six feet, and in much better shape than my office-flabbed body. When we met at the bar, he lifted a lean gin and tonic to click against my foamy fruit concoction, and the pineapple slice and umbrella jostled against each other in my glass. His clothes were of the lean variety also: simple white pullover, khaki slacks, white tennis shoes and no sox. My Hawaiian shirt hung as an embarrassing flag over my paunch, draping down towards my orange shorts. I was a caricature of myself, and myself was none too pleasant a reality. We had shared two uncomfortable drinks at lunch and quickly parted; he babbled on about diving and fishing for tuna, and I confessed that my souvenir shopping was not quite complete.

I had just settled down to my book on the balcony, feet up on the other chair, dangling just out of the rain's reach, when Maximillian called on the house phone and invited me to golf. My protests seemed irrelevant; if you have never played you had to start sometime, if it was drizzling there was no wait for tee times, if you lacked clubs they could be rented. Thirty minutes later I was in a taxi, speeding down the causeway, palm trees waving at me through the wipers. Maximillian continued his elated patter: the rain would refresh us, he was pleased to be my teacher, he just appreciated the company, the greens would be very slow because of the showers.

It was mid-afternoon when we stepped from the taxi, and as I trotted into the clubhouse my backwards glance caught Maximillian strolling slowly after me, drops of water already beaded on his visor. No there was no delay, yes we could tee off, yes I could rent shoes and clubs. A mere eighty-seven dollars found me standing on a grassy rise, club in hand, ocean wind conveying the thin drizzle around my glasses and into the corners of my eyes. Water coated my lenses, and before the first ball was hit it became clear that my handkerchief was inadequate to the job of absorption. Water ran unobstructed down my forehead, tickling my nose before it plopped off my face and onto my shirt. The wind pushed my clothing flush to my body, and the first shivers introduced themselves to me notwithstanding that by then I should have been parboiled in the wet heat. My body vainly pumped some heat up to my chest; I coughed once, then pretended I had just cleared my throat.

Maximillian hit first, and when I lost sight of the white arc and turned to him for guidance his face was pointed down the fairway, his weight forward on the balls of his feet, blue eyes tracking his ball as it landed six or eight feet from the flag. He smiled as he described the splash of impact: wetter than he had thought, but no problem.

Having hit his ball, Maximillian turned to me. Oblivious to what was fast becoming a near-soaking downpour, he patiently positioned my hands on the club he selected and guided my arms and head through the seemingly simple steps of hitting the ball. He ignored the rain, making me too embarrassed to take notice of it myself. We pretended in our own ways that the sun was shining, that soaking day, that day when it never stopped drenching us, that day when after ten minutes you could see the outline of my underwear through the plastered sheet of my clothing as they hugged my frame in bulging outlines and flabby crannies, and we trudged up and down the hills and around and over water and sand pits, all the while he matching par on that deserted golf course as if he were playing some national tournament on some sun-saturated afternoon.

His patience was astounding; I dug deep furrows in the tightly growing grass, the metal edges of my clubs cutting into the saturated sod; I hit over and around the greens, used infinite putts and strokes and hits or whatever they were called as my ball rolled around the holes, each elusive hole, each exasperating infernal hole, each unattainable tiny wet secret hole, each damnable damned and goddamned hole; and each hole became transmuted, from something I cared not a whit about into some essential quest, some desire tempered though my anger, forged through my burning of eyes and shivers of flesh, transcendent beyond all real worth, a sheer physical dedication to the exclusion of all other reality. By the eighth hole the rain had stopped in my mind, my bitter burning maniacal mind, the water no longer reached my skin, the wind slithered around me as I stood hacking on the top of each grassed ritual altar of a hill, cursing my balls as they skittered left and right, rolled down wide expanses of lawn in faint imitation of Maximillian's majestic arching strokes.

I cursed and sweated through the heat-soaked all-encompassing moisture of the afternoon. I injected my own moisture into the great flow of wet air, added my contribution to the Gulf Stream of hot wetness being brewed that afternoon over the Yucatan, a steamy froth to be pumped northward on the boiling oceans to bathe those thousand palm-treed islands that depended on that wet blast, yes I was part of the heat and energy and struggle and wetness that became the Gulf Stream, an energy so large that it would not die except five thousand miles northward in a cold and ice-strewn sea; and each ball I hit and hacked and beat and cursed and yes kicked and coaxed was all part of the design, all necessary to this broader task, and it was wonderful that Maximillian had known, had always known that fact and had been willing, in his own controlling eager way, to share it with me.

Six o'clock found me naked in my room, my clothing collapsed in a leaking pile on top of my sneakers, merging their precious moisture with the rug, unchecked by me, fastidious me. God I was a mess, water dripping from my hair onto my peso bills I had pulled from my pocket and spread to dry on the small night table.

I stared at the chunks of me, the blobs of me, in the mirror, the meaty hunks of wet flesh, bright red through abrasion and wind and water, patches of roughness and worse shivering under the air conditioning that I could not control; my eyes still burned when I blinked, a shallow pain that verified my suffering. Outside, the

Gulf Stream was still being born in a twirl of wind and water; inside I held the yellow golf ball, shivering in front of my mirror, and smiled.

—•—⊨◆⊨—•—

Lately, for some reason, my game has been off, even the guys at the club have noticed. While I still carry my six handicap, and last weekend led my partner and me to another low net score and yet another small brass-plaque trophy, there is an unmistakable loss of crispness. My tee shots are too fat, they do not carry; my chips don't bite the green but roll out of control across the grass; my putts hang on the lip and defy me.

Billy, the club pro who taught me a dozen years ago and has been gratified by my progress, can't understand it; he has suggested that I may be just a little stale. I do play five or six times a week, with thirty-six holes each Saturday and Sunday. Since my divorce – Helen complained of being widowed by golf and there was much truth to what she said – I had taken only two or three vacation days, to coincide with nearby golf clinics, and the pressure of the office was intense of course, having to fit all my work into a four a.m. to noon workday, no breaks. The lack of promotion has long ceased to bother me, and the office and I have reached an easy truce; I pay it Caesar's due and it respects the balance of my life.

Today I was out at the thirteenth hole, which happens to be the furthest from the club house, working on my short irons. The thirteenth is ideal for this drill, an attractive and slightly elevated hole closely protected on the left by bunkers and on the right and behind by various water hazards. It was a chilly early December afternoon, no one else was out on the course, and I hit baskets of balls for longer than I realized I guess because I found myself straining to see the balls as they bit into the putting green a few dozen yards away. I was annoyed, no doubt about it, but I con-tinued to hit; I felt my groove coming back, and the yellow-ness of the balls still could be picked up against the sky before they arced downward.

In fact, the later it got the better I hit.

I hit faster and faster, hit through the third bucket of balls, went up to the green and collected another buckets-worth under the dim moonlight, went back down and hit those balls also. Each stroke felt better, surer, truer. I never had realized before, how when you practice you are looking for your groove, and just when you may find it, just when the flow of your body becomes the idea of the motion you seek, then something happens and you have to stop. It's lunch, or tee time, or you're out of balls, or some other really quite uninteresting reason, and all of sudden, in defiance of logic, you have to stop.

And once you stopped because, perhaps, it was getting dark, then all that extra time afterwards, that just always goes to waste. Or at least, it used to.

It has been about seven months since I started to practice each night. At first there were the typical difficulties; the club was not sure they were happy with the arrangement, what with insurance problems and all, and the office had to come to terms with the new schedule.

If I don't get off the course until, say one a.m., it is not reasonable to expect to do your best at the office if you start in only three hours. But the new half-time schedule from eight to noon is working fine; you know how part-time work is, you get so much more productivity from your grateful workers and the employer makes out like a bandit. Although my new apartment is small – who can afford a house on half-pay? – it is positioned just between the club and downtown, so I no longer waste a lot of time commuting. And if it's been a really tough night of practice,

I can always save a few minutes by going directly to the office and sleeping at the foot of my desk, although I have to be sure to awaken a few minutes before eight because the girls really seem to be upset if they come in and find me stretched out under my blanket.

Interestingly, a few months ago, I found myself thinking of Maximillian again after all those years. One night I was out on fifteen, working on my sand wedge, and it began to rain, rain really hard. Not the warm tropical variety, more a Northeastern wind-blown shiver-your-timbers variety storm. In a minute, my windbreaker clung to my chest, and I could barely see my phosphorescent golf balls as I pitched them up towards the green. The beam of light from my miner's helmet illuminated a tunnel of flowing drops of water but could not penetrate as far as the flat atop the green. I shook my night goggles every thirty seconds, but visibility was hopeless.

I took them off, and then took off my regular glasses also. The wind was cold, my cheeks ruddy on the verge of rawness. If I didn't know better, I would have thought that a drop or two was frozen into sleet, or perhaps even hail. Early Decembers in Boston can be chilly and meanspirited.

Without glasses and goggles, I was more comfortable, and I found that if I shut my eyes the stinging went away. My swing, on which I could then concentrate, immediately became more fluid. The balls wocked and splotched off my club, although I had to suffer no small number of mishits, what with the darkness, the rain, and my eyes being shut most of the time. In fact, it seemed not to make any sense to place the balls on the grass anyway; I was losing a lot of them and besides, it was the flow of the swing I was working on.

This approach showed much promise; golf balls were very expensive for my half-time salary, not to mention the cost and time painting on the phosphorescent paint.

The truth of the matter is that I spent the better part of ten hours out on that golf course that evening, just swinging my clubs. As my arms got tired I alternated woods and irons to feel the different weights, and every half-hour I'd putt for a few minutes until my circulation improved.

Well, I guess that was around the time that I started missing work altogether, even on my new schedule, I won't deny it. It wasn't really unfair when they laid me off. I had my thirty years, so my pension was fully vested, and my medical benefits were continued which proved to be a good thing; all that swinging out on the course late at night through that winter caused no small number of chills, and twice I had to deal with a slight touch of pneumonia. Nothing serious.

I have no family, and after a few months the few people who remembered me from the old days in the office lost interest and stopped visiting. I cannot say that I hold them to task for it; I always stayed to myself, particularly after I learned that none of them golfed very well. I guess it's a case of "live by the club, die by the club." Helen never came, although I particularly asked that she be contacted. Too many years and too few good memories I guess, although I like to believe that I would have visited her under similar circumstances.

My bursitis doesn't allow me to swing a club anymore, and my legs don't work well enough to carry me up and down even the shortest of courses, but I don't mind. About twenty years ago, when I gave up hitting the balls and just concentrated on my swings, I began the slow liberation of my game from tiresome convention. The task was finished a few years after that, when I found that I didn't really have to swing the clubs themselves, I could just close my eyes and sense the flow and rhythm of my swing, trace the straight arms and snapping wrists, imagine my hips and shoulders sveltely moving through the stroke and conveying my power and life force into the ball, dream that ball skyward and then falling in a neat and satisfying downward swoop.

Although originally I found one drawback to this ultimate form of my game—even my oldest golf partners and friends seemed agitated to hear about my rounds, my difficult approach shots and clever club selections—the advantages were so overpowering that I long ago ceased caring, and marked off their agitation to nothing more than sour grapes. After all, I no longer needed to buy golf balls, or even clubs; I could surrender my club membership and, in fact, the savings on dues came in handy because all that golfing had been keeping me broke what with my small pension and only a single earner's social security.

And, best yet, finally I discovered how to take my world-wide life-long golf tour and vacation, and that was one happy day I tell you. It happened that I was walking past my local library when the idea hit me. Rushing inside, I signed up for a card and asked for directions to the golfing section. Although shocked to see that it only occupied half a shelf, and was designated part of some other category entirely, leisure or sports or some such, I was able to find just what I needed anyhow: several large picture books of the great golf courses of the world, complete with photos, schematic layouts of the holes, distances in yards and meters, and narrative describing the unique problems of each hole on each course.

That first afternoon, seated unobtrusively in a simple wooden chair at a library table, I chose the legendary main course at Saint Andrews in Scotland, the holy birthplace of golf. I studied the layout, absorbed the view from the tee, closed my eyes, grabbed my two wood, and stood tall in the Scottish breeze as I drove straight down the fairway. A smile spread across my face as I chipped up to the green, and that smile became a peal of laughter as I sank a thirty-five-foot putt to birdie the hole.

The librarian jolted me with her touch; it seems that I had talked through the hole, consulting with my caddy about the crosswind. I checked the books out and took them home; no need to disturb the library.

I have played all the great courses these last few years, all the great courses of the world. The rugged European courses are hardest, the California sweeps of sensuous green the most lugubrious, but I must confess a partiality to the courses of Mexico. When I close my eyes I can feel the moist heaviness of their air; I remember to adjust my club and stroke to compensate.

When I putt I must make provision for the dense tight grasses nurtured in the intense rainfalls. The wind from offshore pushes my tee-shots, and I turn my body precisely enough to counterbalance the force. Today the nurse has propped up my favorite, an old but verdant friend of mine in Cancun, near the top of the Yucatan peninsula of Mexico. I recall that once, long ago, I have played this course. Oh, not in my mind. I mean by standing on the ground and whaling and hitting and actually playing the game in physical life.

It is an odd feeling, this memory, and it merges with a face, the face of a man taller and trimmer than I am, old but not stooped and not bedridden like me. His voice is flat in that Midwestern near twang that tells you that patience is virtue, and his eyes are startlingly clear and blue. We are standing on the first tee, and I think it is beginning to rain. I do not mind.

As I swing through my first ball, I remember. A smile fills my face as I rest it against my pillow, and I turn to speak to Maximillian, to thank him.

But he is gone.

Everyone Needs a Hobby

I am angry with myself, given my slow start. I almost gave up the whole thing when I realized that here I was, 22 years old, likely one-quarter of the opportunity already had passed me by, at least statistically. Then again, you really cannot expect a child to pick up on this, so maybe I lost only, say 10% of what you might reasonably expect.

I tell you this: if I ever have a kid, I am going to start the collection right from birth and then, when the kid gets the idea, he or she will have a complete set of everything right from the get-go.

I had been saving facial hair since I grew a scraggly beard a few years ago and then had to cut it off for a job interview. It came off in such a neat tuft that it seemed a shame to just toss it out so I put it in a shoe box. It was quite natural after that, when I cleaned out my electric razor, to brush the loose hairs into that same box. For a while I kept the cut beard piece separate in a corner, but after a while I just brushed the cut hairs into the box no matter where they fell. It was a few months into this practice that I realized that I was missing a lot; so, I made a list.

There is of course hair from all over the place; mostly on top of the head although I had started to shave my legs for bicycle racing. Nail cuttings from fingers and toes are easy also. Some of the other stuff was esoteric but completeness counts, I thought (and think) so I set up discrete little glass jars for the stuff that comes out of the corners of your eyes in the morning, and sometimes those thick fingernail coatings of yellow stuff from your ears. At the end of that phase, I remembered that sometimes you get stuff from your navel but I think that years of that stuff would only fill an empty cigarette box.

I was pretty happy for a few months when I caught a bad cold and couldn't stop coughing. At the end I was bringing up these green elastic tendrils from somewhere and that seemed a little gross to me but they were so substantial, compared to some of the other stuff, that it just seemed illogical not to save that and I found an old paint can and started putting it in there and also what came out of my nose which was hard to separate from the tissues sometimes and that is why there are those white bits of paper in there.

I went on the internet and had trouble finding anyone else with this hobby except for this one guy in Portland, Oregon who was shy about it but it turns out he had thought it all through and was also saving saliva without anything in it and also sweat and his waste, if you know what I mean. Saliva didn't seem easy to capture plus you spit all the time and then brush your teeth and how do you save that, anyway? As for sweat, that seemed impossible unless you were willing to save wet clothes and then over time they just dry out, but I did buy some twenty-gallon lawn bags and I am experimenting with T-shirts that I use for exercise.

One night it hit me like a rock as I was brushing my teeth that I had forgotten about the teeth themselves! By now I have all my adult teeth and who knows what my goddamned parents did with my baby teeth, but I bought an old porcelain jar labelled "TEETH" which I think was a 19th Century thing for false teeth, and since I did not have anything readily handy to put in there I asked my dentist to pull my wisdom teeth and I put those in there, as a starter. You will by now notice that I have avoided mention of those noxious extrusions like passing air from either end, not to mention excrement and urine. I was loath to even think about it, for a while, except for the air or gas which it seemed to me was sort of benign if elusive. I do try to belch, when home, into a large glass jar and I have tried to do the same with passing gas from my rectum, but I don't mind telling you that I am having a hell of a time with that part of it and the fact that my collection is so incomplete is, I tell you, depressing on occasion.

Now I view myself as a wholly normal human being and the idea of collecting excrement and urine is repulsive, and the argument that my collection demands no less still cannot get me comfortable with that process.

So here is how I handle it, or at least have handled it for the last couple of months anyway.

Actually, there is no real benefit to your hearing about that part. I think also we can avoid the whole sex thing except to say that when you are alone the collecting is much easier than if you are with someone else, except for this one girl whom we are not going to talk about.

Let me tell you, instead, how I hope to expand my collection.

There are two related collectibles that I have not yet approached. One is blood and the other is actual flesh. The blood is easy although actually hard to collect and when you go to the Red Cross they will draw it but then they do not want to give it to you. My doctor was also very unsettled by the discussion and I don't think he will help, even if I were to go back there again which I doubt. Minor collections into the jar are fine but very slow and a couple of more spectacular efforts scared me as I got woozy the first time and on the second try I actually passed out and wasted a whole bunch and ended up just stuffing the whole red-soaked wash cloth down into the jar which absorbed most of the earlier collections and certainly took away from the purity of the effort to date. But I think I can get the blood thing to work and have begun to discuss it with my girlfriend who says she might help me to do it but was thinking about a trade for what I can do for her in return.

The flesh thing does represent the very edge of my comfort zone here but, then again, I am a young guy and likely can grow into it. Visible impairments will upset friends and parents and ultimately make employment difficult but I am exploring over-eating followed by liposuction as one partial solution. I still have my tonsils and appendix, and these seem benign candidates and I am starting to read about adenoids and gall bladders which, I have reason to believe, also are expendable.

My girlfriend has told me she has something really exciting to discuss with me tonight so, if you will excuse me, I will trim my nails, answer calls to nature, shave, and then head out to meet her. It has been a real pleasure talking with you. Let's do it again sometime.

THE SHIRT OFF YOUR BACK

I went to State U, see. Only for a year and a half, I'm not the studious type, but I was damned proud of it. It wasn't easy and it wasn't cheap, and it's made my life better, fuller if you know what I'm saying.

So one day I'm walking down the street and along comes this guy, looks like about my age, and he's wearing a sweat shirt with cut-off sleeves that says STATE U right on the front of it. I stopped him, said he looked my age and when did he attend, and he says he didn't go there at all. Said he bought the shirt from a street vendor at the beach, it appealed to him for some reason. I was sort of annoyed, ya know? Not in a big way annoyed, mind you – that sort of thing came later – but disturbed at why someone would wear a shirt for somewhere he didn't even go to school.

Now maybe I should have known right off; the blue color was all wrong, sort of a royal blue kind of a thing, not the soft mellow blue of the real State U colors. But anyway, I asked him where he did go to college and he says UC Santa Barbara, which I can assure you is one hell of a long distance from State U in the City, and in more ways than one.

I didn't make a stink with this guy, mind you. It's not the kind of thing to start a big deal over, after all. It's his choice, he can go naked as far as I'm concerned, that's his business.

Ya know, I wish t'hell they'd turn out that light, or at least turn it down at night. It's been almost a year, and I still can't get a good night's sleep; every time I turn over, it wakes me up.

Anyway, the next time this thing comes up I'm on vacation in Arizona, and I'm at the edge of the Grand Canyon looking over and down, trying to see the river that I know is buried somewhere in the gorge, and there's a woman standing on the observation platform a few yards away with a Boston College T Shirt and I was living back in Boston at the time, so I asked her if she still lived in Boston and she looks at me like I'm nuts. She's all confused. I mean, I'm not even sure she knows that Boston College is in Boston, she's so mixed up. So I said to her, "No, hey, I just saw your shirt and I live up in Boston and I just wanted to know if you still lived around there, or if you moved away after College." Well, as you can probably guess she didn't even go to BC, had never even been to Massachusetts in her whole life. And, she's looking at me like I'm crazy for asking the question.

"Ya shouldn't be wearing the shirt if you didn't even go there," I said in self-defense.

"Fuck off!," she replied.

Nice talk from a young woman, eh?

I'm glad you're back because I've been trying to get this straight in my own head, when it really began in earnest, and I think it was in the Fall after I got back from my vacation. It was late August or in September of that year; Sandy went right back to work at the school office and the kids seemed to start right in with classes almost the day we returned. I was out of work, just looking for the right thing ya know, and I'm walking back from the strip mall that was just around from my street when a woman pulls up in a van and asks me where there's a McDonald's. I'm telling her, there are a few kids in the backseat, and I guessed they were hungry, and she's wearing a sweater with a sailboat that says "Cape Cod" over the pocket.

I asked her where she liked to go on the Cape, for vacation or whatever, and I gotta admit, I had a feeling when I was asking that she didn't know Cape Cod from the Bat Cape. I mean, I admit it, I was fishing for the wrong answer, which of course I got because I'm beginning to get the idea that no one, and I mean no one, has any ethics or logic when it comes to shirts and sweaters. They just wear any damned thing that they feel like, because they like the color or they borrowed it or something.

So she's very pleasant and thanks me for the directions and starts to roll up her window saying that she never had been to Cape Cod, or at least not since she was a kid, and I really got mad all of a sudden. I had enough of this crap, ya know?

"Then why the frig are you wearing that sweater," I enquired, but I must have been yelling because she startled backwards and stopped rolling up her window.

So I was able—oh thanks for the cig, mind if I smoke it later?—so I stick my arm in, over the edge of the window which is halfway up, and I pull up the pin and swing the door open. Her little white face went a helluvalot whiter at that, I can tell you.

I am suggesting to her as nicely as I can that she should take off the sweater. I mean, that isn't a big deal, I wasn't saying she should throw it out or anything. She was wearing some sort of a shirt under it, I wasn't making any improper advances or anything. I just said for her to take off the sweater, but I must have been yelling real loud because she started screaming and then I was pulling at her arm and pulled her right out of the front seat. The car started to creep forward at that point, with the two of us standing on the curb and with me still pulling on her sleeve.

So then? No, no trouble finally. I realized there were kids in the back of the car, I jumped over and stopped the car and stood up and she jumped in and roared away like a bat outta hell and it's the last I ever saw of her. Big woman, big shoulders, long dark hair, little bitty face, scared as shit.

But I felt I had accomplished something, ya know? She heard, firsthand, about how you should not wear stuff if it just isn't true. That's very important, and I realized that day, ya know, that not a lot of people understand that fact. Amazing!

I don't mind talking to you, doc, because, face it, who else here will listen? But ya gotta do me a favor, okay? There's a guy in a cell across from me, and he opened a package and it had a Notre Dame T-shirt in it. Sometimes, he just sits on his bunk reading the paper and wearing the shirt. So, I'd like you to take away the shirt. I talk to this guy all the time and, I tell ya, no way that dummy went to Notre Dame.

Then there was this woman, this namby pamby bitch in Gore-Tex, a whole ensemble, she comes running past my house and her jacket is open and she's wearing this T-shirt, and on the front it says in big black letters COED NAKED JOGGING TEAM. What does that mean, anyway? She's fully dressed of course. Jacket, matching pants, a bra I come to find out, shoes, socks, watch, Walkman radio, the works. That mama never jogged naked in her life, let alone coed or on a team! What does that shirt mean anyway?

Well, by then it was later in the Fall and I'd been seeing a lot of shit and I'm getting madder'n a hatter from all this shit I'm seeing. Coed naked everything. More people lying about going to Harvard than you can shake a stick at. Shirts telling me people visited places they never even dreamed of, or that they're gay, or they're horny, or they're God knows what. Now, normal people don't get upset by stuff like this, unless of course it just completely takes over the world and there is no place on earth to escape it, but that is just about our situation we've got right now with these fucking lying T-shirts, sweaters, jackets, sweat suits, whatever.

So I jump into my station wagon and I catch sight of this woman in the NAKED COED T-shirt about one block down, turning into a park where there is a path I sometimes take with Samantha and Todd that leads to a weedy pond with lots of frogs to chase. And I'm out of shape but it's mostly downhill and I pull off into the small lot and hop out and tear down the path top speed, I'm wearing my sneaks so it's no problem; and I overtake her about halfway around the pond in front of the tall cattails and, swear to shit, I don't even bother to waste my good breath 'cause I just know I'll get that same blank stare and crap, so I just grab her around the waist and toss her into the reeds and go in after her and I rip off her jacket which isn't hard because she's still surprised, and then she wakes up and worse yet thinks I am after her sweaty ass, which is a joke, and she starts to thrash around and I have to give her a slug, which I do, and she crumples down and it's easy, I just pull the fucking shirt up over her head and her limp arms and I rip that lying shirt from the neck into both arm-holes and I throw it down onto her stomach, and then I move it up to cover her jogging bra because actually she looks sort of bare; but the shirt is turned downward so you can't see that bullshit printing on the front of it.

And that's it with her. I didn't touch her or anything.

I don't know how that other stuff happened.

It must have been, someone else came down the path after I left.

Then another time this dumbass kid, maybe he's fifteen, skin white as chalk, and he's wearing a big green jersey, says "Boston Celtics" on the front, and the double zero – you know, "00" – on the back. So he's Robert Parish, right? He's now all of a sudden seven feet one half inch of lanky bony black man, playing center for the World Champion Boston Celtics, right?

Right!

Who the hell is he kidding?

Now you're gonna tell me he's just a kid, and everyone knows that he isn't Robert Parish, and everyone in the world wears sports jerseys. Like that makes it okay or something? I mean, that's my very point! That's what's wrong! They're all doing it. They all think it's okay.

I'm not some nut you know, who wants to go out and change the way the whole world behaves to match his own sick, puritanical view of how things ought to be. The judge said so. The judge specifically found that I was not a nut. That I knew what I was doing.

I want you to remember that.

That is why I beat the ever-living shit out of that kid. To show them all, to teach them a lesson.

Him and that other asshole, some Lutheran guy with that "Italian Stallion" shirt. The closest he ever got to Italian was his salad dressing.

But I think ya know, I'm in here mostly because of a white sweatshirt being worn by a beautiful blonde who, I gotta admit, did set my heart aflutter when I saw her. It was almost Christmas now, and most people were deep into the working season, and looking kind of pasty and reddish but, this woman, maybe she's thirty and is she ever looking tough. Real deep tan, like she spends her time in Florida or something.

So by now I'm moved out of the house. I couldn't focus much on construction which is what I had been doing the last few years. I had a good gig going, doing interior work on condo conversions, easy stuff with no finish carpentry, but around then on some days I just wasn't really up to it, and the wife got pissed and told me I was getting weird and I should take my act elsewhere, and she said she was worried about the kids and she even went and got a court order against me staying at home anymore.

So one night I'm at O'Hara's having a few beers and it's getting late, and like the old joke goes that ugly women always look best when you've had a few beers and it's closing time, but there was this woman who was with a group of people I did not know, and they had a few beers themselves, but this woman was really a knock-out. So they come out of one of the booths in the back, and I'm only paying a little attention because you don't want to stare, right, it's not polite. So she comes to the side of the bar and gives me a little polite smile and I'm about to give her one of those return polite half-smiles, when I see she's wearing this white sweatshirt and its stretched tight over her, uh, bust, ya know? And printed on it, and I am very serious about this, it says "JUST DO ME!"

How does she think she can get away with that? Doesn't everyone have the normal reaction to that invitation? Or am I the only person in this whole bar, in this whole damn city, who understands what she is saying?

Now the police were called and kept telling me that it was clear that she did not intend to have her sweatshirt read and interpreted literally. And the prosecutor pointed out to the court that it was unbelievable that I conveniently assumed what no normal person would assume. But, I beg to differ.

And I don't exactly like the way you are smiling at me and trying to hide it with your hand in front of your mouth.

Whoa, stop please, before you call the guard over, no, no just please sit back down and answer me one simple question: do you not agree that people owe it to be honest with each other in matters of normal human social interaction?

Me, I don't even understand anyone who says they disagree, ya know what I mean?

FINDERS-KEEPERS

The ending of this story is a seeming precursor to the above story entitled Everyone Needs a Hobby. You may be disquieted, as I am disquieted, by my seemingly constant interest in such a dark theme, but against the advice of my esteemed editor I have chosen to include both stories; seems I am bad at taking good advice.

One day Hank found a penny. It shined up at him, and he put it in his pocket and ran into the house. His mother looked up from the peas she was shelling and said that it was good to find money and, yes, he could keep it. Hank asked if the person who lost the penny might look for it and be angry. Hank was still young enough to value a penny.

His mother thought that the owner of the penny would not be a problem. "How will he know that you have his particular penny, anyway?" she asked.

Although often she was stinting in her attention, and usually concentrated on shelling her peas or rolling out her batter, she paused in this instance to add another penny to Hank's palm, and to admire his diligence in finding his penny. She even stroked his hair.

After that, Hank walked around looking at the ground. He

found other coins, and once outside the drugstore a dollar bill, and he put them all in a wooden butter box with a splintered end retrieved from the grocer's trash.

⚊⚬⚊ ⚎◇⚏ ⚊⚬⚊

Henry was having trouble writing his lab report and spread his notes and drawings over his desk and table and onto his bed. The floor of the dormitory was chilled to his touch as he bent to place more recent figures and sketches around his feet in a tight arc. A draft rippled the pages, and Henry moved the corner of a large Jim Beam bottle onto one edge as an anchor; the bottle had been filled nearly to the top with pennies, and Henry had to strain to pull it across the tiled floor.

Standing to evaluate his arrangement, Henry carefully tapped the edges of each sheet with flicks of his finger until all were square and even in relationship to each other sheet and to the square corners of the bed, desk and floor tiles. Some pages were in piles and seemed disorderly. He opened a drawer and took out a few small boxes. Selecting one, he undid the rubber band and thumbed through the various paper clips, selecting six of identical size to place on his papers. He resealed and replaced the box in the drawer, putting the box of larger clips, rubber bands (narrow) and rubber bands (wide) and tacks on top. Henry felt satisfied with how those boxes fit together squarely in the drawer, on top of the larger boxes containing his staples, post cards, bottle caps and pennies.

It was a shame that he needed to use drawer space for those rolled pennies in the old White Owl cigar box, but his footlocker finally had been filled with other cigar boxes with pennies and, of course, the beer cans took up so much space no matter how neatly you placed them in rows. The spaces left open by the untouching arcs of the cans Henry had filled with rolls of pennies placed vertically. He had considered collecting and rolling half-dollars

221

which would have more fully filled those spaces, but he had been saving pennies for so long that the mere thought seemed disloyal.

After three semesters at State, Henry finally was beginning to enjoy the campus. Although he stayed to himself, and worked on his collections, he enjoyed going to sports events and concerts; in fact, all the programs for these events were in chronological order on his closet floor. His job at the movie theater took some of his time, but lately Mr. LoBianco began letting him take home the torn ticket stubs. That had greatly boosted his stub collection, which now filled some of the shoe boxes under his bed.

Once Henry stood at the edge of a dance floor at a Sophomore mixer, an old corduroy jacket hanging on his square shoulders and away from his thin body and had smiled at some of the girls. They passed nervously by him, and Henry imagined the sweat beading in his pencil mustache that he carefully raised to give his uneventful face more character. He left halfway through the evening, dancing with no one. On the steps of the gym, his glasses fogged in the early winter air; the music could be heard clearly from inside, and three girls ran past him up the stairs. He imagined that their laughter was about him.

After that, Henry went to parties and dances only at their very end, dressed in jeans or overalls. He would pretend to be part of the clean-up crew, and thus could fill his bags with bottles and caps for his collection. Some of the girls would chug their remainders in an effort to be helpful.

Henry liked lab reports. Even though his measurements often were imprecise and did not match expected results, he was able to type them in precisely prescribed formats, and he bound them all with blue covers. They were on the shelf above his desk, between the green English themes and the yellow history reports. Henry glanced along the shelf at last year's brown, red and gray covered folders.

Henry wrote quickly on his typewriter once he began. The contents of the report, after all, were not very important, and he was comfortable with all the Cs he received. It was not like he planned to go to graduate school; just a simple degree for a simple job. Henry's pleasures lay elsewhere.

He leaned back in his chair and thought again of the plan. A house with a den, a door with a lock. No one could enter except him. His wife, blonde and petite, would leave his cup of soup on a table by the door and retire. Then he could open the door and get his soup and not be disturbed. Inside, the room would be larger than you might expect to find in a modest white colonial. In fact, its shelves and cabinets stretched many yards in each direction. All the labels were black on tan, lettered in a calligrapher's hand that made full use of the power of India ink. All the boxes rolled out on smooth slides or casters, and the vivid colors danced in the intense florescent light: beer cans, cigar wrappers, postage stamps, paper money from around the world, bottle caps, tobacco tins. At one end, an easy chair facing the older classic part of his collection: rolls of pennies, by now thousands of rolls, behind a waist-high plastic barrier, a mountain of rolls, a brown hillside of neatly, tightly rolled coins. One day a week he would maintain this part of his collection, moving among the rolls and resealing the ends with long strips of scotch tape.

When Bill from across the hall knocked on his door, calling out for dinner, Henry's room disappeared around him. He was hungry but remained silent until Bill left. Recently Henry had begun to take his meals late; fewer people were there to stare at him as he poked through the barrels at the tray return.

"What do you mean that we'll sleep on the fold-out?"

"I mean, I need the space." His fingers moved back nervously through his thin brownish hair and held onto his neck; he stretched back against his hand to fight against the tension.

Terri stood up from the table and walked around the kitchen. She shook her head, finding no words. "Do you really, really think that two grown people with a perfectly good bedroom ought to sleep in their living room just to make room for a collection of — of — junk?" Her voice, normally strident in disbelief, had this time a flat monotone that frightened Henry.

"Look, the living room is fine. It's not like we ever have anyone visit."

She looked up. "Is that my fault?"

"Not a matter of fault, a matter of fact," he explained. "It's like having three bedrooms, not two, that's all. Why have rooms designed by someone for their idea of living? Why not have rooms for how we live?"

"Live? Live?" Her voice rose again to its accustomed incredulous stridency. "You call this a way to live? There is so much crap in this apartment, I don't know whether to shit or go blind. I come back from the office, you've been here all day, and I figure at least today he will make dinner, but no. You haven't made dinner for a month. Instead, I gotta run a fucking obstacle course of your shit. And now it's what—license plates? Why? You nuts? I think you're nuts."

Patience, let's explain it again, sometimes Terri forgets. "Look, Ter, it's just a hobby. You knew I collected when we met. You thought it was funny."

"A carton of match books is funny. A closet of wire hangers without clothes is not funny. A carton of shirt cardboards next to my dresser is not funny. Used toothpaste tubes isn't even quaint. It's sick shit, Henry. Sick, sick, sick!"

Terri started to clear the dishes, then put them back on the table.

"Henry, Henry, what's happening? Why do you do this? Why do I stay here? Each morning I get up and I say, this isn't happening, this is too absurd. But it is happening, Henry. What are you doing? What are you doing with your life, with our life? Are you going to ever work again? Are you looking? All day alone, what do you do? Do you call for jobs? Your unemployment is running out. Then how do we afford to live? Or do you – fuck with this crap all day? Henry? Henry? Talk to me, Henry."

There were some crumbs on the table. Henry swept them with the edge of one hand into his other palm. Their sharp texture was pleasing.

"Henry? Oh for Chrissakes! Henry, I'm going to the movies with Helen. Then I'm coming home and going to sleep in my own bed. Do you hear me, my own bed!"

Terri paused but there was no response so she left the room. Minutes later, the front door closed. Silence, she was gone. "Good," thought Henry. Good that she is gone. Good because there aren't enough hours in the day to do what he needs to do. So much to organize, to handle, to arrange. Neatening up the dinner dishes in a stack, Henry walks, smiling, into the bedroom. He strips the bedding and carries the linen into the living room. By the time Terri returns, she'll be so tired she won't care where she sleeps. The square flat expanse of mattress lies before him. Its potential calls to him, and he sees clearly what he shall do. With new surfaces to fill, Henry can expand once more. Even now, he has stored several trash bags in the basement. Now he can bring them upstairs, empty them and arrange their contents onto the bed.

And when Terri returns home and he shows her, Henry is sure that she will understand.

Old Hank moved stiffly in the dawn chill that permeated the kitchen of the farmhouse on the hill. Although he had lived in it for twenty years, ever since his mother's death had given him enough money to buy, finally buy, a home suitable for his hobbies, he never got used to how the wood stove took so long to bite into the chill each morning, particularly since it heated so intensely once it was well-fired.

Old Hank – the kids in town called him that on those few occasions each year that he went down to Mort's to restock – carefully dunked yesterday's tea bag into the cup; a penny saved was a penny earned, and since he collected the printed tabs at the end of the tea bag string he instinctively pulled the string through the staple to disengage it. In the decades since Terri left him his palate had fallen to the simplest of levels; tea and toast, toast and cheese, one or two chops and a potato for dinner. Old Hank always was too busy to bother much with cooking, anyway.

Each morning the ritual was reenacted, although Old Hank knew the ending, knew it as well as he knew the number of bottle caps in the four hundred and twelve shoe boxes in the attic. Each morning he would mentally list his collections and pretend to decide which ones would occupy him for that day. The pennies were no longer any good; they were in the floor-less basement, too heavy to move around in any meaningful way, too damp to be pleasing to the touch. Besides, the bugs were eating the wrappers and the yellowed tape was drying off the end of the rolls, and sometimes when Old Hank picked up a handful of rolls the coins would dribble free and go rolling along the dark earth. With the arthritis in his bones, Old Hank had a devil of a time picking them back up, although of course he would never quit and leave even one on the basement floor; that was what was good about having them rolled, you knew exactly how many there were so you would also know exactly how many were missing.

Smooth stones? Postage stamps with flowers, racetrack

programs, baseball programs, graduation programs, fifty-four separately sorted categories of programs; not enough to sink your teeth into, really.

Of course, that was the problem all along, the problem he noticed about twelve years ago when he went down to Nashua for the first time to attend one of those collector shows. No matter what he had collected for all of those years, no matter how many rooms he filled with his collections, so full that the ten-room house and the barn were bulging and he had taken to sleeping on a cot again, in the hallway, just as he had shortly after Terri had left him.... there seemed to be a collector at the show specializing on each separate thing, and that person's collection was so much grander than his own. The bottle man displayed many bottles that Old Hank had never even seen, and the books of photographs showed even more. The beer can man said he had eleven thousand beer cans at his own home, including nine hundred and forty-five different brands; Old Hank had driven quickly home, and when the dawn arrived and he had finished counting he knew that he just couldn't measure up.

Of course, strangely, each of these people only seemed to collect one single thing. At the stamp section he thought that he had found a kindred spirit or two, but he soon realized that the envelopes and postcards were all different aspects of a single collection of postal materials, and not truly different at all.

Although until then he had collected for sheer pleasure, he now found himself awake most nights, worrying about all his inferior collections. He felt like a failure whenever opening one up, and for three or four days actually stayed in bed without resorting even once; and this with several cartons of rubber bands askew in the very next bedroom!

Then Old Hank found the secret of his unique new collections, collections so special that no one in the world would ever be able to rival them. Old Hank had become the ultimate of specialists, and all at once he had stopped sweating and starving himself. In fact, he found new need for the energy he got from his dinners, and he doubled his rations just to be sure.

Old Hank placed his teacup in the center of his toast plate after he had scraped all the crumbs into his pocket. He placed the plate in the corner of the sink, exactly opposite his dinner plate from last night. He climbed the stairs slowly, sliding his feet on the bare treads, lightly toeing every third or fourth riser just to be sure his footing was sound. At the end of the hall he unlocked the door to the main bedroom and bolted it behind him. Seated at the table he had placed just in front of the doorway, he picked up an empty mason jar, released the top and waited.

He shifted, felt the warmth of the sun obliquely cutting across his face and chest from the un-curtained window, and then tried to relax his body and let it come. Soon, he has able carefully to uncap the bottle, and deposit a soft passage of belched gas. Quickly he recapped and replaced the jar, a trace of a smile edging his face.

It was Thursday, so he could clip his nails on both hands and feet. These remains he swept into an empty dishwasher carton he had picked up in front of a neighboring farm years before.

It was a sunny day, and Old Hank felt good. He couldn't really wait for tomorrow and besides, one day's growth didn't much matter, did it? Pulling the mirror forward, he carefully trimmed his few hairs and let the ends fall onto a white sheet of paper; leaning forward, he carefully clipped his nose-hairs as high as he could reach into his nostrils with his little scissors, and then stood and took off his bathrobe. After trimming his chest hair, he stretched each arm over the paper in turn, cutting carefully because once, last month, he had nicked something badly and he hadn't been able to stop the bleeding for hours. Worse, it was just a slow leaking, and there was no real way to collect and save it.

Pushing his hips forward until the bottom of his torso stuck over the edge of the table, Old Hank adjusted his mirror and trimmed his body hair around his genitals; they fell as gray coils onto the gray and black residue. Finally, he took the shavings that he had caught in the sink the prior evening and dried overnight and shook them onto the small pile. This went into its own Tupperware, which sealed tightly and was so much more effective for saving, well, things like these.

Old Hank always had been quite regular, so he was able to grab two of the appropriate jars and add to those collections in the bathroom next door; for these he used smoked glass jars with tight screw caps and rubber gaskets, because he had heard that released gasses sometime could build up explosive pressure and cause unfortunate problems. With two rooms full of the stuff, he didn't want any surprises.

Although Old Hank couldn't hear very well anymore, the result of too many deep probes into his ears for his wax jars, he was distracted by a shrill call below. Looking out the window, he saw a small fox caught by the leg in the trap he had set for the raccoon that had been at his trash. "Serves him right," thought Old Hank, who nonetheless descended the stairs as quickly as he was able. Grabbing a squirrel gun from the cabinet and two shells, slowly Old Hank lumbered through the hall and kitchen and out the back door. But by the time he got off the porch and around the corner the fox was gone, its gnawed leg already collecting flies in the growing heat of the day as it lay bloodied in the jaws of the trap.

Old Hank cleaned out the trap and reset it, throwing the leg towards the woods. He was halfway up the stairs when he paused, absorbed in some inexpressible revelation, and then he hustled down the steps and thrashed through the tall grass and underbrush until he found the fox leg. He held it by its paw with some distaste, but he carried it into the kitchen and placed in on the table, turning it around with one finger and examining the smooth fur, and the ripped flesh where the animal had gnawed and pulled until he was free.

Looking under the sink, Old Hank found a coffee can with its plastic lid holding a supply of used soap pads. Impatiently he shook out the contents and carried the can over to the table and dropped the leg into it. He covered and uncovered it several times, each time peering over the rim and shaking the can a little. It was good, this leg; it was interesting too. But there was something wrong, something not wholly pleasing. Old Hank was not used to observing solitary things, and the truth of it was that fox leg, rattling around in there, just looked kind of lonely.

Old Hank took the can and replaced its cover, and took a roll of paper towels, and two or three of the thicker kitchen knives, and went upstairs to the bathroom. He pushed aside a few brown glass jars with disinterest and, dropping his robe off his body, began to turn in front of the mirror, figuring out what parts really weren't all that important.

THREE WEEKS ON THINGVALLA ROAD

I often just drove past the sign and didn't think very much about it. Strange name, but just a street sign, green and at my visual periphery. Months later, driving to work in a chilly snowfall, I saw a bundled-up figure trudging down the center line of Huron Avenue towards the bus stop. I pulled alongside and cranked down the window, my face absorbing fine pellets of coldness.

"Hop in."

A hesitation. Wide blue eyes scanned from between wool cap and scarf.

"Come on, you look frozen. I'll drive you to the Square. Or into the City if that's where you're going."

A long few moments passed, while my car, my suit, my aspect were scanned for, I imagined, warning signs of danger. Then: "Okay, thanks." She slid onto the front seat, accompanied by an aura of cold air. "Thank you! Don't usually do this, but it's so darned cold."

"Well, I don't usually pick up people either. Funny how when there are extremes, like cold or snow or rain, or any emergency, people talk when normally they just ignore each other."

She unwrapped her scarf, pulled off her cap, glanced over,

half smiling. Fine red hair framed her face; a small brownish beauty mark set off the redness of her cheek. "Yeah, I noticed that, too," she replied.

My car sloshed and slid down the street. "Where to?"

"Just the Square, okay?" A pause. "I work in the Bookstore."

"Fine. Going right past it," I lied.

An open space of time and words, each thinking for an impersonal remark.

"So where do you live? Where were you coming from?"

"Oh, I'm living with a friend temporarily. Down that side street, Thingvalla Road. You know it?"

"No, not really; just seen the sign. Funny name ..."

I left her in front of the Bookstore that dominated the Square. The wind filled the car, swallowing her thank you. I did not ask her name but remembered her eyes that shone from reddened skin and hair that reflected the sparkle of snow.

A few months later: the first really Spring-like day. The moisture and boggy smell of drying earth were tinged with heat and carried by a mild and constant Southern breeze. I was early and traffic was light. As a lark, really, nothing more, I turned right onto Thingvalla Road.

The entire street was only a few houses long, gray and brown triple-deckers typical of working-class New England neighborhoods, square porches in front, windows set back into the facade mindlessly reflected the dark blue sky and blocking out any glimpse of the interiors. I drove slowly to the dead end, marked by a small widening or turn-around, but saw no one. Ugly little front yards of beaten-down dirt, no more than brown plots waiting for the greening of Spring, running back from the sidewalk to the low red-brick foundations and uneven wooden stairs. All the houses stared out quietly. A silent street, devoid of responses. I drove into the City, still too early for the start of the workday.

In May, when my family was away visiting my in-laws, and I had stayed at home to work on a case, Sunday dawned gray, muggy and dull. I drifted around the house in sweater and jeans, unable to focus enough to drive into the office. After a while, I took my Chevy out for a drive, and found myself at the corner of Huron and Thingvalla Road. Turning right, I drove down Thingvalla. A few children in T-shirts rode rusty bicycles in slow circles. Two tossed a baseball in lazy arcs. Sure that I wasn't conspicuous in my gray sedan, I pulled to the curb near the end of the street and turned off the engine. The entire sweep of the street was shrunken into my rearview mirror: children, muddy non-lawns, a pile of shrub cuttings near the end of one driveway, two teenagers soaping a brown Plymouth, an old lady in a black dress walking bowlegged down the sidewalk. Two small maples with green-tipped boughs flanked the center of the block.

I sat for about an hour, slumped down in the seat and staring through my mirror at the lethargy of the scene. The girl with red hair did not appear. I drove to the office and attacked the contents of my desk.

Next morning, it was pouring heavily and without hope of respite. I loaded my briefcase, umbrella, and raincoat into the car and pulled away from the driveway. At the first corner, I stopped to move everything from the seat beside me into the back, and then drove deliberately and a bit too quickly to Thingvalla Road. I paused at the corner, for how long I'm not sure, until the honking behind me pushed me ever so slowly around the corner. I drove down the street at low speed, peering left and right onto the porches for my red-headed acquaintance, or for anyone else who was bundled up against the rain. No one appeared except for a man in work clothes who jumped into a pickup and roared off without need of my assistance. I turned and sat, engine idling, for a few minutes, but the houses held their secrets. Through one window, I could see white gauzy curtains and a round pull-ring on an old roller-shade. Within this frame, a lamp on a table, its finial golden glass. Shapes moved in the room, unclear and unidentifiable. I drove into the City.

About a week later, I realized that I had become determined to learn more about who lived on this mundane street; I imagined it as a sociological inquiry, the study of the microcosm the better to understand the whole. I learned that Town Hall sold a "police list" for five dollars, disclosing the occupants of each street, house-by-house.

Thingvalla Road had fourteen houses and 151 people. The oldest was 91, a retired hairdresser living at number eight. There were sixty-six children. I could not identify my red-haired friend, if indeed she had ever made the list. The workman with the pick-up truck was equally as elusive: perhaps Hurley at number fifteen, perhaps Johnstone at nineteen. The bow-legged old lady must have been Mrs. Antonelli, aged 78, "housewife."

It was now light well into evening. On the way home, I drove slowly down Thingvalla Road, the police list opened on the seat next to me, imagining occupants, putting them onto the various floors, inventing appropriate dinners for them—starch for laborers, hot dogs for the junior high school students, a six-pack with a slug of beef jerky for John Hurley. I decided I didn't much care for Hurley, with his over-hanging belly and common demeanor. I found myself looking forward to the weekend.

Next Saturday, I packed a thermos of coffee and two swiss

cheese sandwiches (on white with lots of butter) and parked at the very end of Thingvalla Road, car sideways in the turn around so I had a view of the entire street from the driver-side window. I was early, seven in the morning; no sense missing anything, you never know when something interesting is going to pop. I had torn out the page for Thingvalla from the police list, cut away the other streets and pasted Thingvalla onto a stiff cardboard so that it would not get dog-eared.

A few people seemed to leave for work around 7:30, all turning toward the bus stop without a backwards glance. The mailman came between eight and nine; earlier than to my house in my fancy suburb. His small bag emptied in fifteen minutes and he was gone.

Children, all boys, drifting into the street and clustered to no purpose. Mothers in nondescript dresses or black stretch pants, some with small kids, walked towards the store on Cross Street and returned with unbalanced brown paper bags. One child carried an enormous bag of potato chips clasped in front of his stomach, top open, pudgy hand stuffing gold clumps into his maw.

A few cars came and went, cargo and occupants discharged into driveways hidden from my vantage point. A truck delivered oil just before noon. I sipped coffee and ate half a sandwich. After lunch, some residents brought out beach chairs, gaudy plastic webbing woven between rusty metal tubes, and planted them at the edges of the sidewalk. Two middle-aged men sat facing me, passing a large bottle of Coca Cola between them. The breeze carried voices to me in bits and shards. Red Sox. New bus schedules. Paint the porch green why dontcha? Jane Fonda has no tits. The women sat with their backs to the sun; one knit. Their communication was lost in their jowls and housedresses. About 2:30 I needed to go to the bathroom. I hadn't thought of that. As I sat uncomfortably, wishing I hadn't drunk the coffee and considering my options, two men approached my car.

"What's the story, sport?" The smaller spoke; the larger lurked for effect.

"Nothing much. Just sitting and enjoying the day." No good. Makes no sense. "Actually, I'm – writing a book about the town and I'm trying to get a feel for it."

"Didn't I see this car parked here the other day?"

"Oh. Well ... I doubt it. Did drive by early in the week, and decided to come back and spend the day today. Maybe you saw me then. Monday or Tuesday, maybe ... "

"Yeah, well, how about trying another street? You're making my wife nervous."

The bigger man moved alongside the car and rubbed his right fist into his left palm with a circular motion. I was about to ask him if he got that idea from a bad movie but decided against it.

"Sure, sure, no problem." I turned over the engine. "Have a good day," I called, almost gaily. "No offense meant," I suggested. I rolled slowly down the street and drove home, shaking.

When my family went to the beach house in mid-June, to get in some vacation before the summer rentals began, I went to the Ryder Truck outlet and rented a panel truck with dark frosted windows in the back doors and spent a frantic day buying equipment. I loaded into the back of the truck a portable toilet the size of a bucket , a can opener, a lot of food that didn't require heating, a couple of huge water bottles, a flashlight lantern, one of those new portable phones with two power packs, a radio with extra batteries, a few paperbacks, some toiletries and body wipes and a couple of sleeping bags from Sears.

I called the local police to tell them not to disturb the Monitoring Vehicle that the Air Pollution Commission was going to place on Thingvalla Road for a few weeks. I confirmed with my secretary that I was going camping but would call in; off with the guys, family down on the Cape. I called my wife and told her that I'd be with Johnny and Tyler up at Tyler's cabin in New Hampshire as we had discussed tentatively the other evening but would check in when I could get to a pay phone, and thanks for understanding as I had not gotten away for some fishing and hanging out for, God it must be four or five years.

That night I drove to the turn-around at the end of Thingvalla Road, orienting my truck between houses and with a view of the street from the rear windows. Quietly I unscrewed the license plates and put them inside the truck. I placed orange plastic cones in front and in back of my truck, propped a sign in the front window which read "Air Monitoring Study—in case of questions call 556-2020" and set about taping a dark summer-weight blanket behind the two front seats to block any view into the back of the van. Exhausted, I checked the locked doors, dropped down the small curtain that covered the two small rear windows, and collapsed onto the bedrolls. My sweat soaked into the fabric, and I realized that bedrolls were not likely a good choice for my enclosed space. I fought down the temptation to crack the rear door open for ventilation and then tried to fall asleep. It took a really long time. I awoke with a start, stiff and strangely chilled, to a rhythmic thump on the side of the truck. I was afraid to move until I heard the voices of children nearby. I slowly straightened myself under the sleeping bag, crawled to the rear doors and pulled open a corner of the curtain. For a while, I heard only the periodic thump on the side of the truck and saw nothing but an empty street. Then, a thump, a cry of "Oh, shit!" and a ball rolled rapidly away, down the sidewalk, followed by two boys running full tilt, their scabby legs pumping from dirty shorts.

237

I used the toilet, closing the cover quickly but not quickly enough; the space was more confining than I had anticipated and had no circulation. I ate a hard roll followed by a can of soda for breakfast. The sun was going to be hot. Even though I had selected a light tan truck and it was only June, the heat began to build. By mid-day, no one stirred on Thingvalla Road, and I sat in the back, afraid to open the doors, stripped to my shorts, with rivulets of sweat meandering down my face and chest and dripping and pooling on the rubber floor mats.

No air moved in the back of the truck. Enough light came through the dark glass in the rear doors, or leaked around the curtain barrier, so that I could read my paperbacks, but after ten minutes the sweat began to sting my eyes. I turned around and concentrated on the street instead. At four o'clock the men began to return home, the armpits of their green or gray work-shirts stained dark by perspiration. The smell of charcoal fires somehow penetrated the truck, sickening me. I couldn't eat but forced myself to drink a warm 7-Up. The sun finally sank, and children ran up and down the street, yelling, well into the night. The heat ascended from the street but dallied in the torpid pockets of my truck. After midnight, unable to sleep, I opened the rear doors a few inches, feeling the heat and smells roll out into the darkness.

Days and nights became monotonous patterns. I would awake, eat lightly, observe the morning's activity. By midday, the heat sometimes would drive even the children from the pavement. Nothing but heat and my own silent cursing would fill this time. Soon, persistent odor of urine and waste and sweat and old food filled my lungs and mind. All my clothes had been sweat-soaked, and those that had dried were stiff to the touch and sour to the nose. I'd remain naked, because it was easier.

Each weeknight, the men would come home, change into

238

shorts and sit on porches and smoke and drink soda and beer. Their conversations were lost to the darkness, but the hum of voices floated across my mind and taunted my awareness. The younger children played hide-and-seek while the older ones huddled behind my truck and smoked; mostly cigarettes, although the occasional acrid counterpoint of marijuana leaked through the seams of my capsule, lingering long after the teenagers had gone.

One evening, someone pissed on the side of the truck; the metal rang with the force of his stream. Very late one night, a convertible pulled into the turn-around and its two occupants kissed and petted each other in silence for almost an hour. I sat, naked, staring at them but did not get aroused. When they pulled away, I thought I briefly glimpsed the faces of two boys in the yellow glow of the streetlights.

On Tuesday, June 28, my watch stopped, and I started to mark the days in small scratches on the inside wall of my truck. I had given up the idea of calling my family every third or fourth day. If they were looking for me now, that was all right – I knew they couldn't find me. But, I still wanted to be home when they returned from vacation. I hardly ate. I could feel myself getting thinner, sweat continually oozing from my body. I took to sleeping naked also, prone on the rubber floor of the truck to soak up its coolness. The odor inside soon turned rancid, but I dared open the back doors only very late at night, slightly and only for a few minutes. I gave up exercising; the heat and confined space made real effort impossible. Twice, late at night when I could not stand it, I slipped out of the truck and walked purposefully down the street to work out my stiffness. Once I pissed in the bushes, and one night dumped my bucket into a nearby sewer.

Sometimes I read. I read something by Thomas Mann, something by Harold Robbins. I started and put down an anthology of poems. Mostly, I looked out of the truck onto Thingvalla Road. Its patterns soothed me – the boring sameness of its days and nights. The adults had no imagination, no texture to their hours – the same cigarettes burned the same holes into the night from the same chairs on the same porches. Even the children were boring – the same coarse language, the same games with the same playmates. One teen-aged boy from number twelve stood at his bedroom window late one night, the light to his back, and seemed to masturbate. I turned off my lantern and tried to do the same, but I rubbed myself raw in the heat and could not get anything to happen.

A couple of times, my attention snapped out of the window when I was sure I had glimpsed the red-haired girl, but my concentration was so poor, the light at night so unreliable, that I could not be certain. One evening, a girl with red hair climbed the porch steps of the nearest house, her tight slacks creeping into her body. I was so startled that I opened the rear doors of my truck without thinking; I quickly shut them again but had the sense that I might have been observed. That night, I became unsure that it had been she.

My three weeks were coming to an end. I felt that I had, at last, unlocked the secret of that street: it was as prosaic and uninspired as it seemed. Ageless, shapeless people in work shirts spawned crude and listless children destined to replace their parents on these same square porches, drinking beers and lighting Camels or Phillies while their own children hid in the same driveways and sneaked the same smokes and showed each other their genitals and were trained to walk to the buses and work in the same garages or factories. The symmetry left me at peace. Here at last was a street that hid nothing. It was exactly what it had seemed that first Spring day that I had driven down it. I even ceased to care that I could not locate the girl with red hair.

On my last night, I packed the few things I had brought with me, cramming all the food and wastepaper into a large green trash bag. The toilet was almost full again. I sat on the stink in an effort to top it off. Then I piled the books neatly in a corner and lay on the floor in the heat, trying to sleep.

The swelter that day had been particularly intense and a hazy inversion blanketed Thingvalla Road, suspending a corona around the streetlamps. Finally, after midnight when all the porches and windows were dark, I opened the back of the truck. The night had cooled. I moved my face into the stream of air, my sweat drying into my beard almost immediately.

Evenly, deliberately, I filled my lungs with the breaths of summer, my body and mind cleansed and reassured by each intake. As I sucked the night into myself, I thought I heard a noise to my left, up on a porch. I froze, thought I sensed two figures returning my stare, felt a hint of red hair, then slowly backed into the truck and pulled the doors almost shut. I waited a long time, until I was sure nothing was moving and then snapped the lock on the doors as silently as I could. Exhaling in relief, I turned to see my reading lantern lighting the corner of the truck. Stupid of me, to have left the light on when the door was open, but it was my last night on Thingvalla Road and therefore it didn't matter very much at all, not anymore.

— • — ⚒ — • —

"Jesus shit. Look at that!"

"Is that a person in there?"

"Was that a person, don't ya mean?"

"Christ, what a stink ..."

"Not enough to identify him by."

"The teeth. Forensics, they can always figure it out by the teeth."

"Whattadaya think the poor motha was doin' in a truck in the middle of the night, anyway?"

The Sergeant moved around the charred side of the van and saw the blackened rag on the ground, below the gas tank intake. The tank cap was on its side, a few yards away.

"Hey, Cap," he yelled. "Lookit this."

In his bedroom, behind the dirty lace curtain, John Hurley belched loudly and backed one step away from the window frame. "Come back to bed, John," the girl whined. "It's the middle of the night." Her red hair covered the pillow, reflections from the streetlamp dropping highlights here and there.

"Yeah, yeah, in a minute. I wanna see what's happenin' down on the street."

He belched again, and he smiled.

Relationships Require a Sound Footing

I was attracted to Lois by walking behind her. I did not know her. I was walking down Madison on a day where the wind was off the river, driving thin cold rain before it. My view was cast down towards the pavement to avoid puddles and to protect my face.

Her lower legs, knees down, stuck out below her tan raincoat. I first noticed her sneakers, colored Nikes over short white sox. In warmer times I might have followed those legs upward to, well, frankly, review the rest of her posterior. But between the rain and the obvious camouflage of outer clothing, I was not about to pick up my head that day just to be disappointed.

In my focus on Lois' feet, I then noticed that when she stepped forward her left leg snapped out straight ahead of her, but her right leg did not. Her right leg came off the pavement and then, after suspending her foot for an instant, her knee would direct her foot outward away from her body and then, in a tight arc, quickly bring that foot back into the frame of her torso and plant it delicately and directly in front of her.

I slowed my pace, staying a few steps behind, enjoying the rhythmic, inefficient throw of her right foot, followed by its recovery of reason evidenced by that knee intelligently redirecting that foot to the straight and efficient path.

Then I blinked against an upward gust of wet wind, blinked again to clear my eyes, and when I looked up at the next corner realized that, somewhere in the last quarter-block, she was gone. I was looking at a pair of black leather boots over stocky female calves, a pair of muddied brown wingtips sticking out of the cuffs of gray trousers, a small puddle collected in the modest depression between the level of the sidewalk and the slightly higher lip of the curbstone.

That Fall, I started my practice of paying attention to how people handle their walking gait. Fascinating, in a low-key sort of way, I concluded. I mean, there are lots more interesting things than the way that random people happen to walk, not to mention the basic unimportance of the collected anecdotal data—beyond a passing thought that some of these people must be wearing their shoes down pretty unevenly.

Not to be obsessive, but here let me just mention what I have learned. Most people just "walk." Their feet go out straight in front of them. By walking behind them, you cannot tell if their feet are landing on the level or whether they are wearing down the left or right sides of their heels and soles, but to all appearances their walk is unremarkable.

Many other people, however, walk with personal quirks. I am not talking about the old or the impaired. I am talking about ordinary people, if you looked at them standing near to you your reaction would be, yeah, that's a contemporary in age, style, earnings.

Here are my categories of deviant walkers. You may want to see if you also have noticed these types, at least on some level short of creating a formal taxonomy:

Some people, men and women both, throw out one foot to the side. A few throw out both feet, creating a sideways rocking gait unless the knees pull those feet frontward with alacrity. The throw often is subtle, but sometimes spectacular.

Some people walk straight, but land their feet splayed outward, a duck-like Charlie Chaplin-esque effect. For men, their trousers echo the splay with a flap of fabric.

Some are pigeon-toed, you expect them to end up crossing their legs inward and falling over themselves, face-down on the pavement.

Some women wear skirts with narrow clearance. They mince along, unable to stride out, often twisting a rear kick pleat to the less vigorous side, disclosing too much of an unfortunate upper thigh.

Others wear loose, soft-fabric skirts and take controlled steps, often holding one skirt edge to guard against a gust lifting the skirt fabric and disclosing more private territory.

Then there are short-skirted women who stride out with flounce, treating the continuous flash of thigh as a fashion statement; these women always wear at least medium-height heels, or platform shoes, and seem to contemplate their total image, I suspect conscious of their walk and keeping it straight ahead and purposeful.

There are fat people whose body parts are rubbing when they walk, causing a slow gait with feet pointed outward to reduce friction, creating a sideways list to one side, then the other. There are some deeply bowlegged people, I note anecdotally, often women bearing some strange genetic disposition, who carefully place each foot down within the frame of their bodies like a person placing a cane or crutch close enough to maintain balance and momentum.

There are those whose walk reveals familiarity with different modes of locomotion or habitual contact with different surfaces. Dancers prance at irregular intervals. Runners break into jogs to reach crossings before the light changes. Ice skaters slide forward one foot and then the other, extending hands slightly in an echo of a balance, a hint of a crouch evident in their posture. Cross country skiers sweep each leg behind them.

Finally, some folks are just plain uncoordinated. They are the children of Boris Karloff, jerkily lurching down the even cement as if stepping barefoot on a carpet of angry scorpions. One suspects some neurological complication.

＊━ ≣◊≣ ━＊

One beautiful day that following May, I was again walking down Madison on my way to work and, although the weather did not compel my looking downward, I had by now gotten in the practice of looking downward anyway, at least some of the time.

So here I am—picture this if you would—strolling down Madison and I see those colored Nikes again, same type of short sox, and that telltale outward throw of foot on the right-leg step, snapped promptly back in line. I notice now the legs which are delivering this familiar pattern; they are thin but well-proportioned, they disappear behind a skirt a little above the knee disclosing no hint of cellulite but, rather, exuding a nice pinkish glow, none of that upsetting super-whiteness that looks like a slab of chilled sturgeon. Sharp indents just over the top of the sox promise a deep hollow on each side of the now-invisible heel.

We arrive at the corner together. I know this person, she is my—friend. I feel like I have met her before, a feeling which is unfounded and delusional. Reflexively I turn to her, finding a squared profile with severe chin and straight sloping nose set off by blonde bangs and a sweep of hair into which her ears slowly disappear.

"Great to see you again," I say. "How has your Spring been going."

246

Lois turned to me with a half-smile of collegial puzzlement. "Hello. I must say I am not sure I can recall . . ."

The pause becomes evident and I realize I am in embarrassing difficulty here. A very limited number of possible replies suggest themselves and are dismissed; outright lie ("Wasn't it at the gallery opening, you know . . .") to the absurd truth ("I loved your walk with the thrown out right foot from the moment I first saw you last Fall and when I just got a glimpse of your calves that clinched it for me and I just had to talk with you").

"I can't tell you. I'm embarrassed to tell you."

The light changed but she did not move. I stood there also. Her grin morphed into a wide smile.

"You must be kidding me, right? Is this a pickup line? That would be – disappointing . . ."

"Sort of. But I do know you. In a way. It will take some explanation."

"I'll bet," she said, making a show of looking at her watch.

"I'm not a creep," I blurted, realizing that in a way I was now in fact lying. " Here is my business card," I said as I frantically fished for one in my wallet. "I'm a real person!" (Well, that was sort of stupid; even Stalin and Caligula were real persons but, likely, not the best of personal companions.) "May I call you?"

A big smile now. "Won't that be a little hard since I have your card but you do not know who I am?"

Moron. I am sure I am a moron. I am sure she knows I am a moron.

"I will call you. On the phone, you can explain all about this." Stern tone now: "If you are one of those stalkers I assure you I will have your ass, even in your Zegna suit." My spirits soar. She will call me! She noticed my suit, I am so glad I wore a nice suit!

The light changed again and I just stood there as she began to cross. I was about to call after her that I was not a stalker but caught myself that this was not a great thing to yell out while surrounded by lots of strangers.

Later, much later, Lois told me that she was particularly attracted to my compulsion to describe her body in great detail. It proved to be, for her, a form of flattery, that her feet and legs and arms and fingers and hairline could prove so fascinating to another human being. Of course, she told me with salacious leer, that it was also a little creepy, she could better appreciate my affinity for parts of her body other than feet. Her biggest fear to overcome was that I was so guilelessly candid in my admissions, and so skilled in observation, that she worried my curious little predilection was dangerous to the safety of others.

I have found that Lois likes to come back to this theme primarily when we are naked. That's okay with me. Our only ground-rule is that we do not mention any of this to the kids.

Oh, yes. Good stories have a moral. Here is the moral of this story: "Honesty is the best policy."

THE PRODUCER

I am often asked about my working habits. Until now, I have eschewed revealing them. Some may find them bizarre but, more importantly, they are so personal and idiosyncratic that I am certain they cannot be put to productive use if emulated by others.

Success, however, has attracted attention which, in turn, has fostered a combination of vanity and willingness to shock. The devil-may-care liberation of being able to say virtually anything without creating offense—indeed, almost always thereby enhancing my aura—has led me to describe the processes leading to (what many have described as) my colossally powerful oeuvre.

I forewarn you that what follows is my actual process; it is not invented to mock the question, nor as a comedic send-up. I follow my regimen each working day, or rather afternoon. I have never known a great idea which could be attributed to labor expended prior to noontime.

I sit in a conventional office, albeit without telephone. I sit in an inexpensive black leather chair, although my buttocks do sometimes inconveniently stick to the surface as I wriggle. You see, I always work in the nude. In this fashion am I open to all available sensations, as well as having access, as needed, to erogenous zones.

I do have a touch of whimsy, however. It reminds me of the

basic humanity which must be at the core of very great works. I wear a white chef's toque, always immaculately clean, as I "cook up" my productions. And I have never enjoyed being barefoot, and over the years have experimented with numerous shoes and slippers. I have, this past decade, adopted very light running shoes, to "speed" my effort and to keep my feet reasonably cool, as I must maintain air temperature in the mid-seventies.

My computer is my link with my assistant, Bertha Zvik, who sits in the adjacent room but obviously cannot enter my workspace on a regular basis. When I need to instruct her directly, she must put on her blindfold, and then enter and guide herself to the front of my desk by use of the handrail we have installed for that purpose.

I arise at ten precisely, take twenty minutes of stretching, shower with tepid water, and eat half a cold pink grapefruit. I do not like my grapefruit sectioned; I prefer to pierce the moist flesh with the side of a non-serrated teaspoon and segment it from the binding filaments in a deliberate if squirty motion. I wear a robe while eating, to keep the citric spray from my body, as I find that the spray dries to an unpleasant sticky residue. I take one cup of coffee with a generous pour of cream to cut the dark roast, but only one cup; otherwise my need to urinate during work time becomes a distraction. At precisely noon I pass by Bertha, nod my hello, enter my office, remove my robe and place it on the hook, take my fresh toque from the table, walk across the highly polished linoleum floor, and seat myself.

You may be surprised at the linoleum; not the kind of floor covering you would expect in the home office of someone such as myself. As a child, my bedroom floor was covered by a medium gray sheet of linoleum, which my father had carefully rolled out, using an industrial razor to trim the edges and to fit the carved flaps around the feet of my steam radiator. This linoleum had a pattern of darker, ebony squiggles, and with my child's imagination I sometimes awoke with an awareness that those squiggles were alive, moving and malevolent. I would be careful never to let my bare feet touch the floor, relying on a series of close-toed slippers, nor would I allow my bedding to droop onto the floor and allow the squiggles to climb up and onto my mattress while I slept.

At first, I pretended that they could not climb the legs of the bed, but as I grew older I realized that this was implausible. That is when I placed the pie tins under each leg of the bed and filled each tin with water. My parents were stunned by my assertion that squiggles clearly could not swim, but after faint protest and an earnest discussion which I could almost hear through the common wall of our bedrooms, I was told at breakfast that I could maintain my moats—which I did until I left for college.

Now when I set up my home office, my staff could not locate linoleum either in rolls or in tiles that was anything like the design of my childhood, but I found an artist in Soho who undertook the task of creating a huge linoleum-based work in light gray, festooned with squiggles conforming to my best recollection, and I had that installed on my office floor.

It is a reminder of how we move forward from our childhood fears and yet, we are also tied to them in some indirect way. They inform our world view at a very basic level.

Perhaps that is why I am careful never to slip out of my running shoes while I am working.

In any event, I work without food or drink from noontime until I feel myself drained of psychic energy. Or need to toilet. And then I arise, save what is on my computer, lock my handwritten notes and any dictated tapes in my vault, place my toque on the table so staff can replace it for the next morning, resume my robe and leave the work wing. Typically, Bertha will be at her desk, although if I have been lost in creativity I may have worked into the late evening and Bertha may have left. Our arrangement is that if I have not exited by 9 p.m. and have not texted her to stay,

Bertha may leave without formally advising me.

I follow this regimen, while in residence in the City, Tuesday through Friday. On Saturdays I prepare for receptions, galleries and restaurants. On Sunday I read the *Times* cover-to-cover, skipping only the automotive section and anything written by Tom Friedman, as I find discussions of the flatness of the world distasteful, and one never knows when Tom will take off in that direction. Besides, Tom has a derivative mind, although when I mentioned it to him he did not seem to agree.

Mondays are my days of renewal, and information gathering. I walk in the City with a modicum of freedom. The theaters are dark, keeping hordes of undesirables away. Most working drones are attentive to their occupations and are off the streets, particularly after a weekend. This allows me to observe all those people with whom I feel allegiance; truckers delivering stuff, clerks restocking shelves, working women taking a day off, the unemployed, the crazies, the con men, the people of ambiguous intent, the people trying out their new/old hustle ("brother, you are looking really fine today" followed shortly by "I've enjoyed talking with you but now I gotta confess that I find myself coming up just a little short ... ").

I often go downtown for lunch, dim sum or a deli, maybe a dirty water dog from a street cart. I talk to people continually, often turning on a small tape recorder or taking a quick picture with my cell phone so that I can capture the moment and later extract the nuance. Once or twice a year, I travel alone for a week or two, sometimes new places and sometimes old ones. I have given up on France, I tell you. It's a long story, and a shame, but it is fully the fault of the French, and not me. I rather like the Greek Islands, where the locals try to hustle you at backgammon. Retsina has replaced Chambertin Clos-de-Beze as my go-to libation. On these excursions I take no notes or photographs. I just absorb. When people recognize me, which often happens, I smile and chat but never sign. I think it rude they should ask, but do not say so.

That's it. That's my work "process." The mechanics of my life. I owe it to posterity to be accurate so, you should note, I hereby assure you that everything I have told you is accurate, and without hyperbole. Not very interesting but remember that you asked to hear it. I suppose now this information will be bisected, dissected, parsed, conjugated, analyzed, reinterpreted, related to my body of works, speculated upon in my biographies, and otherwise blown out of proportion by people like you. Well go to it. As for me, I am a few minutes behind schedule.

Would you please pass me my robe? Ah, thanks . . .

V

THE FUTURE

The future is not what you think. The future is people of today with minds warped and stressed by what we call science and which is really change. People will snap and crumble tomorrow as they do today.

THE OBITUARY DEPARTMENT SCISSORS

Harry Laughlin was an ordinary man. His desk was next to mine at the *Littleton Star* for a couple of decades. He was already writing for the *Star* when I was hired as a young reporter in the summer of 1957, fresh out of journalism school at Columbia and in such need of a job that I allowed myself to land in the middle of the State at a weekly paper with only 30,000 readers.

If mighty oaks grew from humble acorns, perhaps the *Star* could put down my roots under the *New York Times* someday.

We wrote just about everything, there were only three of us. Harry had the obits, and when I arrived, I expected to inherit that lowly task but Harry was pretty insistent on holding onto that assignment.

"It's the scut-work," I'd say, and Harry would give me that wry smile of his and tell me that "it's peaceful work and besides, I have the groove for it."

Rhoda called one cloudy afternoon to tell me that Harry wasn't coming in today, having failed to awake in a living frame of mind that morning. It was a factual report. Rhoda had worked at the *Star* when she met Harry and had retired to homemaking on their marriage. I knew pretty much what there was to know about Harry, truth be told there was not much beyond the usual dates and data, but I asked my questions politely between my condolences and got enough detail to write the obit on him. I was sure we had a decent file photo somewhere and said I would call the town's one funeral parlor for the rest of the details. A few days later Lou told me that advertising was down, he was adding a stringer to cover some of Harry's work, but would I mind taking over the obits until the economy turned?

That summer, one of those periodic "recessions" had seized Chester County a bit harder than the rest of the state, and it didn't look like the economy was about to veer anywhere, but Harry had enjoyed the obits and, anyway, in our small corner of the world there weren't that many people dying in a typical week. "Sure," I said, as Lou knew I would. I was settled, permanently nestled, into the town, and Anna Louise's salary at the doctor's office and my senior reporter stipend was enough for the mortgage and the Christmas toys for Jillian even if that second bathroom seemed to be on permanent hold.

Harry's desk was larger than mine, and closer to the file drawers for the obituaries and the photographs also. Didn't think Harry would mind if I migrated, and Lou just grunted the next day when he saw me transferring my few personal items. Even the *Star* operated on Darwinian principles.

The *Star* came out on Thursday, the same day of Harry's burial in Town Gardens; it was sunny and hot and we all sweated into our one dark suit. Lou said a few words; Rhoda leaned against her son, a taciturn postal clerk who seemed put out by the drive from the City. The pastor told us that Harry was a good father and husband and wrote a mean column on occasion.

Back at the office, I grabbed that day's paper and sat down to cut it up. Before computers, we kept our files in hard copy, which meant we cut articles out of the paper if noteworthy and filed them in manila folders and buried those folders in quasi-alphabetical order in the mass of gray metal cabinets that ran the full length of what we called the newsroom. Periodically Lou would curse and go through the drawers and throw out the older stuff to make more room, although for some reason the tall file cabinet next to Harry's desk, marked "People," was kept locked and never got cleaned out at all.

My scissors must still have been in my top left drawer of my own desk, but Harry's were right on his desk, stuck point down in a coffee cup that said "Linda's Diner" on one side and helpfully said "Coffee Cup" on the other. These were old black metal shears, very long and very sharp, without any modern accommodations such as padding in the finger holes, but they looked like they would serve. I cut out the "Recipe of the Week" to save for the annual "Recipe of the Year" competition file. I cut out the article about the Town Manager's interview; it was always fun running old quotes that contradicted his then-current view of things. I cut out the local school column, which we kept forever although no one ever looked into that file for any reason.

On page 7 of our eight-page effort was Harry's picture, and under it my bylined obituary. Harry always saved the obits and filed them in the drawers marked "People." Sometimes when an article needed some context we would want to read an old obit, and Harry would take the key out of his pocket, open the drawer and retrieve the information for us. It was remarkable, sometimes, the insights he gave us, things none of us really remembered about persons or events but which were both telling and rang true to life.

Once Harry was out of the office and we needed background on someone who had died recently, but we could not find another key to that file. "Just leave the damned key in your desk. Or unlock the file, everything else is open," said Lou with a bit of an edge. "Yeh, sure Lou, sure," said Harry, but then the moment passed and since we needed the obit files so seldomly and since Harry seemed to sort of live in the office, the issue never arose again.

"Harry Laughlin, Reporter for Star

Harry Townsend Laughlin, 72, senior reporter for the *Littleton Star*, died suddenly on Friday at his home on Farmingdale Road. The cause of death was not disclosed by the family.

Harry graduated from Littleton High School in 1925, where he was fullback on the Tiger's JV football team and assistant managing editor of the Yearbook. Voted "Most Likely Never to Leave Littleton", Harry started working as a copy boy at the *Star* shortly after his military service with the Army and rose to senior reporter responsible for political and social news for all of the County.

"He was a great reporter and a great friend," *Star* owner and editor Louis Vespers said. "His incisive eye for issues will be missed by all."

Harry enjoyed hunting small game and philately; his wife said she intended to give his stamp collection to the local Boys and Girls Club. "Harry always liked the kids, you know," she said.

Harry was laid to rest today at his family plot at the Gardens, next to his younger brother Carter who had succumbed to polio as a young lad. He is survived by his wife Rhoda (Greene) and his son Bradley (Buster), of the City."

Not much for a whole life, I thought as I picked up Harry's desk scissors and excised his denouement from the surrounding advertisements, but then again Harry seemed to lead a happy life and who was I to talk; my life was much like Harry's and I did not even have a family plot. I sorted the articles and started putting them away; they all got filed except for the obit. I could not find the key. I went through Harry's desk twice—he did not keep much of a personal nature in there and not much of anything else either —and checked the walls looking for a hook with a hanging key, but came up empty-handed.

Next morning, I found my desk as I had left it, strewn with cut-up pages of the *Star*, and Harry's obit tucked under the desk lamp in one corner. I pulled over a waste basket and was stuffing the scrap papers off the desk when I thought I saw Harry's face peering up at me midst the trash. I had thought that I had cut out the picture as well as the write-up yesterday, but perhaps not. I reached up to the desktop for a last armful of newsprint when I saw Harry's picture, attached to his obituary, still staring up at me from the edge of the lamp.

"Bedamned!," I thought and I bent over and dug out the scrap papers and spread them on the floor. Found page seven. There was the picture, and under it the obituary text itself. "Another copy I guess" was what I thought but something – different – about the article caught my eye and I picked the page up and smoothed it out on the surface of my desk and began to read.

"Harry Townsend Laughlin, 72, died with an unbelievable pain burning in his chest and running down both arms, in a cold sweat in his bed early one dark morning, unable to call out to his wife Rhoda and not even sure she would have come even if he could cry out which he could not. His last memory was of the warm stream of urine running over his crotch.

Although he liked to write and went out for Yearbook, the teachers never appreciated his prose and his classmates made fun of him for writing and not smoking in the bathroom even once. He went out for football to get those assholes off his back but spent his athletic career sitting on the JV bench. Rhoda was always cold as ice and did not warm up after they married. His son Buster was just like his mother and Harry didn't share a civil word with him after the age of eleven. Harry took out his anger by shooting animals, but he was

260

afraid of the moose and even the deer and restricted himself to rabbits and turkeys. With nothing to do at home, he took up stamp collecting which was mindless but all-occupying, so he did not have to think about his life.

The only thing Harry really liked was the obituaries. He would staple the replacement obituaries to the original, saccharine write-ups and lock them up in his personal file drawers.

If you are reading this now, Steve, then you cut out my obituary with my scissors. The scissors were given to me by Dink Hopewell, who wrote the *Star* obits before me; he got them from his predecessor he told me. Keep a close eye on the scissors because other scissors don't work; I tried. Enjoy, Steve. You now know why I was happy at my work at least.

PS–a copy of the key is taped to the bottom of the wide drawer of my desk, in the back center."

I picked up the scissors, cut out the replacement obituary, stapled it to the original, groped for and found the cabinet key, unlocked the rank of the files and pulled the top drawer outwards. A to D. I found the Ms in the third drawer and there was Harry's folder, all prepared and empty. I slipped the two articles into the folder, locked the cabinet and dropped the key into my pocket. I went out for a walk.

I was back a half-hour later. I had to write up the Grange meeting, which I did and handed the copy to Andy, who set the type with the old-fashioned linotype machine, hot lead lines of words popping down the chute and forming whole paragraphs and articles; we were ten years away from using computers to do the same job in a quarter of the time at a twentieth of the cost. On my walk I had gotten a copy of the key, and I taped one back under the drawer. After I taped it, I went back and taped over it three more times; with a key that valuable one cannot be too careful.

I spent the afternoon reading. The things you don't know about people could fill a book.

Well, fill a revised obit, anyway.

The last town manager died while in Las Vegas, spending some of the embezzled town funds that were never fully recovered; that was about five years ago, near the time that Harry had been able to completely paint his modest house and put a new, expensive slate roof on top of the peeling tar.

That the late Pastor Linkletter was a pedophile had been rumored but never proven; the list of his victims read like a who's who of Littleton, and it did not seem likely that this old story would ever see the light of day.

I learned enough about so many people that I came to understand why Harry was so often able to provide local, shall we say "color," to our sorry little small-town reportage. "Color" indeed. And perhaps why, when Harry went out to interview someone, a rare occasion where we actually tried to report news rather than rewrite rumor, he would come back with sharp commentary from people who were otherwise noted for their unwillingness to talk to the "press."

Lou complained that I had become less productive at the time he most needed me to be on top of my game. Anna Louise commented that I had seemed withdrawn; I missed one of Jillian's field hockey games for the first time and spent two days trying to explain through her tears. I could not wait for people to die; I would energetically write a glowing obit to make the town smile, impatiently wait for the Thursday press run, that night use the scissors to cut out the obit and arrive at five the following morning to use those same sheers to cut out the truth, staple the two together, and place the truth into another locked-up file folder with a smirk on my face and a lift in my step.

262

Thus amused, I watched Jillian graduate from High School and matriculate at State and move, as all the young folks moved, to the City. Thus amused, I watched Anna Louise grow crow's feet and a sagging figure and an increasingly dour view of life and of me. Thus amused, I read my way backwards into the town's history and people and gathered a comfortable sense of self and an awareness of the way of the world. Lou came to the office less and less, I took over as editor, Littleton became unexpectedly a distant bedroom suburb of the City, and the *Star* seemed to grow in readership, so I no longer thought about the *New York Times* and not even of the *City Tribune*.

Lou fell ill, a lingering illness not likely to kill him right away, but ill enough that I began to think of my future. I had an idea. I came back to the office late one night. I wrote an obituary for Lou, as if he had died. I went over to one of those new computers that created press-ready copy electronically, without need of the linotype and of old Andy, who had been demoted to a janitor we did not need but neither Lou nor I had the stomach to fire the old guy. I fiddled with the keys until the larger printer whirred into action and printed a mock page of the *Star* with one single article, Lou's obit, right smack in the middle. I cut the obit out with my trusty scissors, left the article tucked under my new high-intensity desk lamp, placed the cut-up page on my desk, and went home. I couldn't sleep but I forced myself to stay away until 4:30 the next morning. Anna Louise called down the stairs, asking where I was going at such an hour; I yelled back some nonsense about the *Star* and scuttled out into my car and drove into Town.

No high drama needed here. The replacement obit sat right in the middle of the mock page. Halfway down I learned that shortly Lou would make arrangements to sell the paper to a publisher of suburban newspapers, which pretty much told me that my comfortable days as editor and town historian were soon to be over.

I was working longer hours now, and Lou was having mini-recoveries and coming to the office and making more work for me. I was getting home late many nights, but Anna Louise sometimes was not even there when I arrived. She was working late at the office, they had taken in a couple of younger docs as the Town was growing, there was more paperwork, and the insurance companies were driving everyone crazy. Over the winter months she became even more uncommunicative; not so much sullen as disengaged, but with a nervous little laugh I had not noticed before.

There was only one way to find out what was happening in her life. I wrote her fake obit, then next day read the replacement, dated June 11, 2005:

"Anna Louise (Stahlmayer) Beltram, 70, died at Chester County Memorial Hospital yesterday of gunshot wounds received at the hands of what is presumed to be an intruder at her home on State Route 130, Littleton.

Anna Louise's interests included the Horticultural Society, the Daughters of Liberty and the volunteer library committee. Her daughter, Jillian, Littleton High School 1978 and holder of a bachelor's degree and an MS in Social Work from State, told the *Star*, "my mother was a wonderful mother, full of life and love and caring for others."

Anna Louise will be interred in the family plot of her second husband, Doctor Lance Beltram, at the Gardens. She is also presumably survived by her first husband, Stephen Sheldon, former editor of the *Star*, whose disappearance from Littleton five years ago, following a sexual liaison between Anna Louise and Dr. Beltram of which Sheldon became aware, caused a termination of their thirty-year marriage."

I placed her original obituary and the replacement obituary in the *Star*'s small bathroom sink and burned them. The sun was coming up over the Mercantile Block on the other side of Littleton's main street, as I sat down at the computer. I deleted Anna Louise's obituary. I checked my desktop, making sure my scissors were still sitting in its coffee cup.

I started to write an obituary. Why not try to go out in style? Tomorrow's "rewrite" would correct all errors anyway.

"Stephen Langwell Sheldon, 97, died peacefully in a nursing home overlooking the Pacific Ocean in San Carlos. A longtime resident of Littleton, Sheldon was well known as a . . . "

The Ascent of Man

I killed him with my hand around his throat until he lost his air. He was different from me, a short one. I wanted to use his female.

I killed her with a stone on her head, as I was done using her.

I killed the child in the river, until there were no more bubbles from its mouth. It did not float towards the lake so I left it on the sand for the tigers and the birds.

I killed them on the edge of the cliff as their cave was better than ours. They fell over the side.

I killed them with my club when they crept through the tall grass towards the giant beast we had killed.

I killed both with the stone tied to my pike which I used to break the logs for the enclosure so that our birds would not wander. They approached our hut but were not of our tribe. When I looked closely, one was only ten seasons, still three seasons from taking a woman, and one of my women said I should have spared him. I had my other women explain why it was for the best, as I needed to bury them both before darkness. I have no time to explain to women.

I killed them, the two with the hard hats and long spears, because they were dressed like the ones who came last harvest with many in their cohort and told us we must give part of our crop to their leader who lived far away. I do not know this leader. Our elders agreed that if this clan returned and there were not many, we would kill them rather than give them our food. Our whole village helped to beat them, although one female was slain by a long sword before they died of our village beating them about their face and chest. We hid their hats and shields deep in the forest, in case their clansmen returned in numbers, but could not agree about hiding the spears and swords as they were so powerful. Finally the elders agreed it was dangerous to keep them but Ludefor tried to keep a sword.

I killed Ludefor because the elders instructed it, to kill him at night with that sword he kept, and then to drag him and the sword into the hills where we hid all the rest. So I did, as he slept.

I killed one from a horse although he had much armor, as he had killed my lord and overrun the manse with his legions, and had taken many women including my daughter who was still a maiden. So as he lay there with her, his helmet and leggings aside, I drove a knife into his throat and I showed his blood to my daughter, but she lay there with open eyes and did not speak or turn. I saw she was ruined and I kissed her forehead and slew her too, most gently, and cried and let my tears mix with her blood on the gray stones of the floor.

I killed a heathen near the city where our Lord our God had died cruelly by the hand of the Jew, although my King had told us that these heathens were not the Jews, not even such as those in the towns near Shropshire before they were sent away. And I killed many more but we could not capture Jerusalem as there were too many no matter how many I killed by sword and pike and stone.

I killed three men in the pay of a foreign prince though, as I, they did not come from the land of the prince for whom they fought. Word of my bravery against the pirates led the regent of the Frankishmen to seek my sword, and the money was paid first to my eldest son before I departed. They knew I would not run away even though the money had been paid before, as I do not kill for coin and sought the monies only for my son as he is not yet strong in killing.

I killed the red men across the sea, though was so ill by the passage that I feared I had no power for it. They came with axes and simple bows, and by arranging in ranks so there was always fire we were able to slay them all. I know not how many I killed, but our army killed many at a distance. I was told too that I killed also by my seed spread among their women, which caused them and their children to fear and die, but I cannot count those dead except as by the hand of God, as these red men do not know Him nor care to hear of His tender mercies.

I killed the yellow man when he ran towards our ship, which had come peaceably to trade. It was I, as I fired first and saw his head hinge backwards on his neck just before his body melted downward. My companions killed the rest, and praised my first killing, and did not mention that I could not kill further, for the sight of that head dropping backwards like the cover of a hinged box made me sick. But my companions praised me nonetheless, and I smiled and let their praise engulf me.

I killed those in the trenches although they would not fight like men. I threw grenades over the wire and heard them scream. Perhaps they were only wounded, not killed? But they were so numerous that I am sure that many were killed. I never saw a one of them.

I killed uncounted. The bomb sight was not so true as the government would have you believe. And some factories lay next to workers' quarters. I often have wondered if my pilot told his family that he had killed people even though he was only flying and had no control over the release of the bombs. I, myself, never told my family that I had killed them, but that is another story.

I killed one hundred and seventeen men and boys, their heads illuminated and as voluptuous as Crenshaw melons between the fine black lines of my sight. I know exactly as I kept count. I am sure as I am very skillful, and you can see the round black hole begin to fill crimson before the head disappears from view. Twelve were spared. I think those days the crosswinds were difficult.

I killed one person, in a suit, in a hot city on the Arabian peninsula, but I am not cleared to tell you anymore. I was not in uniform.

I killed a small city while sitting at a computer console in the high mountains. The satellite showed the drone explode, the buildings disappearing in white smoke and dust. I do not know the name of the place. I was only given map coordinates.

I killed by beam one warrior designated by the other hemisphere, as my justified laser beam intersected his beam close to his face and particles blew his brains out of his eye sockets and his ears. This was the 664th monthly Mano-a-Mano, but we still train to fight by wars if the Agreement of Peace and Diversion were ever to fail. I am not certain I could kill using the weapons of our fighting force, but I may try to do so next month; as an exalted warrior, I am entitled to kill another in my brigade with a crossbow if I would like to gain that experience.

I killed my second wife today. I impressed my brain on her thoughts and crushed the life from her spirit. Computer tells me that killing once required touching, and that it was accomplished upon corporeal entities.

FYI

(Excerpted from an interview with Fox News; March 23, 2038, with CEO Mort Levine)

Every time I pass one of our Institute billboards, it fills me with pride that we are able to provide such valuable service, deep service, to so many of our fellow human beings. Our patronage grows each year and we hope to be empowered in some other countries over the next decade, as soon as they become enlightened enough to follow America's lead. As ever, we are the moral, social and intellectual leaders and our innovative daring is, rightly, the envy of all peoples except those religious zealots who will here go nameless.

It was typical that people noticed that being young was the key to happiness; our advertising skewed sharply to the youth markets, and people male and female were educated to emulate the styles of the young notwithstanding their vagaries. And people noted that, although icons deteriorated before their very eyes and became objects of scorn and embarrassment, some icons never did suffer that fate. They were those lucky enough to be taken young. Jack always had that youthful open face; Marilyn always had that voluptuousness and those moist red red lips; James Dean forever swaggered across our minds, his jeans too low on his hips for comfortable voyeurism. Janis Joplin was forever the rebel with

270

the obscene leer and imagined sexual debauchery.

So about fifteen years ago, young people started to SD. The movement was small at first and much maligned; religious scruples combined with family angst slowed the spread of the practice. But the advantages of being forever remembered as young, your face unlined, your breasts pert or ripped, your teeth straight and gleaming, your hair silky and shiny – the promise of immortal youth was just too strong a fundamental need to be long denied. The Self-Dying cult expanded until it was not a cult at all, but rather a way of life. There was debate, to be sure, as to several features: what was the very best age to SD; what method was least likely to distort the body in shape or expression and thus impact the after-SD photo essays that were posted on the new social media sites (my favorite always was DeadandProud, although its acronym DAP left me somehow uninspired).

So a few of us were sitting around our tech incubator site commenting on the trend, and believe me it was trending trending trending notwithstanding the grieving parents in the PSAs – indeed, perhaps even in part because of them. And, forgive me for taking credit but I must report the truth, I myself observed that this was a business waiting to be formed, crowd sourced and taken public on a fast track. Thus was born Forever Young Institute and its public facing how-to site FYI.org.

Our kits flew off the shelves, although we were unable to package preferred poisons due to intrusive governmental regulations of the sort that have squelched so many imaginative new economy start-ups. We instead had to explain how the necessaries could be otherwise obtained. We provided literature, guidance to audience management, links to videographers, referrals for professional site development, tips on how to monetize the process even if you were not initially famous or significantly followed, and counselling tips to deal with uncomprehending parents. As State laws, driven by our referendum function, came to accept the concept, we were able to open walk-in clinics where one could have a well-planned event with friends in attendance, or just a natural spur-of-the-moment passage where your contact list could be left with us for publicity after the fact. As no securities exchange would list our shares when we went public, we availed ourselves of over-the-counter trading, but after our third public offering attracted over $2 billion, NASDAQ was forced to relent and now you can follow us daily in your paper or online (trading symbol DEAD). I must say that when our team was invited to the White House Conference on Innovation and I found myself on a panel with Elon Musk and Bill Gates I felt proud to be part of the evolving American Dream. Bill I admit was a bit luke-warmish as he has directed his fortune to saving lives, but Elon realized that life is a choice, and that Bill should direct his attention to those who chose to try for a long existence and should keep his nose out of free choice which, after all, made America great.

I should not close without mentioning our newly developed service; it will be announced in a couple of weeks but I guess there is no harm in sharing with you the general outlines now. Starting this Fall, at selected drop-in centers, older Americans past the age where being young forever seems feasible, now can also participate in this revolutionary movement. In a few short hours, plastic surgery, laser sculpting, hair dying, make-up artists and Hollywood-trained costume designers can transform old people, even up to the age of 35, into their younger true inner selves, and then they can undergo the event and they, too, can be young forever.

Yes, I agree; America is a wonderful country full of innovative people and a daring population. As soon as our lobbyists can move Congress to act, the foolish artificial age floor will be removed and all citizens will be able to stay young forever and will be permitted to elect that status at either earlier or later life points ... Well, I cannot even imagine our stock price in a couple of years. So here's a tip, if I may without the SEC landing on my neck: buy FYI shares now. You will not be sorry.

WAITING ROOM

So there was this screech of brakes and then here I am, sitting comfortably in a green mohair couch that looks very much like the one in our living room when I was growing up. I know without being told I am in the Waiting Room and I am, well, waiting.

This room is echo-y, if you know what I mean. Sounds are muffled but discernable from far back in the room but, when I turn, the light dims after a few yards and I cannot see beyond. It sure is eerie but for some reason I do not feel upset. Strange; normally that kind of thing would drive me nuts.

My mother is eating a celery stalk off of a low flat Limoges plate with a celery stalk design. She always had an affinity for plates that reflected their contents. Our kitchen cabinets were full of platters with embossed turkeys, compote dishes with covers in the shape of some fruit, a tray with a base of green asparagus, a bowl with a cover in the shape of a chicken. Since she had been deceased since 2002, I must confess it was a bit disconcerting to see her but, of course, a welcome sight.

A dull stench directed me to my father, smoking a fuming pipe. His antique smoking stand was next to him, its amber jar holding his dark tobacco, although the slot for matches was uncharacteristically empty.

Cousin Louis always was overweight and when he died of a

heart attack at age 40 or so it caused me to go on a strict diet for two or three weeks, but then I remembered that his father, not my blood relation, also had died young of heart failure and I was thus able to attribute his demise to DNA rather than diet. No reason to pass on the pumpkin pie after that. Louis seems thinner now, as when we were in high school and before his first wife ruined him in many ways all of which ruination seemed to gather at his belt line.

But it was my grandparents, looking gray but still mobile, who really caught my attention; they were deep in conversation with a group of people who seemed vaguely familiar. I got up and strolled over but no one acknowledged me; the words were guttural, poured out quickly, a little Russian I thought, some Yiddish I was sure, something else totally unfamiliar. My mother's mother, who passed at 109 years, was closest to me and I reached out gently to touch her shoulder. My hand rested on her sweater, I could feel the warmth of her body, but she did not turn. Hard of hearing she was, so I leaned near her ear and almost yelled her name. No reaction.

I was beginning to get the idea that this was a bizarre dream. Normally when one recognizes you are in a dream you struggle to awaken. You may not succeed at first, as dreams are deep in you but, as you climb your mind outward, you ultimately succeed. Of course, I was now awake I was sure, the real me and not the me in the dream, and I was not sure of my escape route, but I tried to awaken my real self nonetheless. To no discernable effect.

I had been hungry when I got in the car but dinner at Marcus and Sally's always was great so I had denied myself a snack before leaving. I was still hungry but did not know what to do about it. I wandered back to my couch to find a folding metal snack table, just like the one in my basement at home. A dish of veal piccata with vermicelli dressed in oil and garlic stared up at me; silverware and a glass of pinot noir shared the tray. I did not, all of a sudden, feel like eating and stood with a start.

I almost ran into Richie, a friend of mine when we were both ten or twelve. He was wearing high-top sneakers and a scarf around his neck, covering the place where the fence spike impaled and killed him while we were climbing out back one day in 1950 or so. I tried to stop him, said his name, reached out to his arm, but he kept on walking, a thin smile on his face. I always hated that smile; Richie was quite the snitch.

Around the room I walked, recognizing everyone but afraid to speak or touch again. There were darknesses where the walls should have been, on all sides, not just behind the couch where the muffled conversations drifted towards me. I tried to step into the darkness a couple of times but the darkness kept pace ahead of me. After a dozen or so steps I retreated, unsure of what I was going to find if I continued.

I sat at my couch. My dinner had not gotten cold. With want of anything else to do, I ate. The texture of the food was perfect but I could not taste anything. I examined, looked closely at the food. I rolled a piece of veal between my fingers until the light breading disintegrated and fell to the floor.

There was a feeling then of a new person standing behind me; I turned quickly. Everyone else in the room seemed to turn also, just for a moment. My granddaughter Daphne stood with her soccer ball under her arm. Her long legs stretched from the edges of her orange shorts to the tops of her orange socks, each with the small "L" team logo, the letter reared back as if ready to kick the small orange ball in front of it. Everyone else quickly turned away but I rushed to her, calling "Daphne, Daphne" but she just stood there smiling and then dropped her soccer ball and began to dribble away into and around the crowd.

A tear began to find its way down my cheek but I wiped it away in anger, swallowed and marched off with resolve to find some person or clue to allow me to decipher what was happening; or, I now confess, to confirm or explain away what seemed to me either an incredibly real and depressing dream or a reality so unsettling that it had to be a nightmare.

I do not know how long I have been here as there are no days. I have not slept and seems no one else sleeps either, but all that is without apparent effect. I have examined the faces of everyone I have met here and I know them all. Of course I do. While I have been here I have been visited by Carl Berenson, a business partner of mine and my best friend in the office; and by Rita Goodby, a very close friend of mine in College who did not respond to my entreaties, a particularly sardonic moment given our history; and by old Veonora Sheldrake, who lived down the block in one of those old houses that were destined to be sold by someone's estate if only to be torn down and replaced with a three million dollar mini-manse with more bathrooms than bedrooms.

I have come to terms that while this is a waiting room, I am waiting for nothing. No one seems to leave, or to graduate. The older residents seem to be able to converse, but I do not know if this is universal and shall come to me in my time, or whether this is an attribute that management has discontinued for newcomers. The melancholy thought has occurred to me that I am going to see many more members of my past, family or friends or acquaintances or enemies, too. I have stopped crying; there is no use to fight it. What is happening here is just life. Well, an odd way to think about it, but true, yes?

I am almost looking forward to being able to see some people again, although I do hope their trip here is not traumatic.

There are no animals in the waiting room. I tried to think about that in hopes my pet would appear, in the manner of my favorite veal dishes. No luck.

I do miss my dog.

WHO KNOWS WHAT EVIL LURKS

It's been almost four weeks since I lost my shadow and I thought I would adjust to it by now, but no such luck. I am, frankly, surprised. You don't pay much attention to your shadow, do you? It just sort of follows you around—not to make a joke out of it—and you don't rely on it to navigate or keep your balance or anything.

And I can't even say that people stare at me, or at least not that I notice. Maybe each person's shadow is personal and not of general concern. Or maybe there are enough people these days who have lost their shadows that it has ceased to be a novelty.

Right off let me say: I don't want to tell you the circumstances. Maybe later, but not now. It feels sort of personal if you know what I mean. Or even if you don't, I still don't want to get into it.

But I am going on vacation soon and I find that I do worry. What if I am on the beach on Cape Cod, where shadows are typically more pronounced on a sunny day? What if some kid comes running up to his mother and starts crying, like "Mommy Mommy that strange man, he doesn't have, doesn't have a, [gasp, cry, scream!] shadow!" Not my problem but still ...

I live in the City and walk to work. Most of the time I am in the shade anyway so no one can notice. And at night, well it's night, people really don't have an awareness, light coming out of a shop window might create a shadow but who is attuned to personal shadows at night? But still, I am thinking of taking a different kind of summer vacation, frankly, to off-load this tension I feel. Cave exploring? I laugh to myself. Hiking only in the woods? A staycation where I go to a lot of movies?

My girlfriend, that's another story. Things have not been the same this past month, not at all. She has become more distant. Actually told me one night she had a headache and couldn't come out to dinner. I have started to drop by her building to see if I can catch sight of her when we are not together; it is almost like stalking but I have to know if she is seeing someone else. So far so good, but I continue to, well if you can take a joke about this: shadow her some nights.

⚫─═❖═─⚫

Mr. P presents as a well-groomed Caucasian male of medium height, sandy brown hair, brown eyes, closely shaven; he is 28 years old. Mr. P is employed at a stock brokerage firm in the City and evidences no anxiety about his position or his finances. He came to the clinic first on April 4 in the company of a young woman he identified as a friend and has returned on several occasions over the last few weeks evidencing increased distraction and lack of focus. On this most recent occasion, Mr. P had a trace of a five o'clock shadow and his tie was undone and his collar was opened at the throat.

Mr. P was given a battery of psychological and neurological tests on his first visit, all of which were returned within normal ranges. On the occasion of his most recent visit, another battery of psychological tests (Stratton-Beaumont II) disclosed a lack of an ability to focus on questions both written and verbal and a lack of association with reality in only one area; that area, however, was so intense as to be described as obsessive.

Mr. P claims to have lost his shadow. When, after prodding which made staff uneasy, we agreed to shine a light on his profile as he stood a few feet from a wall, his tension seemed only to mount and he thereafter refused to speak further of his "situation." We prescribed 500 mg. of Zardex taken twice a day, morning and evening, with food and asked him to return next week and to keep a log of his movements and perceptions during that time period to discuss with Dr. Lipper. Mr. P. evidenced a near-panic reaction to learning that Dr. Lipper was on the psychiatric staff here, but we did manage to calm Mr. P. down sufficiently to extract his agreement to come next Thursday to at least explore the situation with Dr. L.

I am not sure Mr. P. will come for his appointment and I have asked reception to remind him both by phone and email on Monday and again on Wednesday.

NB—building maintenance is not sure why no shadow appeared when Mr. P. was in the office but staff suggests that the paint, an off-white with a granular sandy texture, likely diffused the image; it is noted also that the room was otherwise quite bright under the fluorescents . . .

—◆—

Gotta tell ya, I am totally, like, freaking. I mean, I really really liked this guy. Finally, a guy with a real job, a clean shirt, doesn't smell from the gym, and he's like so normal. And he's after me but not in a pushy way and he's got real potential, ya know. So after a few weeks we're hanging out and drinking beers and what the hell, we sort of hook up for the night. His apartment it's even almost neat and nothing weird is growing on the sides of his refrigerator and all.

Then he gets this – obsession thing. Ohmygod, it comes out of nowhere, like one day we're just talking at the bar at Maxie's, just talking and he says something like, did you happen to notice my shadow when we walked in here and I says, like, what are you asking, whaddaya mean shadow. And he looks down and real calmly he says to me, well I don't want you to get upset but I think I have lost my shadow. He then looks up, serious expression, and gives me a half smile like he's embarrassed. So I think it's like a joke and I play around with it, tell him no I didn't notice but I can go back out and check the sidewalk; and he gets all sorts of upset, ya know, like he's serious which is bullshit except it turns out he doesn't let it go. Oh, so then when I think he is going to totally wig out, all of a sudden he just smiles and drops it; but next day is Saturday, we are supposed to go canoeing and all and he then changes it to the movies and I think it's strange cause it's some real nice day out, and like he's all "I want to see this movie" so I say okay but he's nervous and tells me halfway through that he still can't find his friggin' shadow. So I tell him to "shhh" it's a movie and he takes my hand and sorta pulls me out of the movie and I think he's kidding but he isn't.

So I tell him maybe he should see a doctor, like he's getting me scared there, and he says yeah, that's a really good idea, will you come with me. I don't know what to say, I say sure when do you want to do that and he says "right now while I still have the nerve to do it" and we go right down to the Hillside clinic, ya know on Third off Hillside Ave, he waits with me and then goes inside and I wait, and after an hour I ask and they are giving him tests they say. So I went out and got a Starbucks and a magazine and a couple of hours later, I'm really wigged out, ya know, and he comes out all fine and says "thanks for waiting I am so sorry" and off we go to dinner like nothing happened.

Since then he hasn't said a thing about this but he's got some new shit going on, I tell ya.

Like he needs a shave, he used to be real close-shaven which is one of the things I liked about the guy. But now he has stubble half the time and his eyes sort of dart sideways when we are walking and I am beginning to think he's one of those closet nut jobs, ya know what I mean. He's still sweet and all but it's like weird. Half the time I'm like blowing him off and I'll be damned if I'm going to give him the benefits until I figure this all out. And he must like know how I feel, he's stopped suggesting, ya know?

And when we do go out it's always nighttime or, I notice, it's cloudy out. I think he doesn't want to go out in the sun. I think that's like sick. Don't you think that's like sick? I sorta want to insist we go to a picnic or something just to break him of this weird thing he's got.

But then, like I began to think about what if... Well, all I can say is, I am totally friggin freaked out like major league ...

Memorandum : Tribunal Recording Office
From: Recording Secretary
CC: Enforcement; Homeland Security Data Office
Dated: 16-8-55
Re: Mr. P.Case 379493-2055

Subject came before the tribunal 16 February 2055 charged with an 806; found guilty but only in his thoughts, not in actions, so death decree abated. Was sentenced to shadow deprivation for an indefinite period, subject to six-month review. Field report follows:

Mr. P. shows signs of stress; psychiatric eval by Lipper (MD-our agent #XF-440) reveals disorientation, nervous twitches, poor job performance resulting in reduced compensation, recent loss of significant sexual partner (F). Lipper estimates punishment factor (PF) achieved at 4.5 out of 10. Sentencing recommendation was minimum 6.5 given seriousness of guilt and nature of offense. Tribunal this date tabled issue of return of shadow; calendar ahead to 16 February 2056; summons to issue with service by electronics.

I do not know why I did not get it back. They told me they did it; I couldn't believe it, they said it was experimental. I told them that, now that I knew, I could handle the thing, no problemo. Probably a mistake now that I think about it; if they are monitoring PF, how can I get my severity ratio up to whatever they decreed if I am cool about the whole thing so that it doesn't feel like punishment at all?

Shit! Why did I think I was doing myself a favor by being so cocky.

I need to tell Alexandra. She will understand. Maybe. It wasn't really me, acting like that.

Will she believe they can do that to a person? I guess I can prove it if I have to; just run a little demonstration. And how do I handle my firm, I really cannot start explaining about shadow suspension, that will lead into a discussion of that other thing and I can't have that.

I am going to have to rally next time with Lipper, improve a bit so it doesn't look phony, and then start to deteriorate again in the next meetings. What more suffering can I conjure? Can I get away with lying about Alexandra? They know everything you are doing, how can I hide that? Maybe I cannot try to get back together with Alexandra after all . . .

This is crazy. Absolutely crazy. If I could only move to Central City and start all over; but you cannot get a new identity anymore; Homeland Security declared that a risk to the order of things.

◆—◆ ▰◊▰ ◆—◆

Clipped from the *New City Times* 22 December, 2055:

SHADOW DEPRIVATION PROTOCOL ESTABLISHED

Citing the increase in suicides by criminals punished to

shadow impairment, an experimental sentencing model first silently introduced earlier this year, the Tribunal has temporarily suspended the model and established a protocol by which criminals can retrieve their deprived shadows upon payment of ten thousand credits for each Punishment Factor unit remaining on their sentences, failing which payment the criminal is to be remanded to custody for re-sentencing.

The government has issued no formal explanation for why the deprivation of a shadow should be so traumatic, even to those who were subsequently informed that they had received such a sentence. "You would have expected that the anxiety would have been released," said Vigor Lipper of Governance Social Services, director of Experimental Psychology. "It just goes to show you that there is so much about the human psyche that we still don't understand, even at this advanced stage of our society."

Funeral services for the last group of suicides will be held at Hillside Memorial Chapel on Heathenmass morning, 25 December, promptly at ten.

A MAN FOR NEXT SEASON

It occurred to me, around about my 118th year, that I was not about to die, at least not any time soon. At first, I thought it was just a device, that thought, designed cleverly to put me at peace so that, next morning, when I woke up dead, I would be comfortable about it. But then, when day after year it did not happen, it became clear that I was differently calibrated, and that my anomaly was my reality.

I had earlier speculated that aging led to dying in a natural, organic way; your loss of friends and family a preparatory lesson in nothingness. I eagerly read the literature about how one came to accept his mundane-ness, ubiquitous-ness, surely no uniqueness, and that the great arc of life was your fate, you were a cozy part of an endless one-ness of experience. But such, it seems, is not to be my fate.

Fear morphed into bemusement. I awaited each new day just to see its content. I ceased to look at each dawn as a blessing or a gift. I took each new day, then, as my just due, granted by no deity or truth, just another of an endless stream of canvasses on which I could paint my sloppy day-ness; some good, some bad, some forgotten, all assumed, none cherished above others nor even seemingly stolen from an emptying supply of opportunities. Indeed, I came to believe that my opportunity box was, functionally, infinite.

I then entertained a variety of perceptions, lasting some palpable number of days, months, years: superiority over mere mortals; object of awe exuding soothing ease as others rushed to bathe their lives in mine and to support me; power derived from my confidence that I could start new and ambitious projects with long timelines without concern that I might not finish.

I wrote novels. I started esoteric collections of different things, sure I would be able to fill the albums or boxes. I confidently befriended younger people, sure I was not a mere curiosity but rather a true companion. I patiently indulged the parade of those who came seeking understanding of various things: first the gerontologists, then the true scientists with their tests and vials of blood and increasingly sophisticated diagnostic devices, then philosophers, then the lost people seeking guidance I did not possess, next the offended and angry who sought my physical harm as an unnatural abomination sent by various satans, then the clerical keepers of various gods wanting to know what he/she/it looked/felt/sounded like, and then often the just plain people who passed their lives along with mine in annual parallel, the none-too-brilliant who just understood that you live each day until you ran out of them, after which you didn't live them anymore.

I surrendered the often revisited thought that the old view of life was just a comforting sop designed to lull into finally accepting imminent death and thus, ultimately, I came to be young again, putting death on my back burner as far removed from my quotidian existence as to be irrelevant. I ceased fearing my fear, as I had none.

My health remained at some mid-point; my vision decayed slightly; my bicycle rides slightly less robust; my colds slightly more prolonged; my life moving evenly towards some zero point but, like an immutable mathematical slope, never reaching my long black horizontal zero axis on the graph paper of time. Other people dying remained traumatic; I had no greater comfort or understanding. Each death of a grandchild, a great grandchild, a great-great grandchild, or of a new friend, or of a new wife of any age (and they came for me for various reasons or for no reasons, as love comes and goes), all caused the same pain, but each day I arose to feel it, to process it, and then to file it away.

I came to lay down in my cellar the most tannic and long-lived wines, confident that they would not peak after my time; something maturing over decades in its bottle was perfect for my keeping. I selected authors, gathered all their collected works, and leisurely read them stem to stern in chronological order without any sense of haste. I used the monies lavished on me by the wealthy, who wanted on occasion to talk to me, or to learn something from me, or simply to be known in their circle as my major benefactor, to live well but without ostentation; I was never afforded the chance for great wealth when younger and found it just not to be my style.

There were decades when I would, indeed, take some job. I found selling in stores to be gratifying; although the number of stores decreased markedly for a time, thereafter people reinvented them as a mode of human socialization. I spent some time traveling also; as different parts of the earth periodically passed from being war zones to placid I was able, finally, to see all there was to see. I visited the extra-terrestrial places, too, but found myself missing true gravity and large trees. The coastal cities of the Pocono mountains came to be my primary home base, although I did spend some time in the lowlands of Nepal.

Scientists long ago stopped marveling at my skin; it's just skin, like yours. They stopped marveling at my memory, it is all the same, I never could remember faces and names, and never managed to be able to forget just about everything else. I am, finally, just allowed to live, to exist. My historical memories have been recorded in great detail and are open to all at www.smithsonian/steve.org, and few come around to listen to me talk about it anymore. I have said it all, or at least all that is within me. On occasion young people or writers may come to hear stories of how it once was, in the vernacular of the day, imagining telephones and automobiles and flying devices with propellers, but even these voyages back in time have abated; all that information is so accessible in the data banks that no one bothers to access it directly from the source.

And as for the "human perspective" on all that? Well, it is just the stuff of memory, and the human gloss over time has lost its attractiveness to the modern mind.

I have learned much of course, but not what it is like to die or even to fear it, both very important data points. I am intrigued by the subjects, but not enough to precipitate the event. I think I will continue to await, expecting an infinite number of future days. The ones I have been getting are, after all and by and large, reasonably happy. To sum it all up, and so very many people ask me to sum it all up for them so they can go on their way with a lesson in their pockets, I would have to say these things: *change is seldom good, flowers deserve your attention, and you should marry as often as you are able because, at any age, it is good to have a way to warm your feet in bed when you have left the window open too wide.*

VI

NOIR

Not every day in New York looked like the days described in these stories. It only seemed that way. Ordinary people disconnected from normalcy by unexpected circumstance, all set in half-lit rooms. I suspect that these stories are an amalgam of how I like to remember New York in the Fifties, and the influence of noir cinema occupying late nights on WOR and WPIX on my family's round screen Crosley. Upon reincarnation, I hope to travel to Hollywood and work on matching coarse words to the dark shadows, half-drawn venetian blinds and sour-smelling barrooms of those genre movies—if the future holds promise for such things.

THE ADDRESS

THE STOP

THE ENVELOPE

MISFILED

THE ADDRESS

Now I guess if you were writing a modern novel, the kind where each chapter is four pages and there are 75 of them and each chapter really is a scene in the ultimate movie version, you would start my story right now, in my cell. You then go to flashbacks, the story unfolds, and it is unchallenging (you have to know how it ends after all, the movie begins in a jail) but it's that satisfying roundness of narrative that makes you feel afterwards that you have seen a full "story."

What really troubles me is not that they did not prove me guilty, but rather how the facts – what the DA called the "evidence" – incredibly wound itself around my person so tightly that I could not escape. It's not a matter of my thinking I was smarter than anyone else; it's more a matter of how circumstance encompasses reality and thereby dictates the future.

He was an old guy; at his house, number 77, where his widow and children and grandchildren gathered in his memory that night. Sitting on the coffee table, in the front parlor of the brick-front turn-of-the-century neo-Victorian, was a homemade picture album of his eightieth birthday party held that very winter. I knew him well in a shallow kind of way, a perpetual guest at the home of a mutual friend where he and his wife also were regularly invited. I liked him; he had that courtly reserve that comes with guys that age who wear bowties. When I was told of his death, I wanted to attend the funeral but it wasn't convenient, coming as it did on a sunny warm Sunday in early summer. I decided to pay my condolences instead on the next day, after work, when I could stop by on the way home from the City, say the warm things I felt, tell the widow we would stay in touch, and still get home in time for a half-bottle of Pinot and a few smokes along with Sunday's leftovers.

They were digging up the streets and it was one of those muggy Boston days where the trees in Back Bay offered no relief; the heat fell into your car through open windows and was mollified only by cranking up the air conditioning. I circled the block twice, deciphering the parking signs and trying to avoid the red traffic cones around the trenches, angry that I had gotten a late start and was bumping up against the hour when visiting was scheduled to end.

Taking a chance next to a cryptic yellow stripe on the curb that may have meant I was pulling into a tow zone, I swung out of the car, tucked my small purse under the front seat, ran my palms down the sides of my skirt, and headed down the street.

The door was half open, letting into a small vestibule with an inner door beyond. Quietly I shut the outer door behind me and let myself through into the hallway. The dark oak woodwork of a turned banister and paneled stair to my right, pocket doors half opening to a lush sitting room on the left with a couple of couches, chintz around a small marble fireplace, crystal chandelier hanging from a high ceiling with central plaster medallion and dentil molding around; the air was cooled, the room inviting. The room was also empty.

On the wall, a small shelf held a hand-lettered sign on a white card, the script full of seraphs and mock medieval adornments: "Please remove shoes." I slipped out of my heels and pushed them gently to the side of the hallway.

I took a few steps down the hall; black and white photographs on the walls, polished wood floors with rich red Oriental runner, a casual table of vaguely Chinese influence to one side. I walked tentatively back into the house when I was struck by the absolute silence. Could there be a prayer being said, a silent observation of some sort, in one of the back rooms? Holding my right arm out and slightly in front of me as if to ward off a sudden turn in the landscape or to sense a change in surroundings, I walked in small steps further down the hallway, past an empty dining room with glass breakfront and heavy table and chairs with ball and claw feet sinking into an even darker Oriental, then a kitchen redone with stainless steel and granite, surrounded with glass-fronted cabinets. Empty, the stools around the counter standing at unoccupied attention.

I paused and listened; it could not be this quiet! Could people be up the stairs?

Improbable. I leaned into the rear stairwell, somewhere the hum of an air conditioner. Something clearly is not right about what I am doing; I lean farther into the rear stairwell, one foot on the first step, hand gently on the rail and listen without breath. Something is just not right. I turn and walk quickly back down the hallway.

— ✦ —

Mildred is ushering out the last of the visitors, me included. There has not been a chance to speak except for the perfunctory condolences, and now there is that awkward silence when she says "You're going?" and I say "yes, it has been a long day for you." Compelled to fill the ensuing silent moment, I tell her that a funny thing happened to me on the way to her house, I wandered into number 75 next door, I was so flummoxed about being late and all, and it was the strangest thing, the door was open, I took off my shoes, I got all the way into the back of the house and there was no one there of course, I got out as fast as I could once

I realized my mistake, felt like a fool when I looked at the house number and came right over but was amazed that the apartment, lovely by the way, was wide open like that and what was the sign about the shoes all about?

"She's strange. Perfectly nice but strange. Came to the funeral yesterday, you would have met her ... No one on the street locks up, I know it's in the City but we've all been here for years, it is really quite safe. Even when Lou goes out for his late-night walks—well ... " Suddenly Mildred's face sags, her years etch their sorrow on her cheeks as her eyes fill. I am sorry, I started, but can only give her a quick hug, a squeeze of the hands and I am again out in the heat, the contrast to the cool interior makes me perspire, I have to wipe my forehead twice before I can regain the car. I sit back in the driver's seat and sigh. I wonder why my right hand quivers a little, and then I remember and I turn on the ignition.

⊷⊶ ⊨◊⊨ ⊶⊷

"So then what did you do?"

"I told you. I got concerned. Scared actually. The place was clearly empty. It felt empty. You know, sometimes when you just stop and think for a minute and it comes to you, there is no one there. Just a feeling. So I went out into the street and saw I was next door, the numbers are those little brass things, I just went up the wrong steps and the door was open. So anyway I went into 77." He kept his notes in a black and white bound book, what we used to call a composition book in school. It was not a large book, more like half-sized. He wrote in pencil, a small bitten piece of yellow pencil, it made him curl his fingers and hunch over the page as he laboriously recorded whatever it was that inspired him.

"You want coffee?"

"I want to go home. I've been here for an hour and a half. I told you what happened. Didn't you talk to Mildred next door?"

"We have a few things we still have to go over. You sure you don't want coffee?" He was a large black man, Detective Browning or Bronson or some such, he had given me his card and I had slipped it into my purse and didn't want to go digging for it so I didn't use his name. Somehow I sensed that coffee equated to more questions; I waved my hand dismissively.

Browning/Bronson came back into the room with steam coming out of a white plastic cup with playing cards printed on the side in black and red. All aces. "Machine is terrible but it's all we got, the guy next door closes at 4."

"I don't know what more I can tell you. I thought the place was empty. How was I to know someone was dead? I never left the first floor."

"Now that's one of the things I wanted to ask you about." He flipped back to near the start of his notebook. "You know, we got your fingerprints on the railing heading up the back stairs. How am I supposed to believe you never went up there, those stairs go right to the hall outside her bedroom."

"I told you, I was listening up the stairs. I must have put my hand on the railing." I paused. "I am sure there were no fingerprints up the stairs, you know on top. And I'm sure there were no footprints."

"Well, you don't get footprints on a carpet, and no dirt or anything if someone is barefoot." He did not write into his book; an ominous sign? "Why didn't you tell me you knew her?"

"I didn't know her name until I came in here, didn't know it when you called. Why would I tell you that? Or, not tell you that? Look, I don't want to say I am confused or worried but I don't know what is going on here. Why do you keep asking me questions? Should I have a lawyer or something? I didn't do anything and you're acting like I did." My voice squeaked at the end, I wished it hadn't.

"I told you we are just trying to understand what happened. If you want a lawyer go call one, I won't ask any more questions." He glanced up over his reading glasses; his stare said, if you ask for a lawyer then I know you need a lawyer and why would that be, young woman?

"Look, I told you what happened. I don't mean to be uncooperative but I don't have anything else to say. I would like to go home. It's late, I worked all day."

"If I send someone with you and drive you home, can we pick up the shoes you were wearing last night?" His brow made quizzical motions. "Might tell us something. We both know you were in the place, and we both know when, and I am told that the subject died at . . ." pages flip briefly " just around 7:30. That was sort of when you were there?" It was a statement disguised as a question. "The shoes might, well might tell us something about this." I didn't like that question; my heels had been scuffed on the rough pavement around the apartment, where they were digging up the pavement, and I had dropped them at the cobbler on the ground floor of my office building on the way into work that morning. Somehow I was not enthused about explaining that fact, however benign.

"Whaddaya say?"

"I think I want to talk to a lawyer. You're making a big deal out of this and I don't like it."

Browning/Bronson flipped his book shut, looked up and allowed himself a brief, thin smile.

———— ✥ ————

Well, let's not get melodramatic here. I have no idea how they found out about the whole history, maybe it just came out later when they started digging. You really never know, when these things happen, about the sequence of things.

So the grand jury indicted me based on that whole thing in New York and the fingerprint, and then the cobbler was slow as only cobblers are and they found some blood on the bottom of the left shoe and since I had told them I left the shoes at the front door there really was no way that there could have been blood on that shoe if I were telling the truth. I guess. Who knows?

The knife had no fingerprints but where the blade met the hilt was a strand from a rag they found in the kitchen and they figured out someone had wiped the knife clean, and my lawyer thought that ten years was a great trade against the risk of going to trial, which he was sure we would win but then again you never know about juries, now do you?

So here I sit and I am told that the way it worked out the case is over and done with.

Which is good. Because now I can finally say it, and it feels good to say it.

It was dumb luck they lived next door, dumb luck I wandered in, dumb luck she was in bed with the flu, just one of those really really weird things, you know.

But I am just totally glad I killed the bitch. I truly am.

THE STOP

The problem with cell phones is not that they are impolite. It's the guilt. Knowing someone else's business makes you feel guilty.

So when the cabbie picked up his cell and started talking, as if an invisible phone booth had dropped from the cab roof to insulate his conversation, I leaned back to watch the drizzle mist over the streets and tried not to listen. That is not so easy to do, by the way. It reminds me of the old saw that goes something like "Don't think of elephants." All of a sudden you can't think of anything but ...

"Not hardly."

We seemed to speed up, the droplets moved sideways on the window and smeared the stoops and storefronts as we rattled past. Seems the conversation was aggravating my cabbie.

"Ya gotta tell her no way. No effing way."

Some black foreign car, running only with parking lights, fed in from the right, and I was swung into the door by the cab's sudden swerve. The cabbie kept driving with one hand, faster than before.

"What I gotta do, fer shitzake, drive over there and explain everything? We been through it last night."

We had cut through South Boston, a bunch of streets I did not know. I was sorry we weren't on the Expressway. A liquor store flashed bright neon at the cab, its orange reflecting off the mist and making me squint.

"I gotta fucking fare, fa Chrizake! ... Yeah yeah yeah look, okay, okay, in five."

The cell beeped into silence as we turned right down a side street. "Ya ain't in no hurry are ya?"

I leaned forward to make up some lie about being late when I learned that it really wasn't a question: "Cause I gotta make a quick stop."

I got up the courage to ask him to turn off the meter which he did without comment. We were weaving down dark unfamiliar residential streets, triple-decker wooden houses with sagged porches and trash randomly arranged on stairs, sidewalks; wet gutters. I could no longer tell if we were at least heading vaguely south toward my Hingham destination. I never thought I would have deep longings to be home in my condo, but I was starting to get them now. I finally found the spirit to complain, but my wordless reply came seconds later as we pulled sharply into a driveway alongside a dark, old brick storefront.

"I'll be just a minute," he said unconvincingly through the opening between the passenger and driver seats.

"Hey, excuse me, wait up a minute. Just wait. Where the heck are we?"

My tone must have had just enough fear in it to make him stop and turn back to the cab. "Jamaica Plain. Relax. It's safe. Here, I'll lock the doors and leave the dome light on." He was gone before I could think to object, before I could conclude that sitting in a lighted car in a dark alley in a seedy neighborhood was worse than being in complete darkness, before I could realize that I really had to take a piss, before I could figure out how to be outraged.

So I sat there.

Longer than five minutes. A lot longer than five minutes.

Ten or twelve, once I started looking at my watch, which wasn't even right after he left. His boxy shape had slipped into a side door in the brick wall. There were no windows facing me. I could not tell if a light was on inside. I twisted to look out the back window; the wet sidewalk was black, no reflection of light from the storefront window nor from any streetlamp. On the other side I stared at a solid fence, part white paint and part peeled and splintered wood. The rain descended on the roof like a heaving dew settling in nearly soundless waves.

I did not want to step outside, but I really had to go to the bathroom and no one was in sight; no one had come past and although the area was slightly seedy in an urban kind of blue-collar way there was no logical reason to think that I was actually in danger. I looked at my watch under the vivid yellow of the cab's dome light; it was 11:45. Late night in an alley in the middle of a drizzle, first chilly hints of Fall in the air, maybe a touch unusual but not a big problem if you thought about it rationally.

And I wanted to think about it rationally, very badly wanted to, sliding back and forth on the vinyl hills and valleys of the lumpy rear seat had not exactly made me forget the pressure I was feeling from inside. I opened the cab door with a small creak, the cold entering immediately as my body heat fell out onto the alley. The windows fogged first, then my glasses. The cab door made a tinny ding when its edge just hit the brick sidewall and that was followed by a surprising soprano scrape as I shifted my weight to exit. I stood outside the cab listening. Only the rain trickling and hissing down.

I felt better, bolder now that I was out of the cab. More in control, less afraid. There was no sense pissing in the narrow space near the cab, and I walked sideways down the alley a few yards deeper into the darkness and relieved myself against the wall with a long, fulfilling "aaahhh."

Heading back towards the taxi, some voices escaped through the side door, but I ignored it and grabbed the handle to the rear seat.

I should not have been surprised that the door had relocked; it was that kind of night. And in the middle of Jamaica Plain, wherever that might be. I walked to the street: empty. Too much to hope for, another taxi in the middle of this residential nowhere at midnight in the dank and drizzle. Every few seconds a car seemed to traverse along the cross street, but that was half a block away.

The side door in the alley pulled outward soundlessly, but the handle banged when bounced back off the wall. The noise broke my concentration as I tried to decide if any of that distant traffic might include taxis. At first, the darkness hid the person standing near the door, but my eyes adjusted to the dim inside light which outlined a woman. It was not the kind of night that she was going to be young and attractive, and I was not disappointed in my premonition. Tell the truth, my main thought was whether she had come out with the cab keys.

"You with him?" She approached quickly as she spoke.

"Who? Me?"

She snorted. "Who the hell else? You with Lou, or are you gonna let me go past ya?"

I jumped backwards, although I wasn't within five feet of her. "You can go. You can do what you want." I heard myself speaking low, breathlessly, urgently. "I'm just a taxi fare," I added, and was immediately sorry without knowing why.

She scuttled to the end of the driveway, looked left and right, then back to the alley. She was dark-skinned, tall and thin, hawk nose, black hair in something of a tangle. Not young, not old, not pretty, eyes wide apart and wide open.

"I gotta get out of here," she said. Hey me too, I thought.

She glanced into the alley again. "He ain't gonna be inside forever."

She turned into the street, looking back after a couple of steps.

"You comin' or what?"

"Me?"

"Yeah, we both have a better shot if we're together."

"But I'm not involved. I'm a goddammed cab fare, dammit. I'm a passenger!"

"Right, and Lou is goin't be real happy that you let me go."

"I'm not letting you go," I hissed intensely. "You're just going."

"And he's just going to get back in the cab and drive you away, after what you just saw."

"I didn't see anything."

She started walking away; "Whatever, it's your ass."

I watched her speed up, going straight down the street on a chunky pair of heels that clicked and thunked on the wet sidewalk.

"Shit," I cursed, or maybe just thought, and took four or five quick steps back toward the cab and told myself that I'd just sit back down and read my newspaper in the backseat and when the cabbie came back I'd just look up and ask to be taken to Hingham now, and say "what girl" when he asked, and I grabbed the door handle and then remembered I had locked myself out and I said "shit" again except this time I'm sure I said it out loud.

This is not my long suit, these kinds of situations. I'm an

accountant—and I enjoy it!

That doesn't mean I'm boring; just means I am organized. Tonight is not organized. I do not like it.

So, time to get things organized and shaped up. I try all four cab doors; no go. I stick my head into the dim light of the doorway; a gray hall, couple of closed doors at the end, no sound; not inviting. I pat my rear right pants pocket for the reassurance of my wallet, then head towards the cross street with the traffic on it, which happens to be the opposite direction taken by that woman.

◆—◆ ≣◆≣ ◆—◆

Inside, Lou sat in his chair and tried to identify the feeling. It hurt somewhere, but his head was falling backwards and the pain was general. He couldn't quite pull his head forward just yet, so he sat there listening. It was quiet which was strange, because Scotchie and Lettie were there, but maybe they were asleep, it being the middle of the fucking night, facrissake. The neon kept buzzing, which Lou did not appreciate, but he had more important things to deal with. He had to straighten out Lettie, so he was angry at himself for wasting time thinking about the lights rather than taking care of business. Also, he had to get back to the cab though he couldn't remember why. Maybe his head was hurt after all.

Fingers twitching for the edge, Lou grabbed some leverage at what must have been the skirt of a table and pulled forward tentatively. His body slowly moved forward, head still thrown back. Shit, his head did hurt a lot. He was just thinking that maybe he shouldn't try to straighten up when his momentum swung his forehead sharply forward. He felt his chin stubble hit the tabletop an instant before he decided to go back to sleep until his skull stopped throbbing.

Scotchie heard a thump and woke up with a small grunt. Startled, he was still too drunk to move quickly. Languorously, he scanned the room with shuttered eyes. The overhead was glaring. Lou was slumped on the table. He eyed the room twice but didn't see Lettie, which was not good because she was Scotchie's task also, but maybe it would still be okay because with Lou there, maybe he was sort of relieved from duty.

The Shark stood in the window of the bar and watched the drizzle weave a gray curtain. Now that the traffic had thinned and most of the house lights had gone out, the main source of illumination was the dull yellow leaking out the bar's dirty front window. The big elm swallowed the output of the only nearby streetlamp, projecting dull shadows on the pavement.

The guy in the suit had stood outside in the rain for a few minutes, likely looking for a taxi, before coming inside and asking for a payphone. The Shark had walked him back towards the phone booth; the door had been closed so he couldn't hear anything. Preppy sort of a guy, look like he had worked a long day. Square, the kind who usually would carry an umbrella or raincoat on nights like this.

Sullivan was picking his nose and wiping it on the underside of the bar rail; at night he came around front, often as not, to take a load off his feet and get a better view of the Leno show. His legs swung off the stool in time to the theme song.

"So who's the a-hole in the suit?" asked Sullivan.

The Shark kept his eyes on the screen. "Dunno. He asked if I could call him a cab. I says, whadoo I look like, a goddamned con-see-urge or somethin?"

Sullivan shifted his body to improve his angle to the TV, and spoke through the one nostril that didn't have a finger in it: "Didn't even order a fuckin' beer!"

"Smart man there," the Shark allowed, but Sullivan was beyond insults.

Mr. Suit came out of the phone booth, looked around at the five regulars still drinking, picked out the Shark as the likely bet and walked up to him with a tight expression on his face.

"You want to make ten bucks?"

The Shark took a step back to get a better overall view of this joker. "Ten? All at one time? Wow, will ya let me in on the play?"

Mr. Suit ignored the comment. "I need a ride to the nearest cabstand or hotel. I need a taxi. I don't think the Checker wants to come here to pick me up, and I get hung up on at Boston Cab and Towne Taxi."

"Imagine that," observed the Shark to Sullivan. "The Checker ain't anxious to pick up your friend here, and what with all the fares you throw in their direction."

Sullivan grunted his agreement.

"So what do you say?" Mr. Suit was whining now.

The Shark figured the Hamilton was just an opening offer. "Ten ain't a wicked lot of money, my man," he said smoothly, "and, I got expenses in this."

"Expenses? What kind of expenses? I just need a lift to a cab or a hotel that can get me one."

"Well, for one thing there's the matter of paying someone to borrow a car, which I don't happen to have at the moment."

"You don't have—oh, for Gods sake!" The suit stopped sputtering and turned to the bar.

"Excuse me. Excuse me! Does anyone here have a car available?"

No one answered or even turned. Fat Freddie both had a car and was sober enough to drive if he really put his mind to it—but who wanted to have the Shark on his back later?

"Didn't anyone hear me?" There was a half-trembling crack of fear and just plain fatigue in the Suit's voice now. The Shark judged him fully ripe.

"Look, Sport," confided the Shark as he moved close to the Suit and fixed him with his glass stare, "these guys, they're like retired, ya know? Freddie here, he'll lend me his car I guess but it's gotta be worth a twenty just for Freddie, and then there's me to take care of."

Freddie didn't turn but said over his shoulder, "I wouldn't lend you a quarter if you gave me a ten G deposit, you douche."

"Now you begin to see my problem," explained the Shark with a sigh, "or, our problem, if you get my drift. It's pissah."

The Shark gently placed a hand on the suit's shoulder: "So," he inquired as a friend, "what ya doin' in the neighborhood anyhow?"

* * *

A sensitive question. I didn't want to admit I was an abandoned taxi fare, it didn't seem like much of an explanation for this crowd. I also had to concentrate on not backing away too quickly, although the sour old beer mixed with vague foody vapors to create a miasmic rot around this fellow's vicinity.

I turned slowly and started to walk towards the bar, feeling this guy after me in my wake. "I, uh, was brought here by a guy with an office around the corner, I think." No reaction. "A cabbie."

My new friend took a small, quick step back and glanced at the barkeeper, who as it turned out was finally paying attention to the conversation. From the corner, two guys on stools leaned towards each other and whispered.

"Louie the cabbie, like from around the corner Louie?" my friend asked, very low. He wiped his palms once, downward across his tee shirt, rearranging the grease.

"Yeah," I said. Why not Louie? Then I felt the temperature change in the room; and thought uh-oh bad vibes. But no other place to go so I said "yeah, that Louie. What about it?"

"Oh, no, no problem," said my friend. "I mean, ab-so-loot-lee no problemo, it's cool, it's all cool."

The Shark wet his lips and looked at the bartender. "Sully, give my friend here a brewski, I gotta take a piss and then I'm gonna take him to find a cab." He looked down the bar. "If I can borrow your car, Freddie?"

Freddie swallowed hard and nearly blurted that it was okay. In fact, suddenly he was quite enthused with the idea. "Sure, sure; no sweat."

⋆ ⇥◆⇤ ⋆

Lou was in Church, he thought, but he was very hungover. He knew this because the bell kept ringing inside his head and making it hurt. A lot. And also, the bell kept ringing and ringing, calling him to some super-important Mass somewhere, his attendance of vital interest to the Deity.

Lou opened one eye and saw the grains of wood. Table. He opened the other eye. Telephone. Shit, ringing telephone. He sat up sharply, then swayed and felt like heaving. "Focus," he thought. "Focus!" He picked up the phone.

"Louie, that you?"

"Who is this?" Lou's voice seemed to be separated from himself by some considerable distance.

"It's me. The Shark. I'm at Sully's bar. Louie, you listenin' ta me?"

The light made him squint. The squint hurt his head, the back of it and behind the eyes.

Shit it hurt!

"Yeah, I'm listenin' so talk already."

"Louie, there's some guy in here, never saw him before and he's lookin' fer a ride and he says he knows you." Lou thought again that it would be really good to focus.

"Guy in a suit," the Shark hissed, almost inaudibly.

"A suit," Lou mused. "Talk up, will ya, yer makin' no sense."

"Louie, he's right around the corner at the bar and I don't want he should hear. Louie, what should I do with him?"

Lou looked around the room. Scotchie was on the couch, asleep with a Dewar's empty.

No one else was in sight. Then Lou remembered. He remembered everything.

"Sonofabitch, keep him there, will ya? I'm on my way."

It's obvious I'm being stalled, but I don't know why. It has really started to pour outside, and I don't have a lot of options. I sip my bottle of Bud, slowly; Mr. Sullivan has not offered me a glass. Sharkie is sitting beside me, he has introduced himself ("just Sharkie, no Mister, gladtameetcha"), and he has ordered a half yard of some pale yellow ale and he is in no hurry to drink it. Sullivan is nowhere in sight so I can't get a refill, which is something of a shame because I might as well, the beer is the only good thing to happen to me for hours. At least Sharkie is quiet.

Jay Leno is roasting Bill Clinton in his manic unfunny way, it's so boring that even the drunks are attentive.

Then it occurs to me that someone is getting the cabbie. Where's the bartender? Probably on the fucking telephone, ratting me out. (Listen to me; I'm beginning to sound like these lowlifes.) Probably trying to reach Louie, although come to think of it Louie may not be available just now. What if the bartender was walking over to the alley, he's been gone long enough, and walks down some hallway and through some door and finds Louie bleeding or dead?

"Well," said the voice in my ear, all gravel and false cooing, "here I thought I had lost my fare." A large arm slid over my back and a hand grabbed my shoulder with a brief, affectionate squeeze. "Whaddaya say, buddy?"

"Oh," I croaked, "I am, uh, just having a beer."

Louie laughed, more than it was funny, and reapplied his squeeze. "Funny guy. So – where'd she go?"

I turned and was about to sincerely say I didn't understand when Louie smiled sweetly and grabbed my balls gently in his cupped hand and began shaking his palm like he was rolling dice. His arm kept me firmly on my bar stool, my hardware hanging over the edge and rolling back and forth in his large mitt.

"You mean the woman in the dark outfit? Black hair?" I asked quickly.

"Very good," said Louie, and he gave my package a gently upwards joggle. "Glad to see you skipped the 'who do you mean' bullshit."

"She was very upset," I rushed onward. "She ran down the street. The other direction. She said she had to get away."

"She said that, huh? So-you wuz outta the cab then, huh?"

Shit shit shit. No I wasn't? Yes I was? Had to be.

"Yes I was." A short pause. "I had to pee." Pause. "Then I couldn't get back in. Must have locked myself out. By accident."

Someone at the bar snorted, but Louie kept my rapt attention by his growing pressure on my shoulders and by his, well, to say it truthfully, his—jiggling—fondling of my balls.

"Look, you can stop doing this—thing," I said and looked down and raised my eyebrows in reasonable inquiry.

"This? This?" Louie asked. Jiggle jiggle jiggle.

"Yes, you don't need to do that," I said.

"Oh, I'm not so sure about that. Let's just call it my truth machine."

"Why would I lie? I don't know what the hell is going on. Just let me get out of here. I'll walk, to hell with getting wet. I don't even care about the rain ..."

⊷⊶ ⋡◈⋢ ⊷⊶

He's probably telling the truth about that, Louie thought. Why would he lie to me? He's just a fare. He doesn't know anything about Lettie and me and her habits. If she tried to talk to him, well, she's such a friggin' ditz and he's such a stiff, there's no way she could have told him anything he would understand, anything useful—or dangerous. But what the fuck do I do with him now? And what if she did tell him something?

"Okay, chief," I tell him, "back in the hack." I give his hardware one last extra-sharp flick to make sure I have his undivided attention. "Let's you and me try to find Lettie." I'm thinking maybe Lettie needs an attitude adjustment, particularly since she somehow got that rummy asleep in the room to help her skip out, although the poor bastard was probably too drunk to know what was happening.

309

I don't know how the hell he expects to find this woman. All I know is that it's a big city and she walked away over an hour ago and it's almost one a.m., for crying out loud. I'm tired. I'm outraged but too afraid to do anything about it. I have the realization that I am being held against my will, and my stomach sinks. I'm a prisoner! I've been kidnapped! This doesn't happen to real people. That fucking son of a bitch grabbed my testicles and I didn't even do something about it. I disgust myself. I don't even want to think about it, I feel I deserve what is happening to me ... We are driving up and down a bunch of main streets with bars and fast-food joints, but the restaurants are closed and the bars are closing; metal gates are being dragged over doorways. This is Boston, and in a few minutes nothing will be open. She could be a hundred miles away. She could have found a cab, or hitched a ride, or gotten on a bus, or found a friend, or called someone to pick her up. She could have done anything in that much time, it's a goddamned city! Louie pulls up to a bar, hops out of the cab, goes inside for a minute, comes back out and continues on, he's leaving the motor running and I'm too chicken-shit to drive away. All I have to do is just drive away, drive downtown or to a police station or even a hotel and just step out of the car and leave it, he'd never find me, he doesn't even have my name. What this guy must think of me—a prisoner so chicken, so ineffectual that you don't even have to guard him, point a gun at him, even warn him not to run away. Surprised he doesn't give me a loaded gun to hold for safekeeping, so that I can hand it to him real fast when he finally decides to shoot me. Shit shit shit shit shit ...

Down a long dark street is a small bar, its neon window signs are dark and someone in a Red Sox jacket is lowering a metal screen over the front door. Louie stops, cranks open his driver-side window, jams part of his torso outside and yells "McGuire" in a voice too loud for 1:00 a.m. "You seen Lettie tonight?"

310

McGuire is holding a cigarette in his mouth, his hands struggling with a padlock, he is down on one knee; the smoke is curling around his gaunt gray, pockmarked face. He turns over his shoulder, eyes squinted. "That you, Big Looo?"

"Yeah, sure whoyathink?"

"She came in late, maybe midnight. Bummed a quarter to make a call. Then bummed another quarter. Then she got Harry from the MTA to buy her a beer." He rattled the padlock to loosen the hasp. "Imported no less," he added, to no one in particular.

"So where is she now?" Lou's voice was almost a shout, I couldn't understand why someone didn't open a window from one of the houses and tell him to shut up. Maybe they were used to it in that neighborhood.

McGuire turned back to the lock and gave it a hard shake. "Fuckin' rusty piece of fuckinshit thing," he observed in a mutter. He stood up and turned around. "How the hell do I know? One minute she's drinking a beer, next minute I turn around and she ain't there no more. It's not like she checks in with me, ya know." He paused, voice lowering "She back doing that shit again, Lou?"

Louie sounded tired. "I dunno. I don't think so. Maybe. Who the hell knows. I gotta find her."

McGuire came down the street until he was a few yards from the car. "Look," he said, "I'd tell ya if I knew but I don't know shit." He held out his arms, palms up.

"Yeah, thanks, Mac." Lou cranked up the window and started to drive slowly down the block. Nothing, no light or glow cut the blackness. The rain now gently tapped off the cab roof, just below our awareness.

"Louie, you have a lot on your mind I see. Won't you please just drop me off somewhere?" I had a moment of panic, I did not want to repeat my address, although hours ago I had given it to him. "It's too far to my house, I'm exhausted, just drop me off at the Sheraton in Back Bay, I'll stay in town tonight. I'm beat."

The cab stopped and Louie turned almost all the way around to look at me. He looked a long time through the opening that separated passenger and driver. "Holy motheraGod," he sighed. "I fuckin' forgot you were there. Now, what the fuck am I gonna do with you?"

I didn't like the question.

Scotchie didn't like his new guest very much. He also did not like the fact that his guest was tied up, his arms wrapped behind him and lashed to the back of the big wooden chair with all that reinforced packing tape. It was one thing to babysit Lettie, and since she was a friend – sort of – he often watched her for Lou, and they played pinochle and could kibbitz the night away.

At least he had stopped twisting his arms behind him. The thin reinforcing fibers that threaded through the packing tape must have hurt like hell, and there were a few rivulets of blood trickling down the guy's fingers. Even now, after Scotchie had spilled three glasses of water over the guy's hands, the blood smears remained on his wrists, on the chair and on the floor underneath.

After the first day, Lou had put a gag in the guy's mouth. Not that anyone would hear the yells, which became apparent to the guy after the first couple of hours. It just was that he wouldn't shut up. Always arguing, explaining he didn't know anything, then once in a while just sort of weeping and crying like some pussy. Scotchie didn't like this guy at all so the fact that Lou probably would end up whacking him didn't much bother Scotchie, who also was not the one to ask too many questions. Nope, wouldn't bother him one bit. He decided to eat the rest of the asshole's pizza after all, and he sat at the table chewing the congealed cheese and washing it down with Dewars.

Meanwhile, the suit is now babbling to himself: "This idiot's going to kill me! I cannot believe it! How did this happen to me? I just took a cab! A goddamned taxi! Now I'm taped to some chair. Who would have thought that tape could be so sharp? My arms are numb, I don't get enough to eat or drink, my piss is bright yellow and I'm going to die a prisoner in a store fifteen minutes from my office! Who ever heard of such a fuckin' crazy fucked up thing? Crap crap crap, crapshit gotta get out. No sense talking to Lou. Gotta talk to the drunk, but he's so sauced that you have to catch him first thing when he wakes up, and with this goddamned handkerchief taped into my mouth I can't even do that. What is today, anyway? Has it been three days? Is that even possible? They'll miss me in the office but, so what? There's no way anyone can find me. Except maybe the cab company but who knows to ask? I'm so scared I'd even pray if I thought it might do even the slightest bit of good. Maybe he'll let me go. But I don't know who he is, where this place is, who he knows. Then why does he keep me? Why doesn't he just end this? Who can figure out a crazy guy like this? But one thing's for sure, next free moment I am unstrapped to take a dump I'm gonna run for it. Nothing can be worse than this. This idiot's going to kill me . . . "

Lou is pulling his cab into his alley and he's thinking the guy must be getting desperate.

It's four days and he's had lots of time to think. None of those thoughts are reassuring.

And the truth of the matter is, since he's got him tied up in there, Lou is thinking that now there is no way he can let him go. Before was just bullshit but now it's a serious thing. Why did I even tie him up in the first place, Lou is thinking. It was really dumb, and I was tired and my head had started to hurt again from whatever Lettie must have put in my drink. In fact, it still hurts and it doesn't seem to be getting any better.

She shook her head slowly, a gesture meant only for herself. The early sunlight cut across her lap and warmed her hands. The evening had been almost chilly and the blue veins in her arms pulsed lightly but visibly under her dry skin.

"Stupid guy. Wrong guy, wrong place," she muttered. Her words got lost in the vague clamor of the ocean outside.

Now she could leave the Cape; the police had traced the cab and Lou was in jail and not likely to come out any time soon. She felt the hot bolt course across her chest, knocking the *Herald* to the floor along with the needle that had rested on her lap.

A voice came through the door: "Hey, girl. You seen the TV? Ain't that your old man they got in jail up in Boston for offing some suit?"

Her lips started to answer yes but the sound eluded her, and Lettie went to sleep.

THE ENVELOPE

I need you to picture a man about five feet five inches tall, a man with permanent stubble on his hollow cheeks, thin graying hair askew and a bit too greasy to blow in the November wind. He is in a brownish tweedy suit, with the elbows bagged out and the trousers a bit too big, cinched up with a thin black belt almost to his breast. His shirt is white but gone yellow. His cap is in his hand.

The man is thin and his wrists stick out of his sleeves like bony pendulums. His shoulders slope, hiding what used to be some muscle, built up by random hard labor over many years, but there is not much of that left. The man draws on the short stub of an off-brand cigarette, the smoke disappearing between yellowed teeth into his chest, giving birth to a shallow cough.

He is fifty years old. He is sixty years old. He is the kind of guy you cannot tell how old he is but you do not care. He has a history in the lines of his face but you do not wish to share that history. He is invisible and eye contact is to be avoided. His name is Harry. His name is Max. His name is Shorty. Actually, this one is named Jeff.

"Hello there, my name is Jeff. Jeff the Jet they call me. It's a long story you don't want to hear. Pleased to meet you."

"I am waiting for my former wife. She has something of mine,

315

something she kept on purpose when we split maybe fifteen years ago. She remarried right away, didn't wait for any divorce but it doesn't matter to anyone, certainly not to me. Just so long as she doesn't want any money. The new guy—not so new anymore, huh?—he's paid everything for the kid, spoiled him so he doesn't work, a real punk, I see him around sometimes but we don't talk to each other. I know he knows who I am but he never cuts me a break as his father, know what I mean? Never a beer, a game of pool or anything. He'll end up a dickwad, no job, end up running numbers or worse for small change. Well, fuck him. He couldn't lay brick or know how to pick up a 55-gallon barrel or anything useful and I don't think he's sitting at some desk, he's stupid as a post—just like his friggin' mother, the slut."

"But it's my stuff, and I called her a few times and finally she sighs, like it's a big bother even though she doesn't work and has nothing but time, and says if I come all the way to Somerville and stand on this corner here she'll bring it to me if I just promise to not call her anymore which is fine."

"I'm beginning to think she isn't coming and it sure is brisk out here, I put my cap back on although I don't like it, it makes my head itch. The woman who runs the house where I rent a room tells me I need to shower more, rub my scalp, but the water is cold unless you're the first one up and my one big pleasure, now that I gave up working, is to sleep in."

"Well wait a sec, here she is coming around the corner, a small woman still dying her hair blonde, a couple of shades too much towards brass. Wrapped in a blue cloth coat, with a pair of those brightly colored sneakers stepping out from under the coat folds. Her face isn't too bad but then again I choose not to look at it."

"Ya got the envelope," I ask.

"Yeah, I got it. I told you I would bring it. You think I'd haul my ass out here in this weather just to see you again? If I never saw you again it would be too soon."

I bit my tongue. "You look good, Tina. You doin' okay?"

"Here's your fuckin' envelope. Save your sweet talk for your whiskey bottle." She held out a manila envelope, pretty dog-eared but I flipped it over and it still seemed scotch-taped shut. I shrugged and started to walk away.

"Thanks for the thank-you, shit-head," I heard.

I didn't turn around, I just walked away. I was proud of myself. In my old age I have learned something I never got down before: how to shut up. The envelope didn't fit in a pocket so I held it tight against me. On the outside, in my handwriting from a long time ago, the ink slightly smeared, was the word "Lips."

Lawrence Carter was up early, as usual. His terminals streamed Bloomberg and the market data. His iPad had the *Journal*, his cell phone was frozen on *The Economist* article about American economic decline in manufacturing. His laptop was tied to his trading desk. Sitting in his shorts, one of the girls set down a mug of black coffee, Nairobi Dark, his favorite for the morning; at night, it kept him awake, but awake was what he wanted to be in the morning when the European markets were closing and the American markets were coming alive.

"Close the door, goddammit," he yelled, not turning his head from the screens. The women his wife hired to maintain the household never had a clue about what he expected while he was working, and half of them didn't even speak enough English to explain. Most of them thought any conversation was leading up to a proposition, but, between his wife and Lois, Lawrence's dance card was already full up.

From the hallway, he could hear Melissa upbraiding one of

the kids, probably Larry Jr. who was always slow to get ready for school. "I know the feeling," he thought. "The world will beat that shit out of him soon enough," he mumbled to himself, barely audible.

He ran his open hand back over his remaining wisps of blond hair; his forehead had a light sweat, as always when he was trading. His sharp nose was receding into ever expanding pads of fat growing unwanted on his cheeks, out of which dark blue eyes glared with an intensity. His chin, cleft still visible although growing more shallow each year, framed a rounded mouth that failed to reach out to his delicate ears, giving up just about at the middle of his eye-sockets. The Aruba tan was fading, he needed to get back under the lamp in the solarium but who had time these days? The market had returned to volatility.

He scratched his balls through the slit in his boxers and went long ten thousand Microsoft and watched for the market to tick upwards into paydirt.

◆━━━ ≍◆≍ ━━◆

They found the Jet in a marsh out by Logan Airport in the late Fall. His clothes had pretty much disintegrated, and his wallet was gone, but the tattoo together with the teeth led to a positive identification. Larry had put the envelope in his office safe, the one for which Melissa did not have the numbers. Every once in a while he remembered that he wanted to read, to study its contents again, for old time's sake, before he burned it or shredded it or otherwise made it disappear, but the market was still jumpy, who could figure out China, and then there was South America getting tied up in its own history, and he wanted to savor the experience. Melissa would be on the Island with the kids, he would light a fire, open a magnum of Ducru Beaucaillou, maybe the 2000, and relive the days when he was known as "Lips" on account of his quick patter, and he and Sonny and Louis and the Jet used to hang out in the Combat Zone and make money the old fashioned way.

But Lawrence Carter had time, yes indeed he did. He was making money, the Jet had flown away for good, Lois had agreed to the abortion and he had begun to work out, using the gym on the top floor for the first time since he equipped it lavishly five years ago. It was all good, ya know what I mean?

Then someone called, said he was representing Tina. "Tina who," he had asked; he had no idea. "Tina, Jeff's wife," said the male voice, high pitched from nerves. "Tina, she married the Jet."

A pause. Then, coolly: "Oh, yeah, Tina. Say, who is this, maybe we should get together and chat about this."

"Bullshit on that. I don't want to end up like Jeff did."

Now Lawrence was really not happy. "Don't know what you mean."

"Yeah, I know you don't. We'll be in touch. By phone. And we are recording everything, so you should remember what's going down if you screw with us. By the way, interesting reading in the envelope, Lips. Glad Tina made a copy." The dial tone went on for a long time after that, then the recording of the woman telling Lawrence to hang up and dial again. Lawrence locked the den door, warning Melissa not to wait up, he was doing something with Singapore and there was this time difference. He had taken in a sleeve of wasabi rice crackers, a wedge of London Fog cheese and a bottle of Pappy Van Winkle 15, no ice. This was not an exercise for wine, but for something a bit more powerful.

He turned the envelope over a couple of times, then looked hard at the scotch tape sealing it. Yellowed, cracked, but you could see that it probably hadn't been lifted off and then resealed. Of course, he had never seen the envelope, never knew it existed until the Jet had called, didn't even know if this was the original envelope. He had an idea what was in it, but perhaps the material had been opened, copied, and then put into this envelope with some old tape, or tape that had been aged by heat or by a chemical. It would be good to be able to have it analyzed by a police lab, but of course that was out of the question.

Then it occurred to him that you might open an envelope like this, with an overlapping glued seam at the bottom, without touching the scotch tape and the main opening at all: you might get the bottom open, slip the stuff out and back in, re-glue it and who would know? The hell, he thought, and took a letter opener, grabbed its onyx handle and gently worked it along the edge of the tape, which fell apart in stiff yellow shards.

Lawrence used the back of his hand to whisk the cracker crumbs and a few small clumps of cheese off the desktop, then took out his handkerchief and half-polished the area before sliding the contents flat out onto the cherry-wood. He poured a third glass of bourbon and started reading.

Impressively complete. The notes were just stories, they could have been fiction, could have been about anyone. But the Jet had been pretty complete in his package. There were pictures; there were a couple of parking receipts, a cab receipt, and there was a small reel of recording tape that he had no way of playing; that could be a problem but if you had money you could buy anything you needed on Craig's List or eBay including an old-fashioned tape machine, it would just take a little time. Did he have time? There was also a copy of the *Boston Herald's* front few pages, the one with a picture of the body half, but only half-draped with a sheet. You could see Sonny's shoes sticking out of the bottom, and on the ground was the sweater the Lip had lifted from the counter of Filene's basement the week before the thing.

What the hell was the Jet doing? Was this his own personal Hope Chest, until he decided to monetize his memories with the only guy he knew who was solvent? Would he have planned to shake someone down with this, a couple of decades ago? Inconceivable; who would think that way, and who would figure anyone would be rich enough in the future—or even alive, for that matter?

How to deal with this? This was going to be delicate, over the phone; and he didn't even know if he was being conned, which was worse than having to pay if they had the goods. And what would stop them from doing it over and over if it worked once? What was on the tape anyway, who had a tape recorder in 1980? There wasn't enough Pappy to answer all these questions and that was for sure. He was feeling hazy, not enough food to absorb the alcohol. No matter. Not an action item for tonight. Only question is, do I just destroy all this shit right now? Having it laying around sure can't help me any, no matter what next happens. Well, not before I decipher the tape. What the hell am I looking for on eBay? Do I put in my own ad, doesn't that prove something even if it turns out no one can produce a copy of the tape?

It was easier running hookers and selling horse, you just delivered the goods and got paid, there was no mystery. Who needs mystery in their lives? Who needs this shit? Lawrence Carter re-stuffed the envelope, sealed it with fresh tape and put it into his private safe. The crackers were gone, the cheese was no good without crackers, the bourbon was mellow and smoked and only burned a little in the back of his throat if he let it slosh there for the moment. "The morning," he said out loud. He was always at his best in the morning, and tomorrow at least the markets were closed so he would have more time to think.

Luis was sweating in his hands. He had never had perspiration in his palms before, not even when he was high or having sex or stapling drywall in a summer construction job. Luis did not like the feeling.

"How'd it go, whaddaya think?" he asked Tina. It was next morning and they were going to let Carter sweat until Monday or Tuesday.

"How the hell do I know, you was on the phone."

"Yeah, well it went fine I think. But I wish to hell I knew what was inside the envelope."

Tina sighed. "Look, I ain't one hundred percent sure but I know this much from back in the day: The Jet and the Lip were pretty wild, and one of their boys turned up dead after there was this fight, so I figure one of them offed the guy and because the Jet had the envelope I figure he was holding something on Carter so it must have been Carter or at least he was there. I also think there was a tape recording in there; Jeff lifted one of those miniature tape recorders one time, he loved it, he kept writing memos to himself on the thing like he was some bigshot behind a desk, and I'm pretty sure I felt one of them tapes in the envelope there, so there's that to tell him when he gets suspicious. Which he will. I don't have any info but I betcha he's the guy that done Jeff, or his people. This Carter, he's a real rich guy but he got his start down in the strip joints and bars before they cleaned them up, he's a real phony, name isn't even Carter, it was something Italian or Greek like Carterino or Carino or something."

Luis wiped his face and hands with a stained dish towel and rehung it on the oven door handle. "Ya know I don't like this, this is real dangerous."

"Ya think? I'm the one whose name we're using. You, you're just a voice. If this Carter is what we figger, I'm the one with a major problem here, not you."

"Oh, and if they decide to do something you think they won't figure out it's your husband making the calls? I'm in deep cover here, right? Bullshit."

"Bullshit, bullshit, everything you don't like, to you it's bullshit. Grow up. I'm sick and tired of being broke."

"We ain't broke," Luis bristled. "If it weren't for your shithead son sponging off us we'd be fine."

Tina sighed. "We been over this. I don't wanna hear about my son no more. The idea is, we all get healthy, right? This guy's got too much to risk to take a chance. He's gotta play. He's gotta play big."

At about the same time Tina was mentally contemplating her future money, Lawrence was looking through his notebook for the coded phone number of that guy he had hired when the Jet started acting up.

⋆—≡◆≡—⋆

Normie Pockets sat at a table at the back of the coffee house dipping a rock-hard almond biscotti into the narrow top of his espresso cup; the yellow crumbs floated in a thin scum on top, making it unpleasant to drink, but he liked how the warm coffee flowed into the cookie. Normie enjoyed mornings because they were peaceful, he could kick back and think about things. The Italian soccer league game was coming on the TV in a half-hour, direct from Turin. That was good because Normie was not big into reading newspapers. He lit another cigarette.

"Normie, ya know ya can't smoke."

"Tone, ya know I'm alone in here on this shitty morning, what's ya point. If some dumb paisan stumbles in here while I'm smoking and has a problem I'll put it out."

Tony snorted. "Yeah, someone from the neighborhood is goin' ta be real comfortable telling you to snub it out, Normie. Let me know when that happens, I want to tell everyone about it."

Normie's cell rang. He picked up and said nothing.

"Mr. P, is that you?"

"Who is this?"

"My name is – uh, Mr. CL."

"Uh-huh."

"So I need to talk to you about something."

Normie sat up straight. "Old business?" Normie did not prefer revisiting old business, anyone who wanted to talk about old business generally had an old problem, and Normie knew that sometimes old problems were messy problems.

"What? No, this is—new business."

"Well, you know the drill. Tomorrow." Normie hung up. A good call for a Saturday morning. Mr. CL's fifty thou had been a nice deal, above market in the neighborhood but these Beacon Hill types had no idea what the market was, so you could sort of set your own price; particularly for repeat business, because, based on Normie's sizeable experience base, for these guys repeat business really was somehow related to old business that had not quite been fully buried.

Tony clicked on the TV and came around to sit next to Normie. He absent-mindedly reached down onto the table and took a Camel out of Normie's pack.

"Hey, Normie, where's ya lighter?"

—·— ≋◆≋ —·—

Sarah Greenberg swiped her stringy hair up her forehead; it kept slipping down and blocking her eyes and she was trying to concentrate. She had a guy out of the swamp from a month ago and she couldn't seem to get any traction.

Sarah was the stubborn type. Back when she was married to the Asshole and teaching school in Watertown, that streak got her in a lot of trouble. But stubborn was good for a detective. The Boston Police Department liked stubborn. Stubborn got cases solved, if they happened to be one of the small percentage of cases that the Police Department cared about. And they cared about citizens of Boston, when they turned up decomposing in shallow water. Even cared about the least of these, which means they cared about Jeffrey the Jet Redenheimer.

How did this shlub earn a professional hit? His last arrest was thirty years ago. Since then he had become a citizen. A poor citizen, odd jobs mostly labor, and he lived in a dive for sure and his ex had no kind words to say about him, but still, the guys he worked with, the people he worked for, said he was "solid" and smarter than he looked. Of course, when Sarah first got a look at him, what with his eyes and half his nose gone and his hair, what there was of it, all intermeshed with fishing line and seaweed mixed in, "smarter" was hard to picture.

The only interesting thing she had found in his room, aside from a surprisingly large collection of unredeemed pawn tickets, was a phone number stuck to the mirror with black plumber's tape. It turned out to belong to one Lawrence Carter, a well-connected Boston guy with one of those early 19th century red brick houses with the curved front windows and wrought iron gates up on Beacon Hill. Carter had checked out pretty well; she had decided not to talk to him until she researched the rest of the facts, but it turned out there really weren't any other facts; and then, the rash of rapes in the North End took her attention until they caught the guy and now she was staring at the file again, with the picture of the decedent and her useless notes, realizing she should not have delayed so long in talking to this guy Carter.

Another thing was the angle of the bullets. Two in the back of the head, entering the skull at a steep slope. The decedent was short, but how tall was the shooter? He would have had to have been about seven feet tall; unlikely. Unless the guy was kneeling or sitting in a chair . . .

Possible but unusual. She had found a couple of other similar hits in the files, but both were a few years back; one they had tried to hang on this Polish guy, Norman Poduluski, he had been seen in the neighborhood a couple of nights in a row with no reason to be so far from home, but he ended up with a tight alibi and then he had faded from police view.

Greenberg began plucking the hairs from the corner of her right eyebrow; there were not many remaining, it was a bad habit, and with those steel-colored eyes, wide apart and slightly popped and straddling a porcine nose and light olive skin, she looked a little like a flounder with one eye pointed up and the other hiding in plain view. The crow's feet didn't help either.

━━━✦━━━

"I changed my mind."

"Whaddaya mean, changed ya mind? I been spending the last week and a half watchin' this guy. He's a weirdo, doesn't go out much but I got him figured now I think."

"Well, I don't want you to—do it." Lawrence held the disposable phone tightly, hissing into it. The interior of the Lincoln was cold as hell, the weather had turned. The engine had been off for an hour while he thought it over, but it was too risky; he would pay the money, for now, and see if Tina just went away. If she became a regular problem, there would be time enough.

"Look, it's your thing, I don't gotta do it, ya know? It's fine, just let it sit and ya change ya mind you can, ya know, try me again."

"How do I get my money back?"

Norman paused, figured it out right away, and snorted into the cell phone belonging to a nonexistent Verizon subscriber named Ralph Ligouri. "We seem to have a bad connection all of a sudden, Mr. CL." Norman smiled to himself for thinking up such a clever way to phrase it; and right on the spot also. "This is not your regular type arrangement with a deposit, ya know."

Now a pause on the other end.

A short breath inward, a longer pause.

Then, in a calm business tone: "I realize you have expended some—effort here and I am willing to pay for your time, but look, 75 grand for following a guy for a couple of weeks is pretty stiff."

"Whoa, it ain't the time. Let's say it was even five hundred an hour, that's only maybe ten thou of my time. But what about the risk I take? Why am I following this guy? We got a conspiracy here, that is what we call in my business a major crime, to conspire to, well do something." Norman checked himself, he did not like specifics on a phone, even one that could not – theoretically – be connected to him.

Larry couldn't complain to the cops or the Better Business Bureau but did not like being ripped off; he had to salvage something out of this.

"Okay, okay, we'll call it a credit."

"You asking to open an – account in my – store, is that it Mr. CL? You gotta be kiddin' me. This is rich. Absolutely shittin' me, right, you're not serious, right? Cause you ain't possibly bein' serious here."

"Dammit, 75 is a lot of money." Larry felt the swirl as the toilet bowl he was sitting in began to empty even faster, disorienting him as he swished around in ever-shrinking circles. "What are you going to do for the 75? Huh?" Norman was loving it, a righteous shit fit from some rich guy who wanted his refund on a murder! "What am I going to do for the 75? I tell ya what, Mr. CL. For the 75 I will forget this little incident here and not deliver my product directly to you, Mr. CL. That's what you get for 75."

Larry rationalized the click as Norman hung up on him as a positive sign in one way—it was over for now, at least. That kike broad from the police was not a good surprise when she dropped by the house with her load of questions, but she had said she had talked to Tina, so this was no time to have a bad accident happen to Tina's moron husband. What the hell is the Boston Police Force coming to, anyway? Chief Detective Greenberg! It could almost be a bad joke . . .

The more Norman thought about it, the madder he got. He did not like CL. For the hell of it he felt like shooting Luis anyway, as a matter of principle! But then the cops might get CL who would have nothing to lose by giving up Norman at that point. Unless he took care of both of them? All that work, maybe he should think on it.

And what could CL tell the cops, anyway? They would first have to find me, and then put me together with the thing before they would think to try to get an ID, which would be suspect anyway.

"Fuck him!" said Norman out loud.

In her own cop way, Sarah had not liked Lawrence Carter; he was too controlled. Rich guys on Beacon Hill who traded their own portfolio would have been nervous without reason, being dropped in on by the police. They would try to ask questions, try to get the connection. Carter had been smooth as butter, too conversational, too casual with his hand gestures. And he hadn't even asked what was going on, which might mean he already knew? Not enough to get a search warrant or a phone tap, certainly. But maybe enough to spend a couple of days watching Carter.

Which she did. Which was easy. He didn't leave his town house for five full days (and nights). Not so strange; but why did Sarah feel it was? She was going to give it one more day, when Luis was found in his parked car in East Boston with two neat bullet holes descending at a sharp angle into his skull.

After that, it was not too hard to get a warrant.

—+— ᴇᴇ♦ᴇᴇ —+—

Tina took the cash from the savings bank, all $434. She took the cash in the jar, all $117. She took the money she had hidden over the years in a clothes bag in her closet, all $4,918. She left the morgue, dried off her tears when out of view of everyone, took her one packed bag and went to the South Station bus terminal and bought a one-way to Lowell, where her widowed sister was solvent and living in her old wooden Victorian, long paid for by her now-deceased husband, who had left her with a neat lawn and several empty bedrooms formerly occupied by assorted children who could not wait to get as far from Lowell as possible. She knew a guy from the old days who made her on the cheap a social security card in the name of Natalie Carbone, her sister's married last name, and a pretty good Massachusetts driver's license that matched, with a watermark of the State Seal floating below the glossy surface, just like the real ones.

Meanwhile Norman called CL to tell him that the hit was finished and to make arrangements to pick up the second 75 grand.

"We agreed it was off," whispered Carter, and then hissed "let me call you back, how dare you call me on this phone and how did you know where to call me anyway?"

"Oh, ya know, I don't mind this one being on the record and ya know you arranged this so don't try to welch out of this or you may find that breach of contract is not the best policy when you're doing my line of work."

"Fuck you. I'll call you back," Carter snapped as he hung up his house phone and grabbed his prepaid portable and dialed the number. Lou let it ring until it went to voice mail, before he picked it up.

"Sorry I didn't pick right up when ya called back, but I was on the line with my stockbroker."

Carter ignored the dig. "We expressly agreed it was off, you son of a bitch," he spit into the phone.

"Nah, ya see, what we agreed to was that you were welching me out and I was personally offended and the more I thought about it I figured I'd just finish the thing and pick up the rest of my money, sort of teaching you a lesson. So, Government Center parking garage, just before the Bruins game, say 6:45, section 10, row B just like before. And Mr. Carter, sir: I would not be late if I was you."

<hr />

Sarah saw Carter leave about 6:15 that night, wearing a Boston Bruins hockey jacket. Finally, he was going out of his house. She had decided not to use the search warrant just yet. Tina had skipped and could not be found. Something was happening; better to let it play a while.

She had Tracy follow Carter, and the next morning she saw the fuzzy pictures of Carter talking with someone who looked familiar in the Government Center garage. Very familiar. And Carter returned to his house by 7:45; he never went to the game. It took the identification specialists from forensics about half a day to make Norman Poduluski, who had been off radar for years. Later that day, with search warrant in hand, Sarah made sure that the envelope finally caught up with Lawrence Carter.

As for Poduluski, he was still at large but now it was just a matter of time.

— ⚔ —

Tina slumped over the table; it was 10:15, and the diner's linoleum floor had been mopped and the settings for breakfast had been put out; folded paper napkin, coffee mug in beige, knife and fork and spoon at each seat, all twenty-some-odd of them. Her sister was making her pay for room and board, which Tina sort of understood; it was not like she had been civil to her sister for a decade or three; but waiting tables was not easy for someone with varicose veins and a major lazy streak.

The day's *Boston Herald* had been left by someone on her last table. Before tossing it out, Tina saw a familiar face on the front page, and realized it was the detective she had talked to about Luis. Next to it was another picture, a photo of a handsome business type with thin light colored hair and deep-set eyes, in suit and tie.

"Son of a bitch," Tina muttered. "They caught my meal-ticket."

A half- smile invaded her flaccid features. "At least I can move back to the flat," she thought. "Wonder if they cleaned it out and rented it to someone else already."

At about that time, Normie Pockets was sitting quietly in his black Buick, lights off, in front of the Victorian on Maple Street. He did not like loose ends. He sipped his cold Dunkin' Donuts decaf French Vanilla coffee, chewed the curved lip of the paper cup, and half-closed his eyes. The broad better come home sometime soon; his sweatpants were beginning to run annoyingly up his ass. How late were diners in a shithole like Lowell open, anyway?

MISFILED

I once had a relationship, with Nipples Nowitski.

Now before you start jumping to any conclusions here, let me tell you that this is not that kind of story. It is more of a mystery story, but I am not a detective, or a cop, so don't get your hopes up. I'm just a lawyer, in my own office, who has been around a while, and I am known to know lots of people.

Nipples—I have to stop this here and now. Her name is Irene. Irene worked for one of those big law firms downtown, where they still make the men wear their jackets when they go into the hallway. Irene was a paralegal, an assistant with a variety of duties that required some organizational skills, some intelligence, and a comfort level with repetitive boredom in exchange for a modest regular paycheck.

One day Irene's mind wandered; not far, but far enough. She was filling out a report to be sent to a government office in some obscure place, Idaho or Newark or someplace like that, and her eyes fell on the wrong list to copy from the client's company records. Instead of listing the directors of the company, all of whom were upstanding citizens (or at least a decade away from jailable derelictions), Irene blithely typed in the list of shareholders, some of whom relied on the fact that no one knew they had anything to do with that business. The document was mailed on

June 23. Irene went home that night and did her laundry and then unsuccessfully searched the dating website Christian Mingle.

＊ ▬◆▬ ＊

I was reading the paper in my office one morning when Claire buzzed me. I am in one office of a large suite occupied by a couple of lawyers, a CPA, and a few consultants; we share a receptionist, conference room and coffee machine. Claire is everyone's assistant.

"There is a young lady here to see you, Mr. H. She doesn't have an appointment but she says Lou Taylor from Hathway and Jencks sent her over; Ms. Nowitski."

"Is this Miss Nowitski selling something or what, Claire?" I was tired of being pitched for every conceivable software system that had nothing to do with my actual needs.

"I think it is a client matter, Mr. H. Do you want to see Ms. Nowitski now?" Claire hissed the "Ms" so I would not get that part wrong again; Claire was the helpful type.

"Sure, let me clear some of this off my desk and I'll come out and pick her up in a minute."

"I'll get her a cup of coffee, take your time."

I had two matters spread out over my desk. Lawyers can't let one client see the business of another so I started re-assembling papers into their folders. Mrs. Lyon's complaint about defective aluminum siding on her archaic Victorian went carefully into her file; the papers from my own annoying IRS audit I stuffed into an unnumbered red file folder and squeezed it into a desk drawer.

Ms. Nowitski was an open-faced woman with smooth skin over a bit too much flesh, the kind of look that flattens those little age lines around eyes and the corners of mouths. She might have been 30, but maybe 40. You couldn't miss her figure, though;

333

her blouse buttons pulled across her chest, opening modest dark little tunnels into whatever lurked beneath the fabric. She walked ahead of me, slightly pigeon-toed on low heels with her legs pushing against her skirt that managed to be tight and short and still uninteresting. A couple of steps ahead of me, she left a faint aroma of shampoo in the air. Irene sat erect in my wooden guest chair and shimmied her skirt down a couple of inches. Her voice was pleasant and flat, with a mild whistle through the gap in her top teeth.

"Thanks for seeing me. Mr. Taylor, I told him my problem—he's one of the partners I work for—and he said maybe I should ask you for some advice." She paused, eyes down. "I didn't want to involve my firm in my—problem."

"Well, I've known Lou a long time, it's nice he sent you over and I will certainly try to help," I said softly, then paused to wait for the story. Seemingly I needed a more affirmative cue for Ms. Nowitski, who was admiring the texture of my old oriental rug.

"Your problem?"

"Oh ... Well it is embarrassing really and probably nothing but —I think I am being followed."

"Someone is following you?" I immediately tensed; I did not do that kind of work.

"No. Not exactly. I am being followed." Ms. Nowitski looked up, her eyes now wide open and addressing my own. Her gaze was direct, matter of fact. "I mean people are following me. Not all at once of course; different people at different times, but there is someone almost all the time ... " She trailed off.

"How do you know this?'

She inhaled, exhaled and launched into a detailed soliloquy. "One can sense these things. Someone in the aisle at Whole Foods where she goes every Saturday for groceries although it is pretty expensive. Someone always in the Laundromat late Tuesday night where she went because it always was deserted and she could get the machines she wanted. She and Evelyn, that's a friend from work, went to the movies and Evelyn asked 'do you know that guy, he is sort of staring at us' and I looked up and did not know him and he looked away but next week she was walking from the bus and she was sure he was walking just behind her. There is a dark-haired young woman with a beaky nose who is always at Starbucks in her neighborhood. And – hesitation – the other night she was sure that someone had been in her apartment although the door was locked when she got home and nothing was missing but it just felt funny, little things she could not put her finger on. And one lunch she left her cell phone by accident on her desk, and when she got back she could not find it, but she figured it would show up even though it was not where she always put it, but then after break she got back to her desk and there was the phone in the metal basket where she always put it but it sure wasn't there when she got back from lunch and did I think that was possible, that people were following her even in her office?"

"I don't really know, really can't say." Pause. "Anything is possible of course." She looked at me as if I were going to say something else, so I did. "I would like to help but I'm not sure. Not sure why Lou suggested you see me. Maybe the police, or even a private investigator. I could make a referral, this is not what I usually do, you see?"

Ms. Nowitski looked at me in a factual, nonpleading way. "I am not sure about this. I don't want to go to the police. Mr. Taylor, Lou . . . ," slight blush and quick look down, "he said you know lots of people, you could ask around."

I pretended to write something on the pad in front of me while I thought of something to say. What I did say surprised me, although apparently not Ms. Nowitski. "I can make inquiries, yes I can. I can do that. Are you sure you want to incur a—uh—legal fee for this? The police can be most helpful, and you don't seem to have done anything wrong." I started slightly, leaned forward: "That's right, yes? You are not aware of any reason someone would be following you? Something, well . . . "

"I can't imagine. I haven't done anything. My old boyfriend is married and moved to Los Angeles. There is—no issue currently with anyone. I do know how lawyers work of course. I can pay a fee—if it's not too, you know . . . "

"Ms. Nowitski – Irene – I do not know how much I can help you but I will try. Fill out this form with your contact information, give me a few days. I think it best if I do not call your office, unless you think calling your home is too—intrusive?"

She put down her particulars and her cell phone number. I asked her for $500, promising that if I just hit a dead end I would refund the part I did not use. She said that was fair – at her firm, $500 doesn't even get you the key to the rest room – but she gave me two checks for $250 and asked me to hold one until the following Friday so her paycheck would hit her account. We shook hands, she turned with a slight wobble and I followed her out through my office door and watched her walk down the hall in the direction of Claire's desk, her tight skirt hitching slightly higher with each hurried step. I put both checks in my desk drawer and pulled out my IRS file. I had no idea what to do next, but solo lawyers in this city take anything they can get.

<hr />

Next morning I called Tewilliger. Lyle and I met years ago at a bar association committee meeting. He was a good guy, career assistant DA, I saw him now and again at events, and we helped each other out in areas where one of us was marginally more au courant than the other.

336

"Let me buy you some lunch, Lyle."

"So what do you want," he asked, half-affably.

"Advice on a case and I don't know what I'm doing." "Sure, Thursday or Friday, you pay."

We met at The Sizzling Burger. I briefly considered going to some nice discreet place where we could talk but then thought that would make this "matter" seem heavier than it was. Besides, nice discreet places cost more money and I was paying. The advantage of The Sizzling Burger, aside from price, was that it was so noisy that no one was going to overhear us; the real question was whether we could hear each other.

Lyle was trim when I met him and stayed that way over, maybe, twenty years. One of those guys with no butt, wiry and with a graying crew-cut, no bald spot. I recall once he mentioned working out at the police gym a few times a week. Here he was spearing salad greens dripping with low fat vinaigrette while I un-notched my belt to accommodate the "Big Moo," blue cheese on top, a healthful slice of tomato on the side.

"I have someone who came to my office who says he is being followed. Swears doesn't know why. Swears didn't do anything wrong. Swears not a domestic thing. I don't do this kind of stuff. If I gave you his name, can you find out if it's the government? You guys, the State, the Feds fer God's sake?" The Big Moo let out a squirt of warm fatty blood and began its rapid descent down my chin, headed for my necktie.

"Maybe. Tell me more about it." Tewilliger jabbed an elusive carrot shard. "What's her name?"

So I told Tewilliger the story. I did not waste time asking how he knew "he" was a "she." After all, Tewilliger is a public servant, he only gets 55 minutes for lunch. He said he'd check discretely. He said he'd call my office. He said that if he called and said that he could find out nothing that might mean that he could not find out or he could not say what he found. In any case, this conversation never happened. "Thanks for the salad," he said.

I called Irene the day after she came to my office; she picked up her cell on the first buzz, she was sure she was still being followed, the same guy kept showing up on the sidewalk, the same woman with the beak nose at Starbucks. No, I didn't have any word, but soon.

Next Monday it was, Tewilliger called; it was after lunch so I figured he didn't have much or he would have wangled another salad in exchange for the information. "It's not anyone at this end as far as I can tell," he said. "Certainly not the DA or cops, and I don't think it's the Staties because since the 9-11 thing we coordinate pretty well. My buddy at the DOJ says it isn't Federal. Justice is clued into the SEC, the tax people, drugs and firearms. I can't be sure on the FBI and Homeland Security people, their long-suit isn't updating local authorities, but I did make one call to someone who would usually confirm a name and he said it was news to him. Unless it is a really heavy thing, I'd say it's not the Feds either. My best guess is, whoever is breathing down on your client isn't from the law enforcement community."

We exchanged a thanks/anytime thing, and since it was getting more difficult I took one of the checks out of my drawer and filled out a deposit slip for the first $250 and then called Moe Lipschitz. Moe did the investigations for my occasional divorce case, drove by the houses of new clients to see if they were playing touch football after they hired me to handle their disability claims, things like that. Moe had a license and was sufficiently nondescript to be overlooked, which made him perfect for light jobs. Also, he was inexpensive. He offered a day of following Irene for $250 and when I told him I got a total of $500 for the whole case he rolled his eyes and said that for me, he would do two days for $300. So now I am in the hole for $50 because I am not ready to declare Irene a big deal case and take her second check. I figure, it's a nice thing to do, and if I can figure out the case then cashing the second check later will not feel so—greedy.

Moe tells me I am a schmuck for not getting a picture of my client but calls back to say that she is on Tinder so no problem. I cringe that I never thought of that angle as a source of a stalker, but when I log in it is hard to imagine someone following Irene based on a photo that takes a straightforward face and turns it into a click-through.

Moe is going to do Saturday and Monday and call me Tuesday. I consider telling Irene but decide not to, she is liable to start looking around even more than I suspect she is, which will cause total strangers to start staring at her, which will simply prove to her she is being followed even if she isn't. You can see that I am not exactly sure-footed in these kinds of matters, but my heart is in the right place and my client is skating on my fifty bucks so I figure I am entitled to my opinion.

I am absorbed in another case—I actually do work for a living and for the alimony check I send each month—and have my calls held Tuesday until I finish some papers for court. Claire has left a small pile of phone messages on white tear-off sheets in my mail slot along with a lawyer's newspaper and a couple of bills. Nothing from Moe, which is strange, he is fastidious with his commitments if not overly skilled at his craft. No answer on his cell, so I leave a message and go home to watch the hockey game and eat my reheated raviolis.

No answer Wednesday; I called Irene who said there was nothing new and when would I hear anything. I told her that I had had someone observe her for a couple of days but don't look around now because it is all over, and I will get a report and then we can chat. I suggest she not come to my office again in case she is being followed; she asks if I think using a cell phone is so smart and maybe she should give me her office number after all; like lots of cell phone people, she has no land line at home. Another thing I should have thought of, her cell phone being vulnerable. I took her number and promised.

Next day I am at Starbucks. The coffee is okay, their baked goods not so much. I am eating a yellow slice of pound cake with those little dark seeds when I have to stop chewing because there is a squib in the *Herald* about this guy Moe Lipschitz turning up dead of unknown causes while sitting in his car somewhere, under investigation, he leaves no close family and he is—was—fifty years old. I would have guessed 65 at least.

All of a sudden I want to give Irene back her second check, tell her it isn't the government and she should therefore go to the police. All of a sudden I am particularly interested in not meeting Irene again. But then I figure, I can call Tewilliger and poke around. Will he relate an inquiry about Lipschitz to this small-time investigator I am asking about? Likely. Do I care? I don't know, it is beginning to feel uncomfortable and complex. I think I may need a lawyer.

I repress that sardonic thought and leave my pound cake and now-tepid coffee, scoop up the paper and head to my office.

⸻ ⸱ ⸱

I am trying to get back into my client's aluminum siding complaint as a life's work when Claire tells me that Lyle Tewilliger is on the phone.

"Hey, Lyle, I was just thinking about you," I said in most upbeat voice of modest jocularity. "Whatcha got?"

"I got a dead guy with a wallet containing about twenty bucks and a check from you for three Cs." This was followed with the kind of pause we professionals describe as pregnant, as you wait for the jerk to be made nervous by that silence and tell you something that he was not going to tell you ten seconds beforehand. But I too am a trained professional, not to be sucked in.

"So?"

"This could be a bad conversation," said Lyle in a measured voice. "This about the girl? Just tell me."

So I told him. He promised to hold the check as evidence so at least while I was scared I was sort of solvent.

"Irene, is this a good time to talk?"

"Sure; I can take my break now. I may just stop talking for a minute if someone stops by my desk but we can talk. What do you want to tell me?"

"Irene, the police want to speak with you."

There was a gap of a few seconds, and then a low and measured, "You told them about my problem?"

"No. Well, actually yes, I told them about your problem – but not everything," I lied.

"I said I did not want to talk to the police. I hired you so I didn't have to do that." Calm, factual, controlled; better than I anticipated.

"I know. But something came up. As best I can tell, if you were being followed it was not by a policeman or anyone like that. No one from the government. So I asked someone to—observe you, like I told you. And he did. And then he—well, he just died sitting in his car."

Long silence. "Oh," Irene said.

Another long silence.

Then, "how did they know to call you?"

"He—this dead guy—had my name on his person when he was found." No need to get into the check business. "It was just their routine, I guess."

Quietly: "Do I have to go talk to the police?"

That was an interesting question for me, a lawyer who should know the answer and didn't.

"Irene, that's not the point. This may be serious. It may be nothing. We don't know.

"Maybe we should bring in a criminal lawyer." Pause. "I'll pay for it, don't worry about that. Irene, I don't want to mess this up. Maybe we should talk in person."

She sounded worried, then suggested her office. "I can reserve a small conference room. No one would care; sometimes I do that if I have a client coming in to give me some papers. I could even tell Lou if that were better ... "

"Good idea. Can you do it at 4 today, I'll walk over. We should talk. Okay? Good, I'll see you then." I paused. "Maybe you should eat in today? Did you bring a lunch maybe?"

"I'll have a banana. It's fine." Pause, then a small snort, almost a half-laugh: "I should be watching what I eat anyway."

It was a pleasure to work until 3:30; I picked up my attaché case, put it down and started to walk out, then figured it would look more normal if I carried it, went back to pick it up, silently chastised myself for over-thinking whether I should carry a prop with me, and walked out the door.

"Claire, gone for the day. See you tomorrow in the a.m."

I turned down Third, walking quickly, then drew a breath and consciously adjusted myself to a slower pace. I did not notice the man in the sports coat who slipped into step behind me.

I got as far as just before Chestnut when someone gently touched my shoulder. A slight fellow, blue blazer, open-throat button-down blue shirt, loafers and no sox, a very Ivy-looking guy. His English was flat, Midwestern.

"Can I have a minute, counsellor?"

I couldn't place him and I'm pretty good with people and faces but no one's perfect. "If you walk along with me, sure. Where did we meet before, excuse me but I do not recall." He moved next to me, curbside, and slowed down some more and I found myself keeping pace; no worries, I had plenty of time. "I don't know that we've met. But we know about you. All good things, I hasten to add." A bit formal, I thought; not a lot of people "hasten" these days.

"You know about me?" I was nervous, but only slightly. So far.

"No, actually, Mr. H, *I* do not know about you. As I said, *we* know about you."

I stopped to face him. "That's an odd thing to say. Who the hell is 'we'? Are you with a law firm or something? What's this about?"

He smiled and started walking again, slowly. "Let's walk while we talk. You don't want to be late for your appointment."

I had taken a few steps but then stopped again and stood there. He had to turn and go back about three paces, which he did in a smooth round-about swoop.

"How do you know I have an appointment. I didn't say anything about an appointment. Look, this is a strange conversation. Call me tomorrow in my office. Do you need a card or do you know my phone number already, part of the things that the 'we' know?"

"I think we should chat now, while we walk. You don't want to keep her waiting, do you?"

"Look," I was getting angry about my wasted time, "I don't know why you think I have an appointment with a woman, but ..."

"Mr. H, please, I don't mean to hassle you. I just wanted to make sure you asked your client if she ever spoke to anyone outside her law firm about Jarell Services Corporation? Do you think you could ask that and just let me know on your way out?" I was about to say I was getting pissed off and that this conversation was certainly over when he gently tugged at my sleeve. "Of course, I would be pleased to wait for you in the Hathway Jenks building lobby." A small smile cut off any reply from me. I looked at him, he looked back, I turned to continue my walk and then he was no longer at my side.

I crossed Elm, went into the Hathway building and up the elevator without ever looking around.

Irene came out to reception and walked me wordlessly to a small conference room with one window looking across to an opaque window of another office across the alley. There was a little left in an old pot of coffee, and cups with the logo and law firm name on them; a far cry from the unmatched mugs I kept in my cabinet for when a client came to call. I made a mental note to upgrade.

She looked pretty good today, an unworthy thought that found itself, unasked, sitting in the front of my mind. Seated across the table, all I could see of her was her face, of course, and a good deal of her upper body, seemingly trapped in a stretched white top with scooped neck and a hint, an ample hint, of the infrastructure. I am sure she saw me looking, though I did make sure to look away and not repeat myself.

"What do you think we should discuss? I am pretty confused."

344

Her brow was knit, the horizontal lines on her forehead the only place where her skin was not plumped out. She looked confused. In thinking about it, I wanted to play poker with Irene; whatever she was thinking always could be read in the planes of her face, although pretty often it was clear she wasn't thinking about anything.

"I think we have to stop over-thinking things, and stop seeing bogey-men everywhere.

And stop focusing on being followed—even if we are being followed. At this point, what's the sense? We should talk to the police. At a minimum that should also help solve the 'following' problem. I don't think we have any downside, Irene."

I reached for a stern and certain tone here, almost an avuncular aspect. "We didn't do anything wrong, you were followed, or thought you were, you hired a lawyer which is still not a crime around here, and I hired a known investigator and—well, that's where our story stops, well short of a problem for us."

I was pretty happy with how it came out. I almost added at the end "unless you had something to do with the death" but that seemed silly and melodramatic, so I did not.

"Well, can you come with me?"

"Sure, I'm your lawyer, if you want me ..."

She sighed primly; her lips puckered slightly; the space between her teeth was really pretty small, I thought, her lisp more like an accent. Then I remembered my walking companion.

"There's one thing I did want to ask you, though." Her chin stayed down, her eyes looked up. It could have been sultry and it wasn't. "Did you ever hear of something called Jaret or Jarel Something, a company?"

Irene's eyes widened and she let out a low sound that could only be thought of as a groan. I was most unhappy to see her recognition of the name, and I thought of my Ivy-League walking buddy who suddenly acquired an entirely malevolent persona.

"I need to ask Lou, Mr. Taylor to join us," she said in a near-whisper and before I could say that it was a bad idea she was out the door, which closed with a mild swish behind her. I looked out the window, poured the rest of the coffee into my cup, was glad to find the smaller decanter contained real cream, and filled the ten minutes with sipping and worrying.

◂┄━◈━┄▸

"Hey, H, how they hanging?"

"Lou, good to see you. I'm sorry to get you involved – actually not my idea – but this thing is really pretty unclear . . ." I looked up, hoping Taylor would bring all the strands together in a few simple sentences but—well, life often disappoints.

"H, this, uh matter is getting a little out of hand. I suggested that Irene contact you because, well, it is sort of a personal kind of thing and she didn't want to get the police involved and, anyway, now it looks like it positively involves a possible client of the firm and I want to ask you how that happened."

"Lou, can I get another cup of coffee?" I wanted a few minutes to think. "And is Irene coming back in here or . . . "

"No, actually I suggested that you and I could chat first. How do you want your coffee?"

"Creamer is fine. So is this Jaret or Jarel a client of the firm or what?"

Lou looked down. "You know, whether or not someone is a client is itself confidential."

346

I tried to engage his eyes: "And Lou, any information about my client and her personal case, and between her and her lawyer, is also confidential, you know that." Lou was not amused, but he did pick up the phone and asked someone to bring me more coffee so I figured we were going to have a conversation after all, with each of us breaching our ethical obligations but in a good cause.

"So Jarel Services is—was a big client of the firm. My client actually. They changed counsel several weeks ago when we made an error, not seemingly a big error but we filed the names of stockholders with a government office and the names of stock-holders are not public. It was a mistake by a paralegal; actually, it was Irene who did it. I explained to the President—by phone actually, I never had met him, he came to me as a referral. I told him it was just a clerical error. He said something like "some error" and next thing I knew they took their files away. Didn't tell me to forward them to another lawyer, just box them and send them back to home office."

"Did you mention that the filing was made by Irene?"

"Hell, I don't know, I didn't take detailed notes. I am sure I said it was a para's simple mistake. I might have mentioned Irene's name, I really don't remember."

Lou leaned forward. "Your turn, counsellor."

I told him about the guy on the street. He looked at me suspiciously; I did not blame him, it was so improbable that I barely believed my own recollection.

"Don't look at me like that, if I wanted to make up a story I would have come up with a much better one than that."

We sat in silence. I got my coffee from a young woman in very high heels and very low neckline. I had no idea what to do next.

"Lou, I am going to walk out of here and this guy, I bet he is going to ask me what happened. He's going to ask me if I asked Irene the question about any contact with someone outside of the firm about—Jarel is it? I really do not want to tell him I did not ask; don't want to tell him I did or didn't ask but it isn't any of his business. Then I gotta tell Irene something and probably take her to the police who will want to know everything including this conversation."

"Shit, H, don't do that. We—let's both of us talk to Irene now, find out about this."

"Can't let you do that, Lou. I can't let someone listen in on my conversations and advice with a client. In fact I do think I need to talk to Irene, and would appreciate doing it now, without you in the room, even if it is during working hours and you could likely just say no to that, at which point I would have to go outside and talk to my buddy and tell him I was going to ask Irene but then this partner named Lou came into the picture and told me to take a hike ..."

The pause hung heavy for a few seconds, and then Lou said he would get Irene and he turned and left without a good-bye or a handshake.

An hour or so later I stepped out of the building, I was surprised to see that evening was coming on, I fought down the urge to hop into a cab at the stand in front of Lou's building, and started walking back to my office.

"Long meeting, counsellor?" I had gone a couple of blocks and was not surprised to hear the polite voice that had fallen in step to my right.

"The answer is no."

"No what," he asked.

"You wanted me to tell you if she had spoken to anyone else

about Jaret or Jarel. She got spooked. Seems she made some mistake about a company with that name, whatever. She said it was just a mistake. I had to ask her three times if she had spoken to anyone outside of her firm about that. She said she hadn't, didn't understand the question."

"Interesting. So Nipples denies it . . . "

I stopped. "Beg pardon? Denies what? Who's Nipples?"

My new friend smiled. "That's just what we call her. Great bod, don't you think?" His eyes slightly narrowed and he turned to face me, stopping my progress. "You think that's the truth, counsellor? Just your opinion, you know."

"Yeah. Yeah I do. What the hell is this about? Because when my client meets with the police there are going to be lots of questions."

"No need for that. Why would she need the police?"

"Because," I said, "she was being followed, or thought so, and hired me to look into it.

Was that you? Following her?"

"Mr. H, no need for the police. Let's say she no longer will get the feeling she is being followed, what do you think?"

"Not so easy. Seems a private detective I hired to look into this turned up dead and the police put me together with him and they are sort of insisting."

My friend leaned close into my chest and said slowly and quietly, "That wasn't us. We were not happy about that."

"Look, this is very uncomfortable. I am going to my office. This conversation is over. I assume you don't want to give me your—business card, do you?"

A smile traced a thin line above his chin. "Maybe some other time."

I turned to walk away. After about a dozen steps I glanced around and saw his back halfway down the street.

━┥━

"I am telling you I do not know any more than that." The detective was seated at his desk in a communal room with perhaps five or six other desks and some through-traffic.

"So you called her and she just didn't answer?"

"Yeah. Not the first time, not the tenth time. I told you everything. I told you I will look at your mug shots for that guy in the street. Hey, ask her law firm."

"We did first thing when the two of you didn't show up yesterday as we arranged. Said she just quit, no forwarding address. Today we went to her apartment. Furniture and pots and pans there—we ended up needing a warrant to get in—but no clothes, no cosmetics. You sure you don't know where she is, right?"

"Right. Look, this is weird. Ask the law firm about Jaret or Jarel, why someone might be so upset that someone might find out they were shareholders. Run the names for crooks or cons or Mafioso or something. I do not know what this is about. I got $500 in this case to do nothing useful and I need to get back to work and earn a living. Talk to Lou Taylor, take his time, he's a partner in a big law firm, he can afford to do this."

"Mr. H, my people tell me you're okay, but please can the shit. I got a dead guy and no leads except you so we are going to talk as long as I say we are going to talk. Got it?"

So we talked. That day and a few more times. And sat through a bunch of mug shots and two sessions with a police artist. And then it was over.

━┥━

My two checks from Irene bounced, account closed. The IRS clipped me for a few grand, no records to document some deductions. My former wife remarried so I save on alimony. I stopped going to the gym; I am now a 48 portly suit size but I am very happy. My law practice supports me. I have a girl friend who happens to be a para at Irene's old firm; no one has heard from her. The cops never solved Moe's murder; his daughter who lives in Philadelphia called me once to ask me about my "involvement" but that was it.

About three years after all this, I got a postcard stamped in Los Angeles. On the front was a picture of Grauman's Chinese Theater. On the back it said, "Regards, Nipples."

Go figure.

About the Author

Stephen M. Honig is an author and attorney. His chronology is deceptively predictable, growing up just before the Boomer generation in ethnic Brooklyn, New York, slogging through two intense Ivy League experiences at Columbia and Harvard, practicing for decades as a corporate attorney in Boston, experiencing the suburban life, the urban life, the requisite divorce, and four children who have their own success stories. He is a skillful observer of time and place unique in America, has more than a passing familiarity with the underworld, an ear and eye for the ethnic fabric of cities, and has traveled around the globe including two unusual trips to Russia, once on a mission and once as a professor. There were a lot of card games along the way, a few racing horses, the usual traumas with women and with life, some experiences in law that do not fit any mold, and an abiding passion to convey the texture of normality and of the sicknesses of the human condition.

Stephen has published three volumes of poetry: *Messing Around with Words, Rail Head* and *Obligatory COVID Chapbook*. This is his first prose publication. He resides in Newton, Massachusetts with his wife, youngest son and recalcitrant dog, occupying a household wherein he holds the fourth spot in the hierarchy.

CPSIA information can be obtained
at www.ICGtesting.com
Printed in the USA
LVHW020311270721
693764LV00007B/125

9 780578 901954